Raves for the novels of international bestselling author

Maggie Alderson

Pants on Fire

"A witty, smart debut."
—*Daily Mail*

"Fabulously glamorous . . . highly entertaining."
—*Heat*

"Wickedly funny and realistic . . . the perfect read for any girl who's ever wondered if the grass might be greener on the other side of the world."
—*OK!*

Mad About the Boy

"A bubbly concoction of bitchiness, humour, glamour, and eccentricity written with great verve and enthusiasm."
—*Sunday Mirror*

Handbags and Gladrags

Maggie Alderson

BERKLEY BOOKS, NEW YORK

THE BERKLEY PUBLISHING GROUP
Published by the Penguin Group
Penguin Group (USA) Inc.
375 Hudson Street, New York, New York 10014, USA
Penguin Group (Canada), 10 Alcorn Avenue, Toronto, Ontario M4V 3B2, Canada
(a division of Pearson Penguin Canada Inc.)
Penguin Books Ltd., 80 Strand, London WC2R 0RL, England
Penguin Group Ireland, 25 St. Stephen's Green, Dublin 2, Ireland (a division of Penguin Books Ltd.)
Penguin Group (Australia), 250 Camberwell Road, Camberwell, Victoria 3124, Australia
(a division of Pearson Australia Group Pty. Ltd.)
Penguin Books India Pvt. Ltd., 11 Community Centre, Panchsheel Park, New Delhi—110 017, India
Penguin Group (NZ), Cnr. Airborne and Rosedale Roads, Albany, Auckland 1310, New Zealand
(a division of Pearson New Zealand Ltd.)
Penguin Books (South Africa) (Pty.) Ltd., 24 Sturdee Avenue, Rosebank, Johannesburg 2196,
South Africa

Penguin Books Ltd., Registered Offices: 80 Strand, London WC2R 0RL, England

PRINTING HISTORY
Penguin Books edition / 2004
Berkley trade paperback edition / June 2005

Library of Congress Cataloging-in-Publication Data

Alderson, Maggie.
    Handbags and gladrags / Maggie Alderson.
      p. cm.
    ISBN 0-425-20278-X
    1. Fashion editors—Fiction. 2. Periodicals—Publishing—Fiction. 3. London (England)—Fiction.
  4. Photographers—Fiction. I. Title.

  PR6101.L44H36 2005
  823'.92—dc22

                                                                                    2005041052

PRINTED IN THE UNITED STATES OF AMERICA

10 9 8 7 6 5 4 3 2 1

For Peggy

Acknowledgements

With particular love and thanks to Mark Connolly and Josephine Fairley for their friendship, humour and editorial advice.

Heartfelt thanks also to:

All at Penguin in the UK and Australia. Especially Mari Evans, Julie Gibbs, Louise Moore, Tom Weldon and Bob Sessions. Also to former Penguin, Harrie Evans. And the Curtis Brownies, Jonathan Lloyd and Fiona Inglis.

To my treasured writer gal pals Jessica Adams, Kathy Lette and Karen Moline. To Barry Goodman for the Latin lessons. To everyone at *Good Weekend* for being such mates and to my wonderful editors there, first Fenella Souter and now Judith Whelan.

Love and air kisses to all my shows buddies: Mark Connolly (again), Melissa Hoyer, Jane Roarty, Jane de Teliga, Joan Burstein, Albert Morris, Christian McCulloch, Laura Begley, Kirstie Clements, Nancy Pilcher, Alison Veness McGirty, Judith Cook, Jackie Frank, Marion Hume, and anyone I have left out. So many frocks, so many laughs. And thanks for all the limo rides.

To all the PRs in London, Milan, Paris, New York, Sydney and Hong Kong who have given me fashion-show invitations over the years—particularly Jelena Music and Celina Ma—and to the *Sydney Morning Herald* for sending me to cover them.

To the designers for continuing to inspire me, particularly Tom

Ford, John Galliano, Karl Lagerfeld, Alexander McQueen, Phoebe Philo and Miuccia Prada. And to the ones I can really call friends: Jasper Conran and Collette Dinnigan.

To James Hodgson for Kingsdown and Jane Scruton for Garden Cottage.

To Popi Popovic for everything.

And to all of the international fashion pack for the best people-watching on earth. Fashionisti vincit.

1

MILES McCrae wasn't ever my boyfriend. We just had sex a lot. We had sex a lot in Milan and Paris, where we would gather with the rest of the international fashion pack, twice a year, to cover the catwalk shows of the big-name designers. I'd be in the third row with my hardback notebook and special pen, sketching the key outfits to shoot for *Chic* magazine, where I was a fashion editor. Miles would be crushed up with a horde of sweaty photographers taking the shots that would be flashed to news media around the world. And in each fashion city, we would fall into bed together and shag like animals.

Apart from those few crazy weeks in spring and autumn we never saw each other and had no contact except for the occasional coded email, along the following lines.

To: miles@smiles.com.au
From: epointer@chicmag.co.uk
Arriving Milan on Tuesday. Staying at the Principe. Please deliver
film after Prada show.

That's film as in "film." As in "red-hot love rod." Like I say, it wasn't a relationship, it was just sex. Life-changingly good sex, it must be said. Sex that made the top of my head lift off and kept me smiling for forty-eight hours afterwards, but no more than that. Just sex.

It wasn't that I didn't like Miles. He was a sweetheart, as well as a love god from Planet Tharg—well, Sydney. He was cute, funny and kind. With an unusually large penis. A great guy for someone, for sure, but it was definitely just sex between us. Sometimes it's much better to accept the limitations of a liaison right from the start. That's what I told myself when I met him and I stuck to it. You're much less likely to be disappointed that way. There were so many reasons why a full-blown relationship with Miles would never have worked, but the night we met none of them mattered.

It was a wet and windy October day in Milan. I was wearing a sleeveless Balenciaga top, with ultra-tight leggings, a Rick Owens leather jacket and Sergio Rossi shoes with heels so high I felt like I had electric shocks shooting through the balls of my feet every time I took a step. Just normal working daywear for a fashionista at the shows. I'd been wearing it since nine that morning, when I'd had to leave our hotel—always the Principe, or the "Princh" as we called it—with my *Chic* colleagues, to get to the Pucci show, which was being held in an old warehouse way out on the edge of town.

Our limo had crawled painfully through the usual clogged Milan traffic, made much worse by the rain, with *Chic*'s editor-in-chief Bee Fortess-Smith (née Beverly Fortess, married to a Mr. Smith) barking instructions down her mobile to her assistant, Anoushka, back in London. Most of them seemed to be concerning people she needed to have flowers sent to.

"No, Nushka," she was yelling, quite a feat with a cigarette clamped between her teeth. "Scrap that. Send Miuccia Prada the willow tree and send a box topiary to Mr. Armani. What? Oh, just put the usual. 'Bella, bella'—that's 'Bella, *bello*' to Mr. Armani, remember—'Loved it all. Kisses, Bee.' Oh, and send Miuccia a separate letter in my writing—you know, with the brown ink—to thank her for the coat. Call me back when you've opened my post. And don't forget to collect my dry-cleaning. And make me an appointment with Amanda Lacey for a facial when I get back. Oh and NUSHKA . . ." she shouted down the phone, before the poor girl could hang up. "Call that bitch Domenica Stracciatella and tell her that if I don't have a better seat for the Ferrucci show waiting for me at the hotel when we get back later, I will drop the Cameron Diaz cover and their stupid dress with it. But put it better than that, OK? Make it seem nice, that way you do. Thanks, darling."

I often thought Nushka's diplomatic talents were a great loss to the United Nations.

Sitting next to me in the back of the car—Bee always sat up front—was the magazine's famous fashion director, Alice, which she preferred pronounced in the Italian manner, "Alee-chay," Pettigrew. Which was pretty funny considering she came from Tunbridge Wells. Never the easiest of travelling companions, Alice (I always pronounced it the English way deliberately to annoy her), was stuffing stick after stick of sugarless gum into her mouth and silently seething. Bee had been sent the Prada coat *she'd* wanted as a present and worse still, she was wearing it. All Alice had received was a pea-green ostrich-skin handbag. She was gutted.

Such palpable waves of negative energy were coming off her it was like sitting next to a human Chernobyl. My mouth was as dry as a bowl of pub peanuts, after several glasses of red wine too many the night before, but I knew there was no point in even asking Alice for a stick of her gum. I'd done that once, the first time I'd done the shows with the *Chic* team, three years before.

"Get your own," she'd answered, grimacing like I'd asked to borrow her toothbrush. "I *need* this." She was right really. It was just about all she ever ate.

On my other side, the left—not so good for looking at passing shops, which is why Alice always sat on the right—was the more cuddly shape of Frannie McAllister, the magazine's beauty director and fashion news editor. As she liked to say, she was too clever to have just one job. I just called her the sanity editor. Frannie and I took it in turns to have the left-hand spot and the really crap seat in the middle. No way Madame Alee-chay was ever going to sit there.

The seat sharing was just one of many little ways Frannie kept me sane on those crazy trips. They were so intense. The four of us were forced to be together fifteen hours a day for the best part of four weeks, twice a year, under constant pressure always to look good, pay attention and generally outclass our rivals on other magazines. You wouldn't necessarily want to spend that much time with your best friends and as part of my job, I had to do it with one person I seriously detested and one I was seriously terrified of. In that scenario, Frannie was a true blessing—she was so unusually normal.

She was, for example, just about the only member of the *Chic* staff who ate all the food groups, didn't exercise every day and didn't smoke. As a result she was an average kind of female shape— you know, a bit fat—and of even temper. She had long red wavy hair, perfect skin, a face as pretty as a daisy and a great sense of humour. And another little eccentricity in the fashion world—she always wore flat shoes. I adored her.

I was just wondering how I was going to endure the rest of the car ride with the foghorn in front and the dark star to my right, when Frannie nudged me. She tipped her head in Alice's direction, pulled a goofy face and winked. I smiled and winked back, then I put my head on her comforting shoulder and closed my eyes. I was just starting to drift off into a much-needed doze—we hadn't got back from last night's dinner with the Gucci PR until after midnight, and I'd been up at six thirty to do my yoga and hair—when I was brutally awoken by Bee's voice booming out at its usual heavy metal decibels. She had bones as delicate as a bird and a voice like a freight train, that woman. I could never put them together in the same package, but there she was. Roseanne Barr in Gwyneth Paltrow's body.

"Luigi," she was braying. "How far are we from the venue? I recognized that factory we've just passed. Aren't we getting close?"

"Si, Signora Bee," said Luigi, our lovely, long-suffering driver. "We are two minutes."

"Oh shit," said Bee. "How embarrassing. I'm not going to be on time for bloody Pucci. They don't even advertise. I'm only going for the cushions."

Oh, no, I thought, here we go, the Pucci grab-fest. They always put Pucci-print cushions on the seats at their show and the audience divided cleanly into those who grabbed as many of them as possible as they were leaving, and those of us who didn't. If you were a non-cushion taker and hadn't fixed yours in an iron grip just before the end of the show, you would feel it snatched from under your buttocks the minute you raised them a millimetre from your seat. I found the grabbiness of it quite repulsive, but the most surprising people would come out with armfuls of the things. Bee and Alice were big cushion snatchers. Frannie and I, categorically were not.

"Turn off here and go round the block a few times will you, Luigi?" said Bee, lighting yet another cigarette.

I felt Frannie's body slump next to me. She hated the limo. She called it the travelling torture chamber.

"I knew I should have got the bloody tram out here," she whispered to me in her rich Dundee accent. "Now I'll have to sit in her bloody smoke for another half-hour."

We had just turned down a side street away from the rest of the queue of chauffeur-driven cars we had been stuck in, when Bee suddenly turned round and looked at us through her huge dark glasses. Her blonde bob was so straight and perfect it looked as though it had been sprayed on to her head. Well, it had been in a way. Her hairdresser got to the hotel at seven every morning.

"Are you all planning to go to the Ferrucci party tonight?" she said.

I felt Alice's spine stiffen as she sat up straight. I glanced at her and saw her face was lit up by a radiant smile, as though Bee in her new-season Prada coat was like a vision of heaven for her.

"Well . . ." said Alice, in the same non-committal tones she used whenever a newspaper reporter asked her for a quote about what she thought of a show. "There were some lovely pieces . . ." was the best the most hardened hackette would ever get out of Alice. In the same vein, she was clearly waiting to see what Bee wanted her to say before answering this question.

"How about you two?" said Bee.

I shrugged and felt Frannie slump in her seat. Another party, more smoke.

"I dunno," I said. "I might go. I was going to see how tired I was after the show tonight. We've got another big day tomorrow and Marni's at nine in the morning, all the way out here again."

Bee took a deep drag on her cigarette and blew the smoke right at us. Frannie let out a little groan.

"Well, you've all got to go," said Bee. "Because I'm not. Going to plead migraine. Got to put that Stracciatella strumpet back in her box."

She was waving the seating plan that always came with the Ferrucci invitation. She hadn't seen it until she'd opened her file of the day's invitations, when we'd got into the car that morning. The howl that had gone up when she'd noticed her less than ideal placement would have been audible out at Lake Como.

The "day files," as we called them, were delivered to the hotel the night before by Chic International's Milan office, which looked after all the Italian advertising clients, and getting the show invitations—with suitable placements—for all of *Chic*'s eight international editions. It was a job similar to juggling planes at Heathrow on a Saturday in August. I always tore my envelope open the minute I got it to see where my seats were, but Bee never bothered to look at her invites until the last minute. She just assumed she'd always have her rightful place—one of the best seats in the house.

"How dare she put me close to runway entrance," she was still raving. "I'd only be able to see the back of the bloody clothes as they went past. What does she think *Chic* is? Some crummy little freebie magazine? It's only the biggest-selling high-fashion and beauty lifestyle glossy in the British market. We have more AB women readers than any other comparable monthly magazine in the UK and a strong features base, alongside our world-class fashion pages."

Very gently, Frannie nudged me again. Bee's sales spiel cracked us up. She had it down so pat we were convinced she muttered it in her sleep. Frannie did a great impersonation after a couple of drinks.

"She knows I'm runway end or close to it," Bee was droning on. "So I'll make her look really bad to the boss, by not turning up at his stupid party, but I need you all to be there to tell everyone how sick I am."

She chucked her cigarette end out of the window and I saw Luigi push in the car's lighter on automatic pilot. He'd been Bee's Milan driver for six years, he knew the score.

"And do a number on that Giancarlo bloke," continued Bee, extracting another cigarette from the packet Luigi was proffering. "He's the one Antonello's listening to these days about the advertising, not that stupid little slut. Miss Stracciatella's star is fading as fast as her hideous orange tan."

She was still turned round in her seat glaring at us, so we couldn't even close our eyes and block her ranting out.

"I'll do the show, of course," she continued. "And I'll come back out here in a few weeks and have lunch with Antonello myself to smooth things over, but you three can just keep things ticking over for me at the party. Tell them I'm just *dying* of migraine."

She chuckled and sucked deeply on her fresh fag.

"Like I said, I'm definitely going to the party," said Alice, who had told me the night before she definitely wasn't. "I'm going to wear that dress Antonello gave me last season. That's why I brought it with me."

As more of Bee's smoke drifted back to us, Frannie opened her window a crack and pressed her tiny retroussé nose against the gap.

Twelve hours and six fashion shows later, at 9 p.m., with nothing more than five cups of coffee inside us since that morning, there we were sitting on hard seats, packed in like a Tokyo subway, waiting for the Ferrucci show to begin.

As if by magic—but actually thanks to Nushka—we had all been re-seated near the end of the runway, just to the left, with Bee in the front row, still wearing her dark glasses. She didn't normally wear them inside show venues—that was Anna Wintour's thing and there was nothing wanna about our Bee—but it was all part of her party-no-show migraine set-up.

Next to her was Alice in her Ferrucci evening dress, an amazing creation in yellow chiffon, constructed round a corset base, plunging at the neck and slashed right up her golden thighs—Alice was permatanned from fashion trips to exotic places, which she organized entirely around her beauty needs. She had styled the dress in her inimitable way, pairing it with a vintage kimono, a pair of men's flat black lace-ups and a trilby hat. Her long wavy blonde hair was pulled back into a demure pony-tail at the nape of her long neck and she was wearing the dangly antique pearl earrings which were among her many trademark "pieces." She looked amazing. Alice always did.

I was two rows behind her in the same clothes—and shoes—I'd been wearing since that morning, because I'd been forced to go to the hideous show of some ghastly minor advertiser just before this one, while Alice went back to the hotel to have a massage and get changed.

The only other spare time we'd had that day was over lunchtime and it had been a tough choice—eat, or shop. Actually, it wasn't that hard. Food lost. You had to grab your shopping moments while you could between shows and appointments, and the earlier in the week you could get into Prada the better. Every fashion editor in the world was headed in there too, to get the shoes you wanted, in the colour you wanted, in your size. It was brutal.

Milan was always the major shopping feeding frenzy of the shows season, even better than New York, London, and Paris, because all the big Italian labels had gorgeous things on offer in their Milan flagships that never made it to their other stores. On top of that it was cheaper there and best of all—we got discount. Thirty per cent discount. No wonder we all went bonkers. That lunchtime I had bought four pairs of Prada boots. Winter was coming, I would be going to several major cities to do shoots for the magazine, plus I had all the autumn boutique launches and the Christmas party season in London to cater for. I needed those boots.

You could practically hear our credit cards screaming with pain that afternoon as we'd loaded our carrier bags into the car and headed back out to the industrial area once again for the Emporio Armani show. I had lain back and closed my mind to the balance that must be racking up on that card. I'd actually been a bit worried that it might have been rejected at the Prada till, which would have been too humiliating.

I'd already ordered a new card from another bank to give myself a bit of extra credit for Paris. Nushka was going to send it out to the hotel there to be waiting for me. That would make five credit cards, but with trips expenses—which we had to cover ourselves and then claim back—and shopping needs, it was essential. The other pressure to buy up big in Milan was the need to plan ahead for the next shows season. In six months' time it would all happen again, starting in New York in September. It would probably be hot.

I'd been caught out by a New York Indian summer the first time I'd ever done the shows. What a nightmare. All my carefully assembled new winter gear was useless and there had been nothing summery left in store. They start putting snow boots and sheepskin coats into the shops in August, and all the summer clothes disappear overnight.

So I'd been forced to wear a pair of Birkenstocks to the New York shows and pretend it was a deliberate look. Flat shoes. Nightmare. After that I understood it was essential to buy your key pieces for the next season's shows, a full six months away, so I was now buying some shoes and boots to wear immediately, and others not to be touched until the following February, so they would still be box fresh. As I knew all too well, after doing eight seasons of them, you need the logistical skills of a general to cope with doing the shows, plus the physical endurance—and body fat percentage—of a marathon runner.

And people think fashion stylists are airheads.

Several rows behind me at Ferrucci that night, Frannie sat knitting. She usually managed to finish a jumper-and-a-half each season in the many hours we spent sitting in darkened spaces, on excruciatingly uncomfortable seats, waiting for fashion shows to begin. She'd added up that waiting time once on a slow day in the office, when Bee was away in the Caribbean on a free press trip.

"If you do New York, London, Milan, and Paris, and you average thirty shows in each fashion city," she'd said, her pudgy fingers punching her calculator. "Unless you're Miss Alee-chay and skive off half of them—that makes a hundred and twenty shows a season. My arse," she said, looking up at me over her John Lennon specs. "No wonder we're all nuts."

She went back to her calculations.

"OK, if you then reckon that each designer keeps us waiting between forty fecking minutes and the full hour—we'll be conservative and call it forty minutes—you will spend . . ."

Her fingers did a few more taps. Her parents owned a sweet shop; she was good at adding things up.

". . . a grand total of eighty hours a season just sitting waiting."

She tapped the calculator one last time and her mouth dropped open in shock.

"That's three-point-three-three-three recurring—nearly three-and-a-half days, each season, just bloody waiting!" she shrieked. "Jesus Chreesus, that makes six-point-six days a year—nearly a *week*, waiting. I feel sick. I could re-paint my house in that time. With a toothbrush.

"Just think, Emily," she said, looking horrified. "We're both twenty-nine and we've wasted seven weeks of our adult lives—just *waiting*. I feel ill."

A true Scottish grafter, with an overactive work ethic, Frannie hated wasting time and she'd taken up knitting just so she could do something constructive in those three-point-three days. It was the only useful thing she could think of that you could do in the dark, which was also portable. Luckily, her husband was a landscape gardener and appreciated a steady supply of thick woolly jumpers.

The funny thing was, though, I didn't mind the waiting. Even in the gloom there was always so much to look at. From my vantage point in the second, or third row—ideally, the first *raised* row, which is actually the best place to sit at a fashion show—I could see everyone. But unlike Bee and the rest of them, skewered like specimen butterflies in the front row, no one was looking at me. I could have my own private gawkathon. And this one was shaping up to be a beauty.

The Antonello Ferrucci show was always a major circus. As one of the richest and most successful designers in the world he had the cash to put on a major extravaganza, the pull to bring in some serious front-page celebs—flown over from LA in his private jet—and the advertising budget to ensure that every big name in the fashion media turned up, scrubbed up and smiling. After several seasons showing out in a big warehouse in the industrial area, where we had already been twice that day in long dreary limo rides, savvy Antonello had realized that the fashion pack hated trailing over there—where there were no chic boutiques or bars—and that it was colouring our experiences of the collections. Colouring them grey.

So while other designers were moving out to the big cheaper spaces, Antonello had come back to show in the courtyard of his most central Milan palazzo (he had several). We could walk from his show to our favourite restaurants, even in the typical teetering fashionista footwear I preferred. Clever, clever Antonello. But then you don't grow up working on fish stalls in the street markets of Naples and learn nothing about human frailty.

The other effect of this smaller venue was a much tighter guest list, which made the scramble for invitations much more intense—always good for getting a hype going—and which had resulted in Bee's less-than-perfect initial seating arrangement. Even now, forty-five minutes after the show was officially meant to have started, I could see my editor's *bête noire du jour*, Domenica Stracciatella, Ferrucci's head of PR, running backwards and forwards like a demented chicken, as she tried to keep all the front-row guests happy with their seats. Quite an achievement in heels even higher than mine and quite the shortest skirt I had ever seen.

At one point she seemed to leap, like Lara Croft in a lime-green mini dress, across the raised catwalk to the other side, to intercept some new arrivals she needed to shift to different, less fabulous, seats without them quite realizing it. Smothering them with air kisses, her long white-blonde hair and gold bangles whirling, she propelled them into a B-list spot and left them there, dazed but still smiling. Even more amazingly, she did it all without showing her pants. What an operator.

Five minutes later, apart from a small gap centre right, where the big-name celebrities—always the last to arrive—would sit, the front row was in place.

In the best seat in the house was American *Vogue*'s all-powerful editor-in-chief, Anna Wintour. Fashion's Mona Lisa behind her dark glasses and inscrutable amused expression, she looked confidently at nothing, while her loyal lieutenant André Leon Talley—at least

seven feet tall and wearing a full-length red crocodile-skin coat—
talked to her *sotto voce*. Every single person in that venue would have
given their best Prada shoes to listen in on that conversation.

On Miss Wintour's other side sat Grace Coddington, the magazine's universally respected fashion director. A supermodel herself in
the Seventies, she had nothing to prove and always wore a simple
black top and pants, and was probably the only woman in the front
row in flat shoes. She was definitely the only one wearing no makeup.
At the very top of fashion's tree, some people can rise above it. She
was Frannie's total heroine and role model. Especially as they both
had red hair.

Occupying the other best seat in the place was the most important journalist from the press corps, the *International Herald Tribune*'s Suzy Menkes. The only newspaper reporter in the world
equally respected, feared, and adored by designers, Suzy went to
every show, accepted no gifts except flowers and chocolates, and always wrote her sincere opinion.

As a result she was regularly banned by piqued designers, who
all ended up asking her back, because the only thing worse than being panned by Suzy was not appearing in her reviews. Despite this
power, she was as famous for her immaculate manners as she was for
her frankness—and for her signature hairstyle, a Forties-style vic-
tory roll on top of her head. One of the greatest world authorities
on fashion, she was not herself subject to its whims.

A few places along from her was Louise Kretzner. Not so well
liked, but almost as powerful, she was the chief reporter and gossip
snitch for *World Fashion Daily*, the fashion industry's newspaper.
Although it was published in New York, subscribers could read
each day's issue online, or snap it up in photocopied form at show
venues, although the really chic had the copies delivered directly to
their hotels. If you wanted to stay in touch with what was happening in the world of fashion, you had to read it—and with Louise
you were sure of getting the dirt along with her rather poorly written show reviews. What she lacked in finesse, she more than made
up for with insider info.

To the left and right of them were the other American magazines.
All resolutely not acknowledging each other. Then the Italian,

French, Russian and German magazines and papers all grouped by nationality. You could always spot the German editors as they had a penchant for rather severe bleached haircuts and too much leather clothing. As Bee had once said, they dressed more like hairdressers than fashion editors.

The Asian journos were all seated together in what seemed to be an ever-expanding group, as China seemed to have spawned a huge fashion media overnight. They were distinguished by their use of tiny camcorders, rather than notebooks to record the styles. Mixed in with them were the Aussies, who always seemed to be having a good time, despite their crap seats.

Back in our little perch, we were flanked by the rest of the British magazines and press, all of us chatting to each other and joking, except for Bee and Eva Jones, the editor of *pure* magazine—which was always written with a small "p." I always thought *"precious"* would have been a better name for it. Despite the fact that they seriously loathed each other, Bee and Eva—or Beaver as we all called her—were nearly always seated next to each other, and their mutual hatred gave the rest of us a great deal of entertainment.

Beaver was as quiet as Bee was noisy, with a permanently disapproving expression and a classic hen's bum mouth. But the funny thing was, that while loud-mouthed Bee's hair was a perfect shiny blonde geometric curtain, cold calculating Beaver's was an untameable mop of brown frizz. The ultimate control freak had uncontrollable horror hair. Sometimes that fact alone was enough to keep Bee going. "She's got bad hair, she's got bad hair," I had heard her muttering like a mantra on more than one occasion.

Despite the differences in their personalities—Beaver was a teetotal vegan, who sacked any staff member she caught smoking—the magazines they edited were head-to-head for readers and advertising. It was outright war between them. Both claimed to edit "the biggest-selling high-fashion and beauty lifestyle glossy in the British market, with more AB women readers than any other comparable monthly magazine in the UK, etc. etc. . . . ." They cracked us up.

As usual, *pure*'s senior fashion editor, Nelly Stelios, was sitting next to me and we always had a right old laugh about it all. Nelly—real name Nyla—was a north London girl from a huge Greek family, with a laugh as dirty as a drain and a mouth even dirtier. She was quite exhausting to be around, but I loved her. Everybody did.

Her mum and dad had a chip shop, an early environment which still showed on Nelly's hips, but she carried off her curves with the aplomb appropriate to Kentish Town's Sophia Loren, which is how she saw herself. She never wore trousers, always fitted dresses with high heels and red lipstick, her long curly black hair in a falling-down up do. Men adored Nelly—to the great annoyance of many of the self-starvation brigade, who felt that skinny women with straight hair had sole rights to sexual attention.

"Fucken hell," she was saying, pushing a wayward curl behind one ear and sucking on her half-broken biro. "I'm gasping for a fag. Twice over to factoryville in one day in an enclosed space with bloody Beaver. Jesus, what a nightmare. She won't let me fucking smoke in the car. God, she's a stupid cow."

"You should work for Bee," I said. "She never stops smoking. It drives Frannie nuts. She says Bee's turning us into Arbroath smokies."

"Shall we swap jobs, then?" said Nelly.

"All right," I shrugged. "They probably wouldn't notice. We're just faceless drones really, aren't we?"

"Actually," said Nelly, one of her evil grins spreading over her face. "Maybe not. I'd have to put up with bloody Alee-chay and it would take more than a few gaspers to get me through a car ride with her. I'd have to crack open the voddie. Talking of which, are you going on to the party after this?"

"Yes," I said, without much enthusiasm. I was knackered. I just wanted to go back to the hotel, kick off those effing shoes, get out of my clothes, have a bath and collapse into bed.

"Ex-cell-*ent*," said Nelly, wriggling in her seat to the pre-show music. "Party time."

Nelly's appetite for parties defied belief. She went to all of them—sometimes four in one night—right through the fashion season, and still got up for the first show the next morning. She had the constitution of a cart horse. And the legs, it has to be said.

"Hey, skinny britches," she said, smacking me on the knee. "Why don't you ditch the stiffs and come out with me tonight? I'm meeting some people for a drink first and then we're going to hit the party fuelled up and ready. Is prune face coming too?"

She nodded down towards Alice's blonde head. "Is that why she's all frocked up? Looks like an out-of-work Christmas tree fairy. Stupid arse. Look at that chronic hat and what *are* those shoes? For fuck's sake."

"Apart from Bee, we're all going to it," I said, feeling more tired all the time. The temperature in the vast space we were sitting in—basically a giant plastic tent inside the courtyard of the sixteenth-century palazzo—was beyond stifling. Even in my sleeveless top I could feel sweat running down my back. So glamorous.

"Frannie Pannie too?" said Nelly. "Brilliant. Where is she? Let's send her a note telling her to meet us at the door straight after this, so we can give misery guts and Beaver the slip."

She scribbled a note in her messy shorthand pad, tore out the page and got the total strangers sitting behind us to pass it back to Frannie.

"No, not her, you dozy cow," she was saying, standing up and yelling back across the rows. "The redhead. Two rows back. Keep going. The one who looks like Orphan Annie, but fatter. Oy! Franster. Bloody note! Grab it, you silly bitch!"

As Nelly yelled, Beaver half turned round, looking as sour as a pickled plum. She was always telling Nelly off for behaving "inappropriately" at the shows. Last season she'd given her an official caution for taking her knickers off during the Armani show and waving them at a friend opposite. She only got away with it because her pictures were so beautiful. I kicked her on the ankle.

"Sit down," I hissed. "Beaver's giving you stink eye."

"Oh, shit," said Nelly, flopping back into her seat and leaning down towards her editor and grinning beatifically. "Wotcha, Eva. All right?"

Nelly was saved by the arrival of the celebrities, their entrance heralded by an explosion of camera flashes, the paparazzi swarming along with them like a pack of rats, kept at bay by a phalanx of King Kong security guards.

"Who is it? Who is it?" murmured the crowd, who all pretended they were the coolest people on the planet, but who were in fact just as impressed by a famous face as anyone else. Probably more so actually, considering we were a major part of the international conspiracy that made these nonentities into celebrities.

"What silly tart is it this time, then?" said Nelly, standing up again. I yanked her arm to get her to sit down, but before I could stop her, she was off, squeezing along the row and round the end of the catwalk to have a gawp, pushing through the crowd in her Fifties polka-dot dress and red high heels with ribbons laced up around her ample calves.

The amazing thing about Nelly, though, was while she could be coarser than a fishwife, she really was the most brilliant stylist. She had the rare ability to do the all-important "beautiful" shoots, which is the kind of fashion readers really like, rather than the super-duper conceptual stuff people like Alice did. Nelly's pictures always made me sigh, they were so gorgeous. And all the models loved working with her, because she made them look so wonderful. Many a lucrative cosmetics contract had been won by a model's portfolio full of Nelly's pictures. Alice frequently made her models look hideous—because she could. Everyone told her it was "art." Which Nelly had once told her was Greek for "shite."

She quickly came stumping back and I saw Beaver beckon her over. Her brash and fearless stylist did have her uses. Nelly leaned into the thicket of her editor's hair to whisper who it was, because Beaver clearly didn't want Bee to earwig and get the celeb-sighting low-down from a member of the *pure* team.

"Madonna," whispered Nelly to me, as she sat down.

"Really," I said, sitting up like a begging dog.

"Naaaaaaa! You silly cow," said Nelly, punching my arm. "It's never Madonna, is it? Or Kylie. It's Britney and Posh. Again."

She rolled her big brown eyes.

"Who's the bloke?" I asked, peering over. "He's getting as much attention as the girls. It's not Becks is it?" I said, hopefully. I had a major crush on David Beckham.

Nelly looked at me.

"You're pathetic," she said. "You really *love* him, don't you? I bet you've got a poster of him on your office wall."

I giggled. "I have actually . . . No shirt."

"Well, tough shit, babe, it's only George Clooney."

And then, maddeningly, before I could have a proper gawp, the lights went down, the music roared out and Karolina Kurkova appeared at the top of the runway copping a pose in a single spotlight. She was wearing a huge Barbarella wig, a tiny silver bikini and bright pink snakeskin thigh boots. The hair on the back of my neck prickled. The magic had been unleashed. The show had begun.

It was only an hour and ten minutes late.

2

TWENTY minutes later, while Antonello Ferrucci was still taking his bow, holding Karolina's hand—never a good idea for a man of Neapolitan stature—and blowing kisses to Posh and Britney, or more likely, to George Clooney, Nelly was hustling me out of the row, via everybody's feet, so we could make good our escape without Alice seeing us.

Right on cue, as instructed in Nelly's note, Frannie caught up with us at the exit. Nelly blew kisses at the security gorillas, who were gawping at her cleavage, then she grabbed our hands and had us skipping along the cobbled street like the von Trapp family.

"Pardeeeeee!" she yodelled into the night.

"Who are we meeting?" I asked, Nelly's enthusiasm temporarily taking my mind off my feet.

"And do they smoke?" asked Frannie.

"I bloody 'ope so," said Nelly, puffing to a walking pace. "Just a few guys I met through Seamus—you know, the guy that does *pure*'s catwalk pictures? Sexy Irish geezer? Bit on the short side? Anyway, him, some mates of his and a few of the usual suspects. Peter from *The Daily Reporter*—bitchy queen, good laugh—Dizzy from *The Sunday Opinion*, her girlfriend Rani, you know, that model I used for my ball gowns-at-the-circus story? A few others, the usual party crew. And whoever we pick up in the bar."

She chuckled heartily. I often thought if you could bottle Nelly's energy the bottom would fall right out of the drug trade. And the really amazing thing was, she never took them. She was like that naturally.

My phone rang. I couldn't hear a voice on the other end, but there seemed to be a party in full swing. I could hear loud music and a lot of hubbub and screeching.

"Hello?" I said, wondering if one of my friends back in London had sat on their mobile in a nightclub and rung me by mistake. "Hello?" I said again, beginning to get annoyed. Then I could hear someone talking, although it was pretty indistinct.

"No," the voice was saying. "It was a deliberately matt lip . . ."

"What?" I said.

"Oh, thank you, yes. It was mainly inspired by Jane Fonda's Barbarella, with a bit of Liz Taylor's Cleopatra, but modern . . ."

"Who is this?"

"That's right, but there is an 's' on the end. OK, thanks a lot . . . Emily? Are you there?"

"Jacko!" I screamed down the phone, as I heard the deep dark chuckle, like something primal, which was the rumbling gut laugh of my adored best boy pal Paul Toussaints, who I sometimes called Jacko for reasons that went right back to the start of our friendship. Among his other talents, Paul could do a brilliant moonwalk.

"Where *are* you?" I squealed, literally jumping up and down with excitement. He'd been living in New York for over a year and I missed him hideously.

"Backstage at Ferrucci . . ." he answered. "Doing an interview with *Allure* . . . just thought I'd share the moment with you."

I squealed again.

"I had no idea you were even in Milan."

"Make-up director, sweetie. Don't you read the show notes that are so helpfully placed on your seats?"

"Are you kidding? A load of bollocks about what Mr. Ferrucci is 'feeling' this season?"

"Yeah, usually the tight ass of his latest male model. Anyway, where are you, you big slapper?"

"On my way to the Four Seasons bar with Nelly and Frannie and then on to Mr. Ferrucci's party. You?"

"See you in the bar in five. Just have to pack up and I'm outta here." He paused and then added in an even deeper voice. "Don't wash."

Just another of our little jokes.

The Four Seasons bar wasn't our normal territory, it was a bit grown-up for us—and a bit hard to get the bills through expenses—but it was great people-watching, and handy for that night's festivities. The party was being held back at the palazzo we had just left.

As a rule Nelly didn't so much enter a bar as invade it and usually the proprietors were pleased to see her. There was something so big and bright about Nelly's personality that people just reacted to her positively. She seemed like "somebody," because she thought she was. I suppose it's what you call charisma. Well, most people reacted positively, but there were exceptions and we were looking at one.

"Hello, darling," said Nelly to the sourpuss who was seating people in the bar that night. "Got a spot for three thirsty girls?"

He gave us the once-over and was clearly wondering whether he could just turn us away, when Nelly suddenly charged off.

"Iggy!" she was shouting, already en route to the far side of the bar where fashion's brightest new star, Igor Veselinovic, was holding court. He greeted Nelly like the old friend she was. They'd met at least twice before.

Actually, Nelly had been one of the earliest people to latch on to the Serbian designer's talent, when he had just left Saint Martins and was showing off-off-off-schedule in London. She was certainly the first stylist to use his clothes in a major shoot and, unusually in our industry, he didn't seem to have forgotten. He was also gracious enough to acknowledge that Nelly's beautiful pictures had helped him get his new gig as the ready-to-wear designer at Rucca, one of Italy's most prestigious accessories houses, an amazing platform for a young designer. Already people were saying he was the new Alexander McQueen.

And that was how the party began. Firmly attached to Iggy's group, which also included rising fashion photographer Nivek Thims, whom I knew a little from London, a couple of up-and-coming (literally, if Nivek had anything to do with it) male models, the ageing billionaire playboy CEO of Rucca and his Italian starlet wife. Instantly, we were the power posse in the bar. Nelly turned back and grinned at the miserable maître d', who looked furious.

Gradually the rest of Nelly's pals turned up, all with a few extra friends in tow, so that after about an hour we had taken over half the place, with bottles of champagne on constant order. All on Rucca's corporate bill. Even Frannie was happy—the Four Seasons had excellent air conditioning.

That must have been where I first met Miles. He was definitely there, but I have no memory of it. I met so many people that night, as I did just about every night at the shows. It was like being in a kaleidoscope of smiling faces and air-kissing lips, accompanied by lots of laughter about God-only-knows what, but it all seemed hilarious at the time.

I do remember my darling Paul arriving, looking more handsome than ever in a beautiful Dior Homme suit and a crisp white shirt, and I remember him greeting me his usual way, which involved grinding his slender hips into mine, a routine which still made me blush.

"Stop it, you big poofter," I said. "I can feel your manly length."

"Oh, come on," he said, licking my cheek. "You like that, don't you?"

"You are such a perve, Paul Toussaints. Stop it, yuk," I spluttered, triggering one of his belly laughs.

Paul had been my absolutely number-one gay-boy buddy for nearly ten years. We'd met at the south London tech where I'd been doing an art foundation course, and he'd been studying hairdressing. We'd seen each other around the college—at nineteen he was already gorgeous and incredibly stylish, so you couldn't really miss him—but we didn't actually meet until we both happened to be at the same fancy-dress party. The theme was *Pulp Fiction*—well, it

was 1994—and we were both dressed as the Uma Thurman character in black bob wigs.

It was instant chemistry.

"Hey, baby girl," he'd said, shamelessly checking me out from
head to toe. "I like your style."

"I like yours," I said.

"Yeah," he said, adjusting his wig. "Everyone expected me to
come as Samuel L. Jackson, but I told them, you can shove your
racial stereotyping, I just want to look good. Not ethnic."

He laughed that deep chuckle. I couldn't help grinning at him.

"Damn," he said suddenly, clicking his fingers. "You've got better shoes than me. I think we'd better dance."

Not long after that, he'd showed me his moonwalk and had me in
hysterics describing his childhood obsession with Michael Jackson,
the first man he had ever loved. He knew every word of every song
on *Thriller*. So did I.

Within days we were doing our first fashion shoot together, with
him doing hair and make-up, me styling the clothes, and a photography student—my boyfriend at the time—taking the shots. We
sold those pictures to a style magazine and none of us ever looked
back. We all had second jobs to pay the rent—I was a waitress,
my boyfriend was a labourer and Paul mixed cocktails like Tom
Cruise—but from that point all three of us were on the fashion
groove train and we had no intention of jumping off.

Now, nearly ten years later, Paul was one of the most successful
make-up artists on the circuit and he'd left his sink-estate childhood so far behind him it was almost just a bad dream. He lived in
a loft in downtown Manhattan, always flew first class and spoke
like the international style surfer he was. From his accent you'd
never have picked him out as a "Sarf London" boy, if you hadn't
known. But it wasn't pretension that made his voice change along
with his lifestyle, it was just part of his personal metamorphosis.

Professionally, he'd actually left me way behind too—although
he was always trying to get me to move to New York—but we still
worked together whenever we could. That night at the Four Seasons, though, I hadn't seen him for months and we stood there gab-
bling like lunatics, with so much to catch up on. It was ridiculous

really, because we emailed and called each other all the time, but there was nothing like being in the same place together.

After a few minutes someone stood up to go to the loo and Paul pounced on the empty armchair, patting his lap and making pouty faces at me. I sat on his knee and put my arms round his neck. He growled into my ear.

I didn't think twice about it. We'd always had a very physical relationship—not sexual, of course, Paul was rampantly homosexual—but we just felt so comfortable with each other and I suppose it was part of his endlessly teasing personality, to tantalize a straight woman with his glorious physique. It amused him, how beautiful I thought he was. I wasn't the only one in awe of Paul's looks. He'd had endless offers to model, but apart from one cameo appearance in a Yohji Yamamoto menswear show—along with John Malkovich and Dennis Hopper—he always refused.

"Not going to trade on da physical, darlin'," he'd say in imitation of his grandmother's Jamaican accent. "Looks ruined me mama and I'm not going to let them ruin me, praise Jesus."

He had good reason for not wanting to emulate his mother's life. Seriously beautiful as a young woman—he carried a picture of her in his wallet—she'd been led astray by a handsome, sweet-talking bad boy, who beat her, pimped her and regularly impregnated her, so that Paul grew up the youngest of five children, and the only boy, watching their mother being pummelled by their father's fists. When he wasn't in prison.

Once he got away from that Peckham flat, Paul never went back. He said he just couldn't cope with what his mother and sisters had become, but he did stay in touch with his grandma, a devout member of the local Baptist church, who adored her grandson.

My Childhood was pretty gothic too, albeit in a Home Counties setting, and it was one of the many things we had in common. In fact, talking to Paul about his difficult early years had made it a lot easier for me to come to terms with mine. He had a psycho dad and I had a psycho mum, we'd both survived, we'd both moved on. Or run away, depending how you looked at it.

"Bloody Nora," said Nelly's voice suddenly. "Look at those two, they're practically snogging. Anyone would think he fancied girls.

Oy, Paulie, if you want to kiss a girl, I am available." She bumped one hip in his direction, but then she was distracted by the background music.

"Oooh," she squealed. "I *love* the Sugababes, they're London girls, like meeeeee. Lon-du-on," she chanted, like the Arsenal supporter she was. And she jumped up on a table to dance.

As I stood up to stop her—it wasn't the time, or the place, and if it got back to Beaver, she'd be dead meat—I saw Anna Wintour walking into the hotel. I remembered that she always stayed there and it suddenly struck me that she was coming *back* to it from the Ferrucci party. If Frannie and I missed that gig we were going to be in so much trouble with Bee, it really wasn't funny.

"Stay there," I said to Paul. "I've got to find Frannie. Emergency."

I looked round the room for her red head and found it in a corner, deep in conversation with Nelly's photographer friend Seamus. Frannie was reading his palm—a sure sign she was pissed—and if I hadn't known she was happily married I would have thought she was having a big flirt with him too. I almost hated to interrupt her, but this was serious.

"Frannie," I hissed. "We've got to go to that party, or Bee will kill us."

Frannie's face snapped into a rictus of horror.

"Fuck me blind," she said. "I'd totally forgotten about that stupid thing."

She stood up, paused for a moment and then looked down at Seamus, who was staring sadly at his palm.

"Hey, Shuey," she said to him in her richest Scottish burr. "Want to come to a wee party with us?"

"That would be grand," said Seamus in his Irish one; it was like some kind of Celtic voice-off.

I went back to tell Nelly, who had been ordered down from the table by the miserable maître d' and was starting to look bored. Always dangerous.

"Nell," I hissed at her. "We've forgotten the bloody Ferrucci party. Frannie and I have to go."

Her face brightened immediately.

"Fucken ace," she said, draining her glass. "More free booze. Come on everybody."

I have no idea how we all got into that party. There was a great crowd of people milling around the entrance trying to breach security and the door staff were vetting people like the CIA.

Only half of us had invitations; Seamus and his little crew were dressed like roadies, only smellier; we were all drunk; yet somehow when our noisy group arrived, with Paul, Iggy and Nelly at the lead, we were all ushered straight through. It just happens like that somehow, if you know how it works. It's all about confidence.

I grabbed Frannie's arm when we got inside and I saw how big and dark the space was, with lots of curtained-off booths, conversation pits and different party zones.

"I've got an idea," I whispered to her. "We'll tell Aleechay that we've been here the whole time. With this set-up, she'll never know. We'll tell her we ran off to go to the loo after the show and then came straight here. Cool?"

"Cool," said Frannie, shaking my hand. "I love lying to that bitch . . . and look—there she is."

Alice was chatting animatedly with Antonello Ferrucci in the roped-off VIP area and I could see Beaver sitting on her own nearby looking really put out about it. Excellent. Bee would be ecstatic. And Alice would be feeling so up herself about being in the elite area, she wouldn't have noticed we weren't there earlier anyway.

But I was so glad we finally were. Ferrucci's clothes may have been the preferred choice of hookers and gangsters, but his parties were seriously classy. Frannie and I went on a swift exploratory tour and discovered there were several different bars dispensing champagne, vodka, cocktails, made-to-order alcoholic fresh-fruit smoothies, or whatever else you wanted. And in case anyone felt peckish, white-gloved waiters were circulating constantly with perfect canapés, just the right size to swallow in one go, without spitting crumbs over the person you were chatting to.

There were two dance floors with DJs in rotation, an ambient room to chill out in and another area done out like a casino, with roulette and baccarat tables. You exchanged your invitation for a pile of plastic chips and if you won, you could cash them in for special Ferrucci "dollars"—complete with his Botoxed face—which you would be able to spend the next day at his boutique in Via della Spiga.

And, of course, there were masses of beautiful people to perve on. All the models from the show seemed to be there, along with all their male counterparts from Ferrucci's famously erotic advertising campaigns, mingling with faces I recognized from the front three rows of the shows, and plenty of Eurotrash party padding.

While Frannie and I had been cruising around and sorting out our Alice strategy, Nelly had been busy getting things "sorted," as she called it. She'd managed to commandeer a circular booth that she announced was our "party central" and waiters were arriving with bottles of champagne, trays of glasses and pyramids of chocolate-dipped strawberries.

"Let the games begin!" she yelled into my ear, and they did.

What a wild and crazy whirl that night was. I just remember people, loads and loads of people, coming over and chatting and kissing and laughing, laughing, laughing.

Every now and then, I would team up with Paul and we'd do "a once around the room," which was a quick tour of the venue to check out what was going on and who was there to bitch about and squeal with and lust after, and what they were wearing, before heading back to our HQ. I waved at Alice in the VIP area as we went past and I don't know which of us was happier about our relative locations in relation to that velvet rope.

And then, of course, there was the dancing. I remember Paul first grabbing me when our favourite Missy Elliott track came on and after that I didn't leave the dance floor for what seemed like hours. I grooved with him for ages and then with Nelly and Frannie and Seamus and whoever was there. It didn't matter, I was just dancing with life really. And it's amazing the power champagne has to make you forget how much your feet hurt. Then "Starry Eyed Surprise" came on and the DJ had it on some kind of repeat and a whole group of us were dancing together, with our arms round each other's shoulders.

And that's when I did notice Miles. He was on one side of me in our dancing circle, with his arm round my shoulder. He was wearing an old rock-tour T-shirt with the sleeves cut off—trust me to have total recall of the styling details—and I remember noticing the big, brown, muscly biceps coming out of it. In a kind of drunken dance daze I looked along the arm until I got to the face and then somehow he had both his arms around my neck and everyone else in the room just disappeared.

We danced together for ages and if all my other friends were still there I didn't notice them. All I could see and feel and smell was him. Yet, I think if I'd never seen Miles again after that night I don't think I would have been able to pick him out in a line-up. I wasn't aware of him as an individual, he was a kind of universal male presence and nothing else existed.

We danced apart, we danced in a clinch, he held me close and he whirled me round and once he stopped me dead in the middle of it all and just gazed into my eyes. I remember it clearly; my stomach did a backflip.

I came out of my trance when Nelly suddenly lurched back on to my radar, dancing with some guy I vaguely remembered had been at the Four Seasons with us and who, I eventually realized through my champagne haze, was Iggy Veselinovic. Then Nelly and I were dancing together, the way you just are on a night like that, and I don't know what happened to the guys.

Suddenly I badly needed to pee and Nelly and I headed off to the loo together, giggling and talking total nonsense, with her insisting that Iggy was straight, which I found very hard to believe.

"A straight male fashion designer?" I said. "He could join a circus. In the freak show section."

"I'm telling you, babe," insisted Nelly. "He's got my ovaries twitching and Nelly's gonads are never wrong. The man is straight and he wants to shag me."

The ladies' loo was as tricked up as the rest of the party. It was done out like an old-fashioned powder room with skirted dressing tables and stools, and all the Ferrucci make-up and fragrances laid out for us to use. We had great fun squirting each other with the ones we hated the most and trying on sparkly purple lipstick.

After a while I was getting bored of hearing about Iggy and the ghastly perfume was starting to make us both feel sick, so we headed back to party central, where most of our gang seemed to have re-grouped. And then it just seemed to be time to go. Paul told me Frannie had already left and that he had to be up early to prepare for a show, so he dashed off and the rest of us drifted down the stairs towards the exit.

Then Nelly heard yet another of her favourite tracks starting up and grabbed Iggy to go back for one more dance and a couple of people had to wait at the cloakroom for their coats and someone else disappeared back in for a pee and suddenly it was just me and Miles standing on the street hailing a cab, which we both got into.

I said, "Hotel Principe, *per favore*," and Miles said nothing. He just put those strong brown arms around me again and kissed me, very slowly, taking me right back into that zone where nothing existed but him and me melded together on some kind of lateral plane.

And in that state, when we pulled up at the hotel, it seemed perfectly natural for him to throw a twenty-euro note at the cab driver and take my hand as we walked into the hotel, picked up my key and went up to my room.

Where we shagged like rabbits till dawn.

3

I DON'T want to go on about the sex in detail, because it would just sound yuck and it was so, well, beautiful really. Suffice to say that, just like the saying goes, Miles took me to places that I had never been before (cloud-cuckoo-land?) and between, er, events, he was really nice to talk to as well. He was cuddly too. And although he was clearly some kind of Olympic-class sexual athlete, he seemed to enjoy the general closeness as much as the actual rogering.

We spent a lot of the night just lying there on the super-king-size bed looking into each other's eyes and breathing, drinking each other in with that sense of primeval wonder that only sex with someone new can inspire.

"I can't believe I'm here with you," he said.

"Neither can I," I replied, with all sincerity.

"I thought you were getting it on with that black guy at first. Gee, he's a good-looking bloke. Come to think of it," he laughed, "why aren't you with him?"

"Paul? Well, he is a total babe, but he's my best mate and when it comes to his private life, he makes Liberace look butch. He's what you might call a very *active* homosexual, but I don't see much of him these days, hence the smooching."

"I'm glad about that," said Miles, pulling me closer and nuzzling my ear. "I had my eye on you and I was very disappointed when I saw you cuddling up with him."

"When did you have your eye on me?" I asked, stupid girl, loving the flattery.

"You really want to know?"

I nodded.

"For just over a year so far . . ."

"What do you mean?" I asked, equally mystified and thrilled.

"Well, you know I do runway pictures, right?"

I nodded again.

"Well, it gets really boring stuck there waiting for shows to start squashed in with hundreds of other foul-breathed stinking photographers, most of whom I wouldn't want to sit next to on a bus . . ." He paused. "Do you know they keep us waiting for over three days a season, when you add it up?"

"Yes, I did actually. Anyway, go on."

Go on to the bit about me.

"Well," he said, pulling me closer. "It gets really boring and really stinky in the snake-pit so we have a game we play to pass the time: we look at all you girls through our long lenses and decide who we'd most like to root."

"To what?"

"Root—you know, er, 'shag'? It's an Australian word."

"Ah, well," I said. "Gisele, surely. Or maybe Karolina?"

"No, not the models," he said, apparently genuine. "None of us want to root the models. When you look at them all day, they just become objects, sexless objects. I mean the *real* girls, that's who we look at. The audience. Last season I picked you. And I picked you this season too."

I was too surprised to speak.

"I think you're gorgeous."

He kissed me a bit, to prove his point.

"Anyway," he continued. "So Seamus told me he knew the girl who usually sits next to you—Nelly—because she works for *pure* and he invited me along tonight and I came because I thought you might be there too. So when I walked into the Four Seasons and saw you I felt like I'd won the lottery. Until you sat on your mate's knee, but . . ."

"You stalked me," I said, interrupting, feeling a bit weird about it suddenly.

"Yep," he said. "And now I'm going to stalk you again."

And he did, and then I didn't mind so much.

But despite all that lovely flattering stuff and the preternaturally great sex, like I said, I knew I wasn't falling in love with him. There were just so many reasons why it was never going to work between me and Miles and I knew that right from the start.

For one thing, there was the location problem—he lived in Sydney and I lived in Westbourne Grove, and I had comforted enough girlfriends heartbroken over holiday romances to know that long-distance love just does not work.

Then there was his career as a struggling art photographer. He'd told me that he actually hated fashion and he only did the shows to make enough money not to have to work the rest of the time, so he could concentrate on his art. And his surfing. Which might be fine in Sydney, but it's not fine in w11. And I knew myself too well to fall into that trap. Handsome starving artists were all very well, but I was a fashion princess with expensive tastes.

Then there was the small matter of my husband.

And there you have it. I was married. All along. To somebody else. Happily married too. That's why this thing with Miles was so nuts. I wasn't remotely interested in having an extra-marital love affair, or even extra-marital sex, it had never even crossed my mind. I had plenty of sex and cuddles already, yet here I was, doing the thing that unhappily married women do.

So it didn't make any sense—and there was another really weird thing going on too. I didn't feel remotely guilty about it. Not even when I woke up from a brief sleep—the only sleep we'd had all night—when my alarm went off at six thirty.

I just looked over at Miles and wondered if we had time for another quick one before I had to get up to do my yoga and hair. We did, as it turned out, and actually it was rather a slow one, before

I really did have to get up and salute the sun and my blow-drier, and he had to get back to the flea-pit hotel room he shared with Seamus, to pick up his camera equipment and head out to claim his position at the Marni show.

I lay in bed and watched him dress. His body was almost as good as Paul's, I decided, in a golden-brown version, as opposed to Paul's smooth shiny black, and with a little more hair on the chest and down his stomach. In just the right places really. In his old faded jeans and that chopped-up T-shirt, his thick reddish-brown hair standing on end, a heavy growth of stubble on his chin, he looked totally gorgeous. Not handsome in a classic way, but fundamentally male somehow.

He stood at the end of the bed looking at me steadily as he did up his belt. We spoke simultaneously.

"I wish . . ."

We broke off, laughing. We'd clearly both been going to say the same thing: I wish you/I wish I didn't have to go yet.

"The problem with you and me," said Miles, throwing himself down on the bed again and burying his face in my neck, "is that we're too bloody responsible. We should just fuck the lot of them and stay here all day."

He nibbled my earlobe and my back was arching before I'd even realized it.

"But you'd better stop that," he said. "I'm under serious instructions from my boss at the picture agency to get good pictures of the Marni show. I went out to the venue yesterday and marked out my spot and everything."

"Well, you'd better stop doing that then."

He was brushing his hand lightly backwards and forwards over my nipples, which were clearly enjoying it. I moaned, involuntarily.

"I'm going to have to see you again," he said.

I nodded. He made to get up, but I grabbed his hand. I had to tell him. I had to tell him I was married before he told Seamus about us and Seamus told Nelly and Nelly told Frannie and, ugh—it was too horrible to think about. Everybody on *Chic* and everybody on *pure*—in fact, the entire British fashion magazine world—knew my husband.

"Miles," I said. "I've got to tell you something . . ."

He grinned at me.

"I already know you're married," he said, and put his head down to suck my right nipple. "And I don't give a shit," he added with his mouth full.

By 8:45 A.M. I was yoga-d, showered, blow-dried and dressed—in an Alexander McQueen suit my husband had recently bought me, with a very tight skirt and a very waisted jacket, to be worn only with very high heels—and back in the limo on the way out to the Marni show.

For once, I didn't mind the crawling claustrophobic car ride through the grey buildings, in the fug of Bee's fag smoke. I felt so good I was practically singing. Alice was unbelievably cheerful too, full of the party and what a fabulous time she'd had with Antonello—in the VIP area, as she kept stressing—and how George Clooney had kissed her hand.

Bee was particularly thrilled about the part when Antonello appeared to be ignoring Beaver in favour of talking to Alice and how left out and put out she had looked. She kept making Alice repeat it with all the details, like a child wanting to hear the same story over and over again. Bee was also going on about how marvellous she felt after an early night. And I was, quite simply, spunk drunk from my time with Miles. The only one of us who was quiet was Frannie.

"Hey, Franster," I said, not even minding that I was sitting in the middle of the back seat once again, this time in a tight skirt that was riding up my thighs. I could see Luigi was having a private perve fest in the rear-view mirror and I didn't even care.

"Frannie," I said again when she didn't answer, leaning in towards her. "Are you OK?"

She turned her face to me. She looked terrible.

"No," she said. "I feel like absolute shite. I've never been so hung-over in my life. Aren't you? You were putting it away like a Glaswegian last night."

I considered her question. I felt fine. I felt fantastic.

"Er, I did yoga this morning," I said, slightly too quickly. "I think it must have helped clear the toxins from my liver."

"Oh, God," said Frannie. "The thought of liver. Fried liver with onion. Shut up about food, or I'll boke out the car window."

Then a hand appeared out of nowhere proffering a packet of sugar-free gum. It was Alice. Smiling. It really was an extraordinary morning.

We finally arrived at the venue, an old factory even more decrepit than the average set-up, just late enough to keep Bee happy. As they always did, the Marni people were compensating for the early start by providing coffee, orange juice and pastries and the crowd was falling on it. Two-and-a-half weeks into the season, people were starting to look seriously tired.

I saw Frannie—who was normally Miss Organic Food Purity— hoover up three espressos and two almond minicroissants. She must have been taken bad, I thought. I just headed for my seat. I'd had my grated apple back at the hotel and this show was always my favourite for audience gawping, because while the wooden benches we had to sit on were torture on the lower back, the space was full of natural morning light and you could see everybody really clearly.

I'd been sitting there for about fifteen minutes happily looking around and making notes in the back of my notebook about the cool stuff other people were wearing—and which I therefore had to go out and buy as soon as possible—when I suddenly had that feeling that somebody was looking at me. You know that almost prehistoric instinct we have when we are being watched? I put on my glasses— the ones I need to see the clothes properly—and looked over towards the bank of photographers. It was the usual wall of huge long lenses, but one of them was pointing straight at me. As I stared back at it the shutter suddenly closed and opened like a winking eye. Then Miles's head popped up from behind it, grinning.

I snatched my glasses off and felt myself go hot with a blush which started at my feet and went all the way up to the top of my head, with quite a few stops in between. I was extremely relieved when almost the next moment the music started and the show began.

But it wasn't until I had sketched about three of the fabulous outfits that I realized there was something missing. Beaver was in her usual position in the front next to Bee, but Nelly wasn't sitting next to me. And Nelly loved Marni.

I didn't see Nelly all morning. She wasn't at any of the shows. I tried her mobile several times and it went straight to voicemail. I even rang her hotel—the *pure* girls always stayed at the Palace, five stars, but not nearly as nice as the Princh—to see if she had stayed in bed. They told me Signora Stelios was out.

It didn't make any sense. If she'd been sent home to London for bad behaviour—which was a distinct possibility—I knew she would have rung me to bitch about it. Likewise if Beaver had her doing some kind of secret last-minute shoot and she was out frantically sourcing the clothes. Our respective editors would have been horrified if they'd known how little professional discretion existed between us.

It was all so odd, I was actually starting to feel a bit worried about her. It was totally out of character for Nelly to miss shows, however bad her hangover was, but I certainly wasn't going to ask her po-faced boss where she was and draw attention to her absence.

Apart from that—and periodic flashbacks to the events of the night before which made my insides loop the loop—it was a normal day in the abnormal world of high fashion. We were in a permanent rush to get to each show slightly late, which was then always an hour late anyway. We had no time for lunch, but had to go instead to three showroom appointments with hideous minor fashion labels which advertised in the magazine.

As the orange-faced, fire-haired PRs—it was a particular look that Milanese women over fifty seemed to go for—gushed and cooed over Bee, who loved that part of her job, I had to pretend to be ecstatically excited by their ghastly clothes. I would then select, with great enthusiasm, a royal-blue trouser suit, a purple mohair trapeze coat and a white shirt, which was the only thing I would ever actually use in a shoot. It was just a matter of getting them one picture a season, the essential editorial credit which would keep them sweet until they chose which magazines would benefit from their next advertising spend.

And that was one of the funny things about my job. Because while all of us who worked on glossy magazines passionately loved clothes and making beautiful pictures, that unspoken exchange of editorial credits and advertising cash was what really kept the whole high-fashion publishing industry rolling along.

It was a well-known secret on *Chic* that Bee kept a master list of advertisers and each month, when the magazine came out, she had Nushka go through it page by page and make a note of every editorial mention and picture credit each fashion and beauty advertiser had racked up. Then Bee could check that none of them were being under-serviced by editorial. If they were, she would make us shoot something of theirs in the next issue, non-negotiable. These paybacks were never ever openly discussed—and Bee would have blankly denied it went on to anyone who asked her—but it really was that structured behind the scenes.

Most of the time it was OK, but for some of the labels it was very hard to find anything we could bear to use in our shoots and I knew it weighed very heavily on Frannie's conscience having to write about beauty products she didn't really think were great.

"I just think of that reader," she told me once, screwing up press releases and aiming them at a bin on the other side of her office.

"She's me, ten years ago. Sitting in a wee house in Broughty Ferry, reading *Chic* and believing every feckin' word and dreaming of being beautiful and glamorous and saving up from her Saturday job stacking bloody shelves in bloody Tesco to go out and buy some overpriced bottle of shite, that doesn't even work, or thinking she needs three-hundred-pound shoes to be happy. I can't stand it sometimes." She looked at me and laughed. "And then I get invited to a suntan lotion launch on Harbour Island and suddenly I don't mind so much. Isn't that weird?"

Frannie assuaged her conscience by writing as much as she could about emerging designers and beauty products she really did believe in, by banging the drum about organic cosmetics and by holding regular sales of the truckloads of fabulous free beauty samples she received, for the *Chic* staff. We really appreciated the chance to buy gorgeous make-up at cut prices, because we all earned pretty crap money, and Frannie felt better after donating the funds raised to a women's refuge.

Our relatively meagre salaries were another of the great ironies of the fashion world. We all had to look perfect all the time to uphold the magazine's public image, but none of us could really afford the designer clothes we featured in its pages. And not only were we expected to wear them, they had to be that season's pieces. It was fashion death to wear anything older than six months—everyone would know—unless it was ten years old and could be passed off as "vintage."

So we relied on discounts; buying wholesale; generous Christmas presents; the invitation-only sales when the PRs sold off the season's press samples (another reason to make sure you stayed no more than a model size ten) and on freebies from designers thrilled with a great picture.

But most of all we had to rely on our innate abilities to sling together a great look with one key designer piece, some Top Shop and Zara bargains and bits and bobs from Portobello market. And then there were our credit cards, of course. The fashion editor's flexible friends.

Fortunately for my own personal national debt, there wasn't any time to go shopping that day because after our appointments we had to spend ages out at the Fiera, the only Milan show venue worse than the old factory wasteland. The Fiera was a vast exhibition centre, just far enough from the centre of town to be annoying, that consisted of a hideous labyrinth of escalators and artificially lit, low-ceilinged and badly ventilated spaces, divided up by ugly exhibition stands. I hated the Fiera with a serious vengeance. It made me feel suffocated.

Worst of all was getting to the weird cavernous halls in the centre of the vast maze, which involved heaving crowds of impatient people, in uncomfortable shoes, many of them smoking, passing through very narrow spaces. I lived in fear of being trampled to death under a stampede of Christian Louboutin's red soles, or having my face mutilated by cigarette burns. I'd already had a hole singed in the sleeve of my favourite Alberta Ferretti coat by somebody else's bloody ciggie. In a no-smoking area, of course.

Adding to the frustration, the shows always seemed to be sched-uled so there wasn't quite enough time to go back into town (mean-ing: shopping) between them, but just enough to make hanging around and waiting inside abject torture. The Fiera made me feel more tired than anywhere else on earth.

The best thing that had ever happened to me out there was stand-ing right behind Anna Wintour once in the queue for the loos. I had felt close to greatness for those few moments. Apart from the celeb-watching opportunities, the only respite was a secret café hidden away in one remote corner of the building, which only the British press seemed to know about. It had a great Seventies interior and even some windows, providing the luxury of natural light and a few trees to look out at.

I normally escaped to that haven with Nelly and Frannie—mak-ing sure to brush off Bee, Alice and Beaver first. We'd sit on the slatted wooden staircase, drinking espresso (me) and chomping on delicious salami *panini* (Nelly and Frannie). Forced to be out at the Fiera for hours that afternoon—covering minor advertiser shows that Bee and Alice weren't bothering with—Nelly's unexplained absence was particularly distressing. Frannie was feeling so sick she'd gone back to the hotel, so I had no one to hang out or giggle with. I'd actually nodded off in La Perla, as my lack of sleep began to catch up with me.

But despite my weariness, I still didn't feel any sense of remorse about what I'd done the night before. Not even when Oliver—that was my husband—called me up.

"Hey, Mrs. Fairbrother," he said. "How's it going?"

"Hello, Mr. Fairbrother," I said, genuinely pleased to hear from him. "It's going beautifully, thank you. How about you?"

"Totally cool, actually. I went to a great new restaurant last night, in Brick Lane. Laotian-fusian food. Marnie Stallinger did the inte-rior. It's fabulous. I think we should seriously look at moving to E1, it's the new Notting Hill. What have you been up to over there?"

"Oh, the usual," I lied. I couldn't believe how easily it came to me. "Riding around in a limousine, staying in a five-star hotel, eat-ing in great restaurants, a little designer shopping and an A-list fashion party. It's been really tough."

Ollie chuckled, he loved what he thought of as my glamorous life. Well, it was pretty glam really, on the surface.

"Bought anything?" he asked. Ollie was almost as interested in my wardrobe as I was.

"Yeah, I got some fabulous boots from Prada, quite loose with big chunky heels on them. Sort of like biker boots, but much more expensive."

"Oh, I love those," said Ollie. "I saw them in *The Sunday Times Style* section. They'll look great on you with a short skirt. Phwooar."

I giggled.

"What was the party?" said Ollie.

"Antonello Ferrucci. It was a riot. Jacko was there. He directed the make-up for the show."

"Wow, he really is hitting the big time. I'll have to get on to him again about signing up with Slap. 'Paul Toussaints for Slap.' It sounds great, I like the alliteration. He'd be mad not to do it. Let's go over to New York and work on him, when you get back from this trip. I need to see what's going on in New York anyway, so I can justify it all on expenses."

That was my Ollie, always looking for a business opportunity, meaning an opportunity to further his career and an opportunity for him—and me—to have a good time at the company's expense. Mind you, the company he worked for could afford it.

Ollie was the managing director of a fantastically groovy and successful independent cosmetics brand called Slap. It was the make-up everyone wanted to be seen to be using—celebs were always listing Slap's mascara as the thing they would pick up if their house was on fire and that kind of thing—and Ollie had played a large part in getting it to that status. He really was terrifically good at his job.

So good at it, that he had managed to keep it discreetly quiet that Slap was actually a division of cosmetics giant Eudora Lorimer, a massive international corporation, almost like the civil service, which he had been with since he first left university. The other company he had applied to be a management trainee with had been Marks & Spencer, but I only knew that because his mother had told me. He wouldn't have liked anyone to have known that. Not even me.

Ollie and I had met six years before at the Christmas party of *Gorgeous* magazine, where I had been working as a junior fashion editor, before I got the job at *Chic*. All the big cosmetics company PRs and marketing people were invited, but Ollie was the one everyone wanted to see.

Good looking, in a Hugh Grant-ish kind of cool public school-boy way, with a good sense of humour and beautiful manners, he was truly popular with all the beauty editors he had to schmooze to get his products into their magazines. In fact, most of them were throwing themselves at this rare creature—a straight, single, well-dressed man, of good income, who not only knew the difference between Marni, Mani and Armani, but cared about it too.

The night we met was the first proper office Christmas party I'd ever been to. Up until then, from the time I'd left college, I'd worked as a freelance stylist for ultra-cool independent style magazines from which I received very little remuneration, but stacks of credibility credits.

I was also in demand to style off-schedule fashion shows for up-and-coming young designers during London Fashion Week and to do pictures for catalogues, which was what brought in enough money to live off. So while I had plenty of work, I had never really been part of an office set-up before.

I had taken the job at *Gorgeous,* which was a lipstick, looks and luuurve magazine, much more mainstream than the ones I normally worked for, to have some financial security and to get experience of organizing and going on exotic fashion location shoots. Since I'd joined the mag I'd already been to Morocco, Jamaica and Mexico, chasing the sunshine and light you need to shoot summer clothes for the spring issues, which was always done in the dead of winter to fit in with printing schedules.

I had swiftly learned how fashion editors were able to manipulate the complications of a glossy magazine's production cycle—all the pictures had to be ready at least four months before the magazine came out—so that they could spend as much time as possible in fabulous sunny places.

When I met Ollie that December night in London, I had just

come back from the Yucatán peninsula, where we'd been shooting the new spring looks for the March issue. I was very brown, my hair was seriously sunbleached—with a little help from my favourite John Frieda products—and I was wearing a white strapless dress, with armfuls of Mexican silver bangles I'd bought on the trip, and silver stiletto sandals. Yes, that meant no tights in London in midwinter, an act of personal bravery I considered my professional duty. True fashionistas never wear stockings, except for occasional fishnets.

Ollie had popped up next to me at the drinks table quite early in the proceedings and then hardly left my side for the rest of the evening. I could see people—female people—glaring at me from all around the room, but I didn't care. I'd recently been dumped by yet another photographer boyfriend in favour of a seventeen-year-old Ukrainian model and my ego needed a boost from a handsome chap in a Richard James suit, a Paul Smith shirt and Gucci shoes.

I don't remember much of what Ollie and I talked about that night, but like I say, I always remember the styling details.

Unlike my sluttish behaviour with Miles, I hadn't gone to bed with Ollie the night I'd met him. I'd fancied him all right—he was good looking, there was no doubt about that, and I liked his clothes, which was an essential part of sexual attraction for me—but there was something so overwhelmingly confident about Ollie that piqued the contrariness in my nature. I just wasn't going to make it easy for him. He was clearly used to women falling around him with their tongues lolling out and I was just not going to be one of them.

I didn't particularly care about Ollie at that point, let alone want to marry him, but I was still smarting from the betrayal of my last boyfriend and I was nursing a bit of a grudge against the male sex in general. So I decided to teach Oliver Fairbrother, or "Mr. Perfect," as I had actually heard women refer to him, a lesson.

I started by not returning his phone calls. When I did eventually agree to have dinner with him, I cancelled on the afternoon of the date. He sent me flowers and I sent him a short and formal thank-you note—on the magazine's headed writing paper, as though it was a work thing. It was such fun to tease him.

Finally, we went out for a drink and that's all it was—a drink. Well, two drinks at Pharmacy, which was then the place to be seen at. I spent quite a lot of the time chatting to all the other friends I knew in there, to make it clear it wasn't a big deal to me. Then I went home to Hackney. He was clearly mystified by my behaviour and he started to get totally fixated on me.

He continued to pursue me with flowers, phone calls and the entire Slap make-up range, until eventually I did have dinner with him. That turned into several dinners over time, plus some movies, exhibition visits and walks in the park—but with quite a few cancellations, unreturned phone calls, emails and texts thrown in—and a chaste kiss was all he got at the end of any of it. I didn't sleep with Ollie until three months after I met him, when he took me to Babington House for the weekend and I finally succumbed—as I had been secretly dying to for weeks. By that point I honestly think he would have married me just to get me into bed.

But I have to admit that by then what had started out as a game for me had turned into something real. By the time Ollie and I did get it together, I was fully smitten with him. His reputation as the perfect man really did seem to be justified. He was great company, we shared loads of interests and he clearly really liked women, which is not something you can assume with all men, even the straight ones. He also had the undeniable appeal of his great job and financial security. He had a gorgeous flat too.

On the Sunday afternoon of that first weekend, as we drove home from Somerset in the late afternoon sunshine, with the top down on his vintage Karmann Ghia, I felt happier than I had since I was ten years old. He was playing Neil Young on the ancient eight-track tape machine that had come with the car—a museum piece in its own right. He went to car boot sales to seek out the cassettes, he had told me, and this was the best one he'd found yet.

"I love this track," I said quietly, when "Only Love Can Break Your Heart" came on.

"So do I," said Ollie. "This whole album is brilliant. I've liked it since I was a kid."

"Me too," I said, knowing that he would have no idea just how much it meant to me. I decided to tell him.

"My dad used to play this music in his studio."

Ollie was smiling, he could never get me to talk about my family, so I think he was pleased I was finally opening up. That and a shag in the same weekend. Big progress.

"What did your dad do in his studio?" he asked, gently.

"He was a painter," I said.

Ollie turned and looked at me quickly.

"Not *Matthew* Pointer."

I nodded. My dad had been quite a famous artist. They had one of his giant canvases in the Tate Modern and I'd go and look at it sometimes, when I felt sad. Like all his works it was made up of millions of tiny brushstrokes and they shimmered with intensity. He wasn't a super-big name, but people who were seriously interested in modern art had heard of him. I was glad that Ollie had. It meant I didn't have to explain the rest.

"He died quite young, didn't he?" said Ollie, gently.

I nodded.

"Yeah, he was thirty-eight," I said, my voice cracking a bit. I never talked about this stuff, but I was feeling so comfortable with Ollie I suddenly felt that I wanted to.

"I was ten. It was really hard. That's why I never talk about it, but it's nice to hear this music because he often played this when he worked."

I paused and then felt able to say more, although I couldn't get my voice above a whisper.

"As long as I was quiet, he didn't mind me coming in and sitting with him while he painted. I used to love being in there, watching him make those tiny brushstrokes on those huge canvases. To get to the top he'd have to sit on a ladder and I used to hand him up tubes of paint. I can still remember the names of all the colours."

"What happened?" said Ollie quietly, giving me a sideways look.

"He just fell down dead one day," I said, and that was all I ever said about it, but I remembered it very clearly. I was there.

One moment he was working on a commission for the lobby of a major new bank building, the next he was dead on the floor. He'd had a massive brain haemorrhage, or something—while I watched. My life was never the same after that and it was still almost too painful to think about.

Even without these details, Ollie seemed to pick up that we had moved to a new level of closeness, above and beyond the sexual dimension that had just come into the relationship. He was holding my hand as we drove along and as we approached the turn-off for Shepherd's Bush he pulled it up to his lips.

"Don't go home tonight," he said simply. "I don't want to be apart from you. Come and stay with me at Ledbury Road."

He turned and looked at me for a moment. I smiled back at him, squinting at him through my hair which was blowing all over my face. I nodded. I didn't want to go home to the hard-to-let council flat I shared with Paul in a Hackney tower block. I wanted to stay with Ollie.

"I've got a better idea," he said, as we swung off the Shepherd's Bush roundabout into Holland Park Road. "Come and live with me at Ledbury Road."

So I did.

4

LIFE in Westbourne Grove was bliss. It wasn't just the contrast between my former unsavoury dwelling and a gorgeous "apartment"—as Ollie always called it—in one of the chicest parts of town, it was heavenly to be settled with a man I adored.

Right from that first night Ollie and I just clicked together as a couple. I remember we walked over to 192 for dinner and held hands across the table the whole time. And it wasn't just any table either, it was one of the best ones, right by the window, where everyone could see you as they walked past on the warm May evening—and they did. In our claustrophobic little world, we might as well have taken out a full-page ad in the *Evening Standard* to announce our relationship.

Within months we were an established "it" couple around town, a new level of prestige that was enhanced even more when I got the job at *Chic*. It was up there with British *Vogue* as one of the most respected fashion magazines in the world and Ollie was hugely proud of me. I was pretty thrilled too.

I'd first met Bee when Ollie had invited her over to one of our regular Sunday afternoon gatherings at the flat. Those "Sunday salons"—Ollie's term, he had a catchy name for everything—had become a bit of a "thing" that we did. The idea was to mix up interesting people we'd met around town with old friends and anyone who might be useful for promoting Ollie's make-up, at a relaxed—yet fantastically stylish—meal. Which Ollie could then claim on expenses.

They were a bit pretentious, really, but it wasn't just a cynical marketing exercise. I loved to cook and Ollie adored entertaining. His parents were renowned hosts at their place in Hampshire and having people over really brought out the best in him. He could be a bit twitchy and nervous when we were out—usually in case there was somewhere more fashionable we should have been, or a better table in the restaurant we were at—but in his own home he was completely relaxed and great company.

He'd designed the whole layout of his flat—sorry, "apartment"—entirely around the entertaining area, sacrificing the third bedroom to create a large open space which stretched from the front of the building to the back, where there were folding doors onto a large deck. Divided up into what Ollie called "moments," through clever arrangements of sofas, chairs and tables, it was ideal for people to gather in constantly shifting groups, with us all ending up together around the large dining table. That space had a great dynamic, as Ollie used to say. He loved words like that. I used to tease him about it.

The day I met Bee, it was early autumn and although it was still warm enough to have the doors onto the deck folded back, there was just the hint of a chill in the air. I had filled the place with dark red shaggy dahlias from Wild at Heart, edged the deck with Moroccan lanterns and lit my favourite Agraria incense sticks, which I always brought back from New York. And, of course, I can still remember what we were wearing.

Ollie had on a midnight-blue velvet Seventies dinner jacket I'd found for him in Portobello market, which looked great over a collarless white shirt and jeans. On his feet he had dark red Moroccan slippers embroidered with silver flowers, and no socks. Apart from to the office, Ollie never wore socks, just as I never wore tights. I've no idea what that was all about, it was just one of our things. I was wearing velvet too—a hip-length, kurta-style top in deep red with mirror embroidery around the neck, over my favourite Yanuk hipster jeans, with a fabulous brass-studded belt slung low and a pair of jewelled velvet Manolo mules on my feet.

I wish I could say it was a happy accident that we were both wearing that velvet/ethnic combo, but it wasn't. Nothing Ollie and I did was left to chance and we had such fun contriving our stylish lives. We did laugh at ourselves as we posed together in front of the floor-to-ceiling wall of mirror in our walk-in closet, but at another level we believed our own bullshit too.

"You look gorgeous, Em," said Ollie, watching himself give me a big hug in the mirror. I breathed in a big waft of Acqua di Parma from his neck. "You always look gorgeous. You are gorgeous. You are my beautiful, beautiful gorgeous girl and you make me so happy."

He was just giving me a big snog when the buzzer went. It was Paul, arriving first as he always did. He was pathologically punctual.

"Oh, get you two," he said as he walked in, checking out our looks. "Mr. and Mrs. Chic Ethnic Accents."

He handed me a large box of my favourite chocolate-covered ginger.

"Here's some chocolates for you not to eat, Emily. You two look like Pinky and Perky in those outfits. Or Siegfried and Roy." He laughed to himself. Paul always laughed heartily at his own jokes. It was very infectious.

"When's the *Hello!* photographer turning up then?" he said, sniffing my artfully "unarranged" flower arrangement. "Ollie Fairbrother and Emily Pointer entertaining their fascinating and wittily accessorized friends at their lovely west London home."

We laughed, but it was a bit like that. Journalists from the *Evening Standard* were always quoting us in articles about the lifestyles of groovy people around town and Ollie had whooped with satisfaction when we finally made it into a picture on the *ES* social pages, at an opening at some ultra-hip new art gallery in Columbia Road.

Slap make-up MD Oliver Fairbrother and stylist Emily Pointer with artist Jeremiah Hock at the opening of his installation, "Snake Oil," at the Rrrrrrs Gallery.

I'd torn the picture out and put it on the fridge with moustaches drawn on our faces, but Ollie had carefully cut the page out from another copy of the magazine and put it in one of the A3 scrapbooks he kept in his study.

There were eleven of us at the "Sunday salon" the time I met Bee— Ollie thought odd numbers had a much better "synergy" than neat little groups—and the crowd was the usual pick 'n' mix of ages, occupations, nationalities and sexualities, all united by a certain "brightness."

Bee and her banker husband, George, were the next to arrive after Paul. I already knew her face from boutique openings and fashion shows, but we'd never actually met. She knew Ollie pretty well, though, from the mutual arse-licking symbiosis that exists between magazine editors and make-up brands' managing directors. For Bee and Ollie any social contact was a fiesta of mutual backscratching— essential job-preserving advertising revenue for her, priceless bonus- enhancing editorial recommendations for him—although at least with Slap it was a great product, so it wasn't quite so venal as it could have been.

There were ranks of sales people behind the scenes on both sides who did the actual money deals—the mucky part of the business— completely separate from editorial, but Bee was the crucial bridge between the two. And she worked that position as shamelessly as a lap dancer.

As she walked in that afternoon I saw her eyes swivel around the room like a CCTV camera, taking in the whole scenario. From where her gaze momentarily rested—the dahlias, the perfectly placed pieces of mid-century furniture, the ethnic accents, the French lamps, the feature piles of art books, the incense, the collection of vintage black and white fashion photographs in clusters on the walls, the artless heaps of Sunday papers—I could tell she wasn't missing a detail.

That ability to size up and assess—places, people, photos, fashion collections—in an instant, was one of the qualities that made Bee so good at her job. It was almost like a sixth sense with her. Her seventh was her decisiveness.

"So, Emily," she said, as I brought out the autumn fruits jelly that I'd made for pudding. I saw her clock how good it looked, the jewel-like fruits suspended in stripes of coloured jelly in the glass bowl. "You're a stylist on *Gorgeous,* aren't you?"

I nodded.

"Which shoots did you do in the current issue?" she asked.

"I'll show you," I said. I knew there was a copy of it by my right foot, where all our magazines were thrown into a large Kenyan basket, because I'd put it there earlier, just in case of this scenario. And that particular issue happened to contain the best work I'd ever done.

"I did this dress story," I said to Bee, flipping open the magazine and trying to sound casual. "The idea is—'don't stop wearing dresses, just because summer's over, it's a great way to dress for winter too'—a great working wardrobe option we often forget."

Bee was wearing a dress, did I mention that? A classic Diane von Furstenberg print wrap number. My dress pictures—which included a number of von Furstenberg items—were gorgeous and just the kind of thing I knew that all editors love, but rarely get out of their fashion editors, who always want to do "art" pictures. I'd taken them in locations around Deauville. Two models, beautiful natural light, streetscapes, a strong narrative feel, with a slight poignancy—and really beautiful *wearable* clothes. I saw Bee's eyes flicking over the pages like a stockbroker studying a Reuters screen. The market was clearly on the way up.

"I did this little thing, as well," I said casually, knowing it was another sure-fire editor pleaser. "Just a good-ideas-type story, showing how you can mix six different chain-store pieces, for under sixty pounds each, with one pair of Chloé pants—more like three hundred pounds—and have an entire new wardrobe."

By the time we were on to the herb tea and Turkish delight, she was offering me a job. I accepted on the spot—to be a fashion editor on *Chic* was the styling equivalent of my first big Hollywood role. As Ollie was lighting a Cuban cigar for her, she announced the news to the table. His face, behind a thick pall of expensive smoke, was priceless—a struggle between desperately wanting to air punch and yelp with joy, and knowing it wouldn't be cool to do so.

I can't think of any announcement that would have made Ollie happier than my promotion to the ranks of the serious high-fashion glossies, and when we were in bed that night after all our guests had gone he had made love to me with exquisite tenderness.

"I'm so proud of you," he said. "You're my dream woman. You make me so happy. I adore you."

It was good stuff. I just lay there smiling back at him. I'm a total sucker for flattery. Then he suddenly jumped up on the bed. I couldn't imagine what he was doing, but then he dropped back down on one knee—stark bollock naked—and took my hand in his.

"Emily Pointer," he said, gazing into my eyes. "Marry me—please."

So I did. And that's what I was putting at risk for a quick bunk-up in Milan with a scruffy Australian photographer. All that.

What was I on?

Whatever was going on with me, it was clear that weird day in Milan—the morning after my night before with Miles—that something was up with Nelly too.

She finally appeared late that afternoon at the Moschino show. In fact, she was already in her seat when I walked in and she was sitting there with her eyes and her mouth closed, an extraordinary event. She didn't even stir when I arrived, and she was wearing the same clothes she'd had on the night before. All of these were firsts.

"Er, Nelly?" I said, sitting down next to her.

She didn't reply, but her right hand came out and grasped my leg.

"Are you all right?" I said. This was getting spooky. Her only reply was a long loud sigh. Then she finally turned her head, which was still lolling back on her shoulders and half opened her eyes.

Then she let out a kind of death rattle groan. I laughed, it was the only possible response.

"Oh, Ems," she said, slowly shaking her head. "This is no laughing matter."

"Well, what the fuck is it?" I said, starting to get really impatient.

Nelly licked her glossy red lips. What a drama queen.

"Iggy," she whispered.

"Iggy?" I snapped back.

She nodded furiously and gestured with her eyes towards Beaver, who was in her usual position in front of us. I lowered my voice.

"What about Iggy? Is he dead?"

She shook her head violently. Then she grabbed my notebook—my special hardback shows notebook, which I can only get at one shop in New York—and opening it right in the middle, she scrawled something right across the page. In splodgy blue biro. She handed it back to me.

"LUUUUURVE!!!!" it said in huge letters. Then she grabbed the book back and added some more. "Nelly gonads neva wrong."

I finally got the full story on a tram back to our hotels, which were right next to each other.

There was a break before the next show and we had both told our editors—separately, of course—that we had to go off and see some new models we were thinking of using. We'd taken the tram, a total novelty for me, as it was where we were least likely to see anyone we knew.

"Well, you were right about him being straight then," I said.

Nelly just nodded. I had never known her so quiet. Normally when she had a new lover I had to listen to every grisly detail—size of penis, number of rogerings, cunnilingus rating—in full technicolour and sensurround.

"He's amazing, Em," she said, shaking her head. "Such an amazing person."

I waited for more information, but all she would tell me was that they had gone back into the party for that last dance and then they'd come out and walked the streets of Milan talking until they got to his apartment in the Brera, where they'd carried on talking until dawn, when they'd finally ripped each other's clothes off.

The last bit sounded rather familiar, but I said nothing.

"I'm going back to the hotel to pack," she said suddenly.

"What do you mean?"

"I'm leaving the hotel and moving in with him. That's what he wants me to do. I'm going to help him style his show."

"But what about Beaver?"

"What about Beaver?"

"Doesn't she expect you to stay in the hotel with her? How can you help him with his show and do all the other shows at the same time?"

"Beaver can do what she likes. Iggy wants me to help and I'm going to. No more shows for Nelly. I only came to Moschino to find you. I wanted to tell you myself."

"Have you got a temperature?" I asked, laying my hand on her forehead.

She laughed, that filthy chuckle, which was a much more familiar Nelly reaction to anything.

"Yeah," she said. "I've got a serious fever, but not up there, darling."

She stood up to get off the tram—I'd decided to stay on and go into town for a little more shopping—and she leant down to give me big smacking kisses on both cheeks. I grabbed her arm before she could get away.

"One thing, Nelly," I said. "Do I have to keep this a secret?"

"Nah," said Nelly, flinging her arms in the air. "I just wanted you to hear it from me first. Tell the world!"

And then she did a twirl, which the men on the tram must have enjoyed, because her circular skirt flew right up and she wasn't wearing any pants.

When I got back to the hotel—two new Helmut Lang tops later—I ignored the "Do Not Disturb" sign on Frannie's door and knocked on it loudly. I wanted to make sure she was all right. And I wanted to tell her Nelly's amazing news.

"Can't you bloody read?" I heard her shout from inside. "Do not bloody disturb, *per fa*-bloody-*vore*."

"Frannie, it's me," I said. "I want to know how you are."

"Bloody hell," I heard her muttering as she came to the door. She opened it without looking at me and then got back into bed, turned her back on me and pulled the covers over her head.

"That bad?" I said, from the door. "Do you want a doctor?"

"No," she said. "I want my mum."

And she burst into tears. I ran over to the bed and put my arm round her.

"Franster," I said. "Whatever's wrong? Tell me. I'll be your pretend mum. Are you feeling really sick, or is it something else?"

She just cried louder. I sat on the bed beside her, stroking her hair with my hand. I had never seen Frannie, my beloved sanity editor, in this kind of state before.

"Whatever is it?" I said. "You've got to tell me. You can't suffer like this."

Finally she lifted up her face. Her eyes were sore and red.

"I've done something terrible, Emily," she said.

"It can't be that bad," I said. "Murder? Fraud? You've bought some more shoes?"

She wiped her nose on the sleeve of her bathrobe.

"I kissed that bloody Seamus," she said.

I didn't know how to react. I felt my face twitch into an involuntary smile. This was getting ridiculous.

"It's not bloody funny, Emily," she said, pushing me off the bed. "I'm a married woman. I love my husband. I'd never do anything to hurt him and now I've kissed some Irish bloke I don't even know."

"Did you—er—just kiss him?" I asked tentatively.

She looked shocked. "Well, I didn't *shag* him," she said vehemently. "If that's what you mean, but I think kissing's bad enough. I'd be shattered if I caught Andy kissing someone else. I don't know what came over me."

I did. She put her head in her hands and shook it from side to side.

"We all drank a lot last night," I said, feeling like a monstrous hypocrite, because I knew I had no intention of sharing my own extra-marital misdemeanour with her. For a split second I considered making her feel better by admitting that I had "kissed" Miles as well, but some kind of big-picture inner cunning made me stop.

"That party was amazing," I said. "We were all really overexcited. It didn't mean anything. It was just high spirits."

"It wasn't, though, Em," she said. "I *wanted* to shag him."

"You wanted to, but you didn't," I said. "Resisting temptation like that just shows how very much you love Andy."

Unlike me, I thought.

"I suppose you're right," she said, looking a little bit happier.

"I'll tell you what. Have a shower, get dressed and meet me in the bar in thirty minutes and before we have to go off to Alberta Ferretti I'll tell you a story about what Nelly got up to last night, which will take your mind right off your own misery."

She brightened visibly, which was such a relief. I hated to see her unhappy. I left her room, but before I quite closed the door I popped my head back in again.

"Hey, Franster," I said. "Was he a good kisser?"

She threw a pillow at me.

I went back to my room for the first time since that morning. When I'd left there had been plenty of evidence of what had gone on the night before. Sheets, pillows and my clothes had been strewn all over the floor, all the towels in the bathroom had been used, that kind of thing. But the Principe's immaculate housekeeping team had done their stuff and there was now no sign of the torrid time we'd spent in there. It was like the tide had swept in and washed away our footprints.

I could leave it that way, I thought. Put it behind me as a silly mistake on a wild and crazy night, like Frannie was going to. That morning I had been sure I wanted to see him again, I'd thought

I couldn't live without having sex with him one more time. Now I wasn't so sure. For reasons I couldn't fathom, I still didn't feel guilty, but I did think perhaps I should leave things as they were.

I was lying on the bed pondering it all—and having palpitations every time a clear memory of the night before washed over me—when my mobile rang. It was Paul.

"How are you, darling?" he said, disgustingly brightly, considering what a late one we'd all had.

"Tired, but happy," I said. "What a great night that was. Did you have a good time?"

"I sure did. I had a great time dancing with you and I had a great time . . . well, you don't like hearing those details, do you?" He chuckled his filthiest chuckle.

"Not really," I said. "But I'm glad you enjoyed yourself."

"You looked like you were enjoying yourself too, my dear."

"I was," I said brightly. "I had a great time."

"Especially with that hunky Australian."

"What do you mean?" I said in a voice that was very slightly squeaky. "I was dancing with everyone."

"Yes, but you were practically humping him on the dance floor."

"Oh, don't exaggerate, I was just getting on down. I was practically humping you as well in that case."

"Ah, if only, sweetheart."

"Fuck off, Jacko. What are you up to anyway?"

"I'm just hanging out here at The Grey and I don't have anything to do later—well not until *much* later—and I thought we could have dinner after your last show."

I made one of those instant decisions. The sort that some deep dark part of your brain makes without involving you in the process.

"I don't think I can," I said. "We've got to see some stupid advertising clients after Alberta Ferretti." It was a total lie. "I'm not sure whether it's just drinks or the full dinner, so I'd better say no. Perhaps we can do something tomorrow?"

"Perhaps we can," said Paul. "Speak soon."

He hung up. Did I imagine a slight coolness in his voice? Or was it paranoia brought on by guilt about lying to my dearest friend who I hadn't seen properly for ages? Because the strange thing was, I felt a lot worse about lying to Paul than I did about lying to Ollie. And the next thing I did was get on the phone and have a long cosy chat to him, telling him Nelly's amazing news, before going down to meet Frannie.

I was beginning to feel like the woman with two brains.

5

IT wasn't a long drive out to the Alberta Ferretti venue and with Frannie feeling much happier—especially after I'd poured a couple of Bloody Marys down her and told her Nelly's extraordinary tale—and with Bee and Alice still both in amazingly good spirits, we were quite the jolly little gang. It was at times like this that I realized how much I really liked Bee. She was unbelievably pushy and tough when it came to work, but she was also a great person, brilliant at her job, searingly bright and really funny.

On top of that she really appreciated anyone with talent, who was prepared to work as hard as her. She showed her appreciation in all kinds of ways from regular job promotions and pay rises, to little presents and bottles of champagne, which would appear on your desk with a handwritten note. She certainly wasn't a cold-hearted cow like Beaver. It was just tough being cooped up with your boss at such close quarters for so long.

This turned out to be one of those occasions when she made it a little easier for us all. She turned round in her seat and gave the three of us a beaming smile—I was in the middle again, as a concession to Frannie's fragile state.

"Now girls," she said. "I've got a little something for each of you."

She handed each of us a small Prada carrier bag. We'd all bought at least four things in Prada already that week, but those little blue bags still had the same effect on us that a bulging Christmas stocking has on a five-year-old. It's like an illness. Prada-osis.

"Wow, Bee," I said, with all sincerity, as I opened the slim blue box within to find a sleek leather wallet-y thing. I wasn't sure what it was, but I liked it. Alice and Frannie had the same thing.

"They're Prada Palm Pilot covers," said Bee. "Just a little thank you to say how much I appreciate the work you girls do for the magazine. I found them in the men's store on Montenapoleone. I've never seen them anywhere else."

She turned back to the front and took the cigarette Luigi had lit for her, sighing with contentment at her shopping coup.

"I haven't got a Palm Pilot," Frannie whispered to me.

"Keep sweeties in it," I whispered back. "And your tram tickets."

After that we just sat there in the limo in happy silence. Even Alice had her good points, I reflected, in my general state of golden glow. Nelly and I were always taking the piss out of her work, but she was actually incredibly creative and prepared to take risks with her styling, in a way that I wasn't. Alice's stuff didn't always work, but when it did, it was amazing.

I also reminded myself that she was fundamentally and deeply insecure, and had been single for an awfully long time. In fact she hadn't had a proper boyfriend as long as anyone could remember. She just lurched from one disastrous short-lived affair to another and that really took its toll on a girl. I offered her a piece of my sugar-free gum. Fair's fair.

"Where shall we eat tonight, gang?" said Bee, also accepting a stick of Orbit. "We've got a night off and I thought we should go somewhere nice. I've got the concierge to book Le Langhe and Bice and I thought you lot could decide."

"I don't mind," said Alice, with her usual commitment.

"Can't we go to Alla Collina Pistoiese?" said Frannie. A totally unpretentious trattoria serving amazing Tuscan food, it was her favourite restaurant in the world.

"Is that really what you want? Don't you want to go somewhere more glamorous? What about you, Em?" said Bee. "You're the foodie."

Frannie snorted.

"The foodie who never eats food," she muttered.

I jabbed her with my elbow.

"I felt nothing, darling," she said. "I'm nicely padded. If I did that to you my arm would come out the other side."

"Actually, Bee," I said, my mouth working on autopilot, chewing gum and talking all on its own, quite independent of my conscious thought. "I think I might go back to the hotel after this," I said smoothly. "Would that be all right? We haven't got another free night this week and I'm knackered after the party last night. I'd like an early one."

"Do what you like," said Bee. "We'll go to Le Langhe. Tom Ford eats there. I'd like to run into him."

As we sat in the Alberta Ferretti venue—an old garage—on the usual hard, backless benches, waiting as ever in the semi-dark, with people treading all over your handbag to get to their seats, I was keenly aware of two things. Nelly's absence and Miles's camera, trained on me as I sat there. I could just sense it out of the corner of my eye, but I had no intention of acknowledging it. Paul's comments about our dancing had made me more wary, but not enough to stop a warm glow spreading through my trouser area.

After the show, as I was shuffling along with the crush of people filing slowly through the courtyard to get out on to the street, I felt a hand gently cup my buttock. I looked round to see Miles smiling at me.

"Going somewhere nice for dinner?" he said, with one eyebrow raised. I knew exactly what he was really saying.

"No," I replied. "I thought I'd stay in tonight and have room service."

"Good idea," he said, pecking me innocently on the cheek, as if saying goodbye to a vague acquaintance. "Get a nice early night."

He squeezed my buttock again and then melted into the crowd. I couldn't believe how easy it was.

I'd been back at the hotel for about an hour and, after a long soak in my favourite Jo Malone tuberose bath oil, I was lying on the bed watching MTV. I was wearing a sheer chiffon Thirties tea dress I had taken to sporting over jeans and a jumper as a winsome winter look. Just at that moment, however, I was wearing it over nothing.

There was a knock on the door and a voice called out: "Room service."

Unless the Principe had recently taken on some Australian waiting staff it was Miles. I ran to answer it—and I mean that literally, I *ran*. As I opened the door I felt my cheeks burning up; the very idea of him seemed to have some kind of visceral effect on me. And there was the reality, even better than I remembered. He pushed the door open with his foot—he was wearing great old biker boots—while pulling me into his arms. He lifted me up, like a bride, and carried me over to the bed.

"Stay there and don't move," he said as he put me down. Then he stood at the end of the bed looking down at me, as he unzipped his jacket—a really beaten-up old leather motocross effort, if you want to know—and threw it on the floor. He undid his shirt—classic blue Oxford cloth—button by button, and then he pulled his T-shirt—an ancient washed-out old thing—over his head. He was magnificent. Such broad brown shoulders, such a deep chest, such a great big hunk of a man. I swallowed hard.

He paused for a moment, with his head on one side, looking me over from top to bottom, then he very slowly unbuckled the belt I remembered him doing up that morning. He was driving me crazy. I started to sit up, with every intention of grabbing him.

"I said, don't move," he whispered, smiling at me.

My heart was pounding so hard I thought I was going to hyperventilate. Thoughts were rushing through my head. What was I doing allowing a virtual stranger into my hotel room? A half-naked virtual stranger. Was I nuts? What if Ollie rang? And how long was it going to take him to get the rest of his kit off? Just when I thought I would die if he didn't jump on me in the next two seconds, he suddenly turned, sat down on the chair by the window and took his boots off.

"Don't want to get caught with my pants round my ankles and my boots still on," he said, grinning at me.

I laughed, slightly hysterically, relieved to have the tension broken.

"You know what?" he said, a moment later. "I've been wearing these boots all day. Reckon they might need a rabies test. I think I'd better take a shower."

He threw his boots over into the far corner of the room and then he got up, pulling his jeans and boxer shorts down in one go. When he stood up again his hard-on was straining right up against his flat brown stomach. I almost gasped. He came over and grabbed my hand, pulling me off the bed.

"And you can come in with me," he said.

I've never been more glad of the Principe's luxurious bathroom facilities. We spent a long time in that shower and while hot running water is not the ideal treatment for a fragile chiffon frock, I did not, to quote Miles, give a shit. When we finally went back into the bedroom, wrapped up in the thick white hotel bathrobes, I noticed the red message light on the phone was flashing. So was the one on my mobile. Miles saw them too. The noise of the shower must have drowned out the ringing.

"Do you mind?" he said, as he took the phone off the hook. I shook my head and at the same time, I reached over and turned off my mobile.

"Do you often ravage married women in their hotel rooms?" I asked him. "You seem to know the score."

"Never done it before in my life," he said. "Can we get that room service you promised me now? I'm starving."

We turned MTV on again while he ate an enormous burger and I had the salad garnish, carefully avoiding the raw onion. It was weirdly normal, which made it totally weird. I didn't know this guy and here we were being all domestic. For the first time since I'd met Miles I felt a tiny pang of guilt.

For reasons I couldn't quite work out, it seemed OK to shag

another man senseless, but cosying up with him in front of the telly seemed like a terrible betrayal of Ollie. Up until that point I had felt completely relaxed with Miles and I'd really enjoyed talking to him the night before—almost as much as I had enjoyed boffing him, in fact—but now I felt really awkward. I felt even worse when there was a knock on the door. It was Frannie.

"Em," she shouted. "Are you there? Let me in—I can hear your telly. I've got something really funny to tell you. Em? Em?"

Miles and I froze, gawping at each other, until we were sure she'd gone. Then he put his plate down, wiping his mouth on the back of his hand, and lay back on the pillows. He pulled me towards him and kissed my forehead.

"That was a bit close," he said, smoothing my hair with his hand. "Are you OK?"

I nodded, although I wasn't.

"I don't want to make you feel bad," he said. "Do you want me to leave?"

I did, but then I didn't. I looked down at him. So handsome, in a wonderfully brutish way. And apparently sincere too.

"Yes and no," I said. It was the truth.

"You want me to leave, so you don't feel like a sordid adulterer, but you want me to stay so we can carry on doing the filthy sordid things we've been doing, right?"

I smiled at him. Bingo.

"You've totally got it," I said.

"No worries. I feel exactly the same. So I'm going to root you one more time—and root you good, so you won't forget it—and then I'm going to leave you to get your beauty sleep."

He rolled over and gently lay on top of me, opening my legs with one knee, nuzzling my neck and ear gently, and then entering me suddenly in one smooth movement. All awkwardness instantly vanished as I felt myself start to rock slowly beneath him and my brain slipped into a blissful state of neutral.

I have no idea how much time passed in this manner—and several other manners—but finally it reached a natural conclusion so that it seemed absolutely right that I should be, once more, lying on the bed, naked, watching Miles get dressed. After he put on his jacket he came and knelt next to me at the side of the bed. He took my hand and brought it up to his lips.

"Emily," he said. "You're amazing and gorgeous and I'd love to see you again, but you're a married woman and I'm a free agent, so it's up to you. As I said, I don't want to make you feel bad, but if you want me to I'm always available to make you feel good, if you know what I mean?"

I did. I nodded. He ran his lips over my fingers a few times, then he stood up and fished a business card out of the back pocket of his jeans and put it on the bedside table. He walked over to the door and, as he opened it, he looked back at me.

"You've got my mobile number and my email there," he said. "You don't have to give me yours. I won't ever try to contact you, but if you want to see me, just get in touch. Are you doing Paris?"

I nodded. He just raised his eyebrows and opened his hands, as if to say, "It's up to you." And then he left.

I lay there, gazing up at the ceiling, still feeling a distinct throb between my legs. It was up to me.

The rest of that Milan season passed in a state of unreality. I carried on doing my job as usual, doing my yoga, doing my hair, doing my stomach crunches and getting dressed up every morning like some kind of show pony, just to spend days riding around in the car and sitting waiting in darkened spaces. The only times I got to parade the outfits I spent so much time, money and effort assembling was during the brief walks in and out of the show venues, the occasional visits to the shops and at the interminable appointments, lunches and dinners with fashion PRs. It was nuts really, but that was the shows.

What wasn't normal, even in that unreal world, was that I was spending just about every waking moment—and a lot of my sleeping ones—obsessing about Miles. His body, to be exact. His naked body. His hard buttocks. His hard penis. His hard and soft tongue. Even his tantalizing nibbling teeth and the coarse feel of his hair in my hands when his head was, well, use your imagination. Just thinking about him could make me start to hum inside like a little motor.

Still not really feeling guilty, but more than a little confused, I had decided not to see him again. I was happy with that choice, but it was so strange to sit in every show and know he was out there somewhere in the semi-dark, possibly looking at me through his long lens. And there I was, all kitted out as Miss Perfectly Groomed Fashion Editor having the thoughts of a total slut muppet.

The other strange thing about the end of that week was not having Nelly sitting by me. I missed her so much. The shows were always our special time together because, although we talked on the phone a lot, we didn't really see that much of each other back in London. It seemed crazy, but we were both always so manically busy with our jobs and, although we crossed over in the fashion scene and always made straight for each other at crowded launch parties, in our general social lives we moved in totally different circles. I was very much the Notting Hillbilly, while Nelly lived near Old Street and hung out with a much more edgy crowd.

Ollie and I might have been in the *Tatler* "Cool Couples A-List"—another cutting for his scrapbook—but I think Nelly found our lives a bit too straight for her taste. She used to call the highly desirable area where Ollie and I lived "suburbia" and she was one of very few people who were immune to my husband's generally irresistible charm. It was mutual. The two of them were like cats around each other, with their fur prickling up.

She did come over to one of our Sunday salons, but whenever I asked her again, she always found a reason why she couldn't make it.

"Oh, I'm sorry, darls," she'd said on one of my many attempts to get her along. "I'll have to leave you and Little Lord Fauntleroy to it this time. I've got to help my mate Tom move house on Sunday, because he's been kicked out of his squat. Give the A-list my love, won't you?"

Neither of them would actually say it, because they wouldn't have wanted to hurt my feelings, but Nelly thought Ollie was a pretentious posh git and he thought she was unbearably coarse and common. But whatever my husband thought of Nelly, I loved her and I really missed her hilarious running commentary at the shows. She did ring me a few times as the days went on in Milan, but she was flat out helping Iggy—or "my Igs" as she was now calling him—with his show. And the really amazing thing was that far from losing her job, as I had feared she would, she was doing it all with her editor's blessing.

With Nelly's talent for broadcasting developments in her private life, Beaver—along with the rest of the fashion pack, which was frantically buzzing with the news—had found out almost immediately about Nelly's new liaison. And far from being furious that her most talented stylist was missing the shows, *pure*'s editor was thrilled to have one of her staff as the "muse" of fashion's hottest rising star. Needless to say, Bee was as pissed off about it as Beaver was gloating.

"Why didn't one of you girls crack on to Igor bloody Vaseline-o-vich, or however you pronounce it, at that party?" she asked us furiously.

We were having lunch in Cova, our favourite café, with its excellent range of very small, very expensive salads and fabulous proximity to Milan's shopping epicentre. A Milan institution, right on the corner of Via Montenapoleone and Via Sant' Andrea, it was bang in the heart of luxury boutique nirvana—the shopping Bermuda Triangle. It also had a waiter who was a dead ringer for George Clooney. We loved the place.

"Perhaps because two of us are married and the other one was busy sucking up to Antonello Ferrucci and his staff on your orders?" said Frannie with her usual frankness.

"Humph," said Bee, necking the complimentary glass of Prosecco which had just been sent over by the management. "It's so bloody annoying. I couldn't believe it last night in Le Langhe. We walk in and there is Nelly Stelios sitting not only with Vaseline-o-vich but with Tom bloody Ford. At the same table. I nearly puked."

Frannie shot me a look—this was the funny thing she had wanted to tell me the night before when she'd knocked on my bedroom door, while I was with Miles. She had told me about it that morning and we'd been in a state of hysteria ever since. Bee was obsessed with Tom Ford. That scenario was like a nightmare specially scripted to torture her. The only thing that could have been worse would have been Beaver sitting there with him too, but still she wouldn't stop going on about it.

"Christ," she was saying, chewing on a breadstick in her distraction, quite a feat considering she was smoking at the same time. "It must have been the worst night of Tom's life."

"They looked like they were having a pretty good time to me," said Frannie. "He was cracking up most of the time. At Nelly."

Bee ignored her and carried on raving, in between biting along the breadstick at high speed like a starving rat. "I bet they're going to do some kind of insider reportage of the making of the show, with great backstage pics and an exclusive interview with bloody Igor. I've already been told we can't have an interview with him. What kind of name is that for a designer anyway?"

She looked petulant for a moment and then another terrible thought struck her.

"And they'll probably have Tom in it now too," she wailed.

She was right on all counts. Nelly had told me all about it. She was directing the whole thing and the US, French, Italian, Russian, Australian and Japanese editions of *pure* had all optioned it. It was a massive story, at least twelve pages. I also happened to know that a documentary team from Channel 4 were filming the making of the feature too, for a one-hour show.

"Mind you," said Bee, still off on one and waving at the George Clooney waiter for another glass of fizz. "It could all go horribly wrong. I still can't believe there is a heterosexual fashion designer out there, even if he is some kind of Serbian thug. He's probably just using her as a big bushy beard."

She paused a moment and I saw her eyes start to twinkle.

"Perhaps there's a nice lezzo you could chat up, hey Alice? To get us a good story. Isn't that new French designer Marie Millais meant to be a big licker on the quiet? You like her clothes, don't you, Alice? Why don't you go backstage after the show in Paris next week and chat her up?"

By the expression that crossed her face, I could tell Alice wasn't sure if Bee was joking or not. She hadn't seen the wink she'd tipped me and Frannie. Poor paranoid humourless Alice. She'd probably spend the rest of the day worrying if Bee really meant it, I thought, and planning what she should wear for a lipstick lesbian look.

"I've got a Joan Armatrading CD I can lend you," said Frannie, brightly, kicking me gently under the table. "Get you in the mood."

"And you've already got your denim dungarees," I added.

"And your Birkenstocks . . ." said Bee, and the three of us collapsed into giggles.

Alice looked at us, bewildered, with a facial expression that reminded me of President Bush trying to grasp an abstract concept, until eventually, I could see the dawning realization that we were joking. Bee was wiping tears of mirth from her eyes. She whacked Alice on the upper arm, with the gung-ho spirit of the hockey captain she had been at school.

"Oh, Alee-chay," she said. "You silly sausage. You are the most wonderful stylist, but you've got absolutely no sense of bloody humour. I don't really expect you to change sides just to get me a good story. I was joking. You know? Funny ha ha? Now, here's George Non Clooney. What are you going to eat, Alice?" She flashed a mischievous look at me and Frannie. "May I suggest the prawn salad?"

And that just set us off again.

6

"HOW'S your family?" asked Paul, stirring sugar into his coffee.

We had finally managed to find time between shows and work meetings—real and fictional—to see each other and we were standing at the bar in our favourite old *pasticceria*, Marchesi, just off Corso Magenta, sipping nuclear-strength *macchiatos*.

"Oh, you know," I replied. "Mad, bad and dead. How are yours?"

"Much the same, thanks. Knocked up, knocked out and knackered."

"That's great," I said. "Do give them my love, won't you?"

"Of course and do send your mum my best wishes, the next time you visit the loony bin."

We clinked our coffee cups. It was just one of our ritual conversations. It may sound heartless and uncaring, but our game of twisted happy families was really a survival mechanism. In fact, it had been confessing to the equally gothic horrors of our childhoods which had launched our friendship from the merely hilarious into the seriously intense, way back when we had first met as students. As my photographer boyfriend had said, the day he moved out from our shared flat, Paul and I were closer than cling film and it was suffocating him.

The thing was, I hadn't told anyone the truth about my family until I'd met Paul. I'd even got rather good at elaborate pretending games, to try and hide the horrible truth. It had been easy when I'd been sent to boarding school at age twelve. With no one around to contradict me, I could make up the kind of family I wished I'd had. So when I met Paul, who was completely open about his horrendous childhood—he'd almost made it into a party piece—it was the most incredible relief to tell him the truth about mine.

It's a simple story really. Both my parents were highly strung artistic types—my dad was a painter, my mum a so-called poet. They both came from privileged backgrounds and had enough money in family trusts to allow themselves to indulge in their "art," without any of the tempering reality checks of having to earn a living.

We lived in a big house in Sussex—Mum and Dad, me, and my younger brother, Toby—in a quite idyllic setting, and there were many happy days. But my mother's mental state became increasingly fragile after a bout of post-natal depression, followed by a series of miscarriages. As my godmother, Ursula, once said to me, my parents were as irresponsible about contraception as they were about everything else.

Anyway, between getting pregnant and losing the babies, Mum supposedly wrote poetry, although as far as I could tell, she spent most of her time smoking dope, drinking and having very noisy nervous breakdowns—which were really just attempts to get my father's attention. He was so totally absorbed in his painting. And his bong.

Then Dad died, so suddenly, and Mum really flipped out. I mean really. She was always drunk, or stoned, she never got dressed and rarely bought any food. When she did go out, she frequently left me—I was only ten—at home on my own to look after Toby, sometimes not even coming back overnight. I was too frightened to tell anyone in case "they" took us away and put us in a home—those terrible childhood fears—and somehow I kept Toby and myself together enough to keep going to school. Why I thought that being taken into care would be any worse than living with a parent in the state she was in, I can't imagine, but when you're a child you just cling on to whatever you know as normal.

The final blow came when my mum attempted suicide. She threw herself in front of a train, but in her drunken state she even stuffed that up and was hardly even injured.

But that was when the social services did find out about how we were all living. Two children and a deranged, drunken woman in a filthy house. They took my mother into custody for reckless endangerment, and Toby and I went into care for one terrifying night before they contacted my father's brother, Andrew, and he came and got us.

For a while it seemed they were going to prosecute my mother for putting the train at risk—and for child neglect—but after taking medical advice about her mental state the cases were dropped. But not before my mother was completely undone. She was already seriously unstable before any of it happened, but with my father's death less than a year before, spending time on remand in prison and having her children taken away pushed her over the edge. In the end she was sectioned and after several more suicide attempts and a serious assault on a nurse, my mother has never been out of the mental hospital. She's pretty much locked in.

My uncle did take me and Toby to see her a few times, but she seemed not to know us. She just sat there, picking at her skirt and rocking—and holding a baby doll. For two already severely traumatized children it was too much, and her doctors agreed it would be better if we didn't see her for a while. Which for me, I'm afraid to say, became years. It was just easier not to go. Much easier.

So, like I said, it was a gothic horror of a childhood. But I was the lucky one in some ways, because I had my wonderful godmother, Ursula, to look out for me. When Mum was committed it was decided that Toby would continue living with our uncle, but he said he couldn't take me as well. He had three kids of his own and it was too much. It was terrible to be separated from Toby, but really, I was saved a lot of aggro. Ex-Sandhurst, ex-Guards, Uncle Andrew was as manically straight and strict as my father had been bohemian. As a result, my brother grew up in a state of near martial law, but he seemed to like it. When he left school he went into the army and became some kind of superhuman SAS freak. We all have our own ways of coping with trauma.

I, meanwhile, was sent to boarding school, which I adored. It was all so normal and blissfully structured—hot food, clean clothes, lots of lovely rules, everything I had lacked at home—and then in my holidays I went to stay with Ursula, in New York, which was utter heaven.

Really, it was a miracle that my parents ever asked someone as sensible as her to be my godmother, although I suppose the fact that she was a diesel dyke who would have made Gertrude Stein look feminine, would have offset any boringly "bourgeois" tendencies she might have had towards financial security and other—to them—tawdry facts of real life.

My father had known her since childhood. Their parents had become friends when her father was posted to London on some kind of secret squirrel mission during the war and after it was all over, my dad and his family had spent a lot of summers at Ursula's parents' place on Martha's Vineyard. It was a seriously Preppie scene, but Dad and Ursula were united in rebellion and became very close friends. They once put hash into the brownies for a family beach picnic. Everyone had a great time without quite knowing why.

After graduating from Wellesley, Ursula went through a seriously hippy stage—she went to Woodstock and hung out with Janis Joplin, which always thrilled me—then she went into publishing, eventually becoming a very successful literary agent. She represented some of the giants of modern American literature, as well as some of the biggest-selling names in airport fiction, and was very wealthy in her own right on top of what she had inherited from her parents.

Even though she never came over to the UK—she had a morbid fear of flying—Ursula and my father stayed friends and it meant a lot to both of them when she agreed to be godmother to his first child. It was one of the few really smart decisions he ever made. I can still remember going over to Martha's Vineyard the summer when I was four, just after my brother Toby had been born. I realize now that was when all my mother's problems had begun, but at the time I was going through the classic displacement of the first child when a new baby comes along.

Ursula did her best to make me feel special and wanted. We went on expeditions together, just the two of us, combing the beach for shells and crabs, and then we'd sit on the beach eating Reese's Peanut Butter Cups as she told me stories about her childhood and how naughty she'd been. On rainy days we baked cookies and on one very hot one, she showed me how to make real American lemonade and we set up a roadside stall to sell it. I still have a picture of myself sitting there.

Ursula never forgot my birthday or Christmas and often used to ring me up—all the way from New York—just for a chat, which was pretty special when I was eight. I think she knew life wasn't that easy for any of us once Mum got ill, plus I was, she often told me, the daughter she would never have. She called me her "undaughter" and in many ways she was more of a mother to me than my own female biological parent ever was.

"Have you seen Ursula recently?" I asked Paul, as we sipped our dangerously potent coffees. One of the great things for me about his move to New York, was that the two of them had become great friends.

"I sure have," he said. "In fact, I've got some books she sent over for you. And she asked me to give you this too." He took my face in his hands and planted a big kiss on my forehead. "Just there, that's where she told me to put it."

I smiled. Ursula always kissed me on the forehead. It was one of our things. She said it was my third eye.

"Is she OK?" I asked.

"OK?" said Paul. "She's amazing. She's fatter than ever, she's richer than ever, her writers are all over the bestseller charts and she's got an even-younger-and-more-gorgeous-than-ever girlfriend. She's the Hugh Hefner of the isle of Lesbos, that woman."

I laughed. Ursula's ability to attract beautiful young women was legendary. She always had a glorious girl in tow—in total thrall to her intellect and charisma. She allowed them to worship her for a while but she always ended the relationships before they got bored with her.

"And here are the books," he said, pulling them out of his capacious Bottega Veneta tote bag and handing them to me.

One was clearly a "treasure" found during her obsessive trawling of second-hand book shops. Called *Siren Songs* it was a collection of poetry with quite a great Seventies illustration of a hippy chick on the dust jacket, which in my opinion was probably the best thing about it. I put it in my bag without looking inside. I hated poetry. The other book was a shiny new paperback, with the kind of text-heavy cover design that suggested it was some hideous self-help tripe. *Thin Souls* it was called. I read out the rest of the title.

" 'How high fashion creates low self-esteem. . . .' Oh, for God's sake, where does she find these things?" I groaned. "Why can't she send me a nice fat art book, or some racy new novel? I love Ursula with all my heart, but for a literary agent, she has really terrible taste in books. Oh well, I'll tell her I loved them. Anyway, did I tell you about the amazing Azzedine Alaia jacket I've seen in Corso Como? God, I love that shop, I haven't seen that jacket anywhere else. They've got this genius collection of vintage handbags too . . ."

But Paul was looking at me with the tip of his tongue peeping out of the corner of his mouth. It looked so pink next to his black skin. He had a look on his face I knew very well.

"What?" I said, crossly.

"What what?" he answered, still looking at me that way.

"You've got your listening face on," I said. "I know you're thinking something."

"I'm thinking you're the one that needs to do some listening," he said.

"Uh? What are you on about?" I said, getting annoyed. "Have another coffee and get that dazed look off your face, it spooks me out. When are you going to Paris anyway? Are you going to spend some time in London in between? Is that the Miu Miu jacket you were telling me about? It's great. I love that colour on you."

He shook his head at me.

"Nice boots, Emily," he said. "New, are they? Nice bag. Limited edition? Must have been expensive. Great jacket. It's Marc Jacobs, isn't it? Is it size eight? Wow, you must be a really great person."

I just looked at him. What was he going on about?

"There's more to life than shopping, Emily," he said, then he sighed deeply and turned his attention to the barista, ordering us two more coffees.

I looked down at my Prada boots. He was right, they were great.

By 8:45 that night I wasn't so keen on my new boots. They were absolutely killing me and Bee was in such a filthy mood that, despite my pleas, she had refused to let us take a detour via the hotel between our punishing schedule of shows and appointments, so I could change them.

"Suffer," had been her final comment on it when my whining had reached what she considered an unacceptable point.

It was the last day of the Milan shows—the day of Iggy's debut for Rucca—and Bee seemed to have gone into hypermania about fitting in as many advertising appointments as possible. It was the same every season.

There was a lovely cruise-y time in the middle of the week, when she would relax and take us out for lunch and shopping and other treats. During the midweek lull she'd always talk about coming back to Milan in a few weeks' time, to schmooze all the designers and PRs at a more leisurely pace, but as the time to go home approached, she clearly went off that idea and was determined to cram it all into the remaining time. Then she'd go into nightmare editor mode and work us like pit ponies until we got on the plane back to London.

By the time we were in the car on our way to the Rucca show that evening, my face was so tired of smiling at hideous hag PRs and their ghastly clothes, I felt like it was going to crack and fall off. I was seriously over it, but it was quite a contest between all of us in that car, who was in the worst mood. As well as my boots—I was sure I could feel blood seeping into the leather—I was fuming because Bee's insistence at fitting in two more "essential" advertiser visits, one of them with a lingerie company, for pity's sake, had made us really late for the show.

And I mean *really* late, not just fashion late, but miss-it late. It was already forty-five minutes after the time on the invitation and we weren't even there yet. The show was being held in an old book-binding plant so far out of the centre of Milan it was practically in Switzerland and I was terrified we were going to blow it. It had happened. I'd had to stand at the back of Versace once after Bee pulled one of these stunts. I was not going to stand at this show.

"Can't you move over one inch?" snapped Frannie—in the middle seat—at Alice, who was doing extravagant yoga stretches from the comfort of her corner. "I'm not a bloody contortionist."

"Oh, do stop waving your arms about, Alice," yelled Bee simultaneously from the front. "You're putting Luigi off his driving, which is dangerous with an Italian.

"For GOD's sake," she yelled at him as he swerved wildly around an old lady at a crossing, prompting a frenzy of honking and gesticulating from other cars. "What is the matter with you people? Why can't you drive like normal humans? You all think you're bloody Senna and guess what? He's *dead*."

I saw Luigi's eyes crinkle with mirth in the rear-view mirror. He had clearly done it on purpose for his own amusement. He leant over and pushed in the car's cigarette lighter—he knew how to calm Bee down.

"Why do they have to have this show at this ridiculous venue anyway?" she was spluttering on.

"It's only the same place as DSquared2," said Frannie, who was in her most argumentative grammar-school-girl mood. She even annoyed me when she turned into Miss Prissy Know-It-All.

"I know that," snapped Bee. "But it's still a bloody stupid place to have to come at night. Rucca always used to show in Via Sant' Andrea, which was so handy for dinner, but this Croatian idiot has to make it hard for everyone."

"Serbian," said Frannie quietly.

"I really don't care where he's from," yelled Bee, practically snatching the lit cigarette being proffered by Luigi. "He's an arsehole wherever it is. An arsehole with a really stupid name."

"A really stupid name that would look great on our cover . . ." whispered Fran to me, nailing the real problem Bee was having with the whole event. It was going to be Beaver's moment of glory by proxy.

*   *   *

The mob scene that greeted us when we finally arrived at the old factory—now a full fifty-five minutes late—just cranked Bee's fury up a little more. There were hordes of paparazzi and a great roiling crowd of people trying to get into the venue.

"Oh, that's all I need," snarled Bee, reapplying her lipstick in Luigi's rear-view mirror, which she had yanked round to face her. "Fashion students."

I could see her eyes reflected back to me in the mirror and despite the venom in her voice, there was a vulnerable look there. But from the moment Luigi opened the car door to let her out, you would never have guessed it.

She swung her long thin shins out of the car like the fashion royalty she was and glided towards the heaving throng with regal grace, despite the fact she was wearing skyscraper heels, the ground was treacherous with potholes and, except for a few blinding arc lights intermittently sweeping over us, it was pitch black.

Adding to the intensity of the scene, it was raining slightly and the air was booming with the sound of low-flying helicopters. I kept looking up and flinching, even after I realized it was being broadcast from speakers. Dodging choppers that weren't there, I managed to walk right into a major concrete crevasse and gave my ankle a nasty twist. It was the same foot that was bleeding, but it could have been worse, I told myself, I could have damaged the boot's heel. I hobbled on.

"Bloody hell," said Frannie, as we pushed our way into the mêlée, waving our invitations over our heads. Most of the people there didn't even have them and were just trying to get in on bluff, such was the level of hype about Iggy's first show for the label.

"I bloody hate crushy crowds," said Frannie. "I always feel like I'm going to suffocate."

I looked down at her ginger head. She was a good foot below me and I could see there wasn't much air down there.

"That's why you should wear heels, Frannie," I said. "They're protective clothing in this situation."

Standing on my good foot, I used the stiletto heel on my other one as a weapon to deter a skinny-hipped Italian guy who was trying to push in front of me. He was the worst kind of Eurotrash mod-elizer in his jeans and blazer and he wasn't going to get in my way. I got him right down the left shin and as he yelped back with pain, I grabbed hold of Frannie's arm and pushed my Louis Vuitton-clad shoulder into the crowd.

I could just see Bee's head way in front of us, slicing seamlessly through the mob. Something about her bearing made the gatecrashers and the security guards part like the Red Sea and I saw her disappear into the venue. I relied on brute force. A rugby union prop forward could not have got through that crowd quicker than I did, until we were brought to an abrupt stop, faced with a wall of huge bouncers.

"No more," said the one right in front of us, standing there like something out of *The Arabian Nights,* his ham-like forearms folded in front of him. He was so huge it wasn't even funny. They must have made his black suit specially out of old tarpaulins. Frannie's face was practically at a level with his crutch.

"We have invitations," I shouted at him. "With *seats.*"

I showed him my invitation and seat number. GA12.

"No more," said Gigantor. "Full."

"Front row!" I screamed at him.

"Full," he repeated back at me, a glimmer of sadistic pleasure in his primitive dinosaur eyes.

I felt physically ill as I heard the unmistakeable sound of the first bars of "Blue Monday" come throbbing out through the door.

It was Nelly's favourite track. Of course she'd start the show with that. I felt quite desperate. Not only was I going to miss my best friend's boyfriend's show, but the glory of strutting over to my first-ever front-row seat.

At that moment Frannie made a very strange sound. I looked down to see vomit cascading from her mouth on to Gigantor's surprisingly small black shoes. He sprang back in horror. Frannie grabbed my hand and we sprang forward into the venue. We didn't look back, but just made straight for where we thought the catwalk should be in the darkness of the venue—and we walked right into Nelly.

"Where the fuck have you fuckers been?" she screamed at us.

"Bloody Bee made us bloody late," I screamed back. "And then your bloody bouncers wouldn't let us in."

"I've held the show up for you. They've already played this three times," said Nelly, looking at Frannie, who was wiping her mouth on a tissue. "What the fuck happened to you?"

"I vomited," she said, picking bits out of her teeth with her tongue. "To order. Taught myself to do it at school, for when I hadn't done my Latin homework."

Nelly just grabbed our hands and marched us into the black space. I could feel rather than see that it was packed with people and I couldn't imagine how there could be a spare seat in the place, but Nelly didn't falter as she dragged us over other people's feet and bags round the edge of the catwalk. It was so thrilling I forgot I had a bleeding foot and a sprained ankle.

She walked us straight up to the prime position in front of the photographers, plonked us in the front row and disappeared. It took me about three seconds after my eyes got used to the dim lighting, to realize I was sitting next to Anna Wintour. As I nudged Frannie to alert her to our proximity to a deity and frantically scrabbled through my bag for my glasses and notebook, Ms. Wintour didn't even turn her glossy basilisk head, but continued to stare straight ahead down the runway through her huge black sunglasses.

I looked left along the edge of the catwalk to where Bee and Beaver were sitting side by side looking over at me and Frannie—with their mouths hanging open and pursed up respectively. I glanced quickly back over my right shoulder and saw Miles grinning down at me, shaking his head and smiling. And then the show began.

It was, as the saying goes, a fashion "moment." From the minute it started there was a tingling magic in the air that only happens very occasionally at a fashion show—and not even every season. I'd experienced it before at a few shows—Tom Ford, John Galliano, Alexander McQueen and Miuccia Prada had all taken their turns to cook it up over the years I had been doing the collections—and there was always something weirdly emotional about it when it happened.

It was some kind of combination of a pure artistic experience with gross commerce and the absolute certainty that you were experiencing something that would be talked about for years to come. And which would change fashion in a fundamental way. Not just in the rarefied world of designer wear, but all the way down the food chain, so that in a couple of years' time even babies would be wearing clothes influenced by the styles in this collection.

With this show it wasn't just the clothes, it was the whole event. It started with the space going completely black and staying that way for quite a while, until the photographers started to whistle and make rude comments. And then the first noise we heard was almost imperceptible, gradually getting louder until you realized you were listening to a jet fighter approaching at screaming high speed. It made your stomach turn to water.

Then, just when it was starting to get unpleasant, the lights went up—wham!—and the music blared out, Mary J. Blige, in full diva mode, as the first model strutted out, a gold-plated army helmet on her head, her face and entire body painted like camouflage, creating the most amazing contrast with a floor-length electric blue parachute-silk dress, with a huge train.

Sashaying down the catwalk she lifted up her skirt to reveal army-style boots, which had seven-inch stiletto heels and laced all the way up to her thighs, which were also painted like camouflage.

As the music changed to a Keith Richards guitar riff, another of Nelly's favourites, the next girl came out, also painted with camouflage. Even her hair, which was up in a huge beehive, had been sprayed to match—and she had a yashmak across her face. She was wearing a black satin coat with huge epaulettes shaped like the armour on a tank and, as she strutted along, she took one of the shoulder pieces off the coat, and pulling out a strap, hung it over her arm as a handbag.

So it went on, the most extraordinary mixture of disturbing military themes, high glamour and ethnic motifs. But, apart from the spectacle, the thing that made the show really impressive to the thousands of highly trained eyes in that crowd, was that mixed in with the wild styling and over-the-top statements, were truly wonderful clothes—and bags and shoes—that women the world over were going to want to wear.

When the models came out for their final strut along the catwalk, they did it to the poignant strains of a small boy singing John

Lennon's song, "Imagine." It might sound cheesy, but it seriously wasn't. It brought tears to your eyes.

The whole thing was a triumph and when Iggy came out to take his bow the crowd went wild. Anna Wintour was clapping enthusiastically next to me and Frannie and I leapt up to give him a standing ovation and each other a hug, because we were so proud of Nelly. It was then that I spotted something I had never noticed before—Iggy's left hand was missing. Instead he had a hook.

While Frannie and I were still squealing with excitement I suddenly realized that Ms. Wintour—as you couldn't help thinking of her—had quietly left her seat and had climbed up on to the catwalk, along with a huge stream of other people. She was going backstage to congratulate Iggy too. Now, *that* was huge.

"We're going backstage," I immediately said to Frannie. It was something we never did—only the big editors, close friends of designers and total wankers went backstage, but now we felt related to Iggy and quite entitled to go. And apart from anything, I sincerely wanted to congratulate him on one of the most amazing fashion shows I had ever seen.

"We'd better tell Bee," said Frannie, back in good-girl mode, so we rushed over to find her just climbing up on to the catwalk herself. She looked down at us, smiling broadly—but she had tears in her eyes.

"Come on, gang," she said. "Let's go and get in the way of the *pure* photographer."

It was total mayhem backstage, with bouncers trying unsuccessfully to keep people out, models with no clothes on, television crews and paparazzi everywhere and corks popping like 24-gun salutes.

I couldn't see Iggy, but I assumed he was in the epicentre of the tangled mass of cameras. So did Bee because she headed straight for it. Frannie went to find the makeup director to get the low-down about the camouflage effects and I had just taken a glass of champagne from a passing tray, when Nelly came running over. I gave her an enormous hug, while camera flashes went off all around us—the paps clearly already knew she was the girlfriend.

"Oh, Nelly," I said, getting all tearful again. "That was amazing, he's brilliant. I don't know what to say. It's going to be huge."

She gave me another of her killer hugs. It nearly winded me.

I'm so glad you liked it, Ems," she said. "It means a lot to me. Especially as I thought you weren't bloody turning up."

She cuffed me playfully around my head and then grabbed my hand.

"Come and tell my boy how much you liked it."

Nelly shouldered her way through the cameramen and sycophants and pushed me in front of Iggy, who looked pink and bewildered and had about six microphones stuck under his nose.

"Emily loved it, Igs," said Nelly.

I didn't know what to say, so I took his hand—except it was the wrong hand and I had grabbed hold of his hook. I couldn't suddenly drop it so I just pulled him towards me and gave him a big kiss.

"It was wonderful, Iggy," I said into his ear. "Absolutely wonderful."

He kissed me three times on the cheeks and put his arms round me.

"Thank you, Emily," he said, in his heavy accent. "Means a lot. Nelly loves you, so I love you. Come with us for dinner."

I gave his hook one more squeeze and made way for the TV crews.

7

IGGY'S show was the lead on Suzy Menkes's page the next day in the *International Herald Tribune* and was splashed on the front of *World Fashion Daily*. The papers had been pushed under my door while I slept and I sprang out of bed to grab them. Suzy raved about Iggy, describing how he had introduced a new level of creativity and intellectual interest into the Milan calendar and Louise—the ice queen of fashion journalism—was equally effusive in *WFD:*

> *This was the kind of bravura creativity you expect to see in Paris—not in oh-so-commercial Milan. Yet despite the breathtaking drama of the show with its, at times disturbing, bellicose themes and references, there were clothes here—and even more crucially for Rucca, accessories—that women of all ages will long to own. Veselinovic's armoured tote is destined to be the next cult bag.*

They both also reported that top LA celebrity stylists were already fighting over Rucca dresses for their clients to wear to the forthcoming Academy Awards—which was the fashion equivalent of winning an Oscar. And Nelly got a namecheck from them both too, as his "new muse."

I was mentally air punching on Iggy and Nelly's behalf when my mobile rang.

"Have you seen Suzy and Louise?" shouted Nelly.

"Is that the new muse?" I shouted back. "I was just reading them. It's wicked. I'm thrilled for you both, Nelly, stoked, it's brilliant. How's Iggy."

"He's pretty happy, as you can imagine. Want to come and have breakfast with us? We're already on the Dom."

"Oh, Nellster," I said. "I'd love to, but I'm racing to catch the plane as it is. I haven't even packed yet. We're all going back this morning."

I paused. Normally we all went on the same flight—the entire London fashion pack crammed into the first possible plane out of town, because everyone wanted to maximize their time at home before heading off again for Paris. Plus I had a pedi booked at Bliss Spa at 4 p.m. I couldn't miss that.

"Aren't you on the ten o'clock flight, Nelly?" I asked her.

"Fuck that," she said. "I'm stayin' here. With my Ig."

"Are you doing Paris?"

"Not sure yet. If Iggy comes with me, I will. Otherwise, fuck it."

"It's that tight already, is it Nelly?" I said quietly, quite concerned about my impulsive friend. "After—what is it?—*five* nights? So tight you're prepared to risk your job?"

"Are you kidding?" Nelly laughed her throatiest laugh. "Beaver's just promoted me. I'm 'fashion-director-at-large' now. How funny is that? Anyway babes, love ya lots. I'll call you. *Stravo lepina.*"

"What?"

"That's: 'Bye beautiful,' in Serbian."

And cackling with laughter she hung up.

As I whirled around the hotel room, stuffing my things into my suitcase—I had only half an hour until we had to leave for the airport—I came across Miles's business card, which was still on the bedside table where he'd left it. I sat down on the bed and turned it over in my fingers a few times, wondering whether I shouldn't just throw it on to the pile of carrier bags, old invitations and press releases already overflowing from the waste-paper bin.

It was another of those moments I'd been having ever since I had met him, when I felt very clearly that I was at a junction in my life. I could throw away the card, making a statement to myself that the whole thing had been a crazy aberration—or I could keep it and leave open the possibility of seeing him again.

For a moment, as I sat there thinking how nicely done his card was, in dark brown raised ink on vivid yellow card, I envied Nelly and her absolute certainty that staying in Milan with Iggy was the right thing to do. But then, as always seemed to happen in regard to Miles, my body was already acting, while my brain was still mulling it over. I fished my Palm Pilot out of my bag and entered Miles's details in the photographer category. Then I threw the card into the bin.

I always felt strangely sad to leave Milan—it was the thought of all those gorgeous shops I hadn't had time to get into—but as soon as we landed at Heathrow I felt the energy of my home city pick me up like a leaf in a fast stream.

I left Bee and the others at the airport to take the chauffeured car into town and hopped on to the Heathrow Express. It was so much quicker and dropped me off just minutes from home. And I'd had quite enough of riding around in cars with those three for a while. Even Frannie. I was sick of being some kind of Siamese quad and was all too aware that I only had a few days of freedom before it all began again in Paris.

By the time the train pulled into Paddington I was so happy to be home I decided to walk back to the flat. It was an amazingly nice day for early-October; blades of sunshine were piercing the station's glass roof and there was no telling how many more days like that we would have before the tight lid of London's winter sky settled over the city until spring.

I had my luggage in a wheelie bag and although it was on the huge side, I could just about drag it along. I even had sensible shoes on for a change—a pair of Gucci trainers in their logo jacquard—but every step I took closer to Ledbury Road, with my bag rattling along the pavement behind me like an old train, my guilt and confusion about what I had done with Miles got more intense.

Back in Milan I had felt so cut off from my real life, that despite my daily phone calls with Ollie I had somehow been able to keep him—and what I had got up to over there with Miles—separate in my head. Now I was back in pure Ollie territory, it all became one big mess.

Taking in the great-looking people strolling along Westbourne Grove, all of them somehow simultaneously individual and totally in fashion, one of a kind and one of my pack, I realized just how much living in that neighbourhood meant to me. I also remembered all over again that I was only there because Ollie had invited me into his life—and into his lifestyle. I could never have afforded a flat in W11 on my salary, even without my shopping habit.

That thought then prompted a moment of pure panic about how much I had racked up on my credit cards in Milan. The four pairs of Prada boots. The Gucci trainers. Another pair of Sergio Rossi killer heels. A Marni coat. A Dolce & Gabbana pantsuit. A Tod's bag. A handful of T-shirts from Helmut Lang. I mean, it was all essential stuff for the new season, but even with discount, what did that come to? £5,000? £6,000?

By the time I had my key in the lock I felt physically sick about it all—especially when I saw the huge vase of flowers on the dining table with a big heart-shaped note.

Welcome home, darling Ems. See you tonight. I've booked E&O. See you there at 9 P.M.—have PO meetings before. Ollie xxxxxx

"PO" was our shorthand for "phone off," meaning he wouldn't be able to take any calls, so I sent him a quick text—"Hme sfly, c u EnO 9. Lv u. Em xxx"—then I set to unpacking.

It was always crucial to me to get my things unpacked, washed and put away as soon as possible when I got home from any trip and especially with the shows, as it was part of the discipline of being ready to do it all again in three days' time. I couldn't possibly pack again for the next trip unless I was completely unpacked from the last one. Plus it was a great way to keep busy when I didn't want to think about something.

I took off everything I was wearing—including my earrings and wedding ring—pulled my hair back into a tight pony-tail and up-ended my suitcase on the bedroom floor. Then I stuffed everything washable—even things I hadn't worn—into the washing machine. Anything that had been in a suitcase was tainted to me. I hate that suitcase smell.

I handwashed my Chloé tops, TSE cashmere cardigans and Prada underwear, squeezed the excess moisture out by rolling them in thick towels and laid them out on my special drying-flat contrap-tions in the autumn sunshine pouring through the French windows.

I was starting to feel much better as I set to brushing and polish-ing all my shoes, putting aside a pair of boots which needed re-heeling, and then setting them out on the shelves in my side of our walk-in closet, in neat rows. Sandals and strappy evening shoes at the top, coming down through mules, to closed shoes and trainers, with boots along the bottom two shelves, all with the appropriate shoe trees.

I stowed two of the new pairs of Prada boots in a rarely used suitcase, locked it and put it back in our luggage cupboard. I was just about to put the suitcase I'd taken to Milan back in there too, when I noticed the two books Ursula had sent over with Paul were still in the bottom of it. I threw them under the bed, without giving them another look. For a moment Paul's strange comment about there being more to life than shopping came back into my mind. He loved shopping as much as I did, I thought. I couldn't imagine what he'd been on about, so I just pushed it out of my mind again, and went back to my sorting.

I rolled my belts into neat coils and put them in their drawer, ran a soft cloth over the handbags I'd taken with me (five), put them back in their dustbags and stowed them away on their shelves. I folded my scarves and pashminas and laid them carefully in their clear plastic storage boxes, arranged by colour. I smoothed my gloves and put them back into their box and sorted my costume jewellery into sepa-rate cases for necklaces, earrings and bangles.

Next I tipped out and sorted my travel tote and my handbag, putting the stack of Italian magazines I always got for Ollie on his

bedside table and my book on mine, chucking the half-empty bottles of mineral water, chewing-gum wrappers and bits of crumpled
newspaper into the bin—except for Suzy's page featuring Iggy,
which I also put on Ollie's bedside pile.

I transferred my everyday essentials—Louis Vuitton wallet, keys
on a Tiffany keyring, Anya Hindmarch mini make-up bag, Palm
Pilot in its new Prada cover, tiny Nokia phone, Smythson notebook, Lamy pen, tissues in their quilted Chanel pouch—from the
acid yellow Birkin bag I had travelled with into a more casual dark
tan Luella Bartley safari bag.

Next I moved into the bathroom, emptying my wash-bags into
the sink and putting all the products away in the cupboards hidden
behind mirror doors. I wiped out the washbags and put them on
their shelf in the luggage cupboard. Then I sorted my make-up bag,
putting my brushes and other tools back into their crystal beakers,
and separating eye shadows, lipsticks, foundations and blushers each
into their designated Lucite storage caddies inside the mirrored
cupboards.

Once all that was finished I had a very hot shower, washing my
hair till my scalp tingled, blasted it with my hairdryer so I wouldn't
get pneumonia and then got dressed again, entirely in pristine
clothes I hadn't taken away with me: chocolate brown Juicy Couture trackpants with a tiny Bond's T-shirt, and a huge navy six-ply
cashmere jumper over the top, a trusty old pair of Pumas on my
feet. No socks of course.

With everything done, I threw my pedicure flip-flops into my
bag and raced out of the flat, to drop all the non-washable clothes
off at the dry-cleaner's on the corner. The man behind the counter
greeted me like family—Ollie and I were probably his best cus-
tomers. On top of my dry-cleaning needs, which were pretty massive, Ollie had all his shirts laundered there—which was at least ten
a week, as he always changed his shirt before going out at night—
plus all his suits.

Then I picked up a cab to take me down to Bliss Spa, in Sloane
Avenue. I especially asked the driver to go through Hyde Park and
as I looked out at its elegant landscape, the last of the afternoon

sunshine falling in shafts between the trees, any residual feelings of panic completely ebbed away. I felt like I had sorted my brain along with my luggage.

Safely cocooned at Bliss, I lay back in my white leather chair and surrendered myself to *Sex and the City*, which was playing on a TV over the pedicurist's head. With my headphones on I was able to tune out from the whole world, even though Carrie was regretting cheating on her dopey boyfriend with Mr. Big. Oh well.

Forty minutes later, with my toenails a glorious rich dark red, I left feeling completely renewed. Dusk had fallen and the autumn chill nipped my soft bare feet in their black flip-flops, but I didn't care. I was still on an "I love London" high.

I had a litle stroll along Walton Street looking in the windows at the gorgeous jewellery in Van Peterson, all the fragrant goodies in Santa Maria Novella and the engraved stationery in the Walton Street Stationery Shop. I even enjoyed looking at the painted nursery furniture in Dragons, even though Ollie and I had no intention of ever having children.

Strolling back to find a cab at Brompton Cross I popped into Joseph and dropped £130 on a pair of their stretch drainpipe pants in deepest burgundy. I already had several pairs of black, but thought the burgundy would be useful in Paris. A key new variation for my winter look. By the time I got home and dumped the trousers in the closet, still in the Joseph carrier bag, I felt fine again. Miles was safely stored in a box in my head. Tied up tightly with a large red bow. I'd worry about the credit cards another day.

With my brain back in order, it was great to see Ollie when I met him later at E&O. He was a bit late, but I didn't mind, I sat in the restaurant's bar—a home from home for us—showing off my genius new Marni coat and chatting to various people I knew in there.

One I was not so pleased to see was Alice's assistant from the magazine, Natalie, who immediately started probing me for all the details of Nelly's affair with Iggy and info about Nelly herself.

I didn't trust Natalie any more than I did Alice, in fact I thought she was a right little conniver, so I was circumspect in my replies.

Once I shrugged her off I was buttonholed by Nivek Thims— the photographer who had been sitting with Iggy in the Four Seasons the night of the Ferrucci party. Like everyone else in the bar, it seemed, he was raving about Iggy's show, but he was also finding ways of implying—due to how closely they had worked together discussing the possible ad campaign—that he, Nivek, had quietly played a large part in Iggy's success.

"That's the great thing about Iggy," Nivek was saying. "He likes to work closely with a small creative elite of brilliant people that he naturally gathers around him—like Nelly. How is darling Nelly? Have you seen her since the show?"

I knew for a fact that Nelly had never met Nivek until the night of the Ferrucci party, so I was a little surprised when he went on to suggest that we send her a text—on his phone—"just for fun," because it was such a coincidence that we had bumped into each other. That was when it hit me just how major Nelly's new role in life was. Overnight she had become someone that anyone who wanted to get ahead in fashion really needed to know. Nivek just wanted to text her—on his phone—so he could get her mobile number. I pretended I'd forgotten it.

Under this pressure, I was relieved when Ollie walked in, looking pink and flushed and handsome, that lock of dark hair falling over his eyes, his suit, shirt and tie combo as immaculate as ever. Unfortunately Nivek was delighted to see Ollie too—he would have liked a Slap advertising campaign almost as much as he wanted the Rucca one.

After giving me a big hug and kiss, Ollie greeted Nivek warmly, pumping his hand and slapping his shoulder in the public school way he had never quite lost. For a moment I watched him with a strange sense of remove. He and Nivek circled round each other like two wolves not sure which of them was more senior in the pack. Both were friendly, showing lots of gum and presenting their metaphorical butts for sniffing, as they tried to compute which of them had more to get from associating with the other.

So far, it was a tie—Nivek had serious groove credentials for the work he had done with various new independent style magazines with names like *Thrust* and *Wonderdog,* while Ollie had the rare appeal of controlling a cool brand and the big budget to promote it. Nivek had close ties with the agents of super-hot young models and Ollie had access to the world's most cutting-edge make-up artists. And now they both had connections to the new fashion supernova that was Iggy.

In the end, by employing a brilliantly slipped-in mention of "our" *very* close friendship with Nelly, accompanied by a dazzling "fuck-you sucker" smile, Ollie triumphed. It was he who ended the conversation, catching the maître d's eye over Nivek's shoulder, like the old smoothie he was, and steering me off my bar stool and into the restaurant.

When we were seated he took both my hands over the table and smiled at me.

"Hello, beautiful," he said. "How the hell are you? You look wonderful, as always. Is that a Marni coat you're wearing?"

"Bingo," I said. "I had to wear it straight away—it's new. And you don't look so shabby yourself. Have you been working out? Or drinking?"

Ollie laughed heartily as the waiter brought over fresh sea breezes, still our favourite cocktail.

"I have been doing a few of those Astanga yoga moves you showed me," he said. "Opening up my chakras. It's good stuff, gets the brain working. So what else did you buy in Milan?"

I gave him the edited highlights. Ollie was one of those rare men who actually loved shopping and really enjoyed seeing what his wife had bought, but generous though he was—he paid off one of my cards for me each month—I never told him the full story. Indulgent though he was, I knew that even he might think I'd gone a bit far with the four pairs of boots. When I eventually got out the two pairs I'd stashed away, I'd tell him I'd picked them up in the Selfridge's sale. Easy.

After that, our conversation fell into its usual pattern: Ollie telling me about his latest triumphs at work and his plans for even greater market domination and coolness for his beloved "brand"; me telling him all the gossip from the fashion scene. Of course, the thing he wanted to know about most was Nelly and Iggy—their new association had even made it into the British papers that morning.

"So how did it come about?" he asked. "How did Nelly crack on to this Iggy bloke?" He snorted contemptuously. "She's no prize, let's face it, so how on earth did she swing it? And is he really as great as everyone's saying?"

Ignoring his unkind remarks about my dear friend, I felt a momentary hot flush of panic engulf me as a sudden total flashback of the night Nelly "cracked on" to Iggy swept over me.

I didn't think my face had betrayed me, as I had got it under control immediately with one of those split-second crisis responses the human brain is capable of. In that instant I knew for certain that I was going to be able to separate what Nelly had done that night with Iggy from what I had done with Miles. I was actually quite impressed with myself and wondered if this was how international espionage agents had to think. It was like having a split computer screen in your head.

"Well," I said. "Everyone was at the Ferrucci party that night. Iggy was there with a load of people, we were all there too and the two of them just got together, the way people do." A vision of Miles's face came fastbowling into my forebrain from nowhere and I knocked it out again, for six.

Ollie was frowning slightly, as he flicked his signature forelock out of his eyes. He had his mouth open and was investigating his back teeth with his tongue. He looked momentarily rather less than attractive.

"But what could he possibly see in *her*?" he said. "It said in the paper that he's got one hand missing, he's got a hook. Sounds grotesque. Is he fat and ugly too?"

"Ollie!" I said, pissed off. "Don't be so horrible. Nelly may not be your cup of tequila, but a lot of men find her really attractive, you know. Not all men like skinny girls. She's what they call a 'real woman' and I've seen men follow her down the street."

"Maybe she'd dropped something," he said. He wasn't smiling.

"Look, Ollie," I said, leaning in to the table and spitting the words at him. "I know you don't like Nelly—in fact, she doesn't like you either, so you've got that in common. But I really like both of you and let me tell you something. Igor Veselinovic is about to become one of the hottest names in world fashion. He'll be up there with Alexander McQueen and John Galliano very shortly and you and I are both really lucky to have a close connection to him right from the start."

That shut him up. I leaned back in my seat and continued.

"So, you have a choice—you can carry on with this stupid snobbery about Nelly, just because her parents have a chip shop, or you can cash in on her new status. And I don't know about you, but I really enjoyed sitting front row at the Rucca show and I love Nelly dearly and I'm going to make the most of it. So there."

Ollie was now carefully picking spinach out of his teeth with his little fingernail.

"And will you stop that goddam picking!" I said.

It was a habit of his that drove me nuts. Even though I knew it was inspired by his fear of contaminating his dazzling porcelain-veneered smile with green foliage, which was a valid concern, I found the public picking completely repulsive. He was still at it.

"If you want to pick your teeth," I continued, slightly surprised by how cross I felt, "go to the bloody *toilet* and do it, and keep your gob shut till you get there."

I said "toilet" deliberately, as it was one of Ollie's most hated "suburban" words. "Lounge" was another that was good for getting at him, and "settee." They made his skin crawl. He wasn't keen on glass clinking either, or a myriad other little signals that someone was not quite his tribe. He stopped mid-pick and looked at me in amazement—then, to my great relief, he threw back his head and roared with laughter.

"I'm sorry, Em," he said, taking my hand again. "It's my terrible prep-school table manners. We were like little savages at my school and I do sometimes forget myself."

He motioned at a hovering waiter to refill my glass.

"Oh, you do make me laugh sometimes," he said, wiping tears from his bright blue eyes. "OK, you're quite right, I must put my silly dislike of Nelly behind me. It's just that I didn't think she was a suitable friend for you and I didn't want you to be tainted by association. And *toilet* to you too," he added, raising his glass and not clinking it.

"Well, look how wrong you were there, Mr. Snob Guts," I said. I paused and looked at him sitting there with all the gloss and confidence his expensive education had endowed him with.

"You know," I continued, not particularly liking him in that moment. "It's not necessary to have gone to a major public school to get ahead in the fashion business, Ollie. I think you need to let go of that idea. It's not like merchant banking."

I could see he wasn't listening, though. He had a look in his eye that I associated with serious brand strategy.

"I could do with a trip to Milan," he said eventually. "Bit of a cool hunt through the city, see how the brand sits there. It's hard to find the right retail outlets in Italy, because apart from a few unexciting department stores the cosmetics marketplace there is limited to independent perfumeries, so it's very hard to control your brand's environments. I think it might be time to move into stand-alone Slap boutiques there. So shall we go for a long weekend soon? Catch up with our dear friend Nelly and her new beau Iggy? You can take me to all those marvellous restaurants you're always telling me about. On expenses, of course."

I shook my head at him, but I couldn't help smiling.

"You are such an operator, Ollie Fairbrother," I said. "Teeth picking, or no teeth picking. I'd love to go to Milan with you—once Paris is over, of course—and only if we can stay at the Four Seasons."

"Deal," said Ollie.

"But hang on a minute," I said. "I thought we were going cool hunting in New York, so you can try and pressure Paul into signing his life away to Slap?"

"We'll do both," he said, raising his glass again.

"Cheers," I said, raising mine and clinking it loudly with his. "Toilet."

Although I only had three more days at home before going to Paris early on Tuesday morning, Ollie insisted on going ahead with our

Sunday salon as normal. I was quite disappointed, as I thought we could have spent the day together, maybe checking out the new exhibition at the Whitechapel and exploring Brick Lane and Hoxton and having lunch at one of the new restaurants there, so he could show me what he was so excited about.

I did go to that part of town quite a lot to various photographic studios in old warehouses and to see young designers, most of whom seemed to be based in E1 these days, but if Ollie was seriously considering uprooting us from our W11 haven I wanted to have a closer look. It was going to have to be pretty special to get me out of Ledbury Road.

But he seemed strangely unenthusiastic when I suggested it, saying he'd gone off the idea of moving—the property market was still too uncertain, it could go up or down, or so he'd read. So instead we spent Saturday shopping for food and flowers and cooking for the next day's lunch. I was always glad to get back into my kitchen, as I found cooking truly relaxing. I could get completely absorbed in chopping and stirring, with my brain in a pleasant state of neutral. I was really glad that Ollie had no aspirations to be a Jamie Oliver himself, as it was my thing and I liked to shine in it.

For that Sunday, I'd pulled a recipe for a Tunisian chicken dish out of an old copy of French *ELLE* and, with the help of a French/English dictionary, I'd worked out what was involved. We went up to the Moroccan spice shop on Golborne Road to buy the more obscure north African ingredients, which was just the sort of expedition Ollie adored, and as well as the spices we had actually gone for, we came out laden with gold and white filigree tea glasses, a brass teapot with an outrageous spout and two couscous steamers. He was such a consumer, my husband. Suited me.

In between the shopping, and stopping to chat to people we bumped into, Ollie worked his mobile, drumming up suitable types to come to our salon. He had a few people in place already, he said, but he liked the serendipitous effect of leaving it to the last minute, surrendering the final guest list to fate. This calculated risk mostly paid off, and we'd end up with a mix of people you never would have put together on purpose, yet who would strangely seem to click; the whole being greater than the sum of the human parts and all that. Only once had it led to a very intimate meal for six people—two of whom were rival model agents who loathed each other. That had been rather too interesting.

For this one, Ollie said he had already "locked down" five guests, but he wanted about four more for "the mix." I had to find two and he had to find two—but he wouldn't tell me who he had already. Ollie loved to turn everything into a game—a competitive game. I sometimes wondered if he had actually left school, but it was harmless and made him happy, so I went along with him.

Although I knew creating an unpredictable mix was all part of the game for Ollie, I was still quite surprised to hear him call Nivek Thims—a name I couldn't miss—who seemed to accept delightedly, judging by the high-pitched squeaks coming out of Ollie's mobile.

"What on earth did you invite him for?" I asked, as we headed into Tom's Deli for a coffee fuel-up, our shopping complete. "He's such a shameless user."

"Partly because I want to torture him with how close you are to Nelly," said Ollie, grinning, "But mainly because I have a gut feeling about him. I've heard his work is really good and I think he will become a big-name photographer, so we might as well get him on side."

For my two guests, my first choice was Paul, who was spending a couple of days in London before heading over to Paris, but after dialling his mobile and getting his voicemail message, I decided against pursuing it. I knew I would have enjoyed the event a lot more with Paul there, but I had my reasons not to ask him this time. For one, I didn't want to jeopardize my trip to New York by giving Ollie a chance to talk to him about signing up with Slap. Secondly, he'd been there the night I'd met Miles and just for the time being it all felt a little too close.

Instead, I invited an up-and-coming fashion PR I rather liked, who was getting a reputation for representing interesting young London designers and who went by the single name of Isolde. Then, after about three knock-backs and five message banks—one of Ollie's rules was that we weren't allowed to leave messages, we had to get a live acceptance—I got quite desperate and roped in Peter Potter, the poison-penned fashion editor for *The Daily Reporter,* a mid-market tabloid.

A little too far to the bitchy side of bitchy queen for my taste, Peter would never have been a first choice, but he always had brilliant goss, which would delight the other guests, whether it had any foundation in truth or not. Plus he was quite well known through his TV appearances, just the sort of media fame which Ollie found so impressive.

It wasn't until I put the phone down on that call—he was clearly delighted to be asked and already knew all about our last-minute guest lists—that I remembered he'd been at the Ferrucci party that night with us all too. I went cold all over and desperately hoped I wasn't part of his current Milan "hot scoop" repertoire.

As a result of Ollie's unconventional way of assembling the guest list, part of the fun of the Sunday salons for the two of us was seeing who turned up.

First to arrive on this occasion was Felicity Aldous, the editor-in-chief of *Chic Interiors,* the sister magazine of *Chic.* I was quite amazed to see her walk in—a full ten minutes before the invited time—because I really couldn't stand her and Ollie knew it.

It was typical of her to arrive early like that. God, that annoyed me. Why couldn't she just have walked around the block a few times like any normal person? You had to arrive at least five minutes after the appointed hour, preferably fifteen, everyone knew that. I wasn't even properly dressed when she marched in, I was still hopping around on one shoe, and it just added to my already less than warm feelings towards her.

Whenever I saw Felicity I was overwhelmed simultaneously by her pretension and her flying saliva. The spit spray you could dodge, but the carrying on about bollocks could kill you, to quote Frannie. A couple of times a year at work we would have what Felicity called "essential cross-cultural briefings"—and Bee called after-work piss-ups—when the staff of the two magazines got together with a few bottles of wine and some chips 'n' dips, so we could tell them what was going on in fashion and they could fill us in on the latest developments in scatter cushions.

I just couldn't take it that seriously. Don't get me wrong, I love

homewares as much as the next compulsive shopper and no one as
over-concerned with their wardrobe as me could help but be equally
obsessed with poncing up their living space, but those *Chic Interiors*
girls went way overboard. I mean, I can be really silly about a handbag, but I do have a sense of humour about it at heart. You have to,
or fashion will eat you alive.

But not Felicity. She really believed it all. She could come over all
spitty and excited about a washing-up-liquid bottle, reducing me
and Frannie to hopeless church giggles at those briefings, until we
succumbed to lobotomized boredom.

She was quite a snappy dresser, though. I was prepared to give
Felicity that—if you like those over-intellectual kind of designers—
and she was really thin, so she wore her clothes well, which was a
good thing, seeing how plain her face was. With her big eyes,
prominent teeth and bony features, Frannie had once said she
looked like a constipated chihuahua in novelty specs. They really
were the most stupid glasses—I think she wore them to put architects at ease—and combined with that ultra-severe Joan of Arc
hairdo, it was quite a striking look. She clearly styled herself a *jolie
laide*. Jolly well never gets laid, Paul had said when he'd met her,
but he was wrong about that.

The amazing thing was, Felicity never seemed to be without a
boyfriend. Good-looking ones too, with jobs and everything.
Mainly architects, it has to be said, but in London's desperate dating
meat market, they were prime cuts, no doubt about it. She had the
kind of look I totally didn't get—I could never understand girls
who didn't simply want to look as glamorous as possible—but
there seemed to be a lot of men who liked women who looked
about as warm and feminine as a John Pawson kitchen.

But Ollie seemed pleased to see her and I was even more pleased
to notice on the *placement*—he always did one on the sly, filling in
the guests as they arrived—that he had cleverly put her next to him,
with me at the other end of the table. Well out of range of the oral
fountain. Hurrah.

Isolde arrived next and she and Felicity seemed happy to have
the chance to get to know each other. Mind you, it would be a rare
PR who didn't seize the chance to cosy up to a magazine editor,

although I did notice Isolde take a few steps back as Felicity talked at her in increasingly excited tones about a new tap designer she had discovered.

While they were happily schmoozing each other, I cornered Ollie in the bathroom, where he was giving his perfect hair just one more little touch up. He was quite vain about his hair, was Ollie.

"What the hell did you invite the human lawn-sprinkler for?" I whispered at him.

"What are you talking about?" he said.

"Spitty Felicity—why did you ask her? You know I can't stand her."

"Felicity?" said Ollie, frowning. "I think she's really interesting—and we've decided to advertise in her mag. I think homewares is a very important growth area and those magazines are about to become as crucial for niche cosmetics marketing as fashion mags, if not more so. It's the ideal way to reach the more sophisticated end of the lifestyle consumer, so I wanted to cement our relationship with her, OK?"

"Whatever," I said, sighing. I should have known there was an angle on it. "But you may want to wear breathing apparatus while you do the cementing."

"What are you talking about?"

"The spitting, Ollie. It could drown you."

He just looked at me blankly.

"I honestly don't know what you are going on about," he said shrugging, and turned back to admiring himself in the mirror, from several angles. "And please be nice to her, Em. I want her to put this place in the magazine."

He chucked me on the cheek and left the bathroom, grinning to himself.

The next bunch of people arrived in a clump, starting with Ollie's old school friend, Jeremy Trouton and his wife, Sarah.

Jeremy was your classic public-school banker wanker, and I actually rather adored him. He was so straightforwardly straight he was almost eccentric and after the twisted creative weirdos we hung out with most of the time, he was a relief. He was funny too, in a totally unreconstructed sexist, classist, Tory-voter, *Spectator*-reader way. He reminded me of my uncle, but with a sense of humour.

Sarah I found slightly harder work, sweet though she was, as it was hard to get her to talk about anything apart from "our two boys." In all fairness, they were really nice kids and in school hols, if they weren't all "in the country," they came along to our Sunday salons too.

Aged eight and ten, I always had a lot of fun with them, so that was a good basis for Sarah and I to get on, even though her house was decorated entirely from the OKA catalogue and she dressed in head-to-toe Boden. She was always telling me how "clever" I was with clothes before telling me how very little she had paid for what she was wearing.

"It's marvellous, you know, Emily," she was saying to me on this occasion, after I had duly admired her purple needlecord skirt. "If you order within two weeks of receiving your catalogue you get a further ten per cent off. I buy all the boys' weekend clothes from them. Amazing value."

Arriving at the same time was another couple, rather different in their interests. Polly and Ossian were "artists," classic Notting Hill trustafarians, complete with whiteman dreadlocks and quite the filthiest house I had ever been in, although full of the most gorgeous bits of ethnic tat and beaten-up pieces of priceless furniture from their various family piles. They never seemed to do much "arting," did Poll and Oss, in fact their artistic lives consisted mainly of going to the openings of their myriad artist friends' exhibitions. But they had an insatiable appetite for social events, were good fun and I was always pleased to see them.

I loved their upbeat manner—everything was "amazing" or "marvellous"—and I always particularly enjoyed watching them interact with Sarah and Jeremy, because they were really just different sides of the same Sloaney coin. In fact, the four of them knew loads of people in common and got on really well. I used to have this fantasy about dressing them in each other's clothes and seeing if I could tell the difference.

Arriving just after them came Ollie's bore of the week. He always had to have one—someone who was directly useful for his work and who also made the whole event fully claimable on expenses. They were a varied bunch. It might be a rally-driving enthusiast from the media-buying agency he used, whom he was grooming to screw even lower advertising page rates out of magazine advertising sales people—Ollie could never have done something so uncouth himself, as it might have damaged his precious relationship with "editorial."

Or, even more eye-crossingly dull, would be someone involved with "distribution" and his hideous wife, although generally they were more likely to be invited to some kind of frou-frou corporate tent at Henley, or a Genesis concert. I always had to go along and do my corporate wife bit at those events, but I didn't mind because I generally got a new outfit and a John Frieda blow-dry out of it. Fine by me.

Other crucial contacts in Ollie's business world included his retail clients, and this week we were welcoming a high-level executive from a chain of provincial department stores which desperately wanted to stock Slap. Her name was Carol. Although he hadn't told her yet, I knew Ollie had already decided to go with them, but by dazzling her with his glamorous friends and lifestyle, he was clearly intending to impress her into giving him a ridiculously large acreage of floorspace at lower rent than any of his competitors, in the prime position opposite the main door, with free advertising space in the store's cardholder magazine thrown in.

There were a lot of plates to spin in Ollie's job—far more than most people realized—and he never dropped one of them. I really was proud of him.

Carol arrived at the same time as Peter Potter, which already had her seriously impressed, as he was a big name in Middle England. Not only did he have his byline picture smiling out of his page in *The Daily Reporter* every week, he was actually better known for his regular appearances on *Wakey Wakey*, a hugely popular sofa-based women's morning "magazine" show. It was seriously mainstream stuff, but—much as it killed us magazine chicks to admit it—it was probably the single most influential platform for flogging fashion and beauty products in the entire country.

From the moment he arrived that day Peter was even more

brightly "on" than usual, with his excitement at having been "ring-side" when Nelly and Iggy had got together, as he put it. And if he had noticed what I had been up to the same night, it clearly paled next to the big story. Everyone at that table knew all about Iggy and Nelly—apart from Jeremy, of course, who thought all fashion de-signers, except possibly Johnnie Boden, were ghastly poofs. Even Sarah had read about it in the *Daily Mail,* an innocent reference that caused a momentary scowl to cross Peter's face.

"Yes," he'd snapped at her. "They picked up the story from my page and just managed to squeeze it into their last edition, with all the other boring shit their boring readers enjoy."

But apart from that momentary irritation he was positively preg-nant with the scoop of it all and clearly longing to regale the com-pany with the details.

Peter Potter was a small man—in every regard, according to Paul, who'd been there once, as he had to so many other places he later regretted—and he was puffed up with glory at having first-hand in-telligence about such a big story. He was generally quite happy to run with sixth-, seventh-, or even no-hand information in his fash-ion gossip column, so this was a big thing for him.

And it was great for me too, as I could sit back, happily out of the spotlight, as he regaled the table with his memories of the night that Iggy and Nelly got it on.

"Well," he was saying, as we sat down to eat—he had the natural sense of timing to keep his big story until he had everyone's atten-tion. "I had always assumed Iggy was a big woofter, like every other fashion designer in the world."

Jeremy nodded in sage agreement.

"And, of course, there are all those *well-known people* who went to Saint Martins with him . . ."

Peter lowered his voice to a more conspiratorial level. The entire table leant in to hear him. Gotcha! he would have been thinking.

"There are several people—*household names*—who claim to have had more intimate contact with Mr. Veselinovic than those three Serbian kisses, which are becoming *such* a signature of his. Nevertheless, it was quite obvious to me from the start that he was seriously turned on by my Miss Nelly . . ."

"Oh, I never thought Ig was gay," Nivek interrupted, with the self-importance of someone who was very close to the person being discussed. "I was at the Four Seasons with him that night it all happened—before any of *you* came in."

Pause for sickly smile at Peter. Registered. Continue.

"You can see by the way he reacts to models," continued Nivek. "At castings for major international ad campaigns..."—pause for effect—"... his interest is definitely more than just academic. His reactions are more, well, *genital* than cerebral."

Nice work, Nivek, I thought. Good interrupting and I liked the use of "campaigns" in the plural. "Major" and "international" were nice touches too. Especially for someone who hadn't actually been booked for the job yet. It quite cancelled out Peter's use of "*my* Miss Nelly.*"

I glanced over at Ollie, who was watching the exchange with the concentration of a spectator at Wimbledon Centre Court. Nivek was in the Tim Henman role. He might win, but he probably wouldn't.

"Anyway," said Peter, brushing invisible crumbs off the table in a gesture that suggested that it was what he would like to have done with Nivek's contribution. If not his actual head. "As I was saying, despite all the *well-founded*..."—killer look at Nivek—"...rumours, it was obvious to me that Iggy fancied the pants off my little Nelly from the moment I saw them together."

"It's funny," he continued, looking smugger with every word. "Because I know they had met before—Nelly had told me all about discovering this incredibly talented young Serbian designer months ago—but it just hadn't clicked between them until that night. I think it must have been meeting away from a work context for the first time that made the difference. And, of course, having been *so* close to Nell, for so *very* long, I could tell immediately she had the hots for him too. And when my Nelly wants a man, Nelly gets him."

"Nelly's gonads never wrong," I heard myself saying. It was quite unconscious. The words just popped out. Every head at the table swivelled round to me, gripped. "Gonads" had even attracted Jeremy's interest. Carol's mouth was hanging open.

"What?" said Peter, Nivek and Ollie in unison.

"Er, nothing," I said, thinking fuck, fuck, fuck. "I was just mumbling."

"Nelly's gonads never wrong?" said Peter, who was highly skilled at hearing and remembering things people didn't want him to hear or remember. "Is that what she said to you?"

I just laughed. "Oh no, I'm just being silly, just a joke. Silly girl stuff, take no notice. Now, who would like some more couscous?"

I got up quickly and went over to the kitchen area. Peter Potter was next to me in a moment.

"Is that what Nelly said to you?" he said, his hand on my arm, quite tightly. "Nelly's gonads never wrong?"

"What?" I said, trying to play the dumb blonde. "Do you want some couscous, Peter?"

I smiled brightly at him, trying to channel Margot from *The Good Life*, who I always found such a comfort in tricky social situations, but he just narrowed his eyes back at me.

"OK, princess," he said, nodding his small shaved head. "I hear you. And I also hear that your gonads were working hard that night too. It was quite hot and heavy on that dance floor, wasn't it, Emily? Nearly as hot as the *photographers' pit*."

He spat the words out. I could feel the blood draining from my intestines, when he spoke again.

"Very charming, that Seamus. Irish eyes and all that . . ."

He looked so pleased with himself and I just felt like shouting with laughter. He'd seen me dancing with Seamus. I did dance with Seamus that night. Closely. Provocatively. It meant nothing.

"Oh yes," I said enthusiastically. "That Seamus is such a sexy little guy. I love those Irish boys. I'm always teasing Ollie about it. Aren't I, darling?" I said, walking back to the table, leaning round my husband and kissing his cheek, as I put the couscous steamer down on the table.

"I was just telling Peter, how sexy I find Irishmen. You know all about my secret love for Terry Wogan, don't you, Ollie?"

I flashed Peter my brightest Margot smile and he looked furious as Ollie laughed along.

"Yeah," he said, patting my bottom. "Can you believe it? Emily is addicted to Radio 2. She listens to Wogan every morning. She loves the old fart."

"Wogan," said Jeremy with great enthusiasm. "Top man, Wogan. Bloody funny. Eurovision. Hilarious. Very dry, old Wogan. Good man."

Up you, Peter Rotter, I thought, you smarmy little creep.

After that I was relieved to find that the conversation had moved on quite naturally from Nelly and Iggy, as the rest of the table didn't have quite the insatiable appetite for the fashion gossip that was Peter's lifeblood. He wasn't too upset, though, because he managed to regain the spotlight fairly quickly with supposedly "gospel" bits of filthy information about Hollywood stars and their alleged sexual perversions.

I found all that stuff about as interesting as rally-driving stories, it was so clearly rubbish, but if it kept Rotter—as I had now decided to call him—off my back, I was happy to look fascinated and tell him how amazingly clever and in the loop he was.

If the mixture of people was right, sometimes those Sunday lunches took off in a way that was quite magical, with really dazzlingly witty exchanges and stimulating arguments, sometimes turning into a full-on party. This was not one of those weeks.

I was sitting next to Sarah, which rather limited my conversational prospects and it didn't take her long to get round to her favourite topic—after her own children—which was asking when Ollie and I were going to "start a family."

"Are you *trying* yet, Emily?" she always asked me with great delicacy, which made me want to bark with laughter.

It didn't matter how many times I had explained to her that we had made a completely conscious decision not to have children, as neither of us wanted them, she was still convinced we were just putting it off.

"There really isn't a 'right' time, you know, Emily," she was saying, with her customary originality. "But then that means there isn't a 'wrong' time either. Really, they will change your life so much, you will just wonder why you ever waited. And, you do know that it gets much harder to conceive after thirty, don't you? I really can't remember life before we had the boys now . . ." she continued and then she was off, droning on about schools and common entrance and all the other subjects that helped to convince me that I really didn't ever want to be a parent.

I tried to divert her by coaxing Polly and Ossie into the conversation, but they were uncharacteristically subdued, after what they admitted had been a big weekend, even by their standards. So I wasn't particularly surprised when the conversation turned to that most excruciating of all subjects—property prices. Needless to say it was one of Felicity's areas of special interest and I nearly lost it when she came out with her first gambit.

"Of course I've been in the Spitalfields market since the early Eighties," she sang out, spraying all around her.

Oh, how I longed for Frannie to share the joke with. Where else would Spitty Felicity live but Spitalfields?

"Of course, from my *vast* Huguenot house on Fournier Street, I have watched the gentrification of Clerkenwell with horror, Hoxton with amusement and Brick Lane with a certain trepidation," continued Spitty, smiling at us smugly over her novelty specs, which looked like missing parts from a passing Sputnik.

"But my house—for which I paid a little over sixty thousand in eighty-four, is now worth well over a million—and I have used the equity to buy several other properties in the *quartier*. It's such a fascinating part of town and the young creatives who are now moving in are nothing more than the latest wave of refugees to populate it. I see myself as their patron."

And that was it, they were all off with their property stories. It was as bad as drug stories, or drinking stories, or even hearing about someone else's trip to the dentist, because no one was really listening to anyone else, they just wanted to broadcast their own smug good fortune. I could have machine gunned them all to death.

I'd heard Sarah on the subject of the Fulham property boom about a million times before—"I knew when Blooming Marvellous opened up we'd made it as a neighbourhood . . ."—so I knew I'd have to sit through a percentage-on-percentage analysis of that, but

I was surprised when Jeremy chipped in. I'd thought he was too much of a gentleman to talk about money.

Even dreamy Polly and Ossie got in on it. It was like a brain-wasting disease that had infected the entire British middle class. A form of BSE caught from drooling over estate agents' windows and the property sections of local papers. The only ones who didn't join in were me and Ollie. He might have been a hard-nosed business man at work and a bit of a poseur in every other respect, but he thought it was the absolute end to talk about money in a social context. And at that moment, I really loved my husband.

8

ON the train to Paris on the Tuesday morning Frannie and I were nearly senseless with laughter. Peter Potter had pissed me off royally at the Sunday salon, but boy had he got his own back at Nivek Thims for stealing his thunder with the Nelly story. Frannie had bought *The Daily Reporter* that morning along with all her other beloved tabloids—the papers of the people, she called them—and we were in stitches over what the Rotter had written.

> *It's quite amazing, the lengths to which some people in this business are prepared to go, to make themselves seem more interesting than they really are. Turns out "rising" not-so-young photographer Nivek Thims was actually born with a slightly less fascinating name. How does Kevin Smith look on your passport, Nivek? Or perhaps you need a mirror to read it?*

"Kevin—Nivek . . ." I had tea coming down my nose, I was laughing so hard. "But, hang on a minute," I said, scribbling the letters on the edge of Frannie's paper. "Look—Thims isn't even Smith backwards. It should be Htims; he's fiddled with it to make it work. God, what a self-conscious wanker."

"Who cares," said Frannie, handing me a piece of paper. "Check this out."

She'd drawn mock-ups of our *Chic* business cards with the following names on them: Senior Fashion Editor—Ylime Retniop. Beauty Director and Fashion News Editor—Einnarf Retsillacm.

It just set us off some more.

"I don't think Retsillacm really works," said Frannie. "But I'm quite taken with Einnarf. Sounds more Celtic than Frannie, almost Tolkien-esque. I could be a minor elfin queen, Cate Blanchett's little sister, but Ylime Retniop, now that's a winner. It's brilliant. You sound like a Tibetan lama, but sexy. I'm going to call you Y-lime from now on.

"Hey, Alee-chay," she called over to Alice, who was sitting opposite, with her eyes closed. "Have you met Y-lime?"

Alice, as usual, was oblivious to the joke. She really couldn't see anything wrong with Kevin calling himself Nivek—"I think it's quite creative," she had said in all seriousness, when we'd shown it to her, in the deep, whispery monotone voice she thought sounded intelligent. Once she'd closed her eyes again, Frannie had sketched out Alice's new business card and Ecila Wergittep set us off all over again.

"Cilla!" said Frannie, wheezing with laughter. "We can call her Cilla."

Bee was tapping away at her laptop across the aisle, frowning hard, so we couldn't share the joy of Eeb Ssetrof-Htims with her—or Thims, as we made it, in Nivek's style—but it kept me and Frannie amused all the way to Gare du Nord. We really were fantastically immature at times.

A driver was there to pick us up, waiting right on the platform, as per orders, but it wasn't our usual Paris chap. Bee—or Eeb as we were now calling her—looked at him with great suspicion which was very soon borne out. He couldn't even find his way to the car park where he'd put the limo. And he couldn't speak English. The poor man had unwittingly tapped right into one of Bee's tenderest Achilles heels—because our brilliant, sophisticated editor-in-chief couldn't speak a word of French.

"Oh, for GOD's sake," she was practically shouting, the third time he had us patrolling back along the station concourse with all our luggage. "What use is this idiot going to be? Frannie, you speak Frog, tell him I am going to stand outside this station—smoking—until he comes to pick me up."

Frannie duly told him and in the end we all went and stood there waiting until he eventually emerged in the car. It got worse. Getting from Gare du Nord to the Hôtel Meurice, on Rue de Rivoli—one of the city's more well-known thoroughfares—he got hopelessly lost. He didn't even know it was one way and tried to turn left into it from Rue de Castiglione.

Bee was going into orbit.

"What use is he going to be to us? How is he going to find his way to an abandoned bloody asbestos works on the Périphérique if he can't even find the Tuileries gardens? We might as well have Luigi here. At least he speaks bloody English."

"But Luigi's not from Paris," said Frannie, going into top-of-the-class mode, a condition often brought on by exercising her text-book perfect, but hopelessly un-idiomatic command of French.

"No, he's not," said Bee. "But I'll bet you dinner at Caviar Kaspia that this fuckwit isn't either. Go on—ask him, Miss Bilingual Dundee Nineteen Ninety-six."

"*Excusez-moi, Monsieur,*" said Frannie in a perfect Dundee accent. "*A quelle ville est-ce que vous habitez habituellement?*"

"Marseilles," came the smiling reply, causing Bee to smack the dashboard in triumph.

"That's it," she said. "I'm calling Luigi, I'm going to get him to come and drive us. At least if we get lost with him, he'll be charming about it and I can abuse him in a language he will understand."

It was shaping up to be an interesting Paris season.

It got a lot more interesting that very afternoon when I was waiting—sweating—inside the vast plastic tent in the Tuileries gardens that was the venue for the Dior show. I'd accidentally got there on time simply because our hotel was just across the road from the park, and I knew I was in for a very long wait. I'd milled around for a bit outside in the afternoon sun, watching everyone come in, which was always like another catwalk show in itself, until my shoes seriously started to remind me that they had four-inch heels attached to them.

Inside, it was the usual circus, but at least the lights were on, so I had something to look at. All the big players were there in their customary spots, doing their customary things and in this instance I had a particularly good view of the French *Vogue* crew, who I found seriously fascinating. The editor-in-chief, Carine Roitfeld was the ultimate cool skinny French brunette, with legs as fine as crochet hooks and straight dark hair that fell right over her face, which was accessorized with the most astonishing pair of black eyebrows. They looked like Fuzzy Felt. She had an almost simian look to her—but, boy, was this one stylish monkey.

On this occasion she was wearing a killer black suit with a fiercely waisted jacket and a tight pencil skirt, which fitted her tiny body like a glove. Her heels were so dizzyingly high, even I would have been nervous to step out in them and, believe me, I did heels. It was no surprise she was Tom Ford's muse.

The other amazing thing about the French *Vogue*-ies was that they all looked exactly the same. They were all super tall and skinny, with straight black layered rock 'n' roll hair, and they only ever wore combinations of black and navy. Even the one guy who was part of the pack had the look. It was hilarious.

Another face I loved watching was *Allure* editor-in-chief Linda Wells, who was as restrained and icy as a Hitchcock blonde. She even dressed the part in perfectly fitting coats and high-heeled pumps. And she never wore stockings, which was another thing I liked about her.

Then there was British *Vogue* editor Alexandra Shulman, who always looked refreshingly normal compared to her front-row companions, who were all so extreme in their style, they looked almost freakish. Ms. Shulman looked like someone you might actually be able to have a decent chat with, but she worked a killer heel with the best of them.

As well as all the famous magazine babes, there was another whole front-row A-list of buyers, who were usually seated on the opposite side of the catwalk to the media. They were like a separate fashion tribe, with quite a few corporate suit-y men and women, mixed in with the more famous characters.

Of these my favourite was Joan Burstein—or Mrs. B, as we all called her—from Browns in London. She was like the Duchess of Devonshire of fashion. Always immaculately elegant in tailored trousers, cashmere, pearls, kid gloves and a fur, a small crocodile bag in her hand—she had the manners to match her style too. If Mrs. B hated a show, you could never have known it from her face, which she always kept in a perfect, politely interested semi-smile—in fact she did a much better job of not looking bored at tedious events than Her Maj the Queen. She was true fashion royalty.

Among the other buyers I always noticed was the exquisite Hong Kong Empress Joyce Ma, who wore the most amazing jewellery—she had pearl earrings the size of quail eggs. Then there was Kal Ruttenstein, from Bloomingdale's, who suffered from very poor health, and had to be helped in and out of venues on his crutches, but always showed up just the same.

But the most intriguing was Lizard Man. No one seemed to know who he was—although I'd been told he had an upscale boutique in LA—but he must have been "someone" because he always got great seats. What made him stand out was his unique look: he always wore bleached-out jeans and reptile skin—a hat, a jacket and elaborate cowboy boots. Different every day. He had a face as craggy as a komodo dragon, and bleached-out Shredded Wheat hair too. I was mad about him.

After a while, though, waiting for Dior to start, even this stellar people-watching got boring and I seriously missed having Nelly to talk to. If she'd been there we would have been eating sweets—cadged off Frannie—and roaring with laughter by now. I would have loved to have told her about Nivek, Cilla and Eeb. She would totally have got it. I worked out her backwards name on the show running order: Yllen Soilets. Soilets was a classic, but it didn't seem so funny with no one to share it with.

The rest of my posse were all out of reach. Bee was front row, Alice just behind her—three rows in front of me, I always got crap seats in Paris—and Frannie was backstage doing a story on the make-up. I didn't know the women on either side of me and I couldn't be bothered to start a conversation with them. After a while I got so desperate I started playing noughts and crosses with myself. I had just won—and lost—for the third time, when my concentration was broken by a wave of laughter round the tent. I looked up to see Miles walking the length of the high catwalk with his metal camera case and tripod hoisted up on his shoulder.

As he approached the end of the runway all the photographers whistled and cheered and he struck a supermodel pose, one hip out, hand behind his head. Quite a few flashes went off and the audience clapped, before he jumped down and disappeared into the photographers' pit. It was very funny and very unusual, because like all the photographers he always got to the venues as early as possible to bag his position among the throng. So how come he was strolling in forty minutes after the invited time—just twenty minutes before the show would actually start?

They were a tight-knit pack of rogues, the shows photographers, and when they weren't having fist fights with *arrivistes* who were blocking their sight-lines, or who had taken their particular spot— the territory was all minutely marked out—there was a kind of thieves' honour between them. Even photographers who were fierce rivals would save positions for each other, if that was where they normally stood, but there was a limit to how long you could hold on to one square foot of standing space in conditions that would make laboratory rats freak out, even for your best mate.

But that wasn't all that was weird about Miles's runway strut. Apart from the spectacle of a grubby photographer acting up like Naomi Campbell, I was not prepared for the effect seeing him had on me. It was visceral.

He was wearing his same old jeans, his biker boots and his motocross jacket; he was unshaven, his thick hair was standing on end and he generally looked like he could do with a good wash. And I could have jumped up and shagged him right there on the Dior catwalk.

I really hadn't expected to feel that way. In the few short days I'd had at home after Milan I'd honestly convinced myself I had worked Miles out of my system, as some kind of momentary insanity. Apart from the teeth-picking episode, I'd slipped straight back into my cool and comfy life with Ollie and, apart from the odd teeth-picking irritation, was perfectly happy there. Or, I thought I was.

We'd made love that night when we got home from E&O and I'd hardly thought of Miles at all during it. Just as it had always been, sex with Ollie was cosy, comforting and satisfying, like watching *Casablanca* on TV at home on a rainy Sunday afternoon. Sex with Miles had been like flying to Mars. They were two completely different activities and amazing though it had been with Miles, I didn't think I really wanted to fly to another planet as a regular outing. It was too unsettling.

But watching him work that catwalk—just seeing his beautiful bum in those faded jeans and knowing the muscle that would have popped up on his right arm, when he put it behind his head like that—had me instantly convinced I wanted to take the next flight out, destination Outer Space. Not thinking with my conscious brain, but with something more primitive, probably located below the navel, I brought up his mobile number on my Palm Pilot wallet and sent him a text: "2nite?"

That was it. I had a reply very quickly: "hotel?"

I tapped back: "meurice"

And back came his reply. We had texts flying up and down that venue like invisible carrier pigeons.

"room?"

"319"

"time?"

"10"

"11?"

"ok"

"v v ok"

It was that easy.

After the show I strolled along the sandy paths through the gardens wondering what to do with myself. Frannie was still inside with the Dior show make-up artist Pat McGrath, who she was going to be following all week for a big beauty story, and Bee and Alice had raced off to do an appointment before the next show, which I didn't have an invitation for. Without Nelly to hang out with, I felt totally unanchored and, well, rather lonely. I thought about going to Angelina's for a hot chocolate, as Nelly and I would have done, but I just didn't feel like doing it on my own. I also felt extremely unsettled by what I had impetuously organized for my evening's entertainment. I felt like I was possessed by someone else. A total slut.

I sat down on a bench to delete Miles's texts from my phone and found I had another one—which suddenly made the night's arrangements seem even more confusing. It was from Nelly: "We r here. Dinna 2nite? Nelly xxx."

I really didn't know what to do. I had no plausible excuse for not seeing Nelly and Iggy. I couldn't palm her off with some tale about a PR dinner because she knew the score—they didn't really happen in the same way in Paris as they did in Milan; in fact we were usually left to our own devices there after the last show.

And apart from that, I desperately *wanted* to see Nelly. I wanted to hear all her news and I wanted to get to know Iggy better. Not just because he was the latest fashion superstar—although that was not without its appeal—but because he was my friend's new man. It was my duty to check him out.

So I wanted to have dinner with Nelly—but I also wanted to rip the clothes off Miles and the two events were just not compatible. Or were they? I got my Palm Pilot out again and called his number.

"G'day, Em," came a deep voice at the other end. It freaked me out. I had turned him into an abstract concept in my head and now it was all too real again.

"Hi," I squeaked.

"I'm looking forward to seeing you later," he said in that slow drawl.

"Well, that's why I'm calling . . ." I said. "I've got a bit of a problem with it."

"That's a bummer," said Miles. "But no worries, just let me know when you can do it. If you still want to."

"Well, what are you doing now?" I said, boldness returning.

He laughed.

"Funnily enough, I'm walking along the Rue de Rivoli in the direction of Angelina's—where I was planning to have a hot chocolate—and I see I'm right outside the Meurice hotel."

"Go in," I said, my heart starting to pound. "Wait in the lobby. I'll be there in a minute. Follow me up in the lift."

I left the gardens at a run, cursing with frustration when I just missed the lights to cross the busy traffic on Rue de Rivoli. It felt like an eternity until they changed again and I raced over.

I stopped for a moment to compose myself before I entered the hotel and then as I came through the door, I could see Miles, out of the corner of my eye, sprawled on one of the brocade-covered chairs. In that fleeting glance I was pleased to notice he wasn't encumbered by his photographic equipment. I went straight over to the reception desk to ask for a new key card because I'd accidentally left mine behind in my room and then headed for the lift.

I didn't look over my shoulder as I waited for it to arrive, but as I stepped inside I felt Miles's arms come round me from behind. I turned and lost myself in his kiss, with one eye open to hit "3" on the control panel. Then I closed it again and we didn't break off until the lift stopped. I led him down the corridor to my room and once we were inside we fell on each other, not even bothering to get fully undressed. I fear I made a lot of noise.

When we surfaced, I felt quite giddy. Miles sat up on the bed and shook his head.

"Geeze," he said. "I think I'm seeing stars. What's going on, Emily?"

I just shook my head.

"Well, welcome to Paris, anyway," he said, tipping an imaginary hat at me. "Nice room," he said, looking round it. "Can I hit your mini bar?"

I just nodded. I still wasn't capable of speech. Miles stood up and half hopped over to the cabinet, with his pants round his ankles.

"Bloody boots," he said, grinning. He opened the fridge door and whistled between his teeth. "You magazine girls don't exactly rough it, do you? Look at this, Veuve Clicquot. Tasty." He took out a bottle of Perrier. "Want anything?" he said, waving it at me.

"Is there any chocolate?" I asked.

"Good girl," he said. "You could do with a bit of fattening up."

He came back to me with a bar of Toblerone and two Perrier waters with old-fashioned bottle tops, which he flipped off with his bare hands. They were huge, his hands. Huge and brown, with beautifully shaped fingers. They looked like hands which could shoe a horse, or mend a Land Rover with a piece of string. Hands that could make a night shelter out of palm branches. Miles would be a good person to be lost in the desert with, I thought and I sighed suddenly, much louder than I realized I was going to.

"That was a big sigh," he said. "You OK?"

And it seems I wasn't, because the next thing I knew I was in floods of tears. I don't know where it came from, but I was howling.

"Hey, Em," said Miles and he put those strong arms around me, stroking me with those beautiful hands and kissing the top of my head. "It's all right, babe," he said. "You have a good cry. You must need it."

"I'm really sorry," I said eventually, my voice quivering between sobs. "I don't know what happened. I never cry. It just happened. God, how embarrassing."

"Now don't go all English on me, Emily," said Miles. "You obviously needed a cry, so let it out. It's not anything to do with me, is it?"

I shook my head.

"I don't know what it's to do with."

"Well," said Miles, handing me a large piece of chocolate. "Eat that. Give you strength."

We sat chewing for a moment and then he spoke again.

"You know, what happened between us back there, Emily. It's not an everyday event, you know. It's unsettling."

I looked up at him, blinking my eyes which were stinging a bit. He picked up his T-shirt and wiped my cheeks with it.

"You can blow your nose on it, if you like," he said, smiling his cheeky smile. "I often do."

I shook my head, but he had me smiling again.

"So it's not always like that for you?" I said quietly. Although I hadn't thought about it consciously, I think I had somehow assumed that Miles was such a great lover that all his sexual encounters went off the Richter scale.

He laughed heartily.

"Are you kidding?" he said. "It's a long time since Mount Vesuvius last erupted, you know. No, it is not always like that for me. In fact, it's never been like that for me. Here, have some more chocolate."

That gave me something to chew on.

After that we just lay there in each other's arms for a while. We didn't make love again. We didn't need to. I didn't know about him, but I didn't want to do anything else, except to lie there breathing next to him. I loved his male smell. It was all very well having a lungful of Acqua di Parma whenever I went near Ollie, but there was something deeply appealing about Miles's unadorned masculinity.

He was the first to speak.

"I hate to break this moment," he said, almost whispering. "But are you doing Comme?"

And suddenly we were both roaring with laughter. I laughed until my stomach muscles hurt. The very idea of a fashion show just seemed so hilariously ridiculous in that primal situation we were in—man, woman, bed—it was the funniest thing I had ever heard. Eventually I recovered enough to speak. Now he was using his T-shirt to wipe tears from his own eyes—tears of laughter.

"Well, actually, I'm not," I said. "They never give me an invitation. Not important enough. How about you? But it must be too late now anyway, you'd be even later for that than you were for Dior, I think, Mr. Supermodel."

He chuckled.

"Did you see me then?" he said, putting his arm behind his head and pouting, as he had on the catwalk. I'd been right, the muscle on his biceps did spring out. At that moment I could have taken a bite out of it.

"Of course I saw you," I said. "Two thousand people saw you."

"Good," he said, grinning again. "I wanted *you* to see me. That's why I did it."

"Are you serious?"

"Yeah," he said. "I mean, I was late anyway, I'd had a big argie bargie with my email and I was running really late. Seamus was saving my spot and I knew I was cutting it fine, but I didn't really need to walk along the runway, did I?"

"Well, that did cross my mind."

"So I did it for a laugh, to cheer the boys up and to remind you I was in town—and gorgeous. Guess it worked, eh?"

I just shook my head at him.

"You're shameless," I said.

"What's to be shamed about? I'm a lusty man, you're a beautiful woman. I'd be a sad arse if I didn't try."

There was a natural pause. I could tell we were both thinking the same thing.

"So how was it with your old man, when you got home?" he said, sounding a bit apprehensive. "Did you feel bad?"

"For a minute. Then I forgot about you," I said, poking him in the ribs.

"Fair enough," he said. "Good job I reminded you then. Anyway, like I said before Emily, there is no pressure from my end—as it were." He laughed. "But really, you know I'm here, you know I'm willing. It's up to you."

There was another pause and then he spoke again.

"Are you doing Costume National?"

We laughed again.

"Yes," I said. "And Rochas. Lucky that Costume National's just across the road from here. What time is it now? Just before six? Perfect. We'll make it with plenty of time."

"I'm not doing it," he said. "I've still got to sort out my stupid email and Seamus has taken all my equipment back to the hotel—I dumped it all on him when you rang . . ."

"You didn't tell him . . ." I asked, horrified.

"Don't worry. He thinks that call was a model I used to see. Her name is Emma, so I called you Em, rather handy that."

I felt an instant pang of jealousy. Maybe he was still seeing her. And other models, whatever he had said about them that time, being sexless objects. But I pushed the thought away. What right had I to be jealous of Miles?

"I'd better get going then," I said, starting to get up.

He grabbed my arm and pulled me back, kissing me deeply. Then he put his nose to my face and neck, sniffing all over my skin, like an animal.

"Just in case I never get to do it again," he said. "I want to remember your smell."

I just looked at him in amazement. He seemed to have such a direct connection between his feelings and his mouth, with no baggage in between to trip him up. He told you what he felt and that was it. I'd never met anyone like that before, except for possibly Nelly, and I wanted to make a gesture as sincere and uncomplicated as him.

"Here," I said and handed him the extra key card I'd got from the concierge. "Keep it."

He looked at me steadily, slightly raising one eyebrow.

"Just text me first," I said.

By the time we came out of the Rochas show at eight o'clock that night, Luigi was waiting for us. Frannie and I exchanged a look. Had Bee finally gone insane? We had a Milanese driver in Paris.

"Oh, you clever boy," said Bee, kissing him on both cheeks. "You got the first plane over, didn't you? Got the car from the agency? Wonderful. I love people who can be spontaneous. Now, I'll direct you back to the hotel and then we'll get the concierge there to give you the low-down on driving in Paris. You'll be fine."

We got in the car. It was nice to be with Luigi actually, a familiar back of head to look at, and we traversed the short distance back to the hotel without mishap apart from two extra circles of Place de la Concorde, just because he wanted to.

"Now girls," said Bee, as we pulled up. "I'm staying in tonight. Easing into it gently this week. I'm doing some appointments in the morning, but they're all with beauty advertisers, so you don't need to bother yourselves. Have a nice easy one and I'll meet you all here at two o'clock to go to Helmut Lang. That'll be a challenge for Luigi. It's on the far edge of the Sixteenth—practically Belgium."

She chuckled happily to herself and disappeared inside with Luigi.

"Well," said Frannie, waiting until Alice was also out of earshot. "She's looking happier. So where did you say we were having dinner?"

"Hôtel Costes—that's where Nells and Iggy are staying."

"Oooh, very posh, I'd better go and change myself. I feel like an old fish-supper wrapper; greasy, smelly and unwanted."

Dinner was hilarious and my pleasure at seeing Nelly was tripled when Paul joined us as well. Everyone was on sparkling form and while it was not the intimate get-to-know-Iggy dinner I had been looking forward to, it more than made up for it in laughs, turning into one of those big nights you can never plan—they just happen.

Iggy was a great host, generously ordering bottle after bottle of champagne and as he passed me a glass I noticed he wasn't wearing the spooky hook. He had a prosthetic hand on instead and was so natural with it, you hardly noticed, which explained why I had never spotted his missing hand until the night of the show.

After dinner, we repaired to the Costes Bar, which was always a scene. Various *Vogue* cover models were in there and a couple of photographers more famous than the people they shot—Mario Testino holding court in one corner, Stephen Meisel in another. There were unexpected faces in there too, including Roman Polanski and Farrah Fawcett-Majors, but not together.

With Nelly's usual bravado we somehow managed to commandeer a nicely dark back corner and it soon became a hot spot of table hopping, as people came over to say hi—mainly to Iggy and Nelly, it had to be said—while the rest of us basked in their reflected glory.

The ghastly Peter Potter came and joined us for a while, which I was not thrilled about with the scent of Miles probably still on me, but at least chatting to the happy couple gave him an item for his column, which got him off my back. Of course, we both faked being *thrilled* to see each other so brilliantly that anyone observing would have thought we were the closest of pals. It was a game I knew how to play and I was happy to play it. He didn't stay long, to my great relief—there were too many other famous people in the bar to distract his attention.

Our little hardcore group was still there happily boozing and chatting in the early hours, when Paul suddenly sprang to his feet and walked a few steps away from us.

"OK," he said, starting to walk back. "Who am I?"

He had his front teeth in a slightly goofy position, his chin held back into his neck as he lolloped along, swinging straight arms and leading with his hips.

"Karolina," I shouted out.

"Gimme flesh, sista," said Paul and we smacked hands in midair. "Your go."

I got up, immediately knowing who I was going to do. I started walking towards them, taking each step with a high-lifted pointed foot, pouting sulkily, waving my hips from side to side and looking up from under my lashes.

"Naomi!" said Iggy.

"Corrrrrect," I said. "Your go."

Iggy stood up and started to walk like a gangling young horse, with knock knees and a stupid expression on his face.

"OK," he said. "Can you see? This one is vintage piece."

"Claudia bloody Schiffer," said Frannie.

"Da!" said Iggy and they smacked palms. "When I first go to Saint Martins I spend all my time watching videos of old fashion shows—I like late Eighties early Nineties, especially Chanel. That Walk! How did she get job? She walk like *magarac* . . ."

"That's Serbian for donkey," said Nelly, who seemed to be getting fluent in her new lover's language very quickly.

Next it was Frannie's turn and she got up and walked along our imaginary catwalk looking like the proverbial village idiot. Her arms hung straight by her side and she plonked along on flat feet looking as miserable as if she was going to the scaffold.

"What the fuck?" said Nelly.

None of us could get it.

"Give up?" said Frannie, eyes sparkling with mischief.

"Tell us!" we all cried out.

"Any male model," said Frannie and we all fell about.

And so it went on until Paul got up for another turn.

"OK," he said. "This is a work in two parts."

He turned his back on us then he swung back round and strode towards us, his head up, looking left and right, his eyes shining, swinging his legs and executing a perfect of twirl, stopping in a killer pose.

"I know! I know!" I squealed, overexcited.

"Say nothing," he commanded, holding up his hand. "Here's part two."

This time he walked tentatively along not moving his head, his mouth hanging slightly open, looking very unhappy, with a dazed, zombie-like expression.

"Oh, that's horrible," said Nelly. "I can't bear it."

"Ooooooh," I said. "Ouch. Poor Maria."

"You're right, girlfriends, that was Miss Maria Constanza. The Queen of the Runway—then and now."

"It's so sad," said Frannie. "Why does she do it? She's still so beautiful, but you just can't do catwalk over the age of thirty, when all the other girls are nineteen. And she looks so depressed, like she's lost her mojo. I just want to get up there and give her a big hug."

"Da," said Iggy, nodding. "I remember Maria too from videos. With Christy and Linda and Naomi and Helena. She was goddess. I have not seen her now, but I have heard. This very wrong."

"That's what I hate about this business sometimes," said Nelly, vehemently. "It can be so fucked."

"Only if you let it," said Iggy, looking deep into her eyes and squeezing her hand with his one good one.

After that poignant note the evening just melted away. Paul was going "out," as he called it and he walked along Rue du Faubourg St. Honoré with me and Frannie, looking for a taxi to take him the other way to the Marais. One finally pulled up and as he was kissing me goodbye he took my face in his hands and looked closely at me.

"Any chance we might get to see each other *properly* this time, skinny?" he asked. "And I don't count a coffee standing up with you bleating on about shopping as properly, OK?"

"How about tomorrow morning?" I said. "We've got nothing until Helmut the pelmet at two thirty."

"Cool," said Paul. "I'm directing Céline, so I'll have to be there by one. I'll see you in Café Flore at ten."

9

THE next morning, it was such bliss to have time to myself, I got up the minute I woke, did my yoga and hair and walked over to Saint Germain deliberately early.

Still high on my afternoon with Miles and the hilarious night with my best pals, I just wanted to be out there in Paris. It didn't matter how many times I went there, the beauty of that city never failed to knock me over and although I had felt lonely the day before, sometimes I just wanted to be alone in it, to drink it all in undisturbed.

I crossed to the Tuileries, and turned left to look down through the triumphal arch to the Louvre, in the golden autumn light. It was quite brisk, but I didn't care. I pulled my Greek fisherman's cap down over my ears and turned up the collar of my favourite Helmut Lang reefer coat. I was wearing my Gucci trainers and, in what amounted to an act of rebellion, I didn't have a handbag with me. Just my wallet in one pocket, my phone in the other. I felt so free.

I walked all the way down to the central courtyard of the Louvre, so happy not to be rushing to a show there, but with time just to take it all in. I slowly circled I.M. Pei's glass pyramid, looking up at the old building surrounding it, then I turned towards the Seine and went out through the huge gate, waving goodbye to all the statues of French philosophers I had never heard of.

There was no one on the Pont du Carrousel but me. Paris is not a city that gets going early and it was barely nine. I paused and looked east along the river, to the Ile de la Cité and Notre Dame, and west to Musée d'Orsay and the Eiffel Tower. Then I looked over at the trees along the Left Bank. The leaves were starting to fall and behind the branches I could see the magnificent grey stone houses on Quai Voltaire.

Finally I crossed over to Saint Germain, which was the part of Paris where I felt I really belonged. I stopped to look at a very small painting in a very large shop window on the Quai, which turned out to be a Bonnard—a real Bonnard. Then I turned up Rue des Saints Pères, looking in at the antique shops along the way, then left into Rue Jacob and right into Rue Bonaparte, my spirits lifting with every step.

By the time I got to Place St. Germain des Prés, where die-hards and tourists were sitting outside the Deux Magots having their coffee in the weak morning sun, I still had nearly an hour before it was time to meet Paul. I just kept wandering farther into the Sixth *arrondissement,* going left and right as the whim took me, although I knew where I was headed really. I paused in front of St. Sulpice to admire the gushing fountain and then I kept going until I reached my final destination—the Luxembourg gardens— and wandered in, past the magnificent palace and up to the round pond.

Here I stopped, sitting on one of the moveable chairs they provide in Paris parks—and which wouldn't last overnight in London— watching the light play on the water. It was a place with special memories for me. I'd gone there as a child, with my father—just the two of us—and sailed a boat on that pond; one of the lovely wooden boats you could still hire from the little kiosk.

I was seven and it had been one of those rare times in my child-hood when everyone had been happy. We were living in Paris for six months so that my father could take up a special bursary from the French government, to paint—in a studio provided—and to spend days in galleries and museums.

Amazingly, my mother was contented just to be there, in a pokey flat in Rue du Cherche Midi, on the top floor, where she didn't seem to mind being crammed in with two small children and having to drag the shopping up all the worn stone stairs. Every day she took us out for long walks through the beautiful streets, visiting museums along the way. I didn't go to school for six months, but Toby and I learned French by listening and we learned about beauty and elegance, just from looking around us.

It was strange how happy my mother had been there, because in our large house in the Sussex countryside, where we had loads of room and domestic arrangements were eased by a cleaner—until my mother sacked her in a drunken rage—she was mostly depressed, drunk, stoned and impossible.

But for that magical time in Paris, none of that impinged and just for a moment it was nice to sit and remember a time in my childhood when I had been truly happy. I guarded that memory like a treasure.

Paul was waiting for me when I arrived at Café Flore, two pots of hot chocolate and a plate of croissants laid out ready for us.

"Hey, babe," he said, kissing me on the lips, as usual. "You look gorge. You've got the kind of glow guys like me spend hours trying to achieve artificially in photographic studios."

He pretended to hold a microphone under my nose.

"Tell me, Miss Pointer," he said, in a cod American accent. "How do you achieve your amazing glow? Is it rampant sex, or daily applications of rhinocerous sputum?"

"All of the above," I said, quickly. "And walking fast, on a cool Paris morning."

He poured the chocolate and we sipped—it was incredibly rich—and chatted with the instant intimacy only possible between really close friends. We had a good laugh about the night before, he told me all the backstage gossip and what he had got up to in London. I told him about Peter Potter and Nivek Thims.

I wrote his name out backwards on my napkin and we agreed that Luap Stniassuot was not an improvement, in fact it was unpronounceable, but he liked Y-lime a lot. He also suggested—without writing it down—that Eillo Rehtorbriaf was pretty good too. It took me a while to cotton on.

"Eillo," I said, squinting as I struggled to turn the letters round in my mind. "Ollie! Eillo . . . did you do that in your head?" I asked him, amazed.

He just shrugged.

"Your IQ must be off the scale," I said to him.

"Dunno," he said. "Never had it tested. It's always been dwarfed by the size of my penis."

I threw my croissant at him.

It was all very entertaining, but after a while I became aware of a slightly shifty look around Paul's eyes. I had the feeling he wanted to ask me something, or tell me something, and was trying to find the moment. I was desperately hoping it wasn't anything to do with a certain runway photographer—but in the end I couldn't stand it any longer.

"What is it, Paul?" I said, "I can see you've got something on your mind. For once in your life, *spit*, honey."

"OK," he said. "Fully busted. Here's the thing. It's Ursula."

"What about Ursula?" I said, suddenly worried. "She's not ill, is she?"

"God, no," said Paul. "The woman is a force of nature, but she's worried about you."

"Oh, not that again," I groaned, instantly pissed off. "I wish she wouldn't do this—and now you are her latest way of getting to me. I should never have introduced you. What is it this time? And why are you telling me now? Why didn't you tell me in Milan?"

"You wouldn't shut up about shopping and shit, if you remember."

"Oh, well I do apologize, Mr. Serious Pants," I said sarcastically, pretending to joke, but really quite cross. "Sorry, I must have confused you with my *gay* friend for a moment."

Paul looked hurt and I felt like a shit. I sighed deeply. I loved Ursula to bits, but I really hated it when she started interfering like this, and dragging my friends into it was too much.

"OK," I said. "I'm sorry. I know you're only doing your duty.

Ursula's put you in a difficult position and I know you love me, so go on, tell me what she's obsessing on now."

Paul took a deep breath and exhaled through pursed lips like a trumpeter.

"Well," he continued. "For one thing, she thinks you're too thin."

"Yeah, yeah, tell me something I don't know. That's just some weird lesbian obsession. She's always thought I was too thin. Is that it? Or is she worrying about me not having children again?"

"Well, there is that," said Paul, looking unusually uncomfortable. "But the real thing of it is, she doesn't like Ollie."

"I know that as well," I said, leaning back in my seat and shrugging. "She's never liked him and he doesn't like her either. Why do you think we never stay at her place when I go over to New York with him? He always insists we stay in a hotel so he can make the whole thing look like a business trip, but really it's because he feels uncomfortable at Ursula's place.

"She is the closest thing I have to parents and it used to bother me that they don't really like each other, but it doesn't any more. I love them both and that's all that matters." I folded my arms. Case closed.

"Really?" said Paul, looking quite amazed. "You really don't care?"

"No. She made it quite clear to me when I told her I was going to marry Ollie, that she didn't think it was a good idea. But I did."

"Did she tell you why not?"

"I know why not," I said. "Ollie is a straight."

"Yeah, well, that's obvious, babycakes," said Paul, back on more familiar territory. "Or I would have knobbed him years ago."

"Very funny, Paul, but I didn't say 'straight,' I said 'a straight.' Although he definitely is sexually straight as well, despite his fondness for shopping and nice flowers. But Ollie is also a straight—as in fundamentally conventional, mentally limited, not creative. That's what Ursula doesn't like about him." I stirred my chocolate a bit, then continued.

"She's exactly the same as my parents like that. With them it was always 'oh, she's really creative,' or 'but he's not creative,' and that was the only level on which they judged people. It didn't matter if they were clever, or brave, or loyal, or successful, or totally hideous, greedy and venal, all that mattered was that sacred creativity. It's why she and my parents were such great friends. They had the same stupid value system."

"You're creative," said Paul.

"Yeah," I said. "And so are you, darling. My parents would have loved you—black, underprivileged, gay *and* creative—they would have been in heaven. But, while I love creative people too, I don't want to live with them. I've been there, done that, got the bloody T-shirt. I know what happens around creative people and as far as I'm concerned, Ollie's lack of creativity, combined with his ambition and business smarts, is exactly what I love about him. Ursula might not like it, but I do."

I could see mischief starting to sparkle out of Paul's eyes again, which was a relief.

"What now?" I said.

He started to giggle, a low rumble in his chest like a Tube train going under a building. "Does Ollie know he's not creative?"

I laughed too.

"Not entirely. That's why he loves having me around—it's creativity by osmosis."

"So all those little games he plays, those contrived 'salons' you have and inviting people at the last minute, that's all part of trying to be creative, isn't it?"

"You got it. He thinks having a bright pink lining in his suit coat is creative and having a funky old car with a stupid eight-track instead of a proper stereo and collecting fashion photographs is creative, when really it's just join-the-dots stuff. Ollie thinks you can *buy* creative. All that other stuff is just schoolboy games, but it makes him happy so it's fine with me."

"Well, that's good," said Paul. "But I don't think that is what Ursula means. What's worrying her is that you are very vulnerable after what happened with your parents and she's concerned you're not getting proper emotional support from Ollie. She believes he encourages you to live your whole life on the surface, which she doesn't think is a good thing for someone with deep-seated issues."

I rolled my eyes. I couldn't stand all Ursula's therapy bollocks.

"And I've got to tell you one thing, Emily," Paul continued. "You have got really thin lately. Now, you know I do thin—I'm gay, I'm in fashion—but you are getting a little too skinny. Unhealthy skinny. Doesn't Ollie talk to you about that? Doesn't it worry him?"

I sighed. I was so sick of that from Ursula and now I was getting it from Paul too. Why couldn't they see how happy I was in my life and leave me alone?

"I like being slim," I said. "I watch what I eat, because I like to feel good and I like to fit into my clothes. I haven't got an eating disorder, I just don't want to be fat. I don't see what it's got to do with Ollie."

Paul pulled a "whatever" face.

"What I don't seem to be able to make Ursula—or it seems, now, you—understand," I said, leaning forward, "is that I might not discuss my inner child with Ollie, but I don't need to because I get a real sense of security from him. Financial, domestic, social, the lot. And after my childhood, those are the best things I could possibly have—can you dig it?"

"I can dig it," said Paul, raising his glass of hot chocolate. "Security is the holy grail for people like us. I'm just trying to create it for myself, rather than relying on someone else to provide it for me. But, I take your point and I'll tell Ursula to stop fussing."

"That's all right," I said, clinking my cup against his. "I'll tell her myself. Ollie and I are coming over to New York for a visit after this hoopla is over. He wants to get you to sign your life away to Slap."

"Excellent," said Paul. "I'll start looking for the beach house. Now that would make me feel a lot more secure."

After he left to get ready for the Céline show, I still had some time to spare, so I wandered around Saint Germain a bit more, ending up in a tiny little boutique on Rue de Buci which seemed to sell clothes for prostitutes. It was brilliant. I bought a pair of skintight PVC crocodile-effect pants and a shiny PVC bustier. They were outrageous and I loved it.

Then I strolled around a bit more, picking up some lavender bags for our cleaner and the girls back at the office, a few bars of olive oil soap to make a nice pile in our bathroom and a stripey matelot jersey for Ollie to tie round his shoulders for a transeasonal weekend look, before I headed back to the hotel to change for the show.

As I walked I tried not to think about my conversation with Paul. As far as I was concerned it was done with. Ursula's concerns were intrusive and misplaced, end of subject. But as I stood once again waiting for the lights to change on Rue de Rivoli, it did occur to me that if security was what I valued in my life above all else, why was I risking it all by cavorting with a penniless Australian photographer, who now had a key to my hotel room?

I didn't have time to think about that, or anything else, for the rest of the day as the cruise-y down time was seriously over and we had seven shows back-to-back, from Helmut Lang at two thirty ending up with Alexander McQueen at eight thirty. All with Luigi at the wheel.

Amazingly, we got to Helmut Lang's obscure venue—and back—and to all the other far-flung spots on the schedule without going wrong, basically because we just followed other limos. We'd come out of each show, Bee would get on her mobile to find Luigi among the throng of identical cars choking the street—pretty much all dark blue or grey Mercedes—and then we'd just follow one of them and their black-clad passengers to the next venue. It worked a treat.

After that the week went on with its usual pattern, all the shows an hour late, grinding limo rides out to them, tailing another vehicle, hectic dinners at 10:30 P.M. after the last show, sometimes leading on to silly drinks and carrying on, a bit of light shopping in any spare time and, for me, a couple more secret trysts with Miles.

By the time we were on to our fifth assignation—counting the times in Milan—it had started to feel really comfortable. I didn't have any more spontaneous crying jags, we just had a great time together and then parted amicably. He never made me feel pressured, or sluttish, he just made me feel good. Really, really good.

I seemed to be slipping happily into my new role as an adulteress and whenever I spoke to Ollie, which wasn't that often over the week, with my busy schedule and all his "phone off" meetings, he certainly didn't seem to notice any change in me. He was his usual affable self and, despite what I was getting up to behind his back, I didn't feel any differently about him. That may seem hard to understand, but my shows life and my real life were like two separate universes, and Ollie and Miles existed in different ones.

The only people who existed equally in both were my work colleagues and, for once, I was glad about their monumental self-absorption. Bee and Alice were far too wrapped up in themselves to notice any changes in me and the only one of them who may have spotted a certain Ready Brek glow around me—Frannie—was so busy with her backstage make-up story, I didn't see much of her all week. When we did meet it was mostly at dinner and I could put my flush and good cheer down to the red wine.

One of the shows I always looked forward to most during the Paris week was John Galliano and on that Friday night my excitement was quadrupled when Nelly appeared and sat next to me.

"Nellster!" I squealed, giving her a huge hug. "Oh, it's so good to see you. It's just like old times. What's it like being in Paris and not being at the shows? It must be so weird."

"It is," she said. "It's fucking weird. When I look at Suzy in the morning and read about all the shows I haven't been to, I feel really left out and I wasn't going to bloody miss this one.

"Oy, Mrs!" she said, suddenly turning round to the woman behind her. "Can you stop kicking my bloody back? You've already done it about ten times and you're really pissing me off. Sit still, or piss off, all right?" She turned back to me, rolling her eyes and grinning. "Bloody Nora. Some people. No idea."

Ah, my Nelly was back. A little bit of Kentish Town in the heart of Paris. I just sat there beaming at her like an idiot, I was so pleased to see her. I mean, I had seen her several times that week for drinks and dinner, but always in a big crowd, not just the two of us, chatting and gossiping, waiting for a show to begin, like the good old days—the good old days of just over a week before. I never thought I'd look back nostalgically to waiting for shows to begin, I thought to myself, but there you are.

"So, how's everything?" I asked, not knowing where to start.

"Bloody marvellous, Em—still. It's a miracle. Iggy and I just keep getting closer and closer and we're doing amazing things with his work too. I'm officially moving to Milan to be with him. He's coming back to London with me after this—he's gonna meet my parents, that'll be a laugh—and I'm going to pack up my place, probably sling most of it actually, and then head back to Milan for good. Although between you and me, it may turn out to be Paris, rather than Milano, in the not-so-distant future."

She winked at me dramatically. There had been something in Louise Kretzner's column that morning about rumours that Iggy was already being approached by one of the big Paris couture houses to be their new designer, although she didn't say which one. Now it seemed like there was some truth in it.

"So are you going to stay with *pure*?" I asked. "Oh mighty fashion-director-at-large?"

"I dunno," she said with her wickedest smile. "But I'm going to enjoy torturing Beaver about it. She's already asked me if they can shoot our Milan apartment for the first issue of *pure inside*—did you know they were starting an interiors mag? Although pure crap would be a better name for it, judging by what I've seen of the dummy."

"Oh, do tell," I said, thinking how interested Ollie would be in this news.

"OK—it opens with a ten-page story on 'The Vessel'—that's a vase to any normal person—in black and bloody white, so you can't even see what colour the stupid things are. And they're all hideous anyway. Then there's an 'essay'—which means no jokes and no pictures—on the subject of 'sitting.' Sit on *this*, I said. Then for their real triumph they've done Christian Lacroix's beach house—once again, in black and white. Black and white pictures of Pucci prints. How totally fucked is that? What a stupid cow."

"Oh, good," I said. "Sounds like it will give Spitty Felicity some competition in the pretension department, as well as for advertising, then."

"Actually," said Nelly. "They've got loads of Slap ad spreads pasted into the dummy, which I thought was weird. It's not like they make 'vessels,' is it?"

"Hmm," I said. "Doesn't surprise me. Ollie's all excited about homewares at the moment. It's his latest craze. He probably will advertise in it—he thinks those painful magazines are the perfect 'vessels,' ha ha, for reaching the more sophisticated consumer, who no longer reads fashion mags."

Nelly just snorted. The very suggestion that anyone could be less than desperate to read fashion magazines was ridiculous to her. She was 100 per cent fashionista, that girl.

The Galliano show was the usual thrilling extravaganza, a breathtaking spectacle of mad disparate elements of historic and ethnic references, which somehow fitted together as a modern whole. And which you knew would translate into brilliantly cut suits and evening dresses that would make women look and—more importantly—feel amazing.

At the end John Galliano made his legendary theatrical bow, which got more over the top every season. This time he had a bare chest under a white suit, with flowing dreadlocks, bondage pants, brothel creepers and a trilby hat. Everyone came out beaming.

"Oh, that's what it's all about, Em," said Nelly, wiping tears from her eyes. "Bloody brilliant. I'm done with missing shows. Well—I won't do the pissy little advertiser shows any more—but I'm not going to miss the biggies. I've got one more day of this season to enjoy and I'm going to do it all. Can't believe I missed Dior on Tuesday. I must have been mad."

"You were," I said. "Madly in love they call it—that's the mad part."

"Hey," said Nelly, suddenly. "Let's go for a drink. Just you and me. It would be great to have a really good catch-up. I'm supposed to be meeting Igster, but he can join us later. I got him a big pile of early Nineties fashion-show videos which I conned out of various PRs and he's in heaven, watching them in the hotel room."

Frannie was backstage with Pat McGrath again, so I rushed to find Bee and Alice, to tell them not to wait for me. I was lucky to catch them, in the mad mêlée out front. Great crowds of thin women in high heels choked the pavement, shouting down their mobiles as they tried to find their limos and drivers, who were blocking the entire street and causing a state of honking hysteria among the never exactly relaxed Parisian drivers. I grabbed Bee just as she was getting into the car.

"Fine," she said, when I told her I wasn't coming with them. "I wasn't going to wait for you anyway."

They sped off and Nelly and I walked slowly up the slope of Avenue de Wagram with our arms linked, just taking in the scene.

"I bloody love this bloody city," said Nelly suddenly. "I love all of it, even the corny old corner cafés and the corny old lights twinkling on the corny old Eiffel Tower. I seriously hope we do move here. The only thing you see twinkling in Milan are the capped teeth on the gigolos and the diamonds on the old bags they service. It's really not my scene. I love all of this place, not just the groovy bits. It's all great."

And so, rather than peeling off to one of the killingly fashionable bars we normally frequented, we sat in an ordinary little café drinking *kir* and watching Paris go by. I loved it too.

After a couple of drinks Nelly confided that Iggy had been approached by one of the grandest of all the couture houses—Albert Alibert—to be their new designer. It was a huge deal, like being offered Chanel, or Saint Laurent. I whistled between my teeth.

"Crikey," I said. "I thought it might be Givenchy, or even Rochas, but Alibert, that's the serious big league."

After another *kir,* she told me Iggy had already accepted the job and was hanging out in Paris while his lawyers got him out of the Rucca contract, which luckily for him had only been provisional until after the first two collections. It had never occurred to them that their new designer would move on quite so quickly.

"We're looking at apartments here, Em," she said, squeezing my hand. "It's so exciting. Can you imagine? We can live practically anywhere we want in Paris. It's so nice to be able to talk to someone about it—someone I know I can trust."

She was right, she could trust me. I wouldn't even tell Frannie or Ollie. I could be impeccably discreet with other people's secrets. With a family history like mine, it was a necessary survival tool. I also finally got the low-down on Iggy and his missing hand, by just coming out and asking her about it.

"Sarajevo," was her reply. "He lost his hand in Sarajevo. Bosnian war."

I tried to remember who were the goodies and who were the baddies in the conflict. All I could dredge up was hideous images on the evening news, reports of terrible atrocities and someone called Radovan Karadzic—wasn't he a Serb, like Iggy? I asked Nelly.

"He's a Bosnian Serb," said Nelly. "Iggy has had to draw Venn diagrams to explain all this to me, but I think I've got a fairly good handle on it now. It's just like the bollocks in Cyprus, which I can relate to, because my family are Cypriots. We're not Greeks, like you probably think, we're Greek Cypriots and my grandparents' house rather inconveniently was in the part of Cyprus that now belongs to Turkey. Which is how come I grew up in Kentish Town. So I probably had a head start on understanding Iggy's situation, compared to most fashionistas."

She laughed, shaking her head at the ridiculous irony of it all.

"Which side was Iggy on?" I asked tentatively.

"That was the problem," said Nelly. "Both and neither. Iggy's dad is a Serb—but a Serb-Serb from Serbia, not a Bosnian Serb—and they lived in Sarajevo, which is in Bosnia, because that's where his mum comes from. With me so far?"

"I think so, carry on . . ."

"Well, Iggy's mum is a Bosnian Muslim, so he's a mixture. That war was between Bosnian Serbs and Bosnian Muslims and Ig was a really bad mixture of it all. The Bosnian Serbs didn't like him because of his Muslim blood and the Muslims didn't trust him because of his Serbian blood, even though he wasn't an actual Bosnian Serb."

"Phew," I said, struggling to understand. "I can see why you needed the diagrams. But how did he lose his hand?"

"Somebody cut it off," said Nelly. "They were torturing him, trying to get him to spill the beans on the other side, which he was supposed to know about and he really didn't."

"Which side cut it off?" I asked, my voice disappearing almost to nothing. Faced with the enormity of Iggy's life, I hardly felt qualified to ask, hideous little Westbourne Grove princess that I was.

"That's the thing, that's why Iggy is so amazing," said Nelly. "He won't tell. Not even me. He says there was good and bad and right and wrong on both sides. They're both to blame, so it doesn't matter which side actually did it, because they both caused it and because he is of both sides himself, he says he can't take sides."

"That *is* amazing," I said, my whole life suddenly seeming shamefully over-indulged and decadent by comparison, give or take the odd dead dad, estranged brother and mad mother. "What a story—and after all that, he's a fashion designer?"

"Yeah, weird isn't it?" said Nelly. "But it's what he always wanted to do. His mother and grandmother are both dressmakers and the construction of clothes always fascinated him—how they made something with shape and volume out of flat material. That's why his cut is so amazing. Plus, he really loves women and wants to make them look and feel good."

She finished her drink in one. "The funny thing is, though, he says if it wasn't for the war and losing his hand, he never would have got to be a designer. After the torture—his dad copped it pretty badly too—he and his whole family were granted asylum in Britain and he got a scholarship to Saint Martins. Men don't generally get to be fashion designers in Bosnia."

While we were sitting there, with me feeling mildly in shock, taking it all in, my phone beeped, indicating a text. I'd had it on the table next to me the whole time, like a complete idiot. It was just a habit in noisy bars and I hadn't given it a second thought. But the minute it beeped, I knew it was Miles and I froze, staring at my phone like I'd never seen one before. It beeped again.

"Aren't you going to look?" said Nelly.

"Oh, yeah," I said, picking it up. Sure enough, it was Miles. "319 at 12?" was all it said. I deleted it without answering.

"Well, who was it?" said Nelly.

I thought quickly. "Oh, it was just Ollie saying he's gone to bed and not to call. Early start tomorrow."

"On Saturday? He is keen. Shame, I thought it might be Frannie-frangipani, I'd like to see her. Let's call Ig and see whether he's tired of vintage Helena Christensen, yet. He loves Helena, my Igster, he's got great taste in women." She laughed heartily. "That's why he loves me."

I didn't reply to Miles's text until the next morning, the last day of the shows.

"Sorry," I keyed in "bad moment last nite. 2 nite 4 sure?"

I didn't get a reply until after lunch and I was surprised by how jumpy it made me. Every time my phone beeped or rang, I grabbed it, hoping it was him. Eventually it was—live. I ran out of the café where I was sitting with Frannie, Alice, Bee and Luigi, mouthing "Ollie" and spoke to Miles on the street corner. God, I was an easy liar.

"Hey, Em," he said. "Can you talk? Sorry I didn't get back to you sooner, more email nightmares. God, those things can stuff you up. But listen, don't worry about last night, that's totally cool, but I would love to see you tonight. I'm going back to Sydney to-morrow."

"Are you doing Saint Laurent?" I asked, hoping he would get the joke. He did.

"Yeah, I'm doing Hermès and Louis Vuitton and Lanvin and Balmain and Saint Laurent . . . and then I'm doing you, with any luck. The question is, are you and your fashionable friends doing dinner?"

"I honestly don't know, but I would like to say goodbye to Nelly, so I don't know when I'll be back at the hotel. What about you?"

"Well, I do normally have a few drinks with the boys on the last night, but I want to see you more . . ."

"OK—why don't you do what you do with the boys and I'll do my thing and we'll both just go back to the hotel when we're ready? You've got your key, so if I'm not back when you get there, just make yourself comfortable. You can start by taking all your clothes off . . ."

"I love it when you talk dirty," he said, laughing. "Three-one-nine baby."

And then, just to cover my tracks, I rang Ollie who, for once, answered his phone. I was getting scarily good at this.

10

THE last afternoon of the shows was crazy with five big shows back-to-back, including the mighty Louis Vuitton which was always held way out in a giant glasshouse somewhere called Parc André Citroën. It was one of the most crucial shows of the season for new trends—and for advertising—and we nearly missed it, because this one time, Luigi followed the wrong car. It was Frannie who realized.

"Er, Bee," she said. "Can you actually see the people in that car we're following?"

"Why?" said Bee.

"Well, are you sure they're fashion people—because we've just passed L'Etoile back there and that's nowhere near where we're going. In fact I think we're heading for La Défense and that's definitely on the wrong side of the river."

"Shit!" said Bee. "You're right. I can see the woman in the back seat and she's wearing a red jacket. Luigi! Stop! *Basta!* We're following the wrong car, what a nightmare."

I had been happily sitting there—in the middle seat—thinking about what I might do to Miles later and oblivious to everything else, so I hadn't even noticed where we were going. Now I feared we were in for a Bee explosion of the atomic kind. All three of us backseat girls sat up straight and waited for the impact. Even Alice turned and widened her eyes at me and I felt Frannie's little hand come over to find mine. I squeezed it back. Bee could be terrifying when she really lost it.

But she didn't lose it. She looked over at Luigi and started laughing.

"This is hilarious," she said, punching his arm. "We've probably followed some banker and his mistress on the way out to their love shack. Maybe we should carry on, eh, girls, and see where they end up?" She tapped her perfect nails on the dashboard. "Now, let's think, this is quite serious really—what shall we do?"

She put her forefingers to her temples and closed her eyes for a moment. Seconds later, she opened them again and snapped her fingers. "Got it!" she said. "Frannie, you speak the best French, so hop out and get a taxi and tell him where we want to go and we'll follow you. Simple. And tell the cab driver we're following him so he doesn't dash off and lose us. Promise him a big tip, OK? Light me up a ciggie would you, Luigi?"

It was brilliant in its simplicity, if slightly eccentric. I asked permission to go with Frannie—just for larks—and the two of us found a cab fairly quickly, which was a miracle itself in Paris. Bee's plan worked like a dream and we arrived at the venue a mere thirty-five minutes after the invitation time. After that nutty episode we were all in a slightly hysterical mood, compounded by the de-mob fever which always gripped us on the last day of the shows—which, in Paris, is the last day of the entire season.

The sense of excitement geared up even more when we found Nelly already installed in our little Brit-pack area inside the Vuitton venue. When we told her the story about Bee getting Luigi over from Milan and how we had been following other fashion limos all over Paris for the entire week, she couldn't believe it, she thought it was so funny.

"Oh, that is hysterical," she said, her filthy laugh booming around the glasshouse. "That Bee is a classic. A Milanese driver—in Paris. She's nuts."

"But don't tell Beaver," I said. "Don't tell anyone—it's just between us. Bee is being so nice at the moment, we don't want to piss her off."

"Don't worry, babes, I would never give Eager Beaver a reason to feel better about herself, even though she has just given me a very tasty pay rise."

We didn't have any more limo dramas for the rest of the day, cruising from show to show in our unofficial convoy of fashion limos, until Luigi finally delivered us to the last venue of the season—the Rodin Museum, for Yves Saint Laurent.

I'd been to Tom Ford's YSL shows there before, but it still made my hair stand up on my neck, it was so thrilling. You entered via a tiny door in forbidding grey gates and once you were through security, you stepped on to a black carpet—like a red carpet, but black, so chic—that led you up to the fabulous old grey stone mansion that housed the museum.

Adding to the sense of drama, the path was floodlit purple and it was lined with an honour guard of unbelievably handsome young men in black dinner jackets. All of them had jet black hair slicked down like matinée idols.

Nelly arrived at the same time as us—riding in the limo with the girls from the Japanese edition of *pure,* because she was avoiding too much close contact with Beaver. Letting Bee and Alice go ahead, I linked Nelly with one arm and Frannie with the other and walked up that black carpet like Dorothy in *The Wizard of Oz.*

"Check them out," said Nelly when we reached the bottom of the steps up to the entrance of the mansion. The YSL footmen on either side of the door were twins. Incredibly beautiful Eurasian twins. "So fucking cool," said Nelly. "Evening, boys." She winked at them both as we went past. One winked back.

Still on the black carpet we walked into the museum to find ourselves surrounded by some of the most famous sculptures in the world, like it was the most natural thing to do on a Saturday night. There was "The Thinker," "The Lovers" and the famously controversial statue of Balzac, looking like he was wearing an old dressing gown. I wanted to stop and look—I was an artist's daughter after all—but Nelly pulled me on.

"Come on, Em," she said. "Stop gawping. Let's get to the drinks tent. We've got time for at least three."

We came out of the other side of the mansion and down the steps, still on the black carpet, heading for a long sleek white marquee, also awash with the purple light. The golden dome of Les Invalides was visible to the right, through the bare branches of the trees. Napoleon's tomb, in floodlit splendour—talk about drama.

Adding to the general scene were the other arriving guests. Isabella Blow, the fashion director of *Tatler,* was picking her way down the steps in front of us in an Alexander McQueen dress so tight, she could hardly walk in it. She could hardly see either, through the Philip Treacy creation circling her head, like a cylinder of thick black mesh going right across her eyes. Just normal everyday attire for Ms. Blow, who passionately championed the designers she believed in.

Just in front of her was another of fashion's famous eccentrics, from an earlier generation. Holding tight to a young man's arm, Anna Piaggi was wearing a bright blue hussar's coat over tie-dyed purple panne velvet leggings. Her Eton crop, with its signature turquoise kiss-curl, was topped with a miniature top hat, in gold and silver stripes. She was wearing a starched ruff like a Toulouse-Lautrec circus dog and carried a cane topped with a silver turtle. On her forefingers she wore rings with gaudy stones the size of gobstoppers.

It was the full fashion circus. All that was missing were the fire-eaters and jugglers. We entered the marquee, pausing to collect drinks from a handsome waiter at the door.

"Ooh, I dunno," said Nelly, hesitating between two glasses. "Shall I be shampoo, or shall I be voddie? It's make-your-mind-up time, isn't it, at this stage of an evening?"

"We're in Paris," said Frannie, picking up two flutes and handing one to Nelly. "It's got to be 'poo."

We clinked glasses and wandered around the space together looking at all the people—quite a few of whom were looking at Nelly, who was cutting a striking figure in Iggy's electric-blue parachute silk dress and the famous armoured bag. We had just taken up a position by a pillar topped with an enormous display of orchids, when Louise Kretzner came over.

"Well, hello, Nelly Stelios," she said, putting out her hand. "Don't you look great in your boyfriend's frock? Did he have it let out for you?"

"Thanks," said Nelly, ignoring the hand and turning away to grab a waiter who was walking past with a full bottle of champagne.

I saw one of the fearsome hack's eyebrows twitch. She hadn't missed the snub.

"So, Nelly," she continued, her voice hardening. "I hear that you and your boyfriend have been house-hunting in Paris."

"Did you?" said Nelly. "I imagine you hear a lot of things in your job, Miss Kretzner, must be fascinating. That's a very beautiful bag you are carrying, if you don't mind me saying so. Very cute, that, having a little Mickey Mouse to carry around with you."

I felt a just perceptible nudge to my ribs.

"Oh, do you like it?" said the woman I had heard called Louise Crapster, by piqued designers. She had come over all coy and girly. "I adore these minaudières," she said. "It's Judith Lieber, of course."

"Oh, of course," said Nelly.

"I collect them, you know," said Crapster, smiling indulgently at us.

"Oh, that must be interesting," said Nelly and I felt another little nudge, this time from Frannie.

I could feel laughter beginning to rise inside me like foaming champagne. It was agony. I couldn't let Nelly down by losing it, she was handling the situation so brilliantly. I bit down hard on my lip and held my breath.

"Well, Nelly," said Louise. "I'm sure we'll be seeing a lot more of each other in months to come, in Milan—or maybe here in Paris."

"Absolutely, Miss Kretzner," said Nelly. "We must have dinner one night."

"Oh, that would be charming," she said, smiling at Nelly, like a crocodile eyeing up a swimmer, then she put one of her wrinkled claws on her arm. "And do call me Louise, everybody does."

She smiled again—it was almost painful to look at—and sloped off towards her next victim.

"If only she knew what people did call her," said Nelly.

"Oh, Nelly," I said. "You were brilliant. You are really cut out for this new role of yours. I would have told her to get stuffed."

"All part of the service," said Nelly.

Twenty minutes later we walked out of the show feeling even more giddy than we had when we'd gone in. It had been one of Tom Ford's great moments, wonderfully romantic and sexy at the same time, and we came out into the cold night air through a side exit feeling excited to be alive and fashionistas.

We were walking back towards the mansion when we ran right into Bee and Alice. They both greeted Nelly warmly, which was interesting, because they used to ignore her, except for a short period when Bee was trying to persuade her to jump ship and join *Chic*. After she declined, she was on Bee's death list for quite a while, so this was a major reverse.

"Well, girls," said Bee. "I don't know about you, but I think we should celebrate that wonderful end to a wonderful season with a nice cold bottle of champagne in the bar at the Meurice. What do you say?"

Nelly was clearly included in the invitation and I nudged her when I looked over and saw Beaver was coming out of the tent.

"Shit," said Nelly and hopped behind me, crouching down.

Frannie moved over to cover the gap, because that bright blue dress was hard to miss. Bee took in the situation with one of her instant radar sweeps and I saw her eyes crinkle with pleasure. She made small talk about the show for a few moments, until Beaver was safely out of sight.

"You can come out now, Nelly," she said. "She's gone. And if you don't mind squashing into the back of the car, you would be very welcome to join us for a drink."

"Excellent," said Nelly. "The more free piss the better."

The journey back to the Meurice was hilarious. Nelly's dress took up so much room we were squashed into the car like fashion students at the back of a show, and without another limo to follow— we couldn't rely on where the other cars would be going after the last show and didn't want to find ourselves out at the airport—we had to navigate our own way back to the hotel.

We did manage it eventually, by a roundabout route, which turned out to be rather a wonderful sightseeing tour of Paris. We sang and laughed all the way—even Alice joined in occasionally—and when we finally got there, we all clapped for Luigi and Bee asked him if he would care to join us in the bar. We found a nice corner table and Bee ordered three bottles of Bollie.

"Saves time in the long run," she said.

"Bloody 'ell, do you know how lucky you are with her?" Nelly hissed in my ear, taking a big suck on one of Bee's cigarettes. "She's not like an editor—she's just a great girl. Wish I'd known, I would have had your job."

Then she got on the phone to Iggy, who came along to join us, and I sent a text to Paul and he came by, bringing his mates Mark and Karl, two really funny stylists from New York and London, and it just turned into another of those hilarious nights you could never plan.

And I have to say Luigi fitted right into the hysterical mix. I'd always enjoyed having him drive us around in Milan, and Bee's mad idea to bring him over to Paris had actually worked brilliantly, but it wasn't until I'd seen him in this off-duty mode, that I realized just how charming he was.

And any straight man who could hold his own—and in a second language—with Paul, Mark, Karl and Nelly on full beam, had my full respect. Paul was clearly impressed too.

"I'm loving Parker," he whispered to me. "He's a doll. Cute as."

I didn't get it at first.

"Parker?"

Paul rolled his eyes.

"Lady Penelope's driver? Duh?"

"Oh, I see what you mean, very funny. Yes, he is really lovely. It was a brilliant idea to get him over here. He really cheers us up."

"Well, he can cheer me up anytime, although he's clearly not my team. Mind you, that's never stopped me before . . ." He got a dangerous glint in his eye. "Hey, Luigi," he said, grasping his knee. "Can you drive a stick shift?"

We were just starting on the fifth bottle, with only nuts and olives to soak it all up, when Nelly came back from a trip to the loo—or the "carsie," as she called it—looking puzzled.

"That was weird," she said.

"What?" I said. "Did you see your new best friend Louise Kretzner in the loo? She stays here, you know."

"No, but I saw that mate of Seamus's—you know, that Aussie guy, whatsisname? Surfer, really built, great arse—oh, *you* know."

She smacked me on the knee. I did know all too well and I also knew exactly what he was doing in the Meurice.

"I think I know who you mean," I said weakly, wondering if I could turn my phone off without her noticing, in case he rang to see where I was.

"Miles," said Frannie, loud and clear in her I-know-the-answer-Miss voice. "He's called Miles. He's really nice. He's the one who walked along the catwalk at Dior—I didn't see it because I was backstage, but I heard about it. You remember, Em, he was with us all that night at the Ferrucci party. You danced with him. So did I."

She giggled and looked a bit sheepish, no doubt remembering what else she did that night. That made two of us.

"Yeah, yeah," I nodded enthusiastically. "I do remember. He's really nice. That was hilarious what he did at Dior. Really helped to pass the time."

"But what the fuck's he doing in here?" said Nelly, who hated unexplained mysteries almost as much as Frannie did. "He and Seamus stay in a total doss-house, they certainly don't stay here."

"He was probably delivering some pictures—a disc or something," I said, suddenly inspired.

"Oh yeah," said Frannie. "That'll be it. He works for loads of different magazines, that'll be it."

"Yeah," said Nelly. "But I saw him go up in the lift and you need a key card to make it work here, don't you?"

"Weird," I said, shrugging, and turned round quickly to Paul to change the subject, which worked, luckily.

He and his friends were hilarious together, but once I knew Miles was upstairs I lost all interest in the chatter and frivolity in that bar—even when we realized the couple sitting in the corner were Harold Pinter and Antonia Fraser.

"Didn't know they did the shows," said Paul, which made us all roar. "Wonder what Harold thought of Helmut?"

I sneaked a look at my watch. It was after midnight already. I'd had enough, I wanted to be upstairs with that gorgeous man, who was probably already naked in my bed, but how could I suddenly leave without them all twigging something was going on? I tried not to think about it, but I just couldn't sit still.

"What's up with you?" said Paul eventually, pushing me in the ribs, so I nearly fell off the corner of the chair we were sharing. "Have you got ants in your pants? You're twitching like a voodoo zombie."

"Oh, it's just sitting on uncomfortable seats all day," I lied. I did have ants in my pants, large ones, which looked very like Miles. "It's made my muscles all tight. I think I need to go and have a hot bath and lie down."

Lie down on top of Miles.

"Well, I'm sorry if we're boring you," he said, half acting snitty, half meaning it.

I was saved by Bee, who started yawning and said that she was off to bed, she was catching an early train home so she could go straight into the office. I used her exit to commence mine, which involved a lot of kissing and hugging of Nelly, Iggy and Paul, even though I kept telling them I would be seeing them all soon—Nelly and Iggy when they came over to London to move her stuff, and Paul on my trip to New York with Ollie.

When I finally did escape, it took all my self-control not to run to the lift and my heart sank slightly when Frannie appeared at my side, just as I got to it.

"I'm going up too," she said. "I'm knackered."

I was even less thrilled when she started to say something about borrowing the latest edition of US *Chic*, which I had in my room. I had to think fast.

"Oh no!" I said, clamping my hand over my mouth. "There's something I forgot to tell Nelly. I'd better go back."

Frannie gave me one of her clever-clogs looks—as if to say, what could be so important I couldn't call her, or text her, in the morning?—but I just disappeared back round the corner to the bar as quickly as I could. I was planning just to wait by the wall for a minute until the lift had gone, but then Paul saw me as he was leaving.

"I thought you'd gone to bed," he said.

"Well, I had, but then I thought I'd forgotten something, but I just realized I hadn't," I said, lamely.

"Oh fine, Emily," he said, shaking his head. "That all makes perfect sense." He came over and put his hands on my shoulders. He rubbed his nose against mine. Eskimo kisses, another of our jokes. "You are such a weirdo at times," he said. "But I still love you. See you in Sin City." He kissed me, smack on the lips, and left.

At last, I was free. Bugger the lift, I thought, and ran up the stairs—it was only three flights—and along the corridor to my room. By the time I got the door open I was literally panting.

Miles was lying sprawled on the bed, naked in a tangle of sheets—and fast asleep. He looked so peaceful and almost angelic, despite two days' beard growth, with his wiry hair sticking up around his head on the pillow. I couldn't bear to wake him.

I cleaned my teeth, drank two bottles of mineral water from the mini bar—I'd had a lot of champagne, I now realized—and sorted out the mess of handbags and shoes on the floor, ready to pack quickly in the morning. I was hoping he would wake up, but he didn't, so eventually I just took my clothes off and slid into bed beside him.

We'd never actually slept together, I realized, as in actual sleeping, except for about an hour in the early morning of our first night and I wondered how it would be. It was one thing having rampant nookie with another man, but to sleep quietly with one, well that seemed weird.

I almost felt like retreating to the sofa, but as I settled on the bed and turned over, I felt Miles's arm come round me and he pulled me towards him, curling his body round mine, all apparently in his sleep. Almost immediately, I fell asleep myself and neither of us stirred until the next morning, when my alarm split the peace. That was a very strange wake-up call. I don't know which of us was more disorientated, but almost immediately Miles's frown of confusion turned into a big smile.

"I can't believe I slept through it," he said, shaking his head. "Was I great?"

"You were great at sleeping," I said.

And the funny thing was, I had been too, and on the whole I was not the greatest sleeper. I often woke up in the middle of the night, next to Ollie, who was a master sleeper, and I would lie there for hours, worrying.

Worrying about my credit-card bills and whether I should change my job and whether I was getting fat and whether Ollie would always love me and was my brother really OK and should I see more of him and should I go and see my mother in that terrible place or did it just stir it all up for her?

And quite often, in the darkest hours, I would shed a tear for my dad, remembering our happy times together in his studio. It was as though all the demons I kept at bay during the day could get through my defences at night.

"I'm really sorry, Emily," said Miles, rubbing his head with both his hands. "What an idiot I am. I'm afraid I had a few too many with the boys last night and I just crashed out. Actually, I'm glad you didn't see me awake, I was pissed. I was a mess."

"So was I," I said. "I think we probably both needed a good sleep."

"And now we need a good . . ." he said, rolling over on to his front and reaching out for me.

"Shower," I said, slapping his bum, that beautiful bum of his, which reminded me. "Hey," I said. "Nelly saw you here last night. It was a pretty close call."

"Oh shit, it *was* her then," he said. "I thought I saw her, so I jumped into the lift to escape."

"Lucky you did," I said. "We were all in the bar and she would have dragged you in there, if she could have. I think I would have died."

Then, at last, we got on and did what we had been supposed to do all along and then we said goodbye, me heading for Eurostar, London and my cosy little life with Ollie, Miles back to Sydney and whatever that held for him. We stood at the door and Miles took both my hands in his.

"Bye, Emily," he said, playing with my fingers. "It's been great. It's been quite a 'season,' as I believe you fashion babes call it."

I smiled shyly at him. He got that mischievous look.

"Are you doing New York?" he said, with a mock serious expression.

I laughed.

"Probably," I said.

"So, maybe see you in February—well, I definitely will see you, through my long and throbbing lens—but it's up to you, if you want to see me back, or not. You've got my number."

And with one last peck on the cheek, he was gone.

11

AS soon as I got back to London, my life settled down into its usual pattern with almost spooky ease and after all the excitement and drama of the shows season, heightened further by my dangerous liaison, I was perfectly happy about that.

Ollie and I resumed our usual round of work, parties and work parties—some together and some apart. He couldn't come with me if I was going along to keep Frannie company at the launch of a new eyebrow gel by one of Slap's major competitors, so we would meet for dinner afterwards and I would tell him all about it. Every detail. He loved getting the inside scoop on his competitors like that.

But if it was a fashion launch he always came with me. They were perfect networking opportunities for him and he also really enjoyed them. Ollie was far enough on the outside of fashion to remain seriously impressed by it. I found his enthusiasm very endearing and it stopped me from getting too jaded about it all. Some of my colleagues were so spoiled they would chuck their party goodie bags into the nearest bin, within full sight of the venue, if they thought the gifts weren't lavish enough. Ollie always opened his with the excitement of a child with a Christmas stocking.

"Ooh, look, Em," he would say, bringing out some garish tube of hair gel to add to the legions already stuffed into our bathroom cupboards. "More product! Excellent." He kept the carrier bags too. He still thought getting something free was the most terrific lark.

As well as tagging along on my calendar of events he also had a lot of work things of his own to go to, some of which I had to attend as the executive wife, but many—sales person of the month etc.—I was all too happy to miss. Between all this and occasional more normal social outings with non-work friends, we were only at home about two evenings a week. One of those was always Saturday. It was another of Ollie's little quirks, but he simply refused to go out on a Saturday night. He wouldn't even go to the cinema and if friends invited us over he would say we were busy.

It was some kind of atavistic hangover from the days when someone like Ollie would never have been "in town" on a Saturday night and, indeed, if we weren't having a Sunday salon the next day, we would go to the country, usually to his parents' place in Hampshire.

Far from dreading the in-laws, I loved going to stay with Max and Caroline. Ursula was right, they were as straight and "uncreative" as people could be—and that was exactly why I liked them. They weren't dull in a narrow-minded suburban way, they were just very conventional for people of their kind, right down to the books of *Social Stereotypes* cartoons in the downstairs loo and the green wellies in the boot room. Like Ollie's friends Jeremy and Sarah, the Fairbrothers were totally predictable, extremely right wing, but sincerely well meaning and generally great fun.

In all honesty I did find some of Max's views a little hard to take and when certain subjects—asylum seekers, unemployment benefit, working mothers—came up, I had to exercise extreme self-control.

Despite this, they weren't uncultured oafs; they loved opera and went to Glyndebourne every summer, but always to the more well-known productions. Similarly they would know what had won the Booker Prize—from Radio 4 or *The Daily Telegraph*—but they wouldn't actually read it. Max only read historical biographies and Caroline loved Jilly Cooper, and so did I, which is one of the first things she and I found to bond over.

I was never quite sure what they made of me, but right from my first visit, as Ollie's new "friend," they made me very welcome.

Caroline thought her parents had known my mother's "people," so that gave us a basis to start from.

I didn't know how much Ollie had told them about my horror-show family background, but it was never mentioned, so I had a feeling he had warned them off. They knew my father was dead and that my mother was "unwell," but beyond that they never probed and if family ever did come up, my brother's military career always stood me in good stead in their milieu, plus I had gone to what they considered a "known" school.

But despite all these unspoken codes of acceptability, the Fairbrothers weren't snobs—Ollie was much worse than his parents in that regard—they just had certain parameters that constituted life as they knew it. Anything else didn't really register.

I think they thought my job a little strange—*Harpers* or *Tatler,* they would have understood as a pre-marriage toy job—but they found Ollie's choice of profession much odder. His three older brothers had all been brilliantly successful in the City, before graduating on to post-Square Mile hobby lives, two of them farming and one dealing in fine wine. It embarrassed Max slightly that his youngest son was "fooling around with bloody lipstick," as I'd heard him say once in a cross moment, but Ollie always laughed it off, saying it was "just a business" like any other.

In a similar vein I always played down my look when we went to see them and in all honesty, part of the pleasure of those visits was forty-eight hours in jeans and a big cashmere jumper. My only concession to my normal style was a pair of bright pink wellies, which they thought were hilarious.

The only slight cause of tension between the generations was Ollie's and my lack of interest in reproduction, but that was mostly relieved by the constant supply of grandchildren from his brothers. There always seemed to be another one on the way, so the pressure was taken off us to an extent, although Caroline did occasionally make well-meaning references to breeding, as she popped a *coq au vin* into the Aga, or arranged the flowers I had brought her.

"Tick tock, Emily darling," she'd say, tearing my exquisitely arranged Wild at Heart bouquet to pieces and stuffing it into an old earthenware bread crock with some huge pieces of garden foliage.

"That's all I'm saying. Little kittens—time passes—tick tock. There, perfect for the hall. Lovely. Thank you, Emily."

Lazy weekends down there and busy weeks in London made up the life I was happy to retreat back into. But still, occasionally, when my brain was in neutral—squashed in a lift, sitting in a taxi, or when I heard certain pieces of music—Miles would pop into my head.

Mostly, I would push him right out again, but sometimes I would take the memory of him out of its box and enjoy it for a few moments, before putting him safely away again. Even at that remove the mere thought of him could make my insides liquefy, but I didn't allow it to happen very often.

I did have one wobbly moment, though. We'd only been back in the office after the shows for a few days, when Frannie suddenly squealed at me from the art department, where she was looking at some shots with the art director, Tim.

"Em!" she cried. "Come and look at this."

I ran over—ever eager to be distracted by a joke—and came to a halt in front of a computer screen covered in pictures of Miles doing his strut down the Dior catwalk. I felt a flush race over my entire body and was gripped by panic.

"Isn't that hilarious?" said Frannie. "I never actually saw it at the time because I was backstage. I didn't realize he'd done the full thing. He looks great actually—shame he wasn't with us that night at the Costes, he's got that model strut going *on*."

I was relieved she was twittering away, as it gave me a chance to collect myself.

"Yes, it was really funny," I said, trying to keep my voice level. "They are hilarious, those photographers. I sometimes think they keep us all sane at the shows, don't you?"

I felt quite shaky from the adrenaline rush. Seeing a picture of Miles was way too real. Apart from anything, I had forgotten quite how sexy he was. I grabbed the art director's mouse and clicked on a few shots, pretending to be looking at the other pics of the actual show, when all I really wanted to do was gaze at Miles in all his animal glory.

"Gosh, that was a great collection," I said, to change the subject. "Look at this amazing cartoon print dress. Reckon that would make a great cover. What do you two think?"

Finally, I felt able to tear myself away and I relinquished the mouse back to Tim. He clicked it a few times, but it was clear he wasn't interested in the cartoon dress.

"Mmmm," he said. "Check that booty. This guy is seriously horny. Who did you say he was? Yummeeee. Your team or mine?"

I legged it back to my desk, before I gave myself away.

Apart from that scary moment, it was actually great to be back in the office, where I shared a little partitioned-off area with Frannie. Officially she was supposed to sit inside the glass office bit with her assistant and my desk was outside, with mine, but we'd swapped the phone numbers over so that Frannie and I were inside, and Janey and Gemma—our loyal right-hand gals—were outside.

We did work quite hard really, but there were also days spent playing with new beauty products, trying on clothes and dancing to the radio that we had on all the time.

"I can't believe I get paid to do this," said Frannie later that morning.

We were testing new face-masks that had been sent in to her—mine was bright pink mud from Arizona, hers was green algae from Brittany—while listening to Radio 2 (it was my turn to choose the station) and reading the latest American magazines which had just landed on our desks. I was reading *Allure* and Frannie was reading US *Vogue*. I had my feet up on my desk and my toenails were drying, a nice bright metallic blue.

"This scenario just needs one more little element for me to achieve complete nirvana," said Frannie. "Bagels and very milky coffee. Janey!"

Eventually, after we'd washed the masks off and scoffed our snacks, which involved splitting a cream cheese and smoked salmon bagel so that Frannie had the bagel and the cream cheese and I had the smoked salmon, I did finally settle down to some proper work.

I seriously needed to get on with it—I only had half an hour to finish my trends list and story proposals for our all-important "New Season Meeting" in Bee's office. Frantically going through the notes of shoot ideas I had made in the back of my fashion shows sketchbook, I realized I would be lucky to finish in time.

This was pretty stupid because it was a crucial meeting. As well as our lists of what we felt were the key trends from the shows we had just seen, we each had to present a plan of the fashion stories (and beauty in Frannie's case) that we wanted to shoot—which meant photograph, but we called it a "shoot"—for the next six months of issues.

As well as the creative ideas, we had to include the more practical details of locations, photographers and models, and exactly how we would style the pictures, so there was quite a lot to it. And it was essential to make your ideas convincing enough to get Bee's approval, because if she chucked them out it could really wreck your tanning plans.

Get it wrong and you'd be down at Camber Sands in the rain shooting the "Catwalk to High Street" budget fashion pages with unknown models, when you'd planned on spending a couple of weeks styling "Edgy Beige" in a tented safari camp in Kenya, with Karolina Kurkova and a vat of Sisley tanning products for company.

Needless to say, never-late-with-her-homework Frannie had finished her lists the first day we had got back from Paris, then she'd used the extra time to gather together visual imagery to support her ideas, which is why she had been looking at the Dior pictures with Mark that morning. She was even planning to wave around some scene-setting joss-sticks during her presentation, which I thought was taking it a bit far.

"I'm going for the full sensurround experience," she'd told me. "I *really* want to do that Japan trip for my incense story."

But apart from general procrastination and flightiness, I had another reason for doing my lists at the last minute. The previous season, when I had done them nice and promptly, Alice had sent her horrid assistant Natalie to get a copy of them and had brazenly pinched two of my best ideas—a direct lift—and passed them off as her own. As fashion director, she always presented her lists first, so it had left me seriously in the shit in the middle of the meeting hav-ing to come up with new ideas off the top of my head.

To make it worse, she didn't seem remotely ashamed of what she'd done and I just hadn't ever felt able to bring it up with her af-terwards. She was my boss, after all, and maybe she thought my ideas were fair game. I hadn't told anyone else about it either, not even Frannie. It was just one of many reasons I didn't much like Miss Alee-chay Pettigrew.

It soon became clear that my instincts had been right about the risk of this daylight robbery being repeated because my loyal helper Gemma had caught Natalie—or Fatalie as I had been known to refer to her—snooping around my desk the day before. Then, just as I was starting to type up my finished proposal, she came in again.

"Alice wants your list," she said, with her usual charm.

"I'm just typing it up now," I said cautiously.

"So when will it be finished?" she demanded.

"Just in time for the meeting, thank you, Natalie," I said, getting seriously pissed off.

"Well, Alice says you have to give your list to me the day before the meeting in future, so she can have it in advance. This is very un-professional."

"Oh, is it, Natalie?" I said. "Well, tell Alice if she wants the list I will give it to her at the meeting. OK?"

She flounced out and Janey and Gemma both made faces at her back as she strutted off, which made Frannie and me roar with laughter.

"What a cheeky bitch," I said, outraged. "How dare she call me unprofessional—even if she was quoting Alice."

"We have a word for girls like her in Scotland," said Frannie, popping a sugary bon-bon into her mouth. "*Sleakit*. I've met stoats I'd trust more than her."

My lists were still belching out of the printer as everyone started to converge on Bee's office for the big meeting. I half expected Alice to come and snatch them from me as she walked in, but she just strolled past, looking unusually relaxed—well, as relaxed as she could look in the overlarge black-framed swot glasses she wore when she wanted to be taken seriously.

It killed me how Alice always dressed the part. To complete her serious meeting look, she was wearing a severe black pantsuit and her hair was scraped back in a tight pony-tail. She was carrying a clipboard. An Hermès clipboard by the look of it, but still a clipboard.

By the appointed hour we were all seated round the meeting table in Bee's large, bright pink office, but she was leaning out of the window smoking. Even the Queen Bee herself wasn't allowed to light up in our offices, so she got round it by blowing her smoke out of the window like a schoolgirl and frantically chewing nicotine gum when that wasn't possible. She had been known to chew the gum and smoke out of the window at the same time. Really it was a miracle she didn't spontaneously combust.

"OK, my little chickens," she said, tossing her cigarette butt down into the street below—I always gave the pavement beneath her office a wide berth when I left the building, for fear of such smouldering missiles—and joined us at the table.

"This better be good," she said, folding her arms and leaning back in her chair. "I'm not in the mood for crap. Fire away, Alee-chay."

Alice kicked off with her key trends and then we went round the table, each reading out our lists, while Bee's assistant Nushka frantically made notes. This would become the "New Season Trends Master List," which was the backbone of the magazine for the next six months and the basis for the catwalk picture supplements that Frannie put together each March and September. Crucial stuff.

After we'd been right round the table with that, it was clear we all agreed on the key directions, which made Bee very happy—she saw it as a sign we were a good tight team—and it put her in a more receptive mood for our shoot plans. Once again, Alice, as fashion director, went first. Her first word made me nearly fall off my chair.

"Sarajevo," she said.

Sarajevo was the first word on my list too. My big idea was to photograph Iggy's collection there, on models who came from all the different states that had made up the former Yugoslavia. There were masses of beautiful girls from those countries on the catwalks in Milan and Paris, which had given me the idea, combined with what Nelly had told me about Iggy's amazing story.

I had also been going to suggest that we asked Iggy to come with us for the shoot, and to have one of our top writers interview him in his home town. I was really pleased with this as a package, because I thought Iggy's story really needed to be told—but also because I knew Bee would love it.

It had all the elements that would appeal to the "intelligent, politically aware and passionately interested in international affairs" *Chic* readers I had heard her describe on so many occasions. Usually to gormless beauty PRs who were terribly impressed and thought these were just the women who needed to know about their new lip glosses.

I just sat there with my mouth hanging open as I heard Alice spouting my exact idea. She must have stolen it from me, but it didn't make any sense—I had only just typed my list out, so she couldn't have cribbed it. Was it really possible that she had simply come up with the same idea as me—synchronicity and all that? But that seemed unlikely as I didn't think she even knew Iggy's story. Maybe she was psychic.

"I think having the profile as well would add a deeper level of meaning to the pictures," Alice was droning on in her deepest, most monotonous "intellectual" voice. "It would be pretty amazing to hear how Iggy feels about what happened in his country and how that relates back to his work."

"Yes," said Bee, beaming at her and actually *clapping*. "That is absolutely brilliant. Wonderful stuff, Alice. Although I must say I've always been pretty shaky on exactly what happened over there myself. Which side was Iggy on anyway? Is he a Muslim, an Albanian, a Croat, or what? And who were the baddies anyway? Can you enlighten me, Alice?"

I saw a look of naked terror flash across Alice's face behind her Elvis Costello specs.

"Er, I'm not sure," she said, her eyes flicking left and right like a terrified cat. "But I'm sure Iggy will be able to put us all in the picture."

She definitely didn't know his story, I realized. Very few people did and Nelly certainly wouldn't have told the woman she referred to as Prune Face, so how could she possibly have come up with the idea on her own? Now I was really baffled.

"Do you know, Emily?" asked Bee, popping three pieces of nicotine gum into her mouth. "Has Nelly filled you in?"

"Yes, she has actually," I said, looking straight at Alice, who just blinked back at me. She didn't look remotely guilty, just nervous. I was absolutely bewildered.

"And?" said Bee, getting narky with me.

"Er, it's all really complicated, as you said. He's a mixture. His mother is a Bosnian Muslim and his father is a Serb—not a Bosnian Serb, though, a Serb-Serb. He moved to Bosnia from Belgrade—which is in Serbia—to be with Iggy's mum. And his grandfather was Russian actually, which is why he's called Igor, which is not really a Serbian name."

"Fuck me," said Bee. "I didn't know you worked for NATO, Emily. It is complicated, isn't it? We'll have to get a really serious writer on this, maybe that brainy bird who's married to Martin Amis, whatsername? She's been to Albania. Marvellous stuff anyway, Alice. Great to see you thinking about the features angle too. Now, what else do you have for me?"

The rest of Alice's list was more her usual fare. For her big-name designer story, for which she got to choose her pick of the best outfits in the best collections, which always really annoyed the stink out of me, she was going to do "Asian Influences."

This involved shooting a new Chinese model everyone was talking about, *naked* in a bare room, with the clothes being held up in the background by children of many colours. On black and white film. I mentally crossed my eyes. If I hadn't been so furious I would already have been anticipating taking the piss out of it with Nelly.

For "Green" she wanted to shoot on a racecourse—you know, "turf"—with the models running alongside real racehorses, wearing papier-mâché horses' heads. Those were her big art ideas, then there was the usual list of shoots which involved her going to fabulously hot and glamorous locations and working on her tan.

Normally I would have kicked Frannie's foot under the table

when we got to the horses' heads bit, but I was too upset about my Sarajevo idea to care, so I just tuned out and tried to think of another shoot idea quick, as I was now missing one and I was up next. Luckily for me my list already included several of the aspirational-but-accessible ideas that Bee loved, the ones that had got me the job at *Chic* in the first place, which would give me time to think of another idea.

When my turn came I started with the second idea on my list, enthusiastically explaining how I wanted to shoot vintage-style satin dresses in an old hotel I had heard about in Prague—all fabulous fading fabrics and old gilt furniture—on four models with long romantic wavy hair who were sisters in real life.

Then there was an upbeat stripes story to be shot on stripy deck-chairs in a studio—cute and cheap to do, so I knew that was a winner. For beachwear I suggested doing an incredibly glamorous bikini cover-up story in art deco Miami, with the girls getting out of pastel-coloured convertible cars driven by really gorgeous men with slicked-down hair, great tans and no shirts on. Very Cosmo 1975.

Then, desperate to replace Sarajevo, I dredged up that old fashion editor's favourite—holiday packing—and made it up as I went along.

"I thought we could do it as a kind of pictorial narrative," I heard myself saying, with no idea what was going to come out of my mouth next, while another part of my brain was madly trying to decide where I most wanted to go to shoot it. I was determined to salvage something from this disaster. Sun, or shopping? I was mentally asking myself as I spoke.

"I thought we would base it around a capsule wardrobe of mix and match pieces, in the classic way," I continued. "But we'd shoot it in the luggage department of Macy's . . ."

Bingo, New York, that was where I wanted to go. I could see Ursula and Paul could do the make-up. Bliss. Thank you, brain.

"So," I continued, getting into my stride. "We'll show her trying to pack her capsule wardrobe in several different suitcases and trying different bits of it on together as she packs. Then we'd see her getting into a yellow taxi with her luggage and then at the airport, checking in. Next she'll be in her hotel room hanging the clothes up and then finally down at the bar having a drink in her evening look."

I was on a roll. I continued, "And in each shot she would have changed just one piece of clothing, so through the story we will gradually show every piece of the capsule wardrobe, demonstrating how it all works together. Day to night and all that," I added, throwing in one of Bee's favourite phrases for good measure.

I amazed myself. I had no idea where that came from—and I liked it. So did Bee. She was beaming at me between her madly chewing jaws.

"Love it, Emily," she said. "Love it. Classic *Chic* stories all of them, especially the holiday wardrobe. You really get it—practical glamour, that's what *Chic* is all about. Intelligent glamour."

It was all very lovely, but I was so weirded out by the Sarajevo incident I couldn't really relish her praise.

Everyone was on a bit of a high after the meeting, as none of us had stuffed up. With just a few tweaks here and there, Bee had been happy with all our ideas and we were all blissfully relieved it was over for another season, because if Bee didn't like your suggestions, you really knew about it. Six months earlier one of the junior fashion editors had walked out of the office during the planning meeting and never come back, after getting roughed up by Bee over her lame suggestions.

Frannie, in particular, was ecstatic as her incense story had been a winner, which meant she was off to Kyoto—the place she had always most wanted to go. When we got back to our little room, she suggested we nick off for the rest of the afternoon with Janey and Gemma and go to Sketch for tea, to celebrate.

I tried to dredge up some enthusiasm, but although I was delighted that—thanks to my quick thinking—I would now be going to New York and seeing Paul and Ursula twice in the next couple of months, the Sarajevo thing was really bugging me. In fact, that's how I felt, like I'd been bugged. It was really unsettling.

Of course I did agree to go to Sketch, for Frannie's sake and also because I fancied the idea of a stroll past the shops in Conduit Street afterwards.

We sat in the salon de thé and Frannie had three elaborate cakes—arguing that she would lose loads of weight eating all that raw fish in Japan, so it didn't matter what she ate now—but I had to make a real effort to look like I was having a good time. Cake is not really my thing.

But I did my best to hide it because I didn't want to dampen Frannie's excitement—and because I didn't want to tell her what was bothering me. It was just too humiliating. So I just sipped some Earl Grey and filed the Sarajevo incident away with all the other things I wasn't thinking about, while Frannie and the girls stuffed themselves and chattered away.

Then I did what I always did when I wanted to put something out of my mind. I went shopping.

12

LOOKING back it must have been the Sarajevo story incident that made me first even consider leaving *Chic*. I loved my job, I loved my colleagues—well, most of them—I was still really proud to work for such a legendary magazine and I even loved Bee on the whole.

So if that hadn't happened I don't think I would have taken any notice when Ollie started suggesting that I should consider moving on "to broaden my résumé," as he put it. He first brought it up when we were out doing the food shopping for a Sunday salon, just a few days after the new season meeting.

"You've been there three years now," he was saying. "It's long enough. Look at your résumé so far—you've done the street-cred style magazines, the mass-market mag and the classic fashion magazine, which is a great combo, but if you really want to move into the international big league, I think you need to do something really niche. Something which will resonate with the people at the very top end of fashion. Something independent, but highly sophisticated, would be the way to go now to position you perfectly for the next stage."

"I'm not a mascara, Ollie," I said, sniffing a bunch of Kaffir lime leaves to see if they were fresh—I was doing Vietnamese food that week.

"Oh, but you are," he replied, tentatively inspecting a jar of something that looked scarily like pickled cockroaches. "We're all products. You've got to think of yourself as a brand to get ahead these days. Start by giving yourself a sell line: Emily Pointer, luxury fashion stylist . . ."

"And international woman of mystery?" I said, holding two large bunches of coriander up to my head and pulling a face.

"That could work . . ." said Ollie, in all seriousness.

"I was joking, you twit," I said hitting him round the head with the herbs. "Anyway, it's Saturday and I don't want to talk about work. Do you think we should get some of these bamboo steamers to serve the food in?"

We did, of course, and stacks of pretty blue and white rice bowls and loads of lacquered chopsticks in loads of different bright colours. As usual we didn't know exactly how many people were coming, so it was always better to over-cater in our opinion.

Ollie had done all the inviting this time. He said I'd done enough just persuading Nelly and Iggy to come—they were in London to clear her flat and do the parents thing—and I assumed he had worked the rest of the guest list to maximize the benefit of that coup. I left him to obsess on all that nonsense; I was just really excited about seeing Nelly and Iggy.

So was Peter Potter, who was one of the first to arrive. Of course Ollie had no idea how much I had come to loathe the little creep, he'd just been thrilled that inviting him to a Sunday salon the last time had reaped our parties a mention in Peter's column as a "really refreshing way to entertain in w11," with Slap and Ollie getting bold-print name mentions.

I had been glossed over as "his stylist girlfriend," which didn't really bother me in terms of my ego, but confirmed my fears that the poison dwarf had it in for me. I was hardly a "girlfriend," I was married to Ollie, and Peter well knew it, but hopefully this second invitation might make him rather less ill-disposed towards me, as well as boosting Ollie's personal profile a little more.

Nelly was also less than thrilled to see Mr. Potter—or Harry, as she had taken to calling him—after slightly too many mentions of her private business in his column.

"What have you gone and invited 'Arry Potter for?" she hissed at me, when I took her and Iggy into the bedroom to see the fabulous Boudicca jacket I'd bought on my Conduit Street shopping spree. "I mean, he's all right for a laugh, but now I'll have to watch what I say all through lunch. I won't be able to get properly pissed—boring. Why didn't you get Louise Kretzner along as well and really stuff me up?"

She punched me gently on the arm.

"I'm sorry," I said, grimacing at them in sympathy. "It was Ollie, he thinks being friends with Rotter will help get Slap mentioned on the telly."

Nelly roared with laughter. "Rotter! I love it. I'd better be careful or I'll call him that to his face. But your bloody 'usband, Em," she was shaking her head. "He'd do anything to flog that bloody make-up, wouldn't he? I'm surprised he don't wear it himself."

Her face brightened suddenly in a way I knew could lead to big fun, or big trouble, in equal doses. "I think I'll suggest that to him actually," she said, looking thrilled with the idea. "He could double up his market opportunities—as I'm sure he calls them—if he could sell his stuff to blokes as well. Here you are, Ig," she said, going into the bathroom and opening my overstocked make-up cupboard. "Put this lippie on. We'll have a laugh with him."

She started applying dark red lip gloss to Iggy's willing lips. He didn't object. He seemed to think anything Nelly did was marvellous.

"You know he'll end up in *The Daily Reporter* as a cross-dresser, don't you?" I said, watching them from the door.

Nelly didn't even listen. She was coating mascara on to Iggy's already long and luxuriant eyelashes. I went back into the living area to find it full of people I didn't know, although Ollie seemed terrifically happy to see them all.

"Ah, darling," he said, coming over and taking my hand. "I want you to meet this crowd, I don't think you know them. This is Donovan Pertwee—he's a brilliant designer and decorator. Worked with Philippe Starck on the Sanderson, now he's doing that new hotel in Soho—you know, the Wigwam. Donovan—this is my wife, Emily Pointer. She's senior fashion editor on *Chic*."

I shook hands with a small dark-haired man who looked like he had recently swallowed something very unpleasant. It may well have been his own tongue as he just grunted in reply to my welcome. Next Ollie turned me—he had his hands on my shoulders and was manoeuvring me round like some kind of puppet—towards a nervous-looking fellow wearing a brown corduroy suit and a bright purple polo neck.

"Now, Emily, this is Mike Hurleigh-Bromgrove—he has that genius new shop Sweep, in Brick Lane, remember we read about it in the *Telegraph* mag? Sells all those marvellous Romanian dustpans . . ."

This was typical of Ollie's introductions. You never just got the name, you got a potted CV, career history and press cuttings service thrown in too, presumably so you could decide how useful they were going to be to you and could bother with them accordingly. I was shaking hands, how-do-you-doing and smiling like the ambassador's wife I was.

"Now who else don't you know?" Ollie was continuing. "This is Gilda Jansson, the wallpaper designer. Marvellous stuff, it was in *Chic Interiors* last month, remember? This is Emily . . ."

I did remember. They'd wallpapered the inside of cardboard boxes with it as a witty styling idea—decorating for the homeless. Frannie had thrown the magazine across the room with disgust when she saw it. Ollie was still wittering on. "Now Sammie King, you must know, she does the homes pages for *The Sunday Courier* magazine and this is her, er, partner, Elinor, who does amazing tiling. You know, Elinor, I'd really like you to look at our shower, I think it could look great in that Byzantine style you did in that house in Palm Springs . . ."

I was quite dumbfounded. It was the weirdest guest list to invite to meet the world's most exciting new fashion name. I'd been expecting major magazine editors and all the newspaper fashion girls, not a bunch of po-faced interior decorators and wallpaper designers.

Things did get a little more normal as even more guests arrived—I was glad I'd made plenty of *phô* to feed them all. There was Katy Jennings, the lovely beauty editor from *pure* who was a great friend of Nelly's, Frannie's and mine—we'd shared many a wild night together after spot concealer launches. And then, as a special surprise for me, there was Frannie herself and her husband Andy.

They were a surprise to Ollie too, it turned out, as Nelly had invited them on our behalf. I was delighted, because while Frannie was always keen to come over to our place, Andy felt the same way about our salons as Nelly did and after they'd been once I could never get them to join us again. I'd given up asking them, as I had with Nelly.

Andy had only agreed to show up on this occasion, I knew, because it was Nelly who'd called and suggested it. I was glad I didn't know exactly what she'd said to persuade him, but I'm sure the words "that wanker" and "just ignore" featured. I knew that's what they thought of Ollie, but it didn't bother me. I'd decided long before that his tendency to pretentiousness was just a kind of eccentricity and I found it rather endearing. And I could be a tad on the precious side myself, given half a chance.

Now it was my turn to do the introductions and I took great pleasure in introducing Andy McAllister to Ollie's new interiors pals as "the hottest landscape gardener in west London."

"Yes," said Andy, whose Dundee accent was even stronger than Frannie's. "I wear thermal underwear under my woollie jumpers. Two layers. Makes me very hot. So does my flask of cocoa."

The last guests to arrive were two of Ollie's more normal strategic Slap invitees. There was Maeve Fischer, who was the make-up buyer for one of the big department stores—I was never quite sure which one, as she was always changing jobs, although it seemed she was now at Storridges, the hottest store in town—and Hervé Moret, a leading French make-up artist.

The final piece of the human jigsaw—which made fifteen people, a lot, even by our standards—was a woman called Rosie Stanton, who I knew of from around the fashion scene, but didn't actually know. I'd seen a lot of her work, though, and was always impressed by it.

Rosie was a highly respected and rather intellectual fashion writer, a former fashion editor on the brainy broadsheet, *The Sunday Courier,* who had gone freelance to concentrate on books. Her biography of Rudi Gernreich—the man who invented the topless swimsuit—had received brilliant reviews and I had bought a copy, although I'd only ever looked at the pictures.

Despite that, I was really pleased to have the opportunity to meet her properly as I'd always been rather fascinated by her. Mainly because, while she wrote about fashion with amazing knowledge and authority, she was astonishingly badly dressed herself. It didn't seem to matter that she hung out with the world's most stylish and image-aware people, none of it ever rubbed off on her. When it came to pulling together a look, she was a shocker.

On this occasion she was wearing the most horrendous pair of wooden parrot earrings—which kept getting all caught up in her rather frizzy hair—and I really wasn't sure if they were brilliantly ironic, or she truly thought they were great. They could just as well have been given to her by some amazing new conceptual Dutch designer, or her seven-year-old kid sister. I really couldn't tell.

The rest of her ensemble was a bobbly pink cardigan with a ragged bit of velvet edging—"vintage" Voyage—an old Ghost skirt in a murky shade of mauve and some really scruffy Emma Hope yellow satin slippers with black opaque tights in between. Completing her assemblage was an Anya Hindmarch Be A Bag, which featured a photograph of Rosie as a very fat baby in a saggy nappy. It was not what you would call a good look.

Despite her lack of personal style, Bee was always trying to get Rosie to write fashion "essays" for *Chic* and I thought I might be able to use this opportunity to talk her into it and win some major points with the boss. So I was delighted, when I peered over Ollie's shoulder as he hastily revised his placement scheme, to see that he had put me next to her.

We finally had them all sitting at the table when Nelly and Iggy made their re-entrance. His hair and clothes were the same as when he arrived—naturally jet black locks in a sexy Caesar cut, a dark grey Prada suit and a deep raspberry-pink shirt—but he was fully made up. It was quite a sight.

There were two full heartbeats of amazed silence and then

everyone—well, everyone who knew who they were, the decorators just sat there blankly—went nuts cheering, laughing and clapping.

He actually looked quite amazing. Iggy was very handsome in a sultry Gypsy King kind of way and Nelly's over-the-top make-up job had somehow enhanced his features without making him look like a total drag queen. He was overtly wearing make-up—it wasn't one of those tragic "no one will know but you" man tan jobs—but he was such a fundamentally male bloke, he didn't look camp.

"There you are, Ollie," said Nelly. "What do you think? Slap for Chaps. Reckon it will work for you?"

"It's brilliant," said Ollie, jumping up from his chair, he was so thrilled. It was just the kind of idea he could never have come up with himself. "I love it. Wow, I seriously love it."

"What do you reckon, Harry Potter?" Nelly shouted over to Peter. "Reckon you can use this in your column, darls?"

"Should be in news pages," said Iggy, in his strongly accented English. "I am first Serbian man ever to wear mascara."

Everybody roared again and what could have been the weirdest Sunday salon of all time, actually turned into one of the best.

Potter the Rotter was able to boost his ego filling in the decorator set on exactly who Iggy was—and how well *he* knew him. And once they realized Iggy was the designer who had been splashed all over every major newspaper the day after his debut show a couple of weeks before, they clearly felt a lot more excited about meeting him.

Rotter was also stoked up because the man make-up was such a great item for his column, enhanced further when Iggy gave him some great quotes about how he had wanted to try the make-up to see how it really felt to *be* a woman so he could design for them better. Nelly was winking at me over Rotter's shoulder the whole time Iggy was talking, making it clear that she had rehearsed it all with him, which greatly added to my enjoyment of the scenario.

Above all, Ollie was beside himself with glee. He knew the incident would be in Rotter's column and seeing the sacred brand name in print alongside Iggy's would be brilliant for its cool credibility—and his. I could also tell he was genuinely excited by Nelly's whole concept of Slap for Chaps and the next thing I knew, he, Rotter,

Donovan and Mike had all gone off giggling into the bathroom with Hervé and Maeve to get their own looks done. The only man who declined was Andy.

"I'd rather set light to my own hair," he said and settled on a sofa with a can of Guinness and a book about Andy Goldsworthy, which we had featured on one of our coffee-table piles. "And I mean my pubic hair."

I went over to the kitchen to see to the food and Nelly came and leaned against the counter, grinning broadly.

"How do you rate that for damage control then?" she asked me, holding out her wineglass for a refill. "That should keep Harry Rotter off our backs for the rest of the lunch, don't you think?"

"Nelly Stelios," I said with frank admiration. "You are a serious piece of work."

"Yeah, mama," she said and put her hand up for a Paul-style high-five. "Gimme some flesh. Reckon your husband might hold me in higher esteem as well after this. Oh, look, here he comes now—Widow Twankie himself."

And there was Ollie lavishly made up, the full catastrophe. I put my face in my hands and groaned, it was so weird, but when I could stand to look at him again I had to admit it rather suited him. It was a more exaggerated treatment than Iggy's, with rosy spots on his cheeks, pink glossy lips, bright blue eye shadow and a large beauty spot. He looked like a Regency fop and it went perfectly with his personality.

He came over and leaned his face into mine. "What do you think, darling?" he asked, batting his eyelids.

"Er, it's actually quite great," I said. "But please don't *ever* wear it in public. That really would be taking brand loyalty too far. And don't kiss me—you'll get lipstick on my collar."

One by one the boys came in wearing their make-up looks, which were all different and all strangely suited to them. The last out was Hervé who had done himself up like Louise Brooks, right down to combing his spiky hair down into a sleek bob with one of Ollie's many free grooming products. He looked amazing.

They were all so overexcited it was like trying to organize a chimps' tea party, but I did finally get them all back to the table—except Andy, who elected to have his food on the sofa, as he worked his way through our art, interiors and photography "library," as Ollie called it, and the six-pack of Guinness he had brought with him.

Trying to eat just prompted more hysteria about the boys not spoiling their lippie, which reminded Ollie he had a box of promotional Slap mirror compacts in his study and he handed one out to everybody so they could check their *maquillage* between bites.

He also cracked open one of the cases of champagne he always had on hand for such "emergencies" and the party just took off from there. It was the Nelly effect again.

Despite all the squealing and acting up that was going on—all of it being cranked up to greater heights by Nelly and Rotter, who were getting on famously—there was plenty of chat as well and I had a really fascinating discussion with Iggy and Rosie about whether designers really needed to have fashion shows any more.

Rosie, I soon realized, was one of those clever people who make you feel cleverer than normal, because you have to try harder to keep up—rather like playing tennis with someone better than you. The combination of her brain and Iggy's first-hand experience—and a few cogent little observations from me as a third-row veteran—added up to a debate that could have gone straight on to Radio 4.

I was surprised how much I enjoyed it, as a contrast to the hilarious, but rather sillier banter that was my normal idea of a good time. I felt really stimulated mentally and it was a very nice change. Probably, I had to admit to myself, because it reminded me of the kind of conversations that used to go on around my parents' dinner table.

I used to love listening to them from a hiding place under a console table in the hall, where my brother Toby and I would be sitting ready to make raids on the leftover cheese and puddings as soon as the grown-ups left the table. My parents may have had "artistic temperaments" to the point of being actually barmy, but they were rather brainy too.

But needless to say with Nelly present and a case of champagne on the go, it wasn't long before the lost art of conversation was lost all over again in favour of disco dancing. It was great fun, of course, and I even started to like Ollie's new decorator friends, who turned out to be OK once they let go of their off-putting sangfroid.

It was, I realized, just a necessary part of being accepted in their tiny world, just as being as silly as possible was in mine. It was a professional face, a mask, rather than the real person—with the possible exception of Gilda the wallpaper designer, who really was boring and took herself incredibly seriously.

She even danced seriously, making very deliberate shapes with her arms and body, which I'm sure she thought were terribly "graphic." She looked like she was pretending to be an Anglepoise lamp. It was Frannie who pointed it out.

"Would you look at Laurie Anderson," she whispered to me and then to Nelly and Katy, until the four of us were in such hysterics we had to run off to my bedroom together to jump up and down and copy her. For the rest of the evening we just had to catch one another's eye and assume a tiny little angular pose to render the others insensible with laughter. I loved jokes like that.

Ollie didn't get it, though. It was after two in the morning when they had all finally gone home and we were having a post-party post-mortem in the bathroom, as I helped Ollie take his make-up off.

"What do you mean Laurie Anderson?" he said, a bit crossly, as I tried to wipe off the copious layers of mascara Hervé had caked on to his lashes. "Ow! That was my eye. I need that."

"Sorry, darling, try to keep them shut. Oh, you know, all that short hair and severe clothes and the 'art dancing.' You've got to admit Gilda takes herself a bit seriously, Ollie."

"I don't know what you mean. I think she's lovely—and she's a very talented designer."

"She designs *wallpaper*," I said, rather contemptuously, but sensing I might have gone too far and not wanting to spoil such a great day—and night—I tried to make amends.

"I really like Mike and Donovan," I said quickly. "They're lovely."

"Aren't they great?" said Ollie enthusiastically. "I knew you'd love them."

"Yes, and I thought Sam and Elinor were, er, nice too. It made a nice change. So where did you meet all these design people, all of a sudden?"

"Oh, I've been going to quite a few interiors events recently, you know, checking out the market to see if it is the way to go with Slap. I must say, so far, I think it is a very interesting arena, which is not being fully exploited by the beauty market, so I intend to do so before any of my competitors cotton on to it. It's definitely where you'll find your really sophisticated consumer these days."

He amazed me with his ability to spout all that crapola at two in the morning after so much champagne, but that was my Ollie. He really believed his own bullshit. It was sweet, really. I chucked his cheeks affectionately and massaged Eve Lom cleanser all over his face and neck. Then I showed him how to rub it off with the damp muslin cloth.

"Not that I don't still value your world, of course, Emily," he continued, scrubbing frantically at his neck. "Iggy's a great guy and I have to say I was quite wrong about Nelly. She's really a super girl at heart. Terrific spirit. What they did with the make-up—it was amazing. Bloody hell, it's hard to get off, though, isn't it?"

He paused and looked down at the cloth which was quite orange with foundation, blusher and concealer. "God, I didn't know it was such a hassle to get rid of it. Don't think I'll be taking it up as a daily look."

That was a relief.

13

THE next day at work there was a memo on my desk that made it clear it was time to get down to some serious scheming and planning. It was Bee's official plan for the fashion to go into the next six months of magazines, listing which stories she had slated for each issue.

So while I had got over the first hurdle of having her agree in principle to my creative ideas, now I had to do the budgets and travel itineraries for each of them and get her to approve those.

This was a lot less glamorous than the fashion-shows and launch-parties side of my job, but it wasn't enough just to have the poncy ideas—to be a great stylist you had to be able to make them happen too. It was surprisingly complicated and Bee was quite obsessed that we did it all ourselves, so we would fully understand the "macroprocesses" of the magazine.

She was always lecturing us about it and she'd started indoctrinating me on my very first day at *Chic*, when she'd called me in to her office for a welcoming coffee and a pep talk.

"This may look like a glossy magazine," she'd said, waving a copy of *Chic* at me. "But actually it's just a business like any other."

It was so like the kind of bollocky thing Ollie said, I felt my mouth twitch and hoped I wasn't going to get the giggles. Luckily for me Bee was in full flow and didn't notice.

"Here on *Chic* we are all lucky enough to earn our livings doing something creative that we love," she was saying with great sincerity. "But while we are very fortunate in that regard, we are *not* artists—never forget that. We're business women and that's how I want you to think of yourself, as a mini managing director."

My face must have fallen. That is the last way I had ever wanted to think of myself. I suppose I was more deeply imbued with my parents' code of noble creativity than I'd realized.

"Don't look so horrified," Bee had continued. "You'll still be able to swan about swooning over the perfect shade of beige, just inform every decision you make while you work here with this fundamental piece of business wisdom: the less money we spend producing this magazine the more profit it will make and the more secure all our futures will be. Geddit?"

I nodded earnestly. I didn't particularly like it, but I did get it.

"Good," said Bee. "Now go and make me beautiful fashion pictures."

Frannie—whose political views were as red as her hair—used to fume about creative people like us being forced into being mini accountants, as she called it.

"I don't want to be mini anything," she'd said. "I want to be big."

"You will be," I had replied, flippantly. "If you carry on eating all those sweeties."

I knew what she meant, though. The difference was that after four years living with Ollie and his genuine excitement about things like percentage yields, bottom lines, cost appraisals and profit projections, I was more able to mould myself into a "corporate drone"—as Frannie called me.

I still found the budgeting part of the job pretty onerous, though. The managing editor had done it all at *Gorgeous,* and on the style magazines where I'd worked before that, there was no budgeting because there was no budget. On those mags, you got everyone involved to work for nothing in exchange for the prestigious "tear sheets"—which is what we called the actual printed pages of photographs that came out in the magazine. We all worked gratis because those groovy pages got us the boring catalogue work where we made our money.

But although I recoiled from it, I was smart enough to realize it was better to accept budgeting as a necessary evil at *Chic*—and to get good at it. Ollie was a big help, sitting me down at his laptop and showing me what a spreadsheet was and how to use one. It was torture, but I had the enticing carrot of knowing it would help me convince Bee to let me go careering off to Buenos Aires, or wherever, to do a shoot. After that, as long as I kept my mind on the goal, I could be quite the little Uriah Heep with my budget.

Bee had been very impressed the first time I had handed her one of my professional-looking printouts shortly after I joined the magazine. Because while she was very generous with the hotels, limos and dinners while we were at the shows—all part of the magazine's image—she watched every penny when it came to putting the editorial together.

She'd spend when she needed to, when it would make a real difference to the magazine—to get an amazing model for a cover shoot, or to fly a name writer across the world to do an exclusive interview—but the rest of the time she was like a miser with the company money. We all suspected it was because she was secretly on a profit-share deal with the management, but we weren't game to ask her.

Whatever her motives, she was so impressed by my computer-generated budget, she had called Alice in to see it.

"Now, Alee-chay," she'd said. "Look at this. A proper spreadsheet. This is how you need to do your budgets. I don't want to see any more of those terrible little sums you do on the back of envelopes, and if you learn to do it properly, like Emily here, you won't keep going over budget with your shoots and I won't have to keep bollocking you about it. And believe it or not, I don't actually enjoy doing that."

I was mortified. Alice had just stood there, looking like a naughty schoolgirl—and, no doubt, all too aware that she was inappropriately dressed for the occasion, in a drippy cheesecloth sundress and flat Greek sandals. She'd just come back from shooting at Jade Jagger's house in Ibiza. It was not a power look.

Adding to the misfortune of the timing, I was wearing a crisp black poplin shirt-dress, tightly belted, with high heels. I looked like Smart Businesswoman Barbie and I was a good head taller than Alice too. I sat down quickly. You don't survive a girls' boarding school without learning the catastrophic implications of such moments.

But Alice didn't look at me with the loathing I was expecting. In fact, she didn't look at me at all, until Bee brought me back into the conversation. She was clearly hoping that if she ignored me hard enough I would cease to exist.

"I tell you what, Emily," said Bee. "As you are clearly so good with computers and figures, why don't you show Alee-chay how to do this?"

Now, I realized, I had a chance to redeem myself. It meant sacrificing serious points with Bee, but I really didn't want Alice to hate me when I had only just started my new job. She was my immediate boss, after all, and she could make my life hell if she wanted to. I also didn't particularly relish the artificial goodie-two-shoes role I had been pushed into. So I plunged in.

"Actually, Bee," I said. "I have to confess it was Ollie who showed me how to do all this—I didn't have a clue where to start. I've never had to do a budget before."

Bee roared with laughter.

"I should have known," she said. "That husband of yours can manipulate figures like a bent chancellor, especially to show why he should pay less for advertising in this magazine. How very funny."

"I'm sure he'd be happy to show Alice—and all the editors—how to do this as well," I said, quickly. "He'd do anything to butter you up, Bee," I added, unable to resist a small arse-lick.

So the following week, Alice, Frannie, the two junior fashion editors and all the fashion assistants, had gone over to Ollie's offices for a morning's training in how to do budgets on a computer spreadsheet, followed by a low carbs lunch and a bumper Slap gift pack as a going-home present—Ollie never missed a marketing opportunity.

I went along too, so as not to feel outside the team, and found it quite a fascinating insight into my new colleagues. Like most of them, Frannie just sat there resignedly and took it all in, but it was quite obvious that despite Ollie's charismatic presentation skills—and he was a great teacher—Alice didn't have a clue what he was talking about and couldn't care less either.

I wondered whether she had ever actually turned a computer on, she looked so blank throughout the whole thing. She didn't jot anything down, or even open the folder of colour-coded tips and hints that Ollie had specially prepared.

Luckily for her, she'd brought Natalie along, who sat right at the front, making copious notes and answering all Ollie's questions with great enthusiasm, her plump brown bosoms heaving with excitement. At the end of the session, Ollie had awarded her a special prize as the star pupil—he was very keen on motivating people—and I would have sworn she was flirting with him as she accepted it. Little fucker.

But that all seemed a lifetime ago, as I sat down to do my fashion shoot planning, and apart from Alice, who left them entirely to Natalie to do, we had all become pretty slick at doing our spreadsheets since then. I'd even taught a new junior fashion editor how to do it all by myself.

Now, with six months of shoots to plan, the first stage of the process was for me and Gemma to sit down with Bee's memo, our diaries and the magazine production schedule and make a plan of which photographs we needed to have ready by when, to get my stories into the issues they were planned for. I quickly saw that my first one was needed in just over a month. We had a lot to do.

Flights and hotels had to be booked—or scammed in exchange for editorial mentions—photographers had to be hired in and models secured, a process so complicated we had a dedicated "bookings editor" to look after it all. We had to, because the people we worked with were in constant demand and their agents juggled them relentlessly to get the best gig for them. It was like some giant game trying to match the required dates with the optimum people.

Quite often you'd get the whole thing in place, only to have it fall apart when your model suddenly got offered a major advertising job. Then you'd lose the photographer as well, because he was only doing it to work with that model, and then the superstar make-up artist and household-name hairdresser would drop out because they only worked with that photographer.

It was quite normal to see a fashion editor banging her head on the desk after such disappointments. At least, that's what I used to do. Frannie would send out for doughnuts when her shoots fell apart and, as far as we could tell, Alice just used to disappear and leave Natalie to sort it out for her.

Then, finally, only when all that structure was in place, could we start to call the bloody clothes in. And that was another whole number. You couldn't necessarily just snap your fingers and get the dress, suit, or coat you fancied photographing, oh no.

First of all you had to check that the thing you had liked on the catwalk was ever actually going to be made—many of the more showstopping outfits were just run up to grab the attention of tabloid newspaper picture editors—and then if it would actually ever be on sale anywhere in the UK. And if it wasn't, you couldn't feature it in *Chic*. Bee was firm on that.

Even once you had established these points you had to duck and dive to get the press samples of the pieces you wanted and hope that they hadn't already been nabbed by other stylists for their shoots. Designers only had one set of samples for each season's collection to lend out to all the magazines and newspapers, and it was really competitive for the "key" pieces.

It could wreck your whole story if *Vogue* had already flown down to Rio with the particular outfit you wanted to take to Rajasthan. FedEx made a fortune flying hot pants from one part of the world to another on such occasions.

And then, of course, there were fashion editors who had been known to hold on to samples deliberately because they knew other stylists wanted them; just to fuck them up. It was brutal.

Sometimes it worked the other way, though, and there had been a hilarious day when I had been shooting on one part of Flamands Beach on St. Barths, and Nelly had been working a few hundred yards along with her crew. We had spent the whole day running up and down the beach in bikinis trading outfits along the lines of: I'll

give you this Lanvin, if I can have that Balenciaga. It was hilarious.
If Bee and Beaver had only known . . .

After a couple of hours of pencil chewing, Gemma and I had our
action plan for the season in place, and she went off to talk to the
travel editor about deals for New York and Prague, while I got on
the phone to Ollie to discuss dates. I didn't want to organize all my
work travel and then find it clashed with some Slap event he desperately needed me to go to, or the flights he would be booking for
our planned trips to Milan and New York.

I left three messages with his secretary and two texts on his
"phone off" mobile, before he finally got back to me. Sometimes it
was a royal pain having a high flier for a husband.

"Hello, darling," I said cheerily. "Busy?"

"Frantic," he said. "You'll never guess what's happened—Peter
Potter has told the paper's features editor what happened on Sunday and they're doing a whole feature about Slap for Chaps. A
double-page spread. It's fantastic. I've had one of their reporters in
here all morning doing an interview and just now a researcher from
Wakey Wakey called up. They're going to do a big segment on it
too. I've sent Nelly flowers and the entire Slap range to thank her."

"Aha," I said. "I wondered why your assistant asked me where
'Miss Stelios' was staying when I spoke to her earlier—one of the
many times I spoke to your assistant today . . ."

"I'm sorry, my angel, Steffie did tell me you'd been calling. I've
been frantic. Now you have my complete attention. So what can
I do for you?"

"I just want to talk about travel dates—I'm trying to fix my
shoots up and I wondered when you were thinking about for our
trips to Milan and New York."

There was a distinct pause—very unusual for Ollie, he very
rarely needed to stop to gather his thoughts.

"Ollie?" I said. "Are you still there?"

"Yes, yes, of course I am. I'm just thinking about those trips, you
see, the thing is, I think this Slap for Chaps idea might take off—I
mean *really* take off—and I don't want to miss any opportunities

by being away between now and Christmas. Then it's the New Year and we have our audit coming up in January, as you know, which is always huge and then it's sales conference and then you're off to the shows again, so I don't really see when we can do it."

I was amazed. Ollie loved our trips together, he'd never cancelled one before. Even if it had meant going to New York for just two nights, we'd do it.

"So you don't want to do Milan *or* New York?" I said slowly, honestly not sure if I had properly understood what he was saying.

"I'm sorry, Em, I hate to disappoint you, but I really don't think I can do the whole New York jet lag thing—not to mention all the partying we'd do there. Not with all I've got on at the moment."

"OK," I said, flatly. I was really disappointed. I loved going to New York with Ollie, we always had an amazing time, but I made a quick decision not to whine about it, because at least I was going there for my fashion trip.

"But what about Milan?" I asked him.

I wasn't prepared to let that trip go so easily. I'd really been looking forward to hitting the luxury brands Bermuda Triangle with Ollie and his credit cards by my side.

"After yesterday I don't feel I need to go rushing over there to bond with Nelly and Iggy," said Ollie, back to his usual quick and slick replies. "We're fully bonded. I think they're both great."

I certainly wasn't going to tell him that they might not be living there anyway.

"But what about looking at Slap's Italian retail opportunities?" I said, still thinking I might be able to persuade him. "I thought that was important too."

"Well, that is important, Emily, you're right," said Ollie, in his most corporate mouthpiece voice. "So I thought I might pop over there next April for the Milan Furniture Fair and then I can see what that's all about. That fair is the absolute epicentre of the whole design world apparently, so I think Slap might have a stand at it, and then I can reconnoitre the retail at the same time. Much more efficient way to do it."

"Well, I hope you have a lovely time with yourself," I said, quite tartly, but Ollie seemed oblivious.

"Yes, sorry about that, darling, but we will get other trips in later next year. I'd better go now, Steffie is making take-this-call faces at me through the glass partition. It's probably something else about Slap for Chaps. Bye, my angel."

And he hung up, to take whatever phone call it was that was more important than talking to me.

14

THREE weeks later I was sitting in Ursula's apartment on 83rd and Fifth. We were in her wonderfully chaotic study, which had books floor to ceiling on every wall, going right over the doorframe and lying in precarious piles on every flat surface.

We were facing each other across her huge marble-topped French desk which was covered, as always, in a mess of manuscripts, toasting each other with champagne from a bottle of vintage Krug, which had just been brought in by her maid, Manuela.

"Welcome home, special girl," said Ursula, blue eyes twinkling. "Welcome back to New York. The city where you should be living."

"Thank you, Ursa," I said. "It's great to be here—in the city I love to visit."

I'd called her Ursa since I was tiny and when I'd discovered it meant "bear" in Latin, it had seemed all the more appropriate to carry on using it. A short round woman, with cropped wiry grey hair, Ursula looked just like a cuddly teddy bear to me. I towered over her, even without my heels on—she always made me take them off to protect her parquet—but her personality and intellect more than made up for what she lacked in feet and inches.

"Size doesn't matter," she always used to say when the subject of height came up. "Trust me—I'm a lesbian."

My stubbornness about living in a small and dull provincial town called London, rather than the throbbing metropolis Ursula considered to be the epicentre of civilization, if not the entire universe, was an ongoing debate between us. Apart from anything else, her flying phobia made it impossible for her to visit me at home, so she had to rely on me going over to New York to see her. Ursula didn't like the passive role.

"I can get you a Green Card in a minute," she would always say to me. "Wouldn't that ambitious husband of yours love the chance to live in the real big city? The opportunities to social climb here are limitless. He'd love it. And I could babysit."

I knew this constant nagging was just because she wanted to see more of me—her un-daughter—and she desperately wanted me to have kids, so she could be an un-grandmother as well, but having scoured out a cool and cosy niche for myself in London, I had no intention of changing anything about it. It was too hard won.

Our other constant source of friction continued to be my weight.

"Did you read those books I sent over to you?" she was asking me, as I leaned back in a beaten-up leather armchair breathing in the unique scent of that room—books, brandy, leather, dust— which was so nostalgic for me.

For a moment my mind was blank—what books?

"The books I sent over with Paul?" Ursula continued.

I remembered, groaned inwardly, considered lying, then considered telling her off for involving Paul in our ongoing wrangle, but decided to leave it be for the time being. I was too happy to see her, to have a row straight away and although her nagging irritated me, I could never stay cross with Ursula for long.

"No," I said, bluntly.

"Did you even open them?"

"No."

Ursula laughed and shook her head.

"Did you even look at the covers?"

"Yeah," I said, sighing deeply, like the sulky fourteen-year-old I had once been in that very room. "One was some dumb poetry thing and the other was hideous self-help tripe about fashion making you fat, or was it thin? Something like that."

"I should have known you wouldn't even open it," she said. "I've met fishing lines that were better padded than you. And better read. But when are you going to face up to it? You are putting your health—and your fertility—at risk pursuing some completely false notion of feminine beauty dictated by a cabal of homosexual men with complex mother issues. Do you eat at all, Emily?"

"From time to time," I said, sucking my cheeks in and pulling a face. "Of course, I eat. Just not as much as you do."

I stuck my tongue out at her. She responded by opening a drawer in her desk and taking out a large tin of Fauchon marrons glacés. She reverently took one from its rustly gold wrapper and brought it to her nose like a connoisseur with a Cuban cigar. Not breaking eye contact with me she inhaled deeply and took a bite, chewing slowly and making appreciative noises.

"Mmmmm, delicious . . . sugar . . . sweetness . . . heavenly melting texture,' she murmured ecstatically and offered me the box. Would you like one, Emily?"

"No thanks," I said. "I've just had a banana."

"You're too thin, Emily," said Ursula.

"You're too fat, Ursula," I replied.

It was a fairly routine exchange between us.

"Well, at least you drink," she said, topping up my glass. "So, where shall we have dinner—sorry, I mean where shall I have dinner, while you toy with an undressed salad and a tragic piece of denuded chicken?"

"Elaine's," I said immediately. We always went to Elaine's. It was one of our many special places in New York and one of the things I loved about that city was that those special places never seemed to change. And I loved going to them with Ursula, because we always got a good table.

That night we got a really great table—by the bar, the third one along—and it was the usual crazy hubbub of people coming over to greet the powerful agent while she gave me a hilarious *sotto voce* commentary on everyone in the place. I loved being temporarily immersed in a world as complex, conniving and petty as the fashion scene and not knowing a thing about it. It gave me some perspective on getting too wound up by my own life.

"See the guy over there, who looks like he just swallowed ground glass?" said Ursula, in a low voice, as the waiter filled our glasses with dark red wine.

"The one with a stupid haircut like a superannuated Tintin?" I whispered back. Ursula barked with laughter.

"That's him. Lawrence Selwyn. He's hoping for a Pulitzer for his second novel. He's not going to get it. He doesn't know yet, but I do. He also doesn't know that I know he didn't write the book. He took a first-draft manuscript written by his late boyfriend and with a little work, made it his own. A recently ex-new-boyfriend is spreading it around. Going to be a huge story when it breaks. The question is, though—does it matter? It's a great novel. I wish I represented him."

She shrugged and took a big slurp from her glass. I gawped appropriately.

"See the woman by the bar?" Ursula continued. "The blonde with the tight-ass body in the tight-ass suit?"

I looked. "The red Versace suit, with the corset lacing up the back?"

"Yeah, the one with the great tits. She's one of that strange tribe of author groupies—they get off on bedding bestselling bookish types—but the thing is, that particular Martha is really an Arthur. Hasn't had the entire op, if you know what I'm saying. Not that she cares who knows, she's a great girl and totally open about it—but you'd be amazed how many well-known literary gentlemen profess not to have known what was still lingering down there until it was too late. And by then, what could they do?" She pulled a mock innocent face and raised her glass to me.

Even though I knew none of the characters, this was as good as sitting in the Princh bar with Paul. It got even better later on when he joined us, arriving shortly after Ursula's latest lover. Like all of Ursa's girlfriends she was very young, very pretty and very impressed by Ursula. This one was called Snapdragon.

"Trust-fund hippy parents—well, briefly hippy," Ursula said to me, by way of explanation. "Knew her dad back in the day. These days, however, he's a Wall Street tax lawyer and not talking to his old buddie Ursula, is he Snappie?"

Snapdragon shook her head, which was cropped in the same brutal style as Ursula's, serving only to emphasize her classic bone structure, dark skin and improbably full lips. She had tattoos up both arms, studs and rings all along one eyebrow, a big fat steel ring through her septum and a big stud on the end of her tongue. For a girl who had grown up a couple of blocks from where we were sitting and who was now a graduate student at Columbia, she was quite exotic.

"Gorgeous, isn't she?" said Ursula, seeing me staring at her. "Mother's Brazilian. Would like to have me killed, but is going to come to a few of my parties first."

Ursula's parties were legendary. She had four a year—one for each season—as her apartment had great views over the park which set the scene beautifully. I had always liked the winter parties best, with Central Park transformed into a snowscape and the hall coat-closet stuffed with floor-length minks redolent of expensive scent.

Apart from the flowing booze and excellent catering, what people came to Ursula's parties for were the other people. She had a Rolodex that spanned interesting identities from every microculture in Manhattan, from the Lower East Side crowd of unknown conceptual artists and radical opera directors, to Upper East Side Brahmins, with every shade of intellectual and pop-culture guru making up the middle ground. She even invited people from Brooklyn. I'd arrived one time and found myself in the elevator with David Auster and RuPaul. They were getting on famously.

The fall party had been a few weeks before and it had been Paul's first experience of Ursula's entertaining style.

"That was what I call a party, Ursula," he said, giving her a big kiss. He gave me one too—on the mouth as usual—then he kissed Snapdragon on the top of her shoulder. "Hey, beauty," he said to her. "Safest place to kiss you. Don't want to get caught up in the ironmongery."

He sat down and held Snapdragon's exquisite chin between his thumb and forefinger, turning her face from side to side. "Such bones," he sighed. "Decided when you are going to let me put you in a photographer's studio and make an object out of you yet?"

Snapdragon shook her head.

"Never," she said.

"I'm trying to get this girl to make a few bucks out of her looks before she loses them," said Paul, to me, putting an avuncular arm round her. "Then she can go and shrivel up in a library for the rest of her life."

"You've always refused to make a buck out of your looks, Jacko," I reminded him. "And you've had plenty of offers."

"Good point," he said, nodding slowly. "Do you know that parallel had never occurred to me? All right, Snappie, I'll stop bugging you. You can go off and write your Ph.D. thesis. What is it about again? Labial imagery in . . . ?"

"Medieval annunciation paintings," filled in Snapdragon, earnestly.

"That's right," said Paul. "Lovely. Wonder if Prince William will be studying that aspect of art history as part of his course? What do you reckon, eh, Urse?"

"As an extra-curricular activity, I hope he is," said Ursula.

After that dinner I didn't see Ursula again until I'd finished the fashion shoot, when I had arranged to stay with her for a few days before going home. And there were times during that project when the idea of being cocooned back in Ursula's apartment, the safe haven of my childhood, was all that kept me going. It was not one of my easier jobs.

Taking heed of what Ollie had said—and others, there was an increasing buzz about him—I was using Nivek for the pictures. It was the first time any of us on *Chic* had booked him, so I hadn't had any warning how difficult he was.

Really, I think, if Paul hadn't been there to gee me along, I might have walked out in the middle of the shoot, he was such a pain. He was one of those photographers who just would not take direction. Suggestions from the stylist were simply not tolerated, it all had to be his idea.

Considering that it was the first time he had shot anything for *Chic* I found his attitude almost unbearably arrogant. I felt like stamping my foot and yelling at him, but I knew it wouldn't have had any effect except maybe to have him storm out. He was that much of an arse.

In some ways it would have been a relief if he had quit, but while I could have found another photographer at short notice more easily in New York than anywhere else on earth, I did not want to lose the model. She was serious cover material. Mind you, she wasn't the easiest little bunny either and it was only Paul's ability to make her feel like the most special girl in the world that stopped her sulking the entire time, instead of just most of it.

Apart from his general creativity and technical skills, that was the secret of Paul's success as a make-up artist. He didn't just make models look good, that was a given, he made them *feel* good too and that's almost more important—because a lot of them are truly convinced they are ugly, foul and fat. That's modelling for you. Talk about a sick industry.

Paul had an amazing knack of being able to suss out people's tender spots in an instant, and with tricky models he always knew which ones to tease, which to flirt with and which to talk to about books and politics. Because while most of them just wanted a laugh, some needed to feel sexy—and others needed to feel that someone understood they had a brain as well as a pretty face.

This girl—Amica, she was called—was a complex mixture of all three. She was astonishingly pretty, to the point where even I was impressed and beauty is something you get inured to after a while in the fashion world. But Amica had one of those faces like a delectable little kitten, combined with amazing legs, golden skin and long dark-blonde hair kissed with blonde highlights—natural—that did what it was told.

She also had a more indefinable quality that made her perfect for this shoot. As well as being young and sexy, she had some kind of innate class. You could have put her in leather hot pants and a lurex boob tube and she would still have looked ready for lunch at Hyannisport. She was the ultimate *Chic* covergirl.

It was a two-day shoot and the problems started with the very first picture. We hadn't been able to get any of the big department stores to agree to us shooting in their luggage departments—they were too worried about security—so I'd got a discount warehouse down on Orchard Street to agree to it instead.

The guys there, full-on religious Hasidic Jews, were really nice and pleased to let us do it in return for a plug for the shop, which was fine with me because it was a great place to buy luggage. They knew me, because Ursula had taken me there to buy my school trunk and I'd bought my cases there ever since, which made Nivek's attitude to them all the more terrible.

He had walked into that place with an expression on his face like he had just stepped in dog doo. He stalked round with his arms folded, not saying anything until he finally came back to where I was standing next to old Mr. Himmelfarb, who had just been asking after my mother—actually Ursula, but I didn't disabuse him—and hoping she had her health.

"You *are* joking," was Nivek's first remark, completely ignoring Mr. Himmelfarb. I said nothing, because I was actually speechless. Nivek still had plenty to say. "I mean you really cannot be serious about this. What exactly am I supposed to do with this place? I mean—look at it. Lino tiles. Horrendo." Then he snorted.

"Excuse me, Mr. Himmelfarb," I said to him. "I think I need to have a word with Mr. Thims here, would you excuse us?" I steered Nivek out on to Orchard Street, which he looked up and down with the same curled lip he had treated the interior of Himmelfarb Brothers to—we were south of Delancey, not the newly trendy part of it. "What exactly is your problem, Nivek?" I said in the most measured tones I could muster.

"What is *your* problem, that you think this is a good place to shoot a fashion picture? It's so gross!"

"It's a luggage store, Nivek," I said, dearly wanting to call him Kevin. "We're doing a narrative story here, remember? About packing and going on holiday? We're not doing landscapes, or interiors, the backgrounds are just settings for the story. The clothes and the model are what will make the pictures, and I think the functional appearance of this shop will add to the shot. The model will pop out against it."

He sighed, like I was a complete idiot. "Emily, Emily, Emily," he said, shaking his head and actually patting me on the shoulder. "There is a basic minimum aesthetic below which you cannot expect me to work."

"Oh really?" I said, removing his hand and dropping it. "Well, go tell that to Bruce Weber and Corinne Day. I'm going back in there to apologize to Mr. Himmelfarb and then I'm going into the location van to see how Paul is getting on with the make-up. Meanwhile, why don't you have a think about where *you* think we should do this shot—seeing as no department store will let us in and Bee insists on the opening picture being in a shop buying the luggage. It was her idea."

That was a total lie, but I was desperate. Mr. Himmelfarb was charming about it.

"We are in retail," he said, shrugging. "All day we see people, some nice, some not so nice. You do what you want. No problem."

I did some yoga breathing on my way to the van, reminding myself not to be indiscreet in front of Amica. I could retain my professional discretion even if Nivek couldn't. And there was the hairdresser to consider too. Mitch was a buddy of Nivek's, that he had insisted we used—against my wishes—and I was well aware that anything I said would get straight back to Mr. Attitude.

"OK, hon?" said Paul, instantly picking up that I wasn't. "Amica and I were just talking about magical realism in Latin American literature." He winked at me over her head.

"Oh, that's great," I said. "I love Isabel Allende. Wow, you look gorgeous, Amica. Really fresh. The hair's great too, thanks Mitch."

I hated it actually, but we could sort that out later. At that moment I couldn't take any more friction.

"Everything OK, out there?" said Paul, raising an eyebrow meaningfully at me. He'd already sussed that Nivek was not going to be a joy to work with. He'd asked to see Paul's book before the shoot for one thing. No one asked to see Paul's book any more. When you directed the make-up for Antonello Ferrucci's shows and advertising you were way beyond that.

"Oh marvellous," I said, crossing my eyes. Amica had hers closed while her mascara dried, so she couldn't see me, and hairdresser

Mitch was absorbed in a bodybuilding magazine. "Nivek is just sussing out the location." I pretended to strangle myself.

"OK," said Paul, laughing with his eyes. "I see. Well, we're doing famously here and we'll be ready whenever you need us. Hey, Ami baby?"

"Sure," she said. "Whatever."

I decided the best way for me to deal with Nivek was to have as little to do with him as possible. So I sent my loyal right-hand girl Gemma out to talk to his assistant.

"Go and ask him what the silly fucker wants to do," I said to her, just outside the van. "I'm going to get Amica ready in the first look anyway."

Gemma was back quickly.

"Kent—that's the assistant's name, honestly, it is," she said. "He's from North Dakota but he lives here now. Anyway, Kent—he's quite cute actually—Kent says Nivek *might* be able to work in one corner of the store, so he's just setting up to do some test Polaroids. Kent is going to come and tell me when they're ready for Amica. Although it's just a *trial,* of course," she added, with heavy irony.

"Oh, of course," I replied and we all knew he was going to shoot there. It was just his way of torturing us to feel he was still in control, but my Bee ruse had worked. Advantage Miss Pointer.

It was a similar story in all the locations. It's hard enough when you have five different shots to do in one day, in different parts of any city, but New York is even harder than most, because of the crazy bustle and press of the people and all the hassle with permits.

And then Nivek did just about everything he could have done on top of that to make it harder, including being rude to a cop, when we were doing the taxi shot—which we should have had a permit for and didn't. We only got out of that one by another intervention from Gemma, who could bat her eyelids for Britain. And very pretty eyelids they were too. I was beyond being able to bat anything, by that stage, apart from possibly Nivek's head with a heavy golf club.

His ill grace infected the whole first day, with Amica refusing to wear a couple of the outfits, for no good reason, and even Paul getting quite testy at times. His problem was that he loathed Mitch the hairdresser on several different levels, not least of which was that he kept giving Amica terrible overdone hairdos, which had nothing to do with the exquisitely natural looking make-up Paul was doing— appropriately for a girl going on holiday. Mitch kept making her look like something out of a Miss America pageant.

In the end, when he refused to take down a full-on Priscilla Presley beehive no one had asked him to do, I sacked him. That was a moment. I'd never actually done it before, sacking someone on a job, but on top of Nivek's posturing I'd just had enough.

What was really driving me nuts was that I loved the concept of the story and maddening though he was, I could tell from the Polaroids that Nivek was doing seriously beautiful pictures. It was almost annoying how good they were, but I kept reminding myself to stay focused on the endgame and that I just had to put up with these two days of torture to have a wonderful story in my cuttings book for ever. If I could only sort out the hair.

We'd done three shots when I told Mitch to go. I could see Nivek waver for a millisecond as he decided whether he should chuck a full tantrum and leave with him. Mitch clearly expected him to, but Nivek was enough of a player—and enough of a shit—to know that an eight-page story in *Chic* was worth a lot more to him than his friendship with Mitch, whatever that was based on and I had good reason to believe it wasn't strictly professional.

I'd asked to see his book before the shoot—mainly because I'd never heard of him and partly tit for tat for the Paul book insult— and it had been conveniently "lost" by the courier en route to my hotel. Now I knew why. It probably only contained local photographer shots from an Idaho hair show.

With Paul doing the hair as well as the make-up, the shoot got much easier. Amica relaxed and it subtly shifted the balance of power away from Nivek, a state which was enhanced further by the glaring fact that Kent was absolutely smitten with Gemma and would do anything to make her happy. She was playing him like a trout; it was beautiful to watch.

By the time we'd finished on the second day it was after ten at night. We hadn't done the shots in order and the last one we did was the unpacking-in-the-hotel picture, for which we had used a suite at the Soho Grand, where Gemma and I were staying on an editorial credit deal. It was Paul who came up with the idea that we should keep the suite on for a post-shoot party—we'd already messed it up.

His initial plan, which we cooked up while Nivek was down in the bar having a cigarette break, was not to tell him about the party plan and have everyone go away and then come back half an hour later. But as we plotted, I started looking through the Polaroids again. I put them in narrative order on the bed and called Paul over to look. He whistled between his teeth when he saw them.

"Shit, that looks good," he said. "That fuckwit can really take a picture. How annoying."

"I don't know whether to be thrilled or furious," I said, laughing. "He's a loathsome toad, but these are fantastic. They've got exactly the mood I wanted. The crazy thing is that obnoxious though he is, these are so great I'm going to want to work with him again and even if I didn't want to, Bee would make me. These shots have that luscious feel that makes you want to rush out and buy all the clothes. He's really good. A really good wanker and we've got to have him at the party, Jacko. I've got to learn to like him."

The surprising thing was that Nivek seemed sincerely excited about the party idea when we told him and the final shot went off without any rudeness or attitude from his quarter.

By the time we finished there was actually a great atmosphere in the suite, which was cranked up further when Paul's friends Mark and Karl turned up, along with a few buddies of Kent's, and Amica's likeable banker boyfriend. We had a wild old time, ordering champagne and snacks on room service and generally acting up.

Everyone was carrying on in the sitting room—Mark had initiated dancing to MTV, which at this point had him attempting to spin on his head—and I sneaked off to have another squint at the

Polaroids in the bedroom. Nivek came out of the loo and found me looking at them. And the man I had wanted to kill earlier turned into a small boy.

"Do you like them?" he asked, uncertainly.

"Like them?" I said. "I love them. They're brilliant. Thank you so much, Nivek. Bee is going to adore these pictures, you know."

His whole face lit up. It was such a striking difference from the person he had been earlier, I just had to come out and ask him.

"Nivek," I said, tentatively. "Why were you such a pain on this shoot? What was that all about?"

He looked shifty and then something in him seemed to deflate. I patted the bed next to me and he sat down, hanging his head.

"I was scared," he said. "I care too much about my work. As a photographer you only get one go and I always get absolutely terrified that I am going to fuck it up and no one will ever book me again."

"You idiot," I said, punching him on the arm. "The only thing that nearly fucked this shoot up was your attitude. Chill out, Nivek—you're really talented, but you've got to relax a bit and learn to trust other people."

He looked up at me with such a vulnerable expression, I almost wanted to give him a cuddle. Almost.

"It's teamwork, you know, this thing we do," I told him, gently. "I mean, you click the shutter and you'll be the one with your name in lights on the page, but it's a combination of my styling and Paul's make-up and—well, we'll gloss over the hair—and Amica's beauty. Even Kent and Gemma played a big part too. Go with that, don't fight it."

"You're probably right," he said. "I think it comes from being an only child, I think everything revolves around me." He picked up the Polaroids and looked at them thoughtfully. "They are good, aren't they?"

"They're brilliant—but don't go all maudlin on me. I'm serious about this. If you can just learn to relax we can do a lot of great work together . . . Kevin."

It was a risk. There was a moment's silence and then he burst out laughing.

"You cow," he said.

"You can call me Y-lime," I said, pushing it a bit further. He thought for a moment and then roared again, pretending to cuff me round the head. Paul came in a moment later to find us hugging.

I tell you, fashion really is a funny old business.

15

THE combination of such an emotionally charged shoot, the great work we had produced together despite it all, the pleasure of spending two whole days with Paul and the high spirits at the party left me feeling pretty wired.

Things didn't wind down in the suite until after 1 A.M. when Paul and his pals—including Nivek—decided they had to go off to some new boy bar. I declined the offer to join them and then, as I sloped off to my room, I caught sight of Gemma and Kent kissing passionately in the corridor. It was quite clear what was going to go on there and I felt a sharp pang of envy. Well, not envy exactly. The truth of the matter was I felt fantastically sexed up.

I sat in my lonely hotel room all too aware of what Gemma and Kent were probably getting up to in hers and feeling quite mad with desire. And it wasn't random sexual desire either. I didn't just want sex, I didn't want sex with Kent, or even Ollie. I wanted sex with Miles.

So I did what drunk and horny women so often do, I drank—a shot of brandy from the mini bar—and dialled. I hadn't even checked what time it was in Australia, but Miles answered straight away and sounded fully awake. Just hearing his voice say hello sent a tremor through my loins.

"It's Emily," I said.

"Hey, Em," said Miles, sounding surprised and pleased. "How are you, darls?"

I let out a big sigh and then I told him.

"I'm horny," I said. "Horny, horny, horny, just like the song, quite pissed, alone in a hotel room and thinking about you."

"Is that right?" said Miles in a voice which was all smile.

"You're not in New York are you?" I asked him, half seriously. Well, stranger things have happened.

"If only," he said. "I'd be right there, but actually I'm here in Australia, on the beach at Seal Rock. I've been surfing all day, I'm just about to leave, but I can't tear myself away from the waves. Listen . . ."

I could distinctly hear the sound of waves crashing on a beach.

"Can you hear it?" he asked me.

"Oh, yeah," I said, wanting him more than ever. I would have done a *From Here to Eternity* with him right there on that beach if I could have.

"Can you hang on a minute?" he asked. His voice sounded more Australian somehow over the miles. And even sexier. I held on and heard what sounded like a door slamming.

"OK," he said. "I'm in my panel van. What are you wearing?"

"In your what?" I said. "And what do you mean, what am I wearing?"

He laughed.

"It's a van-type car thing. An 'estate,' I think you Poms call them. And I mean, tell me what you're wearing—as you take it off. Have you still got your shoes on?"

I had. Very high heels, as usual. No tights, as usual. Low-rise jeans. Layered T-shirts. A bright pink Agent Provocateur thong. I described everything as I took it off, until I was lying naked on the bed.

"Don't lie down," said Miles.

"How did you know I was lying down?" I squeaked.

"I could tell by your voice. Don't lie down until I'm ready. I want you to sit up and watch me. I'm pulling down the zip on my wetsuit now—can you hear it?"

I could hear it and in my mind's eye I could so clearly see it, I nearly fell off the bed with desire. And so it went on, until I realized I had just had what is known as phone sex. It wasn't as good as the real thing, but it was something.

We didn't ring off immediately, but just lay there—well, I lay there, I suppose he was in his car seat—breathing.

"Emily?" he said eventually.

"Yeah?" I answered.

"I'm glad you called," he said and then he paused for a moment. "I miss you."

I swallowed hard. I wasn't expecting that. I missed the sex, but did I miss him? I couldn't allow myself to.

"Well, I'll see you here in New York in February," I said cautiously. "I'll email you, nearer the time. Or I might call you again, before then."

"You do that," said Miles and finally we hung up.

Even though I hadn't had much sleep I woke up the next morning feeling almost as good as if I'd had live sex with Miles. Just lying in bed stretching and thinking about it made me want to ring him again. So I did.

This time, I had clearly woken him up. It took him a moment or two to come to, but when he realized it was me the smile came right back into his voice.

"You are a horny little girl, aren't you?" he said.

"Not particularly until I met you," I replied, in all honesty.

"Well, what can Dr. Feelgood do for you tonight—or this morning, or whatever it is with you? It's midnight here."

So I told him—in graphic detail.

I went out into that New York day feeling ready to take on the world. It was a bright morning for mid-November, with an invigorating chill and a bright blue sky. I had so much energy I decided to get the hotel to send on my bags and set out to walk all the way up to Ursula's.

I counted it later; it was over eighty blocks, more actually, as

I didn't take the most direct route, but wound through SoHo for a while checking out the shops, stopping for coffee at Café Havana and cruising through Nolita, before drifting along Lafayette Street and up to Union Square.

I spent some time browsing in the huge Barnes & Noble, then hit Fifth Avenue to take me all the way up to 83rd Street, with detours en route into Bendel's and Bergdorf's. As I walked I thought about Miles. All the way. For once I let my mental brakes off and just gave in to enjoying the memories. I was intrigued by what he'd said about me being "a horny little girl." It just wasn't a way I had ever thought of myself.

I mean, I liked sex well enough, I certainly wasn't frigid, but I didn't obsess on it like some of my friends. Nelly was always going on about it, in gory detail, which I had always found a bit much. I was happy when it came along, but didn't think about it much in between. Until now. When it seemed I could think of nothing else. It was quite weird, really.

Ollie rang me when I was in FAO Schwarz buying Christmas presents for his nieces and nephews, and Barbie accessories for the girls at the office. As I heard his familiar voice, I was struck once again by my total lack of remorse about what I had done the night before—and that very morning. It just didn't seem anything to do with my relationship with Ollie, it was something that happened elsewhere; in another part of the world and another part of my head.

When Ollie commented on how upbeat I sounded, I attributed my perkiness to the success of the shoot, spending time with Paul, my anticipation of a few days cocooning with Ursa and that famously infectious New York buzz. All of which were part of it as well.

Ollie was chirpy too, getting really excited about Slap for Chaps, which had now been picked up by the broadsheet newspapers. Even the mighty *Today* programme had interviewed him about it.

"Wow," I said, trying to sound slightly more enthusiastic than I felt. "Radio 4. That is grown-up. Anyone would think it was August. Make-up for men is silly-season stuff for them surely?"

"Well, you'd think so," said Ollie. "But there is something about Slap for Chaps that has got them interested from a sexual politics point of view and they are always looking for that angle. *Woman's Hour* is going to do something too. Iggy's comments about trying it out 'to feel like a woman' seem to have given it some kind of intellectual credibility. They've got Germaine Greer commenting on it and stuff like that. Suits me, Emily.

"Oh!" he added suddenly. "Did you know our friend Iggy is going to be the new designer at Albert Alibert? That's helped give the story legs too, because now he's really in the big league."

"Wow," I said again, although I already knew. Like I said, I really can keep other people's secrets. "So it is happening, that really is fantastic. Hey, I might be front row at that show in the future, that really would be a blast. I'll call them when I get to Ursa's. I'm on my way there now."

"Well, you carry on having a good time in New York, my darling," said Ollie, in winding-it-up tones. "I'm holding the fort here. I'm going to be Phone Off a lot of the time though, with all that's going on, which is why I've rung now, just to let you know I'm thinking about you."

We said goodbye, with all the usual soppy stuff and then without missing a beat I carried on walking up Fifth Avenue, with a throb in my groin and credit cards burning a deeper hole in my pocket with every step I got closer to Barneys. By the time I had studied every floor of my favourite store in detail, picking up a few bits and pieces along the way that I wouldn't have been able to get in London, it was after five before I got to Ursula's.

I had planned on nipping into the Frick before going to her place, but by the time I got to 70th Street I had so many carrier bags I decided to go the next day instead. I could do the Met and the Whitney as well, pop down to MoMA and make it a total art day. Manuela opened the door and told me "Missis Lorimer" was out at meetings, but would be back to have dinner with me at home.

I went to my old room and lay down on the bed I had slept on since I was eleven years old. Ursula had changed nothing in there in the intervening years. My old teddies were still there. Pictures my dad had drawn for me were framed on the wall. My Barbies were still ranked up on the bookshelves—even though I knew how much Ursula hated them—and there were pictures of my family looking remarkably happy on every surface.

I loved that room and always looked forward to sleeping in it, especially since Ollie had started making me stay in hotels when I went to New York with him. The only time we had stayed at Ursula's place together I'd asked her if we could go in the guest room instead, because it just didn't feel right to stay in my childhood bedroom with him. For one thing it only had a single bed, but when I was there on my own, I couldn't wait to get into it.

It still was very much my room; it even said so on the door in the bright china letters Ursula had glued up the day I had arrived from England, a shell-shocked little casualty of the bad places unbridled creativity can take people. At least that's how I saw it. My father's death was just a ghastly stroke of fate, but I felt somehow that the unbearably intense atmosphere in our home had hurried it along. He was only thirty-eight when it happened, after all.

Living with my mother's moods and excesses would have put a strain on anyone's health and he had a fair dose of "artistic temperament" himself—which as far as I was concerned was a euphemism for too much drinking and too much thinking about yourself. In my opinion, my mother's mental illness was another version of the same thing.

And that was how I had come to see the catastrophe of my parents' lives. Death by emotional self-indulgence. Living death in my mother's case. There is no doubt they were both intensely creative people; my father was truly gifted, my mother I wasn't so sure about in that regard, but she was a published poet.

The problem was, as they were both also blessed with financial security, they had no reality checks to keep them earthed and they just disappeared up the fundament of their artistic endeavours—and their pot pipes. Not even having kids was enough to ground them. They had too much freedom to express themselves.

Most of the artists I knew who were my contemporaries had to do other jobs to fund their "real" work and it seemed to keep them relatively normal. Ossie and Polly were a case in point—they were rich kids, much better off than my parents actually, and they never really did anything. Without the balance of an innate work ethic, or some kind of fundamental humility, I had come to the conclusion that inherited wealth could be a curse for the naturally creative.

It was great how I could analyse all of that now in a relatively detached way, I thought to myself, as I lay there looking at a lovely black and white photo of my father holding me up—a chubby smiling little girl—in front of one of his paintings. It was the one that was now in the Tate Modern, I realized. Time was when I couldn't even look at that photo, let alone think about it all, but since being with Ollie, doing well at work and starting to feel relatively secure, I had gradually been able to allow the memories of those times—good and bad—to seep back into my conscious mind and I seemed to have assimilated them in some way.

Of course, I did sometimes feel racked by guilt and wonder whether I should go and see my mother again, but I always came to the same conclusion. It would upset me horrendously—and she wouldn't know who I was anyway, so what was the point? I had once asked Ollie if he would come with me to see her, but he had looked so horrified at the prospect I had never brought it up again. Suited me, really. I was jogging along very nicely in my life as I was and I didn't see the point of upsetting myself for nothing. It worked for me as it was.

Although Ursula had urged me constantly over the years, I hadn't ever had any therapy or counselling; I hadn't even ever discussed what had happened with my brother—in fact, that was the main reason I didn't see much of Toby. If I didn't see him, it couldn't come up, easy. I had found that on the whole, the less I disturbed all those memories the better I was and without needing to resort to the prop of therapy, I had sorted it all out in my head, in my own way.

Ursula never seemed to believe me, though. She had mother issues of her own—which was understandable when you'd met her terrifying parents—and because it had worked for her, she was convinced it was the answer to everything and everyone's problems. It was just about the only thing that really got me down about her.

The "you're too thin" nagging was just an irritation, which I actually found quite amusing, seeing how overweight she was. I found it hilarious that she could tell me that it was "emotional blockages" that made me so "obsessed" with staying slim—or thin, as she always called it—when years of therapy had failed to sort out whatever was keeping her fat.

Then there was the baby thing. She just refused to believe that I had made a free and happy decision that I didn't want to have children. She was convinced that somehow Ollie had brainwashed me with his own "selfishness," as she called it.

So although I had been annoyed when she had dragged Paul into our squabbles about these things, I was pretty much used to them, but the therapy thing really got me. People like my mother—mad people—needed therapy. Not me. I was fine.

As we sat down for dinner that night in a cosy little nook off her huge Fifties kitchen, I wondered how long it would take her to bring up her favourite subjects—particularly Dr. Claptrap, or whoever her latest brilliant, perfect-for-me, analyst discovery was.

Longer than usual, I was thinking as we polished off the bottle of Meursault 1998. Ursa was a wine connoisseur and enjoyed sharing it with me. She'd taught me to appreciate it, starting me with one glass with dinner from when I had first arrived at her apartment. Along with books, art and music, she thought it was something civilized people needed to know about.

So far she hadn't brought up my weight; why I should move to New York; my shallow, selfish, venal husband; my self-deluding attitude to having children; or my need for therapy to sort out any of the above—so I'd been chattering happily on, telling her all about the shoot and what I'd been up to.

We'd discussed how wonderful Paul was, especially considering his grim upbringing, I'd marvelled appreciatively about Snapdragon's beauty and Ursula had announced she was getting bored with her. A sure sign she was going to end the liaison before Snappie cooled off on her.

I had experienced what happened after such a parting. There would be snowdrifts of daily letters, poetry delivered by hand, hung-up phone calls and the apartment buzzer going in the middle of the night—for about ten days, before the girl got over it.

Just once I'd seen what happened when Ursula didn't end it first. A woman she had been more seriously smitten with than usual—someone closer to her own age and sophistication—had cooled off on her and told her she wanted some "space." Ursula had retreated to her bed for a fortnight and it had taken her a lot longer than that to get over it fully. It was the only time I had ever seen my human rock falter.

By the time we were halfway down a bottle of 1985 Margaux to go with a hearty *boeuf bourguignon*, I was beginning to wonder what was going on. It never took Ursa this long to start probing me. It was quite a novelty, so I just went with the flow, telling her all about Nelly and Iggy—including his extraordinary life story, which got her quite excited about doing a book deal for him—which eventually led me on to the Sunday salon and Slap for Chaps.

Ursula listened intently, her face not betraying much, then as I was telling her about my latest conversation with Ollie, how he had been interviewed on the *Today* programme about it and was going to be on a discussion panel with Germaine Greer—an old pal of Ursula's—she finally came out with it.

"Are you having an affair, Emily?" she said. Just like that, out of nowhere.

I just gaped at her, I was so amazed. How did she know? And was I? Was this strange thing with Miles an affair? I had never thought of it that way.

Ursula took a long drink from her wine and raised an eyebrow at me.

"Well, it's either that, or you're pregnant," she finally said. "And I don't think you would have drunk two bottles of wine with me if you were. Anyway, having a baby might make you fat and I'm sure you wouldn't risk that, much as I long for a grand-un-daughter. So, are you going to tell me?"

"How did you know?" was all I could croak out.

She threw back her head and laughed and then surprised me, by jumping up from her seat and coming round and giving me one of her special bear hugs. Hugus Ursus I called them.

"Oh, you funny little girl," she said. "I'm so happy for you. Enjoy it."

Then she started clearing the plates from the table and asking if she could tempt me with any of the cheesecake she had bought specially from Payard—the only pudding I couldn't resist. It took me a moment to realize I was actually disappointed that she hadn't asked me more questions. I got up and followed her into the kitchen.

"Is that it?" I said. "You're going to spring that on me and then not ask me anything more about it?"

"Well, do you want to tell me?" she said.

"I want to know how you guessed," I said, jumping up to sit on the kitchen counter while she put the things in the dishwasher.

"You have a glow, Emily. A post-coital glow. It's as simple and corny as that." She chuckled to herself. "When you have known as many women as I have, you can spot these things."

I pondered for a bit.

"Did I have the glow when I saw you on Tuesday? When we went to Elaine's?"

"A little. I noticed something different, but not so much as tonight. The minute I saw you this evening I knew." She paused a moment. "Is he in town?"

It was my turn to chuckle.

"Only on the end of the phone," I told her.

She roared with laughter.

"Well now, that *is* an affair. I was going to play it cool with you, but now I am fascinated. Who is he? Or she?"

"He!" I said indignantly.

"OK," she said. "Don't stress. I just don't make assumptions, that's all. And it quite often takes a *complete* change to make someone glow the way you are. You look radioactive."

She got the cheesecake out of the fridge, put the open box on the worktop between us and got out two spoons. She handed me one and dug hers right into the middle of it.

"So," she said, pausing with the spoon at her lips. "Spill."

I dug my spoon into the cheesecake and filled my mouth with the heavenly sweet creaminess. I paused for a moment with my eyes closed to savour it—and then I told her everything.

16

IN the strange half-light on the plane home to London, I sat and wondered whether I had done the right thing telling Ursula about Miles. But I couldn't have lied to her I concluded, not to her. And especially not after she had sneaked up on me like that.

I was actually quite surprised what a relief it had been to tell someone about it and Ursula was definitely the person to choose. She didn't make any judgements, in fact she seemed quite pleased about the whole thing.

Her eyes had twinkled with vicarious delight as I'd told her how it had all happened. I left out the more pornographic details of course—I might have been her un-daughter, but Ursula was enough of a parent figure for that to seem embarrassing—and she seemed truly thrilled to hear about my adventure. She didn't mention therapy once all evening and best of all, she didn't say anything to make me feel guilty about what I'd done. She didn't even mention Ollie, which seemed a little odd in the context, but suited me.

"How delicious, darling," she'd said, as we scraped the last two spoonfuls of cheesecake out of the box. "Nice name, Miles. And I like the idea of a surfer. Very primal. You just enjoy it. A much better distraction for you than all that silly shopping and brainless socializing you do." Then she paused and seemed to consider what she was about to say, as she licked her spoon.

"I'm sure I don't need to tell you this, Emily," she said finally. "But I'm going to anyway. It sounds to me like you have exactly the right sense of proportion about this little 'entente,' shall we call it? So enjoy it, savour it, grow from it, feel alive—but don't get silly about it, OK? Keep it in context and don't confuse it with real life."

I had the distinct feeling that she was advising me to treat my affair as she treated hers—like a box of chocolates rather than a proper meal, as she had once explained it to me. Still, I was glad she'd said all that, as it was exactly the attitude I had been taking to it, apart from that one day of obsessing as I walked through New York, but telling all to Ursula had enabled me to move on from that. Miles was safely back in his box. A beautiful pink Charbonnel & Walker chocolate box, tied up with a big satin bow, but a box nevertheless.

Once I got back to London, back to Ollie and back to the office, I hardly gave Miles a thought. Certain sexy songs could make me think of him. And stills from certain fashion shows—especially Dior, of course. Seeing a cute guy on the street in worn-out jeans and a leather jacket. Anything on the telly about Australia. Or surfing. And sometimes he would just pop into my head unprompted. But mainly, I managed to keep him filed. And I always managed to around Ollie.

Not that I seemed to see my husband very much. Slap for Chaps had gone ballistic. It was everywhere, one of those things that seemed to enter the national consciousness in a unique way in Britain. Comedians made jokes about it, it came up on quiz shows, people wore it to fancy-dress parties and children played it, until it became quite normal to see a little boy walking along in full make-up as his face paint of choice, when he might have once been a lion, or Spiderman. David Beckham had worn it to a party.

Even really butch blokes wore make-up to work to raise money for charity, culminating in a whole fire crew being sponsored to wear Slap for Chaps for a week, in aid of Children in Need, with Ollie providing the make-up and the make-up artists to apply it. That was all over the telly. Especially when one of the make-up artists got engaged to a fireman. Talk about a feel-good story.

There was even a dedicated blokes' makeover TV show under discussion, to be sponsored by Slap, with full naming rights. So on top of his already crowded work schedule, it kept Ollie very busy.

I was busy too. It was always my nuttiest time of year at work, as I had to fit in at least half my shoots before Christmas, as well as it being prime time for boutique launches and the Christmas party season itself, which was always full-on for both of us.

As well as two Slap parties—a big client number and a smaller office piss-up—I had all the designer and PR drinks to go to, Ollie had all the other magazines' dos and I had to go with him to a lot of corporate booze-ups of varying gruesomeness.

The *Chic* party, however, was the major event. All London's hot young fashion designers, photographers, models, make-up artists, hairdressers, agents, writers, PRs and general faces around town came, and we always had it in a suitably cool venue. We usually racked up the odd visiting celeb as well, which was always thrilling.

That year we were having it jointly with *Chic Interiors* and they had found the most brilliant venue, in the half-finished spaces of the Wigwam hotel, which Ollie's decorator pal Donovan Pertwee was designing. The work-in-progress feel was really rather great.

Ollie was in his element catching up with all his new interiors buddies, as well as the *Chic* crowd he already knew really well. Handsome, well dressed and always in a good mood, Ollie was a popular party guest and I didn't mind a bit when he asked Bee to dance and stuff like that. It was all rather familial and nice, as I danced with her husband George as well.

I also got on down with Frannie's Andrew, who was a surprisingly good dancer, and with all the girls together, dancing round our handbags as a joke. It was that kind of a night.

I was not so thrilled, however, when I looked over mid-chat with Rosie Stanton, who had been writing for *Chic* since she'd been to our Sunday salon—major Bee points to me, tee hee—to see Ollie dancing with Natalie, of all people. Just as I noticed, Gemma stumbled past—she'd had quite a bit to drink and was having trouble with her shoes.

"Look at that little slapper dancing with your husband, Em," she said, leaning down and wrestling with her ankle straps. "*Fucking* shoes, that's it, I'm taking them off. That's better."

She stood up again, several inches smaller, but looking much happier and looked over at Natalie and Ollie again. Natalie was positively shaking her copious suntanned cleavage—she'd just come back from a shoot in Bali with Alice and she always baked it like a roast chicken—in my husband's face.

"She asked *him*, Em," said Gemma. "I saw her do it."

"Right," I said. "I'm putting a stop to this."

But as I tried to get over to where they were, I kept bumping into make-up artists and hairdressers and model agents and other people I knew and I couldn't just ignore them, so I had to keep stopping to air kiss and chat and graciously accept compliments about how great I looked, in my emerald green Dolce & Gabbana mini toga. I did look hot, if I say so myself. I had a genius hairpiece on too, in a high pony.

By the time I got over to the side of the dance floor where they'd been, Natalie had disappeared and Ollie was gyrating enthusiastically with Spitty Felicity, so I left them to it. He'd do anything for editorial mentions, I reckoned, my husband.

Christmas itself was the usual trip to Ollie's parents and I was more than happy about that, because Caroline and Max really knew how to do the whole yuletide thing. Log fires, a huge tree in the hall, loads to drink, a whole Stilton on the sideboard, swathes of holly— Bing Crosby could have turned up at any moment to shoot a Christmas special.

It was exactly the same every year and that's just why I liked it. Caroline even had a service of special Christmas china which was used only then, which I thought showed real commitment. It didn't have the glamour of the Christmases I'd spent on the Upper East Side, or up at Martha's Vineyard, with Ursula, but I still loved it. I loved anything to do with normal family life.

Over the four days we were there, all of Ollie's brothers came and went with their families and it was lovely to have children running around, mulled wine on tap and endless games of charades, Boggle, Scrabble and snap on the go.

Caroline even let me help with the food, which was a great honour—none of her other daughters-in-law were allowed near the Aga—but she'd sussed me out early on as a keen cook and was eager to encourage me. She made a couple of comments about me needing to eat a bit more too, but I just ignored them.

As another indication of my true acceptance into the Fairbrother clan, Caroline had even asked me if I wanted to invite my brother there for Christmas. They'd met him at our wedding and a couple of times since, and clearly thought he was the right kind of a chap. I was a bit thrown at first—he did ring me quite regularly, but I tended to keep Toby slightly at arm's length, for fear of what he might stir up in me. But then I'd thought it over and decided it might be really nice to have an actual family member beside me as we sat down for the turkey. He was my brother, after all.

I turned to look at Toby's face as Max said grace. His head was down with his eyes closed and I realized he was starting to look more and more like my father as he got older, with one marked difference: Dad had always been ghostly pale from spending all his time in his studio and Toby's face had the ruddy tinge of skin constantly exposed to harsh weather. Pushing himself to physical extremes seemed to be Toby's way of coping with all the things he didn't want to think about.

As a result of his formative years with our Uncle Andrew and his subsequent superstraight education, Toby fitted perfectly into Fairbrother-land in his chunky cords and checked Viyella shirts. You'd never have guessed he was the son of a wayward artist and his unhinged poet wife, or even that we were related. I watched him pulling a cracker with one of Ollie's sisters-in-law, a toothy blonde in a bright pink Boden cardie and pearls, who was squawking with excitement at the fun of it. Two hearty Sloanes in perfect harmony.

Toby and I were like some kind of sociological experiment, I thought. I was eleven when I went to live with Ursula, he was seven when he moved in with Uncle Andrew and his family, yet we both seemed completely defined by those years. He was leaving on Boxing Day to go to Andrew's—he had a strong sense of duty to the people who had given him shelter—and before he left he asked me to go for a walk with him.

Even though I hadn't seen much of him over the years, I was still very fond of Tobes. He may have gone off on a completely different tangent to me, but we did have those crucial seven years together. We'd hardly seen any of our parents' relatives when we were little, so he and Ursula were just about the only people left I had any shared childhood memories with.

We met in the boot room and set out across the fields behind the house. They were still crisp with the hard frost glittering in the midday sun and the trees on the horizon were outlined starkly against the pure white sky.

I breathed in deeply, filling my lungs with the cool clean air which seemed uniquely English somehow. I could see the steeple of the village church in the distance and smoke rising from the chimneys of cottages nestling in the folds of the landscape. I'd missed those ageless English days when I'd lived in New York.

We walked along chatting lightly about how nice the Fairbrothers were and Toby's plans for life after the army. Max had taken him off for a man-to-man chat about the City after breakfast that morning and he said he was giving it serious thought.

The conversation gradually petered out and as I saw Toby's shoulders rise towards his ears inside his Barbour, I knew he had something to say to me; something he was having trouble getting out. I remembered him doing that thing with his shoulders when he was tiny and had been told off. I trudged along for a while admiring the effect of my pink boots against the white frost, but in the end I couldn't stand it any longer. I stopped and turned towards him, putting my hand on his waxy sleeve.

"What is it, Tobes?" I said. "I can see you've got something on your mind. Tell me."

He looked relieved, as he turned to look at me, but still constricted by whatever it was he needed to say. He sighed deeply and then took a breath, like someone about to jump off a high board.

"It's Mum," he finally got out in a strangled voice.

"What about Mum?" I said, trying not to let an edge come into my voice, but it did anyway. I couldn't control my reaction to her any more than Toby could be at ease with his emotions.

"She's asking for you," he said.

I laughed. I don't know why, it's just what happened.

"Em," said Toby pleadingly.

Now it was my turn to sigh deeply. I didn't want to have this conversation any more than he did.

"What do you mean she's asking for me? And how do you know?"

"I go to see her," said Toby in a tiny little voice.

I was stunned. I had no idea. I did a quick sum in my head. I hadn't seen her for nearly ten years. The last time I'd gone she hadn't seemed to know me and had kept telling me to get out, so I had. Gladly.

"When do you go to see her?" I said. I realized I was shaking. I wasn't cold. It was some kind of shock. I never talked about my mother and I didn't want to now. Not even to Toby.

"I go every month," said Toby, looking down. "The, er, hospital is not far from where I'm based. I went once just to see how she was and she seemed much better. She recognized me. So I've carried on going."

He looked up at me. His face was even redder than usual. He looked like he could cry.

"The *loony bin,* you mean," I spat out. I had no intention of continuing that conversation and I strode off up the hill to get away from it. I heard Toby call after me, but I didn't turn back.

I just kept walking until the white frost underfoot and the white sky overhead merged together through the tears in my eyes and wiped my brain clean like one of those Etch A Sketch pads.

And I didn't go back to the house until after he'd left.

17

CHRISTMAS melted into New Year, which Ollie and I cele-
brated in high style in Paris with Iggy and Nelly, at the
house-warming for their new apartment, a wonderful sprawl-
ing place in the Palais Royal.

It was quite a party, with a lot of the men—including Iggy and
Ollie—fully made up. There was a great turnout, with Jean Paul
Gaultier and John Galliano both making appearances and, as Peter
Potter—who had been invited by the cunning Ms. Stelios—wrote
in his column, it established Iggy and Nelly as the new "It" couple
of the fashion world.

Then it seemed like I'd hardly got over that hangover and there I
was again, picking up my dry-cleaning ready to pack for the shows.
It was mid-February and the whole crazy fashion circus was about
to take off once more, starting in New York.

It was just going to be me and Alice in New York—Bee felt she
couldn't spare the time this season—but we had a brief to keep UK
Chic visible there, especially at Calvin Klein, Ralph Lauren, Donna
Karan and all the other American designers with big fragrance advertising budgets.

I was sitting at my desk in London pondering whether to cancel
the booking that had been made for me to stay at The Mercer with
Alice, so I could spend more time with Ursula while I was there,

when it struck me. If I stayed at Ursula's, I wouldn't be able to sneak around with Miles. Even though she knew all about it, I couldn't imagine seeing him outside the anonymity of a hotel room—and I certainly couldn't countenance having rampant sex in my childhood bedroom, with the teddies, and my parents, looking on.

By that point, with all the Christmas and New Year jollies—and sales—to distract me, plus some quality time with Ollie, I really had almost stopped thinking about Miles, so I was quite surprised by how vividly that fully formed thought popped into my head. The next thing I knew The Mercer's address was going into the press accreditation form that Gemma had just put on my desk.

I skipped my yoga class that lunchtime, staying in the office when all the other girls went off, which was very unusual, but I wanted some time alone, with no risk of anyone casually looking over my shoulder. I had a private email to write.

Twenty minutes later I had written about fifty different versions and still wasn't happy with it. I understood enough about the lack of internet security to be very circumspect with what I wrote, but I was still agonizing over getting the tone right. So far the best I had come up with was this:

To: miles@smiles.com.au
From: epointer@chicmag.co.uk
Re: Are you doing New York?
Arrive NYC February 6. Staying at The Mercer. Look forward to
seeing your work.

I still wasn't sure about it. I felt it needed to be a little less assumptive that I would be seeing him, but then something happened that made me hit send with an instant reflex. Natalie suddenly appeared in the office. I don't know which of us was more surprised to see the other. She clearly hadn't expected anyone to be in there.

"Hello, Natalie," I said, trying to recover from the slightly sick feeling that I had sent an email I wasn't entirely happy with. "Can I help you with something?" I asked pointedly, hoping to make her feel as uncomfortable as possible.

Her eyes darted around the room making her look particularly "sleakit," as Frannie called it, as she tried to come up with a good reason why she had come into our office, at a time when we were all usually out. I saw her eyes rest for a second on the form on my desk.

"Alice needs your accreditation form," she said, far too quickly.

"Oh, does she?" I said, picking it up. "Well, here it is, Natalie. You can take it to her. I'm sure she will be racing back from that lunch I saw her leaving for half an hour ago, just to look at this form. How lucky you got it for her just in time."

My sarcasm was not lost on her and she snatched the form from my hand and stalked out. As I watched her big round bottom wobble away I couldn't remember when I had disliked somebody quite so much.

The next morning I got in early to check my emails—the way Natalie was creeping around I wouldn't have been surprised if she was hacking into our computers as well—and there was a reply from Miles in my Inbox.

To: epointer@chicmag.co.uk
From: miles@smiles.com.au
Re: Re: Are you doing New York?
Can deliver shots to hotel as required at the end of each day.
Will await instructions.

I was beaming as I deleted it and then emptied my Deleted Items file and re-started my computer.

The New York shows were as dull as I remembered them and the weather as terrible, but the shopping and the nightlife I squeezed in around them were stellar—plus I got to see Paul most days and fitted in a few visits to Ursula.

Apart from a really grim moment when three of my credit cards were refused one after another in Sigerson Morrison and another when I ended up trudging miles through filthy melting New York snow in my pristine Prada boots—one of the pairs I'd put aside back in October—I had a great time.

I didn't have to see much of Alice for one thing. She had a lot of contacts of her own in New York, so apart from sharing the limo, which I didn't even use all the time—hence the boot nightmare—we went our own ways.

And then of course there was Miles.

I saw him first at the Marc by Marc Jacobs show. It was about the fourth one I'd been to and while I had tried not to rubberneck too obviously in the direction of the photographers' pit at each of them, I'd had a fairly good look and hadn't been able to see him. It was quietly driving me nuts.

But I resisted the temptation to send him a text saying "R U Here???" because while I was almost desperate to see him, there was part of me that also wanted to string out the exquisite agony of the anticipation—and another, smaller, part that knew it might be better in the long term if I didn't see him at all.

But then, suddenly, as I walked up the stone steps into the venue, he was at my side. He didn't say anything, just appeared next to me. It was his battered old boots I noticed first and when I jerked my head up, there was that familiar face—much browner than before, especially against the winter-pale faces all around—with that big squinty grin beaming down at me.

He was wearing a navy wool beanie pulled right down on his head which made his white teeth look whiter and his green eyes look greener. In some kind of reflex action I gripped my Birkin bag to my stomach, just to have something to hold on to so I didn't fall over.

He said nothing and neither did I—I couldn't—he just held my gaze for one extended moment, as snow fell gently around us, then he touched my arm with the lightest of pressure and strode off to shoulder his way into the venue. As I watched his broad back disappear into the crowd I realized I had come to a complete standstill, with rivers of people streaming past me on either side.

I sat on the exquisitely uncomfortable metal bleachers—promoted to the second row on Alice's invitation, as she was in Bee's front-row spot—all squashed up with my coat, hat, gloves, pashmina, handbag, specs and notebook, and feeling vaguely unreal.

It was so weird to know Miles was in there somewhere, probably thinking about me—possibly looking at me—but I didn't know where. The particularly long wait before the show began gave me a chance to sneak plenty of looks down to the photographers' pit and after a while there was one long lens that did seem to be trained on me.

I was fairly certain it was Miles, so I stuck my tongue out in its direction and coquettishly licked my lips. The woman sitting next to me gave me a very funny look, but I didn't care. A couple of seconds later, my phone beeped. I looked in my Inbox and there was Miles's number with a message to check my emails later.

I tapped out my reply: "2 nite? 11?"

And back came the answer: "U bet."

The rest of the day passed in a blur, during which I picked up some new underwear at the fabulous Prada store in SoHo—paying cash to avoid card problems—before I went back to The Mercer to drop off my shopping and change.

I felt really mucky after a day rattling around in Manhattan in the snow and slush and wanted to look my best at Donna Karan, where I was sitting next to Alice in the front row, as a result of the ongoing confusion over who was actually there from UK *Chic.* It was fine by me.

I ran a bath, but before I got in it, I checked my emails. There were a few from Gemma keeping me up to date with travel arrangements for Milan and Paris, some jokes from Frannie, and Ollie had emailed to say he was going away for a special work conference in Bath for a few days and would be "phone off" for most of it.

Then there was one from Nelly telling me she was going to be in Milan—yippee!—the usual spam offering me a larger penis and a cheap loan, and then finally the one I wanted. It was a picture of me at the Marc by Marc Jacobs show with my tongue poking out.

The reunion with Miles was everything I had fantasized it would be, on the few occasions I had allowed myself the luxury of thinking about it. Four months had passed since I'd last seen him and I was all too aware that, give or take the odd phone call, I could have built the whole thing up into something it wasn't.

But from the moment I opened my hotel-room door to him I knew I hadn't. He was still wearing the woolly hat and he had augmented his usual jeans and motocross jacket with a big chunky polo-neck jumper. His cheeks were pink from the cold and he was grinning at me so cheekily, my stomach did a spontaneous backflip. I just stood there in the doorway gawping up at him. There was something about Miles that was so quintessentially male, it just did me in.

An image of Ollie at Nelly's party, painted and powdered like a Regency fop, complete with beauty spot, flashed across my brain. I deleted it instantly as Miles thrust his tongue into my mouth.

After we'd got to know each other again, as it were, and I had come to terms with the fact that I wouldn't be wearing those particular pieces of overpriced chiffon underwear again—they were in shreds on the floor—we just lay there, looking at each other.

"G'day," he said, tipping an imaginary hat at me.

"How do you do?" I replied.

"You tell me," he said.

"You do good," I said poking him in his rock-hard stomach. "You're looking seriously fit, Miles," I said. "You're even more toned and tanned than usual. Quite the Calvin Klein model. You'd give that Travis a run for his money right now."

"Summer," he said, with a contented smile. "Since I last saw you, I haven't done much except surf and lie around. There's only so much of this fashion bullshit world I can take—I don't know how you stand it—then I just have to go and sit on a beach for a while to get my head straight. I took a few photos, of course . . . on the beach." He laughed. "And I travelled around a bit in my van. Spent Christmas way up north. It was bloody hot and wet, but still beautiful. What did you do?"

Even as he said it, I saw his face constrict and I felt mine do the same, as my whole body involuntarily stiffened.

"Shit," he said. "Don't tell me. In fact, please erase that question from the records, OK? Let's stick in the here and now, shall we?"

I nodded dumbly.

"And right here and right now, I'd like to do this . . ." said Miles and I sank back into blissful oblivion.

I saw him twice more after that, late one night and then for a delicious rendezvous over lunchtime on the last day. Straight after he left, I raced uptown to meet Ursula for tea at The Pierre.

She was waiting for me in her usual spot in the Rotunda room—it was her favourite venue for meetings with writers—and when I walked in she burst out laughing.

"What?" I said, looking down to see if my skirt was tucked into my knickers or something. "What's so funny?"

"Oh, Em," she said. "You might as well take out a billboard in Times Square—look at you!"

"What?" I said more tentatively, as I had an idea where this was heading.

"He's in town is he?" said Ursula.

I grinned at her sheepishly and nodded. She nodded back.

"Just left him, have you?" she continued.

I sighed indulgently, as I sank into my seat.

"Oh, *you*," I said, kicking her foot with mine. "How do you always *know*?"

"Because being able to judge people by the tiniest little signals is a big part of what I do. A twitch of a mouth can net me another fifty grand if I read it right. Plus, of course, I've been around for about a million years. Here, have some tea and I'll order you a sandwich. You must be ravenous."

And for once, I was.

Another funny thing happened at that tea. Ursula gave me a book of poetry. There was nothing unusual about that, she was always trying to get me to read stuff I had no interest in, but this one was different. It was by my mother.

I just sat and looked down at it. It had a really nice cover with elegant hand-drawn type. I turned it over and on the back there was a beautiful black and white picture of my mother wearing a daisy-chain around her head. I'd never seen the photo before and, more to the point, I didn't know she had ever produced an actual whole book of poetry. I thought she'd just locked herself away in her study for hours as an excuse to smoke dope and ignore us kids.

"Open it," said Ursula. "Look at the dedication."

I did what I was told and there it was, in print for all to see: "For Emily."

I just sat looking down at it. I was lost for words. And I was try-ing not to cry. I'd been trying not to think about her since my walk with Toby at Christmas and now here it all was again.

"Go back a few pages," said Ursula gently after a while.

I turned back and saw that on the title page there was an inscrip-tion in my mother's writing, in her customary pretentious green ink.

"For my precious Emily. My bud," it said. "On the occasion of her becoming a woman."

It was dated the year I was born. I felt a chill go down the back of my neck.

"What is this?" I said to Ursula, when I was able to speak. "And why are you giving it to me now?"

"Your mother gave me that book, the year you were born, in trust. She was convinced she was going to die young . . ."

"She did," I said.

"Emily," said Ursula sharply. "Listen. She was convinced she wasn't going to see you grow up—which was true, really. So she said I was to give this to you when you became a woman. I think she meant when you had your first child, so as I don't see that hap-pening for a while, if ever, I feel this is the time to give it to you. And you have your mystery friend to thank for that."

I looked down at the book again and ran my finger over the cover. Then I looked back up at Ursula. She was smiling at me so fondly I had to go over and give her a hug.

I didn't open the book again until I was on the plane. There was something about the suspended time and the anonymity of those moving spaces that made me feel able to allow brain space to thoughts I would have pushed away in real life and time.

It was called *Paeanies*. The pun hadn't struck me before. Peonies had always been her favourite flowers, I remembered, and while I couldn't balance a cheque-book, I knew all about poetic metre, as it was the kind of thing my parents would sit and discuss for hours. When they were talking to each other, that is.

At first I just flicked through the pages. Most of the poems looked quite short and spare and each one was illustrated at the top with a line-drawing of a flower. Despite the difficult associations, it was a nice thing to have, I decided, and put it away in my tote bag. But after just a few moments, something made me get it out again.

I looked at the first poem. It was called "Bud."

> *Tiny flower*
> *Once a bud*
> *Now unfurling*
> *Your folds*
> *And creases*
> *Smoothing out*
> *Growing up*
> *Towards the light*
>
> *A vital mass of cells and water*
> *That is*
> *Love*
> *That is*
> *My daughter*

A tear slid out of one eye and then out of the other. I wiped them away and then I sat and read all the poems in the book one after another. By the time I got back to Heathrow I knew quite a few of them by heart.

18

IT was after nine on Saturday night when I got back to the flat from Heathrow, and Ollie wasn't in. I knew he'd been at his sales conference in Bath until that morning, but I had expected him to be back by then. I made repeated calls to his mobile but just reached the message bank. I sent him a text and got no reply to that. It was a bit weird—I mean, it was Saturday, I knew he wasn't out on the town.

When he wasn't back by eleven I started to get worried. I thought about ringing his parents to see if he had gone down there, but I didn't want to worry them. I rang Jeremy to see if he had gone to visit them rather than stay in on his own, but their machine was on, so they were clearly in the country.

After that I was completely flummoxed. Ollie was such a communicator, he prided himself on always letting everyone know where he was at all times—"accessible management" he called it—and that included me. Trying to take my mind off it, I did all my unpacking, stashing everything away, sorting out what I needed to take to the cleaner's and putting on the first load of washing.

When I came to my inflight bag I took my mother's book out and after looking at "Bud" one more time, I hid it in the back of my bedside cabinet. I didn't feel ready to show it to Ollie yet.

After that I went to bed, but I just lay there, too worried to sleep.

I was starting to have horrible visions of his yellow Karmann Ghia skidding on black ice at high speed and as the night crept on, and there was still no sign of him, I began to feel almost delirious with worry and somehow it got all caught up with feelings of guilt about Miles.

Maybe I was being punished for my terrible behaviour with him—and for not going to see my mother—and Ollie had been killed in a car crash and I'd be left all alone and penniless. I was such a bad person, I'd probably lose my job as well, my fevered brain told me, and go bankrupt from all my credit-card debt and get really fat from grief.

At 2 A.M., I couldn't stand it any longer. I got up, put the clean washing in the drier and a second load into the washer. Then I just paced around the flat, trying Ollie's phone endlessly with no success. I made myself some camomile tea to try and calm myself, but the worry combined with jet lag—it was still only 9 P.M. in New York—made it impossible. I turned on the TV for distraction, but at that time in the morning it all seemed to be nasty violent films and gangsta rap music videos.

I went back into the bedroom and grovelled around under the bed to find the books that Ursula had sent over to Milan with Paul. I chucked the one about body image back under there and got into bed with the other one, the collection of poems.

Siren Songs it was called, with a line underneath saying: "New works by emerging women poets." I turned to the contents and sure enough there were three poems in it by my mum. I looked at the publication date—1973, before I was born—and then I read her poems. They were OK, but I could tell they weren't as good as the ones in *Paeanies*. They were rather naïve and hippy-ish, but sweet in their way. I put the book in my bedside cabinet with the other one and turned out the light.

It was after four—and I was trying to remember how long you had to leave it before you could report a missing person to the police—when Ollie came in. I sprang up from the bed when I heard his key in the lock and ran to the door.

"Hello, darling," he said, like it was the most normal thing in the world to get home at that time in the morning, without letting anyone know.

"Where the hell have you been?" I said furiously, feeling like I should have been standing there wearing an apron and wielding a rolling pin, but the moment I'd heard that key all my guilt and anxiety had turned to anger. It was so thoughtless of him.

He seemed surprised by my tone.

"I've been at the conference in Bath," he said, like that was an explanation.

"I thought it ended this morning," I said.

"Well, it went over," he said shrugging. "They often do, you know that, Heffalump. Anyway, how was New York? How's Ursula? Has she got a new girlfriend yet?"

I shook my fuddled head trying to make sense of what he was saying.

"Forget New York, Ollie," I said. "And forget Heffalumps. If you knew you were staying on at the conference until four in the bloody morning, why the hell didn't you ring me and let me know? You knew I was coming back today. I just don't get it." I realized I was waving my arms in the air like someone in a cartoon, but it was that kind of situation. "I've been so worried. I was wondering whether to call the police."

My voice broke a little, from the combined worry—and a little lingering Miles guilt. He laughed affectionately.

"Oh, you silly sausage," he said, trying to put his arms around me.

"Don't silly sausage me," I said. "I'm really pissed off. I haven't had a wink of sleep worrying about you and I was already knackered by the flight and everything. I'm going to sleep in the spare room."

I started to stomp off. He came after me and grabbed my hand.

"I'm sorry, darling," he said, looking all wounded. "I thought you'd figure it out—you know how these things drag on—and by the time I realized I was going to be so late, I didn't want to disturb you with a phone call. I knew you'd be exhausted. Come on, come to bed with Ollie."

"Oh, all right," I said, too tired and weirded out to argue any more. "But don't ever do it again. And don't try any funny business either. I'm not in the mood."

I needn't have worried about Ollie exerting his conjugal rights, he went straight out the moment his head hit the pillow. I still couldn't sleep, though. I was too confused.

It was so out of character for him not to let me know where he was, but at the same time what right did I have to criticize him when I had spent a large part of the last five days bunking up with an Australian surfer in my hotel room? And the real reason I didn't want to make love with my husband was that I was so sated from jungle sex with Miles. What a bloody hypocrite I was.

I lay there for what seemed like hours angsting over it all—plus all my usual nocturnal anxieties about whether I should go and see my mother. Reading her poems was making me feel more curious about her, but I had been so devastated by my last visit, I didn't think I could ever go through it again. It's not something I could ever have told anyone, but often in those wakeful hours I wished she had succeeded in one of her many suicide attempts. A dead parent you can grieve. The living dead just haunt you.

When I finally woke at a jet-lagged ten fifteen Ollie wasn't there. Instead there was a note on his pillow:

Gone to Sunningdale to play golf with a couple of key Scottish retailers from the conference. Too good a bonding opportunity to miss. Didn't think last night was the time to tell you... Back this evening. We'll have dinner somewhere nice. Will keep my phone on as much as possible—but not allowed in clubhouse. Why not spend the day at The ESPA Spa at Mandarin Oriental? Slap's treat. Your Ollie, xxxxxxxx

I did. And I took Gemma with me. I would have liked to have taken Frannie really, but I knew that she and Andy would have been cosying up at home—like any normal couple on a freezing cold February Sunday. How Ollie could even contemplate stomping round a muddy golfcourse on a day like that was beyond me. Actually, how he could play golf at all was beyond me. I wondered if he would be doing it in full make-up. That would make an impression on his clients.

Gemma was thrilled to be invited to my spa day, as she was going through a painfully single phase. She was still moping over Kent and I knew she found Sundays particularly lonely, because both her flatmates had boyfriends. We were lounging around in something called "the Amethyst steam room" when she suddenly stood up.

"Look at me, Em," she said, doing a slow twirl, with her arms above her head. "Am I deformed? Am I foul? Am I ugly? No. Look at my thighs—do you see cellulite? No. Look at my stomach. Is it flabby? No. Look at my breasts. Are they way too small? Well, yes, actually—but really, I'm not a hideous monster, am I? I've even had a bloody Brazilian bloody wax. So why haven't I got a boyfriend? Tell me, *please*."

"I wish I knew, Gemma," I said, with all sincerity. "You're not only gorgeous—you are the loveliest person. Loyal, smart, funny . . . they must be mad not to have snapped you up. You're a prize."

"Blokes in London are all such tossers, Emily," she said slumping back down on to the bench. "They're all so obsessed with being cool they don't even ask you out in case their friends don't rate you. They just treat women as accessories to enhance their image. You might as well be a mobile phone. It makes me sick. They're not like that in New York—look at Kent . . ."

I had been wondering when we would get on to Kent.

"He said he just knew immediately he liked me and that was it. Why can't men be direct like that here? Oh, I wish he would come over to London, or I could go over there again. He's always sending me funny emails."

She sighed deeply. I felt really sorry for her. It's terrible to be twenty-three and feel like you'll never be kissed again.

"You know, Emily," she continued, flicking water off the ends of her post-modern Purdey cut. "Sometimes I think you and Frannie got the last two good straight men in London. It must be so wonderful to be married and living with a gorgeous man in your own home and knowing that you'll never have to spend a weekend by yourself again." She was right, I agreed, it was wonderful, but the funny thing was—so far I had pretty much spent that one by my-self.

Ollie got back from golf just after seven, looking rosycheeked and generally pleased with himself. I was in a good mood too after the spa and happy to see him.

I felt soft, smooth and invigorated after the steam room and an energizing aromatherapy massage and I was standing in my under-wear deciding what to wear to dinner—something to show off my freshly buffed and pummelled shoulders—when he came in. He got undressed, stuffed his golf gear into the laundry basket, and put on his dressing gown.

"Would you mind if we stayed in tonight, Em?" he said, hardly even looking at me, as he admired himself in the bathroom mirror. "I thought it would be nice just to watch a movie and have some-thing delivered. I'm shattered after all that corporate backslapping and we've got London Fashion Week starting in two days, and I'll have to be on top form for that."

I was really disappointed. I hadn't seen Ollie now for over a week and I'd been looking forward to dressing up and going some-where swanky. If I'd known we were staying in I would have had the relaxing aromatherapy massage.

"OK," I said, shrugging, and put my dressing gown on too.

As we watched the film—an old Cary Grant classic that Ollie had brought home one night, I think he was hoping to pick up some smoothie tips—and ate our Thai takeaway, something alarm-ing occurred to me. Miles was coming over to shoot the London shows. In fact, he had probably already arrived.

We'd talked about it in New York and how I couldn't possibly see him in my home town, because it would have felt just too tacky—but what I hadn't factored in was that Ollie also went to a lot of the London shows. Slap sponsored the make-up at half of them and he had to go. He also loved it, of course.

Slap for Chaps was having a stand at the selling exhibition as well and he'd probably be parading around wearing it, I realized, with a sinking heart. I knew it had done amazing things for the precious "brand," but I still didn't enjoy seeing my husband got up like Hugh Grant from the neck down and Eddie Izzard from the neck up. It was creepy.

I now felt slightly sick at the realization that over the next few days I would be sitting in venues with Ollie and Miles in the same space. I didn't quite know why, but I hated the idea of Miles seeing Ollie—especially with that bloody pancake on. Normally I was so proud of my husband, but for some reason I didn't like the idea of him through Miles's eyes. They belonged in different boxes and the idea of them being in the same one was all wrong.

Combined with residual jet lag and mixed up with the green curry that seemed to be dancing the macarena in my stomach, it all added up to another sleepless night.

The next day I was relieved to find that Ollie had got up and gone to the office without waking me up again. I got ready for work and on my way to the dry-cleaner's, I dialled Miles's number.

"Em," he said. "G'day."

"Hi," I said. "Are you in London?"

"Yeah, I'm having coffee somewhere in Portobello Road and it's shithouse. You really don't know how to make coffee over here, do you?"

My stomach turned over. He was so close to my home base.

"Don't we?" I said, weakly. "We have Starbucks—isn't that good coffee?"

"You are joking, aren't you?" said Miles, laughing heartily.

"Oh, I don't know," I said, a bit crossly. "I'm not a coffee expert, but, um, you see, the thing is, Miles. It's all a bit weird, because you probably don't know it, but you are about five minutes' walk from my flat right now and that's the kind of thing I'm ringing about. You see, my husband will be coming to a lot of the shows this week and it's just suddenly hit me how weird that's going to be."

"Hmmm," said Miles. "That is weird. Well, don't worry. I won't come near you. I won't even look at you. Not even through my longest lens. OK?"

"Thanks, Miles," I said. "I feel really, really strange about this."

And I don't want it to spoil this thing we have, I was thinking.

"I'll see you in Milan then?" I added.

"Cool," said Miles in his most smiley voice. "You just text me when you're ready."

God, I was a slut.

Despite Miles's assurances I still felt odd about the situation and spent the whole of London Fashion Week as jumpy as a flea, trying not to hang out with my own husband more than necessary and exercising extreme self-control not to look at the photographers' pit.

Maybe it was this state of high tension that caused me to react so strongly at the Huw Efans show. He was the latest Saint Martins-trained sensation to emerge on to the London catwalks, with a powerful vision that did not flinch from using shock tactics to make an impression. He did actually design really beautiful clothes, which I often used in my pictures, but he was better known for doing schlocky things like putting live rats on the catwalk and holding his shows on rubbish tips.

Normally I found it quite entertaining, but this season he did something I really couldn't cope with. The entire collection had been inspired by the film *The Shining* and everything was fine until the big finale when he reproduced that horrendous river of blood moment, at the top of the catwalk.

Of course, it wasn't real blood and I knew that, it was some kind of special-effects-department Kensington Gore, against a video loop of the moment in the film when the lift doors open and the blood pours out. But although I knew all that, the dark red liquid that suddenly gushed all along the catwalk *looked* just like blood and I completely freaked out.

I screamed, I jumped up out of my seat—which was close to the end of a row, luckily—and then I fainted, crashing to the ground in the full view of the entire audience.

The next thing I knew I had woken up on the floor outside the venue with two nice ladies from St. John Ambulance attending to me and Frannie bobbing up and down behind them, trying to see if I was OK. I was, but still very shaken and, worse than that, I was hideously embarrassed.

"Oh God, Frannie," I said, when I could speak again. "Did everyone see me?"

"Only the people right next to us," she lied, like the friend she was.

I didn't feel up to going to any more shows that night, so Frannie took me home in a cab and just moments after she left, I had my confirmation that my freak-out had been visible to everyone present. Peter Potter called on my mobile.

"Well, Emily," he said in his most smarmy darling/bitch tones. "That was *quite* a display you put on at Huw's show just now. What was that all about? Don't like Thirties evening gowns with plaid shirts?"

I laughed as gaily as I could. There was a pause.

"So?" he said, a harder tone coming into his voice. "What was all that about?"

"I don't like blood," I said. "I've got a full-on phobia about it. I do the same thing if I cut my finger chopping onions."

"Are you serious?" he said, not exactly sympathetically.

"Yeah, I'm serious. It's not that much fun actually, Peter, and I dearly wish I could control it, but I can't. I know people who are like that about snakes and birds, but with me it's blood.

"I tell you what, though," I added, trying to lighten the tone. "It's lucky I've only ever seen *The Shining* on video, because if I'd seen that river of blood thing at the movies, it would have been even worse than it was today. It really is my worst nightmare."

"Making an idiot out of myself at a fashion show would be mine, Emily darling, but each to their own."

And he rang off. There was no getting away from it, he really wasn't going to forgive me for not giving him that Nelly gonads story—and Peter Potter was famous for nurturing his grudges.

Not long after, I had another call. A nicer one. My phone beeped to tell me I had a text. It was from Miles and it was very simple: "R U OK?" was all it said.

I called him.

"You saw me as well then," I said.

"Yeah," said Miles. "I was actually in that bank of photographers quite near you and I heard someone scream. When I looked over and I saw it was you, it was all I could do not to rush over. Are you sure you're OK?"

"Yes, I'm OK," I said. "I just have this thing about blood. I really, really hate blood."

"I understand," said Miles. "I really, really hate spiders, which is not great when you live in Australia and spend a lot of time in the bush. So you're sure you're OK then?"

"Yes, I'm fine, it's just the shock and the humiliation, but thanks for checking, Miles, it was sweet of you." I paused. "I'll see you in Milan . . ."

About two hours later I was starting to feel better and was sitting in bed reading my mum's book, when Ollie called.

"Darling," he said. "I've just come out of a meeting and heard what happened at Huw Efans. Are you all right? I know about you and blood, you poor thing. That stupid little arse, that's not big or clever, it's just poor taste, vulgar shock tactics. That's why we don't sponsor him."

"I'm OK, Ollie," I said. "I feel a bit shaky, but I'm fine. I'm in bed. I'm going to sleep soon."

"Well, call me if you need me. I've got to go to three more shows we're sponsoring tonight, as you know, but I'll see you later. OK?"

The next day at the first show everyone was terribly felicitous to me, which just made it all the more embarrassing. The only person who wasn't being nice about it was Bee.

"How could you, Emily?" she was saying. "I was so embarrassed. Thank God you weren't in the front row, that's one blessing, but couldn't you have controlled yourself? I know you don't like blood, but it was only paint or something stupid and what do you think that kind of behaviour does for the image of the magazine? I was mortified."

"Give me a break, Bee," I said. "I didn't do it on purpose. I can't help it. It's a phobia. I hate blood like you hate," I racked my brain for a comparison. "Like you hate—losing an advertiser to *pure,* OK?"

"Gosh, is it that bad?" said Bee. "I'll let you off then."

Then as if it wasn't all humiliating enough, just when I thought it had all been forgotten, up it popped in Rotter's column.

Chic *magazine stylist Emily Pointer looked anything but when she freaked out at the sight of a little stage blood at Huw Efans' brilliant show on Thursday. Not what you'd call professional. Lucky for her she had handsome husband Ollie Fairbrother of Slap for Chaps fame to look after her when she got home.*

Yep, I thought, as I aimed the paper into the nearest rubbish bin, the little shit really did have it in for me. And he had his facts wrong as usual, because as it turned out, Ollie hadn't been there for me.

19

AFTER the tension of the London shows it was a relief to get over to Milan and surrender myself to the familiar routine of claustrophobic limo rides, freezing rain, back-breaking waits on hard benches and the various moods of my colleagues. I may have whined about the shows along with the rest of the fashion pack, but really, I loved them.

Slipping back into that crazy routine was always strangely comforting, and as I looked around the venue of the first show, at all the people in ridiculously high-heeled shoes, carrying handbags that cost as much as the deposit on a small flat, I felt I was back among my own tribe.

As well as all the famous bigshots I was always pleased to see again—Hello Anna, Hello Suzy—there were all the other fashion-shows faces I recognized from season after season, but I had no idea who they were, or where they worked. It was an odd kind of long-term anonymous relationship and it was funny to think that as a regular attendee myself, I was probably one of those known-but-unknown strangers to other people.

I always enjoyed seeing what they turned up in. Oh, I'd think, she's got a new coat. Or, that's the same bag she had last season, time for a change. Or, she's put on weight. You'd see a baby bump one season, notice she wasn't around the next one and then she'd be back showing off the photos. It was like a weird extended family of total strangers, and I loved it.

Bee seemed to be pretty cheerful on the whole too, which was a good thing, because Alice was whey-faced and monosyllabic to the point where I was almost worried about her. I mean, she was never what you would call easy company, but she had dark shadows under her eyes and gloomed around the place looking like some kind of fashion zombie.

Bee didn't seem to notice, mainly because Alice snapped into wide-eyed alert mode whenever being addressed by her mighty editor-in-chief, but also because it would have been a terrible inconvenience for her to acknowledge that her star stylist was ill-disposed during Milan, when she needed her in maximum schmooze mode. She was a tough old boot, our Bee.

In the end, though, Frannie and I agreed we couldn't watch Alice suffer any longer—or, at least, we couldn't stand being around it twelve-plus hours a day—and we decided that we had to do something about it. We'd snuck off to have coffee with Nelly, who was in town, with Iggy in tow, doing selected shows in her fashion-director-at-large role, and Frannie came back from the counter with a couple of paper straws.

"Go on," she said, handing them to Nelly. "Emily and I will draw straws for who's going to ask her what's wrong and you can oversee it as the neutral party."

"I don't know why you're bothering," said Nelly, tearing one straw in half and concealing them both in one hand so they looked the same length. "She's just a moody cow and a crap stylist, who should leave the magazine as quickly as possible, so Emily can have her job." She chuckled loudly. "OK, which of you two bleeding hearts is going first?"

We tossed a coin for that honour—while Nelly rolled her eyes—and I took the first turn, pulling out the torn straw.

"Oh no," I said, groaning. "Not me. Oh, go on, Frannie, can't you do it? Please? You're so much nicer than me . . ."

"Forget it," she said, taking a big bite out of her *panino*. "I'm not that bloody nice."

*   *   *

From that point on the pair of them didn't give me a moment's peace until I had my "little talk" with Alice. It had just turned into a big game for them—especially Nelly.

"I tell you what," she said to me one afternoon, while we were waiting for Prada to start, and she had been teasing me mercilessly about my forthcoming Oprah Winfrey moment, within very close range of Alice's ears. "I'll stop giving you a hard time, in fact, I'll help you do it."

"You will?" I asked, amazed.

Nelly's cleavage started shaking as the laughter welled up inside her.

"Yeah, I'll watch. Reckon I could scalp a few tickets for that. Actually, forget Oprah, we could make more of a Jerry Springer-type show out of it. I can just see it: 'Alice—Talentless Moody Bitch;' 'Emily—Wants to Help Crap Saddoes.' It would be great television."

I put my hands over my ears until she stopped.

My big moment finally came the next day, when Alice and I ended up alone together in the limo on our way to the Antonio Berardi show. Bee was tied up in a meeting with the head of *Chic* International and Frannie was doing an interview with Iggy's replacement designer at Rucca.

Alice was looking particularly miserable, I noticed, as I snuck a sideways look at her in the car. Even her usual gypsy tangle of vintage and ethnic jewellery, and a fanciful antique lace petticoat and army boot combo did little to dispel the miasma of doom around her. She looked as grey as the Milan sky.

I took a breath.

"Alice," I said. "Can I ask you something?"

She turned and looked at me with dead eyes.

"What?" she said, with no enthusiasm.

"I just wondered, um, if you are OK? It's just that you seem a bit low. You don't seem quite yourself and I felt I had to ask . . ."

I petered out in the force of her gaze. There was still no animation in her eyes, but there was a cold malice in there.

"That's what you'd like, isn't it?" she said eventually.

"What?" I said.

"You'd like there to be something wrong with me."

"Of course, I wouldn't," I said, quite taken aback. "It's just that you don't seem your usual self and I was concerned."

"Concerned how quickly you can get my job, Emily?"

I just stared back at her horrified.

"I know what your game is," she said. "Ever since you arrived at *Chic* you've been trying to get me sacked so you can swan around with your long legs and your handsome husband and your Sunday salons in Peter Potter's columns and your great friend Nelly Stelios and her famous boyfriend—and *my job*. You want it all, don't you? But you can't have my job, because I'm not going to let you. And it doesn't matter how many times you try and humiliate me about Croatia and spreadsheets and with all your clever ideas, you will never *ever* get my job."

I started to speak. I had been going to say I didn't want her job, but that was such a lie. Of course I wanted it—but not enough to try and get Alice the sack. I was just looking forward to the day she decided to leave, like most other people on the magazine.

"Alice," I said. "You've got me all wrong. I don't want you to get the sack. I'm not plotting against you. I really can't believe you think that. And it's not just me who thinks you're looking pale, Frannie has been worried about you too."

She laughed, bitterly.

"Oh yes, you and your little gang of cronies," she said. "I might have known you had them in on this too. Well, I know what you're up to, all sitting in your little office, laughing at me behind my back and trying to make me look bad in front of Bee. You think you're so clever, but it all gets back to me, you know, Emily. Well, you can all go and rot."

Then she put on her big black sunglasses and turned her head away from me. I didn't say anything, because I couldn't think of anything to say.

It was quite extraordinary, but Alice managed not to speak to me for the rest of the time we were in Milan—and without Bee noticing. She was never what you would call the chatty type, but it was amazing how she totally avoided making eye contact with me, despite our ridiculously close proximity twelve hours a day in the limo and at shows.

Even at intimate PR dinners for eight people she managed never to address me, refer to me, or look at me, without anyone noticing except me. It was very discomforting. Not even Frannie noticed, but then she wasn't looking out for it, because I hadn't told her or Nelly the truth about how Alice had reacted to my well-meaning enquiries. I just said she'd told me she was really tired after too much travel and left it at that, partly because I was still in a state of shock about it.

I'd really had no idea Alice felt that way about me. Of course I knew there had been some unfortunate incidents, like the spreadsheet scenario right at the start of my time on *Chic*, but I thought I'd done my best to defuse all that. I didn't think she liked me particularly, but I thought she felt that way about everybody.

I didn't want to tell Nelly what had happened because I knew it would have been foghorned all over town in a moment as a hilarious anecdote, but with Frannie it was more complex.

For one thing it would just have added credence to Alice's paranoid delusions to have had the two of us exchanging looks about her in the back of the car and nudging each other, which is exactly what would have happened. Because in some ways, Alice was right.

Frannie, Gemma, Janey and I did sit in our office and laugh at her pictures when the magazine came out. We did have running jokes at her expense about stupid things she'd said in ideas meetings. Gemma had even paraded around the office on several occasions dressed in pastiches of Alice's signature whimsical outfits—gumboots with a gypsy skirt, a ballet tutu with a chunky fisherman's jumper and a top hat, that kind of thing. Oh, how we'd laughed.

And then, of course, there was the simple fact that I did want her job. Perhaps at some unconscious level I was trying to undermine her, I thought. I didn't think I was that ruthlessly ambitious, but after years living with Ollie, maybe it had rubbed off on me. He was certainly convinced that I should leave *Chic* if I wasn't promoted to fashion director in the next six months and was always reminding me of it.

With Frannie busy with her big profile on the new Rucca designer, Nelly wrapped up in Iggy, Bee obsessively chasing advertisers—she'd lost a couple of key accounts to *pure* and she was on a mission—and Alice iceberg-ing me, it was adding up to being a pretty miserable Milan season for me. The only nice thing about it was Miles.

He'd been to see me in my hotel room late at night a couple of times and we'd had a few heart-stopping moments of eye contact on our way in and out of shows, then on the very last day, I ran into him completely unexpectedly at the Fiera.

Frannie was away watching the Rucca fittings and I'd sneaked off to our secret café on my own to have a break from Bee's advertiser mania and Alice's gamma death rays. I was just deciding what to have when I realized Miles was standing right next to me at the counter. We looked at each other in amazement and I couldn't stop myself grinning at him like a fool.

"Hey, Emily," he said, pecking me on the cheek, like it was the most normal thing in the world for us to run into each other. "How are you doing? Want a coffee?"

We took our macchiatos off to one of the tables and sat there chatting like the casual fashion acquaintances we supposedly were. Really, what was so surprising about a catwalk photographer and a fashion stylist with loads of friends in common having a quick coffee together? Well, nothing, if I hadn't been hyperventilating and practically swooning off my chair.

Just looking at the way his strong hand circled the cup made me dizzy and when he leaned back in his chair, stretching out his legs and running his other hand through his hair, I couldn't take my eyes off him. I wanted to bite chunks out of him.

Miles seemed much more in possession of his faculties than I did, but then he always was the classic relaxed Australian.

"Gee, that Franco Belducci show was a crock," he said. "Do you think anyone would really wear that shit? They looked like drag queens. Ugly ones."

"No," I said. "No one will wear that rubbish, but they'll buy the black trouser suits and he advertises with *Chic*, so we all have to go smiling to the show and I have to use something from that hideous collection in one of my stories in the next six months."

Miles frowned.

"You have to use things you don't even like in your pictures?"

I nodded and shrugged. "It's just part of the business. I do get to shoot the things I love as well, so the crap like Belducci is just a pay-off."

Miles shook his head.

"Is that why you have to go out for all those dinners with PRs as well?" Then he lowered his voice. "When you could be having me for dinner?"

I felt my face heat up like my straightening iron.

"You've got it," I said.

"God, it's bullshitty, what you do," he said. "And you do it all the time. I only do it for a few weeks a year and that's bad enough. I think I'd go nuts."

"It's worth it," I said. "For all the great stuff I get to do as well." I giggled. "And for the Prada discount."

"You're a hopeless case," said Miles, punching me lightly on the arm and smiling indulgently.

We sat there chatting a bit more and I gradually calmed down. I even managed to keep it together when various people came over to say hello to each of us. When we were alone again, Miles got us two more coffees and as he was walking back to the table with them, I noticed he was looking at me with a more serious expression on his face.

"Are you OK, Emily?" he said when he sat down.

"What do you mean?" I said. I hoped he wasn't going to tell me to eat more.

"Well, we've seen quite a bit of each other this week and I do also sneak the odd look at you through my long lens, and I've noticed you looking a bit low. You usually strut around the shows like such a haughty little princess, and this week you seem a bit, I dunno, flat."

"I am," I said, and then I told him what had happened with Alice, the whole story, which I hadn't told anyone else.

Miles listened carefully, made a few perceptive and supportive comments and generally made me feel much better about it all. It didn't really matter what he said—although his suggestion that people were always going to be jealous of someone as beautiful as me, was delicious, of course—it was just such a relief to have told someone. Someone who wasn't in any way involved in it, or affected by it. Apart from Ursula, I didn't have anyone else like that in my life, I reflected.

Eventually it was time for us to leave, Miles had to get away to mark out his space at the Versace venue and I had to do three more advertiser shows before that. We strolled out of the café doors together and I was just about to turn left towards the escalators and the exit, when Miles grabbed my arm and pulled me towards the staircase.

"Go up," he hissed at me. "I'll follow."

He knelt down and pretended to sort out something in his camera bag and I did what I was told and went up the stairs. I stopped when I got to the next landing, not sure what to do. It was dusty and deserted up there, and it seemed a million miles away from the frantic main spaces of the Fiera.

A couple of minutes later Miles joined me, his filthiest grin splitting his face. He took my hand and led me up the next flight of stairs, to another landing, where there were a few old plastic stacking chairs lying about in piles and it looked even more abandoned. To one side there was a recess with a door in it and Miles led me to it, pushing me gently against the wall.

As his mouth joined mine I flipped straight into the zone where nothing existed but me and him and flesh against flesh. I was panting so hard, I felt like I might vomit. My stomach was churning with desire for him.

I had my hand down his pants and I was grinding myself against him while we kissed and then moving more out of instinct than conscious thought, I tried to move one leg up over his hip, but my tights and skirt made any further developments impossible. Miles pulled away from me and started laughing.

"Bloody tights," he said. "Bloody winter clothes. Bloody Europe. If we were in Australia, I'd have had you by now. No wonder they're into all those pervy stockings and suspenders over here."

I smiled back at him, it was funny. Then he put his mouth against mine and kissed me again, very tenderly, without closing his eyes. When he pulled away again, he put his hands up around my face.

"But that's OK, isn't it, Emily?" he said, his eyes gazing searchingly into mine. "Because it's not just about the fucking, is it?"

I stood there gazing back at him. That was a question I really didn't want to answer. Not even to myself.

I couldn't believe it, but Alice carried her cold face right on over into Paris, where it was even easier for her to ignore me, as we didn't go round in such a tight little family *Chic* unit there anyway.

Even having Luigi arrive from Milan to drive us again, with the associated hilarity of following strange limos around Paris and Bee's happiness about having her champion cigarette lighter on hand, didn't do much to lift the mood between us. I felt self-conscious about everything I said and did in front of Bee and Alice, in case it added to her conviction that I was out to stitch her up.

In the end, I was acting so weirdly, it was my moodiness that Bee ended up being concerned about, not Alice's. The two of us were walking through freezing fog over to the tent in the Tuileries to see Lanvin when she asked me about it.

"Is something wrong with you?" she asked, with her usual bluntness, her high heels crunching harshly on the frozen sandy path.

"No," I snapped, much too quickly. "Why?"

Bee looked at me with narrowed eyes. Our breath hung in the air between us.

"You seem unusually quiet, Emily. I'm used to you and Frannie chattering away in the back of the car like a couple of entertaining schoolgirls, but now you seem to have hit surly adolescence. That display you put on at Huw Efans was bad enough, but now you've got the sulks and I'll tell you straight, it's a fucking bore. I know it must be humiliating having your husband parading around like Lily Savage in a Savile Row suit, but has something actually happened?"

"No," I lied. "I'm just a bit tired."

She sighed impatiently.

"We're *all* tired at the shows, Emily. Dealing with it is part of the job and I've already got Alice's moods to endure, without you pulling the prima donna act as well, so snap out of it."

Then she slapped me quite hard on the upper arm with her bright green kid leather gloves and stalked off into the fog.

In every regard it was turning out to be one of my less fun Paris seasons. I didn't see so much of Nelly there as I had in Milan because she was pretty much Paris fashion royalty now, in the front row at most shows and caught up with Iggy's working scene every evening.

He wasn't showing that season—he was going to debut for Albert Alibert in October—but she was so wrapped up in him and making their new life together in Paris, she just didn't have the same time for her old London mates. Not in any snobby way, just the practical facts. We did have dinner once and a couple of drinks and coffees, but there wasn't the same feeling of being in a gang.

I still had Frannie, of course, but she didn't seem interested in going out at all. She wasn't drinking or having late dinners, because she was on some kind of super-strict de-tox diet she was researching for her big annual "Bikini Beauty" story for the June issue. It was boring even by my standards of food consumption, but there was nothing I could do to shift her from it.

The final disappointment was no Paul. For the first time in years he wasn't doing Paris, because he'd been offered a car commercial at such a ridiculous fee his agent had threatened to sack him if he turned it down. It had all happened at the last moment and he'd rung me from the shoot in Rio to tell me.

"Repeat after me," he had said down the phone, when I'd groaned with disappointment at the news. "Beach. House. Fire. Island. The. Pines. OK? Have you got that?"

There were just two things—or, rather, two people—that made

Paris bearable that March. One was Miles, who came over to the Meurice late, several nights that week—I'd given him a key again—but the other was more of a surprise to me. It was the writer, Rosie Stanton.

I'd seen her a few times at Christmas parties and launches, since she'd come to the Sunday salon and when I bumped into her at Junya Watanabe on the first morning of the Paris shows, she suggested we "catch up" for dinner, as she put it. I'd been a little vague at the time, not wanting to commit myself until I'd seen what other invitations were coming in. But by the Friday, when there were no exciting dinners of any kind on offer, I was more than happy to accept her invitation to go out after Alexander McQueen.

We went to Brasserie Lipp, where she seriously impressed me by getting us a table, not only downstairs—most foreigners were instantly ushered up the spiral staircase to Social Siberia—but in the front section where only the chosen few were ever seated, and strictly locals. We were actually next to Sonia Rykiel, who ate there practically every night.

It was Rosie's perfect French and intellectual appearance—i.e. hopelessly ungroomed and badly dressed—that had swung it, I realized. My French was OK, a result of that six months in Paris as a child and the expensive education that Ursula had given me, and it was good enough to tell that hers was pretty much native.

"I read French and economics at Cambridge," she told me, when I remarked on it, raising her glass of burgundy to chink my *kir royale*. "And I lived here for several years. That's how I got into fashion writing actually. I was living over here as a correspondent for *The Sunday Courier*, mainly covering French politics, but one day they got me to interview a young designer who couldn't speak any English, because their fashion editor at the time couldn't speak any French, and when she left I got the gig."

At least that explained her dress sense, I thought, taking in the details of that evening's outfit, which was as apparently random as usual. This one featured some kind of terrifying long-line crocheted cardigan in ecru string, over a black polo neck and a flowery summer skirt, with heavy black knee boots.

When Alice mixed heavy boots with floaty dresses it was some kind of a poetic statement, but on Rosie it just looked like a horrible accident. She had flaking pale pink metallic varnish on bitten fingernails, and her hair was in its customary un-style, centre parted and limply hanging. It wasn't helped by the black macramé beret—string was clearly a theme for her that season—that she'd just taken off.

Despite our lack of taste convergence and her rather intense conversational style, I enjoyed Rosie's company. As I had found at the Sunday salon, she stretched me in the brain department. Talking to her about shows made me think about them quite analytically rather than just going on about how "divine" something was, like I did with everyone else. Which really meant how great I thought it would look on me.

Not that I got to say much. "Talking" to Rosie one-on-one was rather more about listening than speaking, I had discovered, but at least she was worth paying attention to. Over the course of the dinner she gave me quite a detailed lecture comparing and contrasting Jean Paul Gaultier and Alexander McQueen, both of whose shows we had seen that day.

"Gaultier is essentially inspired by retro aesthetics," Rosie was saying, fixing my gaze intently over her gigot of lamb. "But he is interested in how he can make them relate to current mores. McQueen, on the other hand, takes contemporary concerns and imposes them on to historical styling. The interesting thing is that although he goes back much further for inspiration, in the current context—with its universal sense of apocalyptic inevitability—he is the more modern designer."

It was quite amazing really, I thought, how she could eat, talk, think and drink simultaneously without choking herself.

"In the Eighties," she continued, stuffing in a large piece of bread, "before the current vintage boom, when most designers were interested in designing for a putative twenty-first-century utopia, or an ironic mis-topian take on that, Gaultier seemed paradoxically more innovative than his contemporaries."

She paused to smile at me, rather smugly, while I chewed and nodded.

"But now that we are beyond that rather metaphysical sense of millennial uncertainty," she continued, "replaced with an actual environment of chaotic change and apocalyptic insecurity, the more distant past becomes more relevant as a reference point, than recent decades. Fundamentally, McQueen's is an aesthetic of anxiety, which I think is very interesting."

I thought I pretty much got the gist of what she was saying and I was rather impressed. Impressed with her and impressed with myself for understanding and even enjoying such a conversation.

Then she started droning on about Rei Kawakubo, who was not my favourite designer, mainly because I never got an invitation to Comme des bloody Garçons, and my mind was floating off into autopilot, wondering whether I should text Miles to see whether he was up for a post-prandial parlez-vous, when Rosie said something that made me snap back to attention.

"Are you happy at *Chic*?" she asked, apparently out of nowhere, although I realized that she had just been talking about how she was enjoying working for magazines after ten years on newspapers.

I was really surprised.

"Well, yes," I said. "It's one of the great fashion magazines of the world and Bee is a wonderful editor. I love working for her."

"And you're senior fashion editor, is that right?"

I nodded.

"How would you like to be a fashion director?" said Rosie.

"On *Chic*?" I asked, suddenly getting concerned that Rosie might be on a secret mission from Alice.

"No," she said, slowly stirring her coffee. "On *Surface*."

"What's *Surface*?" I asked, with intense relief.

"It's a new magazine of which I have just been made editor-in-chief," said Rosie. "I've been given carte blanche to choose my staff and I would like you to be fashion director."

"Gosh," I said, almost spluttering with surprise. "That's very kind of you, Rosie. I'm really flattered. Crikey, you sprang that on me. What kind of magazine is it going to be?"

"It's going to be a glossy fashion magazine, like *Chic*, or *Vogue*, or *Bazaar*, but with less fluff and more analysis. A fashion magazine for women who think."

She smiled at me. One of her front teeth was quite grey.

"There won't be any relationship rubbish in it," she continued. "Or horoscopes, or beauty coverage. Our reader isn't interested in mascara. But there will be more fashion shoots than in most glossies, interspersed with essays on trends and in-depth profiles of the more interesting designers by important writers. I interviewed Junya this morning, for the first issue." She flashed her rather smug smile again. "Imagine *The Economist,* but as a fashion magazine."

I was still trying to imagine a woman who wasn't interested in mascara but who would be interested in looking at loads of fashion pictures. It sounded a bit potty to me, but it's always nice to be offered a job, so I didn't say no immediately. Then something struck me.

"If you aren't going to have beauty coverage," I said, "how are you going to get the advertising revenue to finance the magazine? Most fashion magazines are mainly bankrolled by the beauty industry, not fashion, as you know."

"We believe that if the fashion and writing are good enough to attract the right readership—and they will be—the beauty houses will feel they can't afford not to be in *Surface,* but we won't be at their beck and call for editorial coverage. In fact they'll come begging to us."

"Well, that would be nice," I said with all sincerity. "They torture Bee and Frannie." I laughed ironically. "My husband is one of the worst."

She smiled again, as if to say—I rest my case.

"So are you interested?" she said. "Does 'fashion director' appeal as a title?"

"Well, of course it does, but to leave *Chic* would be a huge step. I would really have to give it some very serious thought and I'd need to know a lot more about—er—*Surface,* first. Like, where did you get the name from, for example? And who's publishing it?"

"When we get back to London, I'll show you the dummy," she said, glossing over my questions. "I'm sure you'll love it. The first issue isn't coming out until September, so you've got a bit of time to make up your mind."

I promised to think about it, although I didn't think I was remotely interested at that point. But then again, I thought, on my way back to the Meurice in a cab—"Emily Pointer, Fashion Director."

It did have a certain ring to it.

20

I HANDED in my notice at *Chic* less than two weeks later, straight after the new season ideas meeting.

Up until that moment I had only been thinking vaguely about the job at *Surface*. I'd seen the dummy and had been impressed by the art direction, the number of fashion pages and the salary Rosie had offered me, plus, of course, the fashion director title appealed more and more. But I still didn't think I wanted to leave *Chic* for an untried start-up mag.

The only thing that made me start to give it more serious consideration was Ollie's reaction. He'd clapped with delight when I'd told him about Rosie's offer. We were having a post-Paris dinner at Locanda Locatelli and he'd immediately ordered champagne to celebrate.

"But that's perfect, Emily, darling," he'd said. "A highly sophisticated, internationally focused product, with a respected editor, nicely niche and intellectually edgy, but not way-out streety, and the right job title for you at last. You'd be mad not to take it."

"Are you sure, Ollie?" I said. "We don't even know who the bloody publisher is. It could be some seriously dodgy porn baron, or an arms dealer. I'm on a good gig at *Chic*, I know Bee likes me and I haven't been there that long, so it's not like I'm stagnating. I'm really not sure, but you seem to be absolutely convinced."

"One hundred per cent, sweetheart. You know I wouldn't encourage you to leave *Chic* on a whim. I'm convinced this is the right move for you."

I took more notice of Ollie's opinions on these things than anyone, but I still hadn't decided to do it—until I sat in that new season meeting and heard Alice reel off every single story on my ideas list one after the other. The Sarajevo thing last time had been a shock, but this was like being in the *X Files*. Especially as I had typed up my list and printed it out at home to be double, triple sure she couldn't get hold of it, but somehow she had.

The ideas Alice suggested weren't exactly the same on every detail of photographers and locations—although even some of those were identical—but the basic story concepts all were. I just stared at her in disbelief.

After what she'd said to me in Milan I kept expecting her to look over at me at some point in triumphant disdain, but she didn't. She just stared at Bee, waiting for approval in her usual rabbit-in-the-headlights way, who praised her lavishly. For my ideas.

I was in such a daze I didn't even realize immediately that her performance had just left me with nothing to read out and I was on next—any minute. I felt completely panicked. While I had come up with my packing idea under extreme pressure last time, I didn't feel remotely up to spontaneously producing a whole list of them, so I did the only thing I could do in the circs. I ran out of the room.

"Sorry, Bee," I said, putting my hand over my mouth like I was just about to vomit. "Carry on without me, I'll be back in a minute."

I ran out of Bee's room, out of the *Chic* offices and right out of the building without stopping. I was in such a state of shock all I could think of was getting some fresh air. I also didn't want Bee sending Nushka round to my office to find me.

I leaned against the wall of the building, panting, my breath hanging in white clouds in the freezing March air. I didn't have my coat, bag, or any money with me, so I couldn't ring Ollie, but I knew I could seek comfort from the Greek guys in the café across the road. They knew me so well, they were happy to give me a cappuccino on the house and at that moment I found their normally irritating line of "lovely laydee" patter quite comforting.

I sat there with my cooling coffee for about an hour, alternately staring into space and drafting my resignation letter on a paper napkin. Between scribbling, I did consider alternatives. I could go upstairs—show Bee my ideas list and tell her what Alice had done, then and the previous two seasons, but somehow I just couldn't bring myself to do it. It was all so nuts I didn't think she'd believe me. And somehow, although Alice's behaviour had been so appalling, I still couldn't shop someone like that.

So, with much crossing out and rewriting, I kept going with my resignation letter and then I wrote it out clearly on a second napkin. When I'd finished I asked Demetrios if I could use their phone. First I rang Rosie, to make sure her offer was still open—it was—so I accepted it, and then I rang Nushka.

"Are you all right, Emily?" she said, sounding genuinely concerned. "We were about to send out the St. Bernard. All your stuff is still here, but you just vanished."

"No, I'm not all right," I said. "Is the trends meeting over?"

"Yes."

"Is Bee available?"

"Yes," said Nushka, who had the perfect PA's instincts about when her boss needed to be made instantly available.

"OK then," I said. "I'm coming right in to see her."

My heart was beating so fast as I walked back to the office, I really did feel physically ill. The more I thought about leaving *Chic,* the worse I felt, but how could I carry on working with Alice after that?

Gemma sprang up when I walked past her desk on my way to Bee's office, but I just brushed her away. I had to get it over with before I lost my nerve. Bee was leaning out of her window smoking when I walked in. I knocked on the glass partition to get her attention.

"Emily!" she said, flicking the fag end down into the street. "What is going on with you? Are you ill?"

"No," I said and handed her the paper napkin.

Bee glanced over it and pointed at a chair.

"Sit," she ordered, coming over to join me at her big round meeting table. "What the hell is all this about, Emily? You were already acting like a freak in Paris and now you run out of the ideas meeting, and then come back to resign one of the best jobs in fashion—on a serviette. Have you gone mad?"

"I don't think so, but I want to leave. I'm really sorry, Bee."

She narrowed her eyes and popped two pieces of nicotine gum into her mouth.

"Have you got another job?" she said after a few life-giving chews.

"Yes," I said. It was by far the simplest explanation.

"Aha!" said Bee, clicking her fingers. "I knew there was something going on in Paris. What is it then? Not something at *pure*, please . . ."

"God no, but I can't tell you where. It's a secret project."

"Oh, no," she said, shaking her head. "It's that dopey thing Rosie's doing, isn't it? That's interesting, I thought she might try and steal Alice and she's gone for you. How interesting. I wouldn't have thought your work would be pretentious enough for her. She must be savvier than I thought."

"How did you know?" I squeaked.

Bee just rolled her eyes. Of course she knew. She always knew.

"But you can't be serious, Emily," she said, her voice softening. "You can't leave *Chic* to go and work on some pretentious start-up with no reputation, no job security and an untried and appallingly badly dressed editor. You're doing so well here, you know I love your work and—even more importantly—I love working with you."

She gave me a deep nod with raised eyebrows that said it all. She was telling me she liked me more than Alice. But it wasn't enough. After what had happened at that meeting I couldn't stay on at *Chic* for another day. I felt like Alice was going to appear wearing my clothes at any moment.

"No, Bee," I said. "I'm really sorry. I love working here, I think you are wonderful, but I need a fresh challenge. I'd like to leave immediately, if you don't mind. It's a good time for me to go, I've done all my shoots for this season and . . ." I petered out, thinking: and Alice will be doing all my shoots for the next one.

Bee sighed and stood up, lighting a cigarette, en route to her usual spot at the window. She looked really, sincerely, disappointed. I felt rotten.

"Emily, my dear girl," she said. "If you really feel you need to go now—go. But I know there is more to this than you are telling me. Something has happened and I will find out what it was, but hear this first. I am giving you one month's grace to change your mind about this crazy idea. Just one month, OK? Here's the deal—I'll give you a hefty pay rise if you stay and I'll change your title to deputy fashion director, if that would make a difference."

I just shook my head, laughing inwardly at the irony of it, and then just hung my head. I felt absolutely sick.

Gemma got all tearful when I told her, Janey and Frannie my news.

"You can't leave," she said, actually sobbing. "You *can't*. I can't bear it if you leave. I'll probably *die*."

"What are you talking about—leaving?" said Frannie. "What the hell's going on?"

"I just need a new challenge," I said, determined to stick to my story. I just couldn't cope with trying to explain that Alice had psychically stolen my ideas for the second time. I'd sound like a nutter. And with my family history, that was something I was not prepared to risk.

"Well, I've got some news for you too," said Frannie. "If you do bloody leave you're not going to get to see me get really, really fat— because I'm three-and-a-half months bloody pregnant and you won't be around to watch, you big idiot."

"You're what?" I said and gave her a big hug. "Oops, mustn't squeeze you too hard. That is the most wonderful news. So that's why you weren't drinking in Paris, you sly dog," I said, leaning down to kiss her tummy. "Well, I won't see you every day, but I'm not leaving the country. I'll still get to see you turn into a human barrage balloon. I wonder if it will show much?"

She punched me on the arm, but Gemma was still wailing.

"Where are you going?" she sobbed. She wasn't up to taking in two such big pieces of news at once. "Can I come with you? I might get someone really horrible as my boss, instead of you. Oh, you can't be serious, Emily. Tell me you're joking."

But I wasn't and it didn't take me long to gather up the few things

I was going to take home with me that night. Gemma would pack up my other bits and pieces and bring them over at the weekend.

By the time I was ready to go, word had got round the entire office and Tim the art director and most of the rest of the staff had come round to our office with bottles of wine they'd had stashed away to give me an impromptu leaving party. I was touched by how shocked and upset everyone seemed to be that I was going. Bee even came in and told them all they hadn't seen the last of me yet, if she had anything to do with it. I knew better, I thought, but I smiled weakly at her.

By seven o'clock people were beginning to drift away, with lots of hugs and good wishes and "you'll be backs" and I decided it really was time for me to leave. But first I had to confront Alice. She and Fatalie were just about the only people who hadn't come to say goodbye to me. I told Frannie and Gemma I was going to the loo and walked round the corner to Alice's office. She wasn't there, but Natalie was. Sitting in Alice's chair, tapping away on Alice's computer. Wearing one of Alice's signature hats,—a vintage stetson.

"Where's Alice?" I asked her, taking in the scenario.

"Gone home," she said, leaning back, her arms folded behind her head, her overcooked cleavage quivering with excitement. "To celebrate."

"Oh really," I said, in my most ice-maiden tones. "I hope she enjoys herself. She might even smile; that would make a change. Well, I'm off then. Goodbye, Natalie."

Julie Andrews couldn't have done it better, I told myself, but as I turned to walk out of the office she called my name. With that irritating instant reaction we all have, I turned back round and was immediately furious with myself I hadn't just ignored her.

"By the way, Emily," said Natalie, with a fake smile. "Fuck you." And she gave me the finger.

21

OLLIE had seemed delighted I'd actually made the big scary break, but when it came to my first day at *Surface* two weeks later he wasn't there to see me off. He'd gone off to Milan for the furniture fair, where Slap was having a stand. He sent me a text to wish me luck the night before, but that was it. I had rather expected flowers.

When I arrived at the magazine's offices in a rather obscure corner of Bloomsbury, near King's Cross, half of the furniture still hadn't been unwrapped. In fact the first thing I had to do was to set up my own room, which was more like a generous broom cupboard, wrestling acres of plastic sheeting off a really nasty pale grey desk and chair. The rest of my facilities comprised a second-hand filing cabinet. I didn't have a computer yet—or a phone.

The staff weren't particularly welcoming either—all one of them. The first issue was due out in just over four months and at that point the only person in place, apart from me and Rosie, was the art director, a lanky young man called Steve, who she had recruited from *Wonderdog*.

Although I did think he was very talented, Steve, in person, was not my scene. He had multiple piercings, overcomplicated facial hair and a shaved head. We looked each other over and in that first instant I knew we were unlikely ever to be buddies. It was clearly mutual and I hoped we could just rub along. The ad sales were being handled by an outside agency—all part of Rosie's determination to keep the two sides of the magazine completely separate—so there wasn't even a jolly commercial team to pad things out and lighten the atmosphere.

At least Rosie made an effort to make me feel welcome, inviting me into her office for a rosehip tea, before realizing, after a few minutes scrabbling on her desk, which was covered in great piles of paper, books and unopened envelopes, that she only had one mug. I tried not to compare it with Bee's office, with her immaculate glasstopped desk that she cleared of paper every night before she went home, and Nushka walking in with freshly brewed espressos in Limoges demitasses.

"It's great to see you," said Rosie, clearly doing her best. "It's really starting to feel like a magazine now you're here."

"When is everyone else arriving?" I asked.

Rosie looked at me blankly.

"The rest of the team?" I continued.

"This is it," said Rosie, apparently surprised that I had expected there to be more than three people. There were thirty on the staff of *Chic*—and that was just editorial. There was a marketing department and a big ad sales team as well. That was when I realized there were an awful lot of questions I hadn't asked Rosie before taking this job.

"But what about my assistant . . . ?" I asked, hesitantly. That was one thing I had made a point of raising with her and I remembered very clearly that she'd said, "We'll sort it out when you get there."

I'd taken that to mean, we'd sort out the details of the salary and starting date when I got there, and had been planning to ask Gemma to join me.

"Well, obviously we can't take anyone else on the staff at this stage," said Rosie, as though it was the most normal thing in the world to do an international fashion magazine with three staff. "But once we are more established, you'll be able to have someone part time. For the time being, you can use fashion students. It would be great experience for them."

But probably not for me, I reflected.

"What about your assistant?" I asked, starting to feel quite alarmed.

"Oh, I've got work experience people booked from Saint Martins and the London College of Fashion, to cover all that, and Steve's going to use graphics students to help him when we get nearer the deadline, and the odd freelancer for the really busy time."

I was horrified, but she seemed so confident about it all, I decided I just had to go and get on with it for the time being and hope things improved. I sat at my desk and wondered what to do with myself. It was so weird to be in what was supposed to be a magazine office and not be surrounded by endlessly ringing phones and overexcited people. It was almost creepily quiet in there.

I unpacked my office essentials —a photo of me, Frannie and Nelly taken at a Jasper Conran after-show party, a handwritten thank-you note from Karl Lagerfeld, a postcard of my father's painting from the Tate Modern and my shoot kit. This was a Prada washbag—a Christmas freebie—packed with safety pins, tampons, aspirin, Sellotape, tit tape, scissors and other essential emergency supplies of my trade. Paul had once slipped a packet of condoms into it as a joke.

Then I went looking for the stationery cupboard to try and make my little cubby-hole look more like a working office. There wasn't one. I sat in my horrid grey chair for a moment feeling quite stunned about it all, then I roused myself and made lists on envelopes I had floating around in the bottom of my handbag, of all the things I needed to bring in to the office and all the people I needed to ring with my new details.

But what new details? I didn't have a phone number or an email address to give out, for a magazine no one had ever heard of. Feeling more and more wobbly, but still determined not to allow panic to set in, I decided to use my mobile to let a few key PRs and agents know where I was. There was no signal in my so-called office, so I spent the next hour crouching in the building's drafty stairwell making my calls and telling them all to use my mobile number for now.

It wasn't until I went back into my broom cupboard that I realized that if any of them did ring me, I wouldn't be able to pick up the calls in there. What an idiot.

As I sat there my mind drifted inexorably to what it would be like in the *Chic* offices that morning. It was mid-April and everyone would be wearing their new spring looks and comparing purchases. There would be lots of excitement as they packed to go on trips to impossibly glamorous places. Rails and rails of gorgeous clothes coming in to be selected for shoots. Pre-release CDs blaring out from the features department's stereo.

There would come Bee, clicking through the office in new Prada sandals with a perfect pedicure, a freshly sprayed-on tan and gleaming hair. Frannie would be sitting at her desk eating for two. Gemma screening calls like a pro, between reading out Kent's horoscope from the *Evening Standard* as evidence he was just about to call her. Janey throwing darts at a notice-board with a *pure* cover pinned on to it. Tim squealing over some hot bod he'd found on the internet. I shed a small tear, then slapped my cheeks and told myself to keep it together.

Despite the unpromising start, I was determined to give *Surface* a fair go—out of pride, more than anything. Rosie had promised me a phone number and an email address the following week and as the days went by, with a few of my fashion pictures pinned up on my walls, a newly purchased Roberts radio playing and a large vase of flowers on my desk, I was starting to feel a little better.

Art director Steve was about as communicative as a speed hump when I tried to engage him in office banter, and I still hadn't found anywhere nearby to do my lunchtime yoga, but I set my mind to staying positive. Even with nothing to do. I kept trying to have meetings with Rosie about planning some shoots, but she seemed to be perpetually busy.

Her office door was always closed and her phone—the only one in the entire office at that stage—had started to ring non-stop as *Surface*'s number had finally been published in London's fashion PR Bible, *The Diary*. Her response was to leave it off the hook. We must have been the only magazine office on earth it was impossible to contact, I reflected.

By the end of the week I was getting so frustrated I typed up a memo with a list of shoot ideas on Ollie's computer at home and took advantage of one of Rosie's occasional mystery disappearances to get into her office and put it on her desk.

I wasn't snooping, but she had left her computer screen active and as I put my memo down I saw what was keeping her so busy. She was finishing her book on the Fifties American sportswear designer Claire McCardell. I knew that's what it was because she'd told me all about the project ages before, in one of her mini lectures. I'd just assumed she would have finished it before she took on a magazine editorship. It was getting more and more weird in there.

I left the office at lunchtime that Friday, because I still had nothing to do, and I thought it would be nice to cook Ollie a special welcome-home-from-Milan dinner. He always appreciated that kind of gesture. As I walked back from Fresh & Wild with the ingredients, I waved to the man in the dry-cleaner's. He waved back and gestured for me to come in.

"I have your husband's shirts," he said and handed me seven of them, freshly laundered on hangers.

When I got back to the flat I went to put them away on his side of our closet and as I hung them up the way he liked them—stripes, checks and plains all in separate blocks—I noticed something strange. They were all duplicates of shirts he already had. It must have been some kind of new grooming system he was introducing, I thought, making a note to ask him about it later.

He got back just after 3 P.M. and judging by the surprise on his face when he opened the door, he hadn't been expecting me to be home.

"Em!" he said. "I thought you were at the office."

"Surprise!" I said. "I came home early to make you a special dinner."

"Oh, that's great, but damn," he said, clicking his fingers. "I'm such an idiot, I've just remembered I left something important at Paddington, in the left luggage. I'd better go back and get it."

And he disappeared again, apparently taking his luggage with him. It was most peculiar. He came back about twenty minutes later with his bags and seeming a little more normal.

"Are you here now?" I said, handing him a glass of chilled white wine.

"Yes, yes," he said. "I just needed to collect another bag and put some stuff in the car to take straight to the office tomorrow. I picked up a load of reference material over there and I didn't need to clutter up the house with it."

I didn't think any more of it. Ollie was always shunting stuff about. It was one of the inconveniences of being a consumer on his level. We always had bags of crap going out of the house to make room for all the new crap coming in.

Dinner was fun. We rarely ate in, sitting at the table, just the two of us, and it made a nice change. He was very excited about his trip and the amazing response he'd had to the Slap stand and all the great connections he had made for promoting cosmetics to a whole new market. He listened attentively when I told him about my strange first week at *Surface* and was very reassuring.

"New offices are hell, Emily. It's always like that. I'm sure you'll get a proper assistant once you actually start pumping out issues. Start-ups are scary and hard in any kind of business, but very exciting as well. Wait until you have that first issue in your hands and the fashion world is swooning, desperate to be in your pages."

The only sour note in an otherwise lovely evening was when I opened the present he'd brought me. Usually, Ollie was a first-class present giver. I'd been quite stoked up about what he would buy me in Milan and had dropped a few hints, but even without any help I knew he always managed to find me the perfect thing and was generous too. But not this time. It was a toothbrush.

I just looked at him when I got it out of the bag. He was beaming at me.

"It's—a toothbrush," I said. Wondering if it was a joke and the real present, in a large Prada carrier bag, was about to appear. Maybe that was what he had been collecting from Paddington.

"Yes," said Ollie, in his most enthusiastic mode. "Isn't it great? It's by Marnie Stallinger. It's her first venture into mass-produced universal consumer objects. It's brilliant isn't it? It's going to be an iconic piece and you have one of the first hundred to come off the production line. I've got the next one in the series. They're numbered.

They'll be worth a fortune in twenty years' time, as long as we don't take them out of the packaging, of course."

I looked down at it again. It was an over-designed purple plastic toothbrush. I didn't even like it. I only used clear plastic GUM toothbrushes I bought in bulk in New York. This was an ugly toothbrush I couldn't even use.

"Thanks, Ollie," I said flatly. "That's great. An historic toothbrush. I'll put it away for posterity."

I got up to clear the table, so disappointed I forgot to ask him about the duplicate shirts.

The following week I made huge strides forward at *Surface*. Ollie gave me a spare laptop to take in and I got an email address and a telephone, of my very own. Rosie seemed to have given up working on her book and was keeping her office door open. Making it look even more like a real office, the first fashion student had arrived to assist her, which seemed like progress. It was just unfortunate she had the phone manner of a serial killer.

It took her two days to master the system for putting calls through to Rosie's extension and even once she could do it without cutting the caller off, she had no discrimination about which people to put through and which to take messages from. I sat in my office trying not to listen to the telephonic PR catastrophe that was going on out there, until in the end I couldn't stand it any longer.

"Shona," I said brightly, going to sit on the edge of her desk. "Shall I give you some hints how to deal with the phones?"

The girl just looked back at me from under her bright green fringe and carried on popping her bubble gum.

"OK," I said, determined not to give up. "When the phone rings, you pick it up and say: 'Hello, *Surface* magazine, how can I help you?' Sound friendly. OK?"

Shona said nothing. She certainly didn't look friendly.

"Then you ask who's calling. If you don't recognize the name as someone important—like Giorgio Armani, or Alexander McQueen, ha ha ha—or someone you have heard Rosie talking about, ask them: 'Will she know what the call's about?' If they then go into a long explanation, or they are clearly a PR, take a message, including their name, phone number and what they are calling about. Obviously do the same if Rosie is out."

I handed her an exercise book.

"Write the messages in this book with the date and time, the person's name and a reply number, and give it to Rosie to look at twice a day, OK?"

Shona carried on looking at me like I was asking her to walk around Hoxton in a Laura Ashley dress.

"OK?" I asked again. She popped her gum at me and went back to reading the manga comic she had brought in with her.

I went back to my office and heard her answer the phone.

"Yeah?" was all she said, then she put the call straight through to Rosie.

I couldn't stand it. I went over to her desk again.

"Shona," I said. "What did I just tell you? You have to announce the magazine. It's really important. You are the first point of entry to Planet *Surface* and it is really important people get a positive impression."

I sounded like Ollie, but I didn't care. I was right. But Shona clearly didn't think so. She put her comic into her army surplus bag and stood up.

"I'm not a bloody secretary," she said and walked out. She didn't come back and I got the blame for alienating her.

"They're only kids, Emily," said Rosie, quite crossly. "You can't expect them to know how to be a top-flight PA. And anyway, this isn't British Airways, we're a cool magazine, we don't have to do all that corporate image bullshit."

I just looked at her. How could I answer her without being incredibly rude?

"I just didn't think she was giving people a very good impression of *Surface*," I said. "And I thought you might like a bit of call screening."

"Yes, well, just leave it to me in future," said Rosie tersely, and I saw her pick up the message book and look at it curiously.

That was when it hit me. She'd never seen one before, because she'd never actually worked on a magazine before. She'd worked on a newspaper—but mainly out of the office as a correspondent—and then as a freelancer on magazines. She didn't have the first idea how magazine offices worked. Or any office for that matter. The seriousness of this situation hit me again when I finally had a planning meeting with her that Friday. I had now been there for two weeks and it was the first time the entire staff—all three of us—had sat down together to discuss what we were going to put in the flaming magazine.

I had my list of ideas ready and it seemed like Steve already had his reactions to them ready too, because he didn't like any of them. He thought they were all "lame," "old," or "obvious." Rosie clearly didn't know what she thought. Because after I presented each suggestion she would say "great, I like it," only to change it to "actually that is quite predictable" after Steve had made his comments.

After an hour of this we were no further towards having a shoot schedule in place and Steve and I were deeply established in mutual contempt.

"OK, Steve," I said to him in the end, determined to keep trying. "What do *you* think we should shoot for the first issue?"

Upon which he came out with a string of ideas which were basically on the same themes as mine, just put more wankily. Looking positively at the big picture—it was getting exhausting, but I forced myself—I decided that at least it meant I could go ahead and shoot what I had wanted to in the first place and just make him feel like they were all his ideas. For a moment I had thought he was going to start asking me to do things with papier mâché horses' heads.

But despite my best Pollyanna efforts it went seriously downhill from there. After we had established a basic list of the fashion stories we were going to do, I brought up the subject of locations.

"There isn't any budget for foreign travel," said Rosie.

"What?" I said. "Do you want me to do the whole first issue in the studio? With a few exotic shots from Camber Sands?"

Now this was something I had made a point of asking her about before I took the job and she had promised I would be able to do exactly the kind of trips I had done at *Chic*. "As behoves a parameter-redefining international fashion magazine," she had said at the time with the self-satisfied smile I was starting to detest.

"What's changed, Rosie?" I said. "This is not what we discussed. I didn't come here to shoot catalogue pictures."

She looked uncomfortable.

"That's just the way it is at the moment. When we get more advertising, we can start to do more trips. For the time being, if you can get freebies, that's great, but there's nothing in the budget for travel."

That was when I went back to my office and called Bee. It was the last day of her one-month deadline and I was going to take her up on her offer to come back. It was so nice to hear Nushka's welcoming professional voice when she answered the phone, I could have wept with relief.

"Hello, *Chic* magazine, how can I help you?" she had said, all sophisticated warmth and *Chic*-ness. "Oh, hi Em, it's great to hear from you. We really miss you. But I'm afraid Bee's all tied up this afternoon. Will she know what it's about?"

That was when I knew I was buggered.

Two hours later it was all confirmed. I'd popped out to the nearest café to get a coffee that was slightly less emetic than Rosie's herb teas and found I had a tearful message from Gemma on my mobile asking me to ring her. I did and got the news like a bucket of cold water in the face.

Natalie had my job.

22

THREE weeks later, the emotional decompression chamber of the business-class compartment of a long-haul jumbo jet gave me the time and the space to look at my work situation with some detachment. In between reading my mother's poems—which had become a bit of an inflight fetish—I considered my situation.

So far *Surface* was a total fuck-up and there was no going back to *Chic* now my least favourite person had my job. Bad. But looking on the good side—at least Rosie had given me complete freedom to shoot whatever clothes I wanted on this trip, which was quite a wild prospect. She had seemed quite surprised when I had asked her to come into my office so I could present the clothes for each of the three stories I was going to do, before I set off.

I'd arranged all the outfits on a clothes rail—which I'd had to go out and buy myself, because Rosie had said there wasn't money in the budget for one—complete with their accessories, and a list detailing the designers, prices and UK stockists. In other words, just the way Bee had always insisted we did it at *Chic*.

Rosie had just looked perplexed and waved me away saying I was the stylist and she trusted me to do the styling. She didn't even want to see what I was thinking of for the cover tries. I thought she was nuts and realized I missed the creative bounce around of such discussions. Bee had often made my shoots much better by restricting me a bit in what I wanted to use and making really helpful suggestions, but Rosie didn't want to know.

"You don't get mixed up in the words, Emily, and I won't interfere with the pictures," she had said patronizingly and completely missing the point.

That was exactly what an editor-in-chief was supposed to do—interfere, control, change, infuriate, and generally spice up the crazy brew that made a fashion magazine great. As Bee used to say, magazines are not democracies, they're dictatorships, with one vision steering them, and that's the only way to make them work.

But as Rosie clearly had no concept of any of that, I decided I was just going to enjoy the freedom while I had it and if the magazine turned out to be as cruddy as her management skills, I'd just leave and go freelance until something better came along. At that moment, though, I was rather excited about the adventure I was embarking on. I was on my way to Sydney, for the first time, as the guest of Australian Fashion Week.

The week after the disastrous planning meeting Rosie had received an email inviting *Surface* to attend, with the flights and hotel paid for. I was amazed they'd even heard of us, but Rosie's reputation as a writer was international and they'd written about us on WGSN—the best fashion news wire service—and they seemed keen for us to go. I jumped at the opportunity to tack some shoots in great locations on to the end of the free trip.

Ollie had been really excited about me going to Sydney and had asked me to do a serious recce of the city and how Slap sat in the market there. He was so geared up about it, rushing into his study and producing a file of cuttings he'd saved about groovy things in Australia, I thought for a moment that he might come with me.

And I had seriously mixed feelings about that. Normally I would have loved to share the excitement of visiting a new city—a new continent—with Ollie, but this was different. Miles lived in Sydney. If Ollie had come there with me, it would have been as weird as when Miles had been in London. Weirder.

Which was also why I hadn't told Miles I was coming over. I knew how I had felt when he was in my home town, so I thought I should respect how he might feel about having me in his. I didn't know anything about Miles's private life outside our hotel-room bubble—and I didn't want to. Not seeing him while I was there seemed the cleanest way to handle it.

Of course the twenty-four-hour flight potentially gave me plenty of time to think about all that and the implications of it, but I just blocked it out with the free champagne, the movies and my mum's book. It was funny how I could use her words to push away the things I didn't want to think about, when normally I used anything available—to stop myself thinking about her. Somehow, though, reading her clipped, economical lines enabled me to allow her into my brain, without having really to confront the situation. It was the perfect balance.

I was so brain lagged by the flight when I arrived I could hardly take in anything about Sydney at first, but I was aware of a very big blue sky and a very short distance, compared to most cities I knew, between the airport and the hotel, which was in an old converted wharf sticking out into the famous harbour.

I had the most amazing view of the water from the little balcony off my room and I sat there feeling slightly dizzy and unable to take my eyes off the sparkling view, framed by wooded headlands and an atmospheric old naval depot to the right.

I started unpacking and then, despite everything I knew about conquering jet lag, I just had to lie down. I went straight to sleep until I was abruptly woken by the phone ringing next to my head.

"I can't believe you didn't tell me," said a familiar voice. "I can't believe you didn't tell me you were coming over."

"Miles?" I said, faintly.

"Who did you think it was?"

"But how did you know I was here?"

He laughed. "I went in to the Fashion Week office just now to get my accreditation pass and there was one sitting there with your name on it. It wasn't hard, Emily. But what is *Surface* magazine?"

I groaned. "Don't ask. I've changed jobs."

"Well, you can tell me about it over lunch. I'm coming to get you."

So there I was, just a couple of hours after landing in beautiful

Australia, in the arms of a beautiful Australian. As welcomes go, I thought, as Miles lifted me up on to the balcony railing, gently biting my neck as he entered me with great tenderness, it would have been hard to beat.

"So this is a panel van," I said to him, as I climbed into a hideous bronze-coloured thing, like an estate car, but with no side windows.

Miles grinned at me.

"Yeah, ugly bugger, isn't it?"

"What's the attraction?"

"Room for your surfboards. And your woman . . . There's room for two to sleep back there. As long as you don't mind lying on top of each other." He grinned at me again and squeezed my knee, "I'll take you on a little tourist tour, before we go to the restaurant," he said. "Show you my city. It's better than yours."

I have no idea where we went. He seemed to drive me all over the place, and the harbour and the ocean kept popping up around corners when I was least expecting them. We definitely went over the Sydney Harbour Bridge a couple of times and although I had seen it a million times in films and photos, I was blown away by the famous opera house view in real time.

My first impression was that I'd never been anywhere that made such an instant visual impact on you. The cities I knew and loved— London, Paris, New York—were more about aggregate impressions of lots of wonderful details and experiences, but Sydney just leaped out at you, the whole fabulous thing in one eyeful. It was like a city designed by John Galliano.

Ollie would have loved it, I couldn't help thinking, as we drove along a pretty tree-lined street of interesting-looking boutiques, cafés, and galleries, in what seemed just minutes after leaving an amazing white sand beach.

I already loved it. It was supposed to be autumn, but the sky was bright blue and it was warm enough for us to sit outside for lunch, on a chic restaurant terrace looking out over the sweep of Bondi Beach, complete with surfers. It was only as I leaned back in my seat with my eyes closed, enjoying the sun on my face after months of crushing European winter, that it really hit me. I was doing something normal—and public—with Miles.

My eyes snapped open again and there he was. Even more tanned, wearing his usual rather tight old T-shirt and ancient jeans, his brown feet in Birkenstocks, still gloriously male and looking at me, not grinning for once, but quite seriously. Then he smiled at me slowly, very different from his normal cheeky smirk, and reached out across the table to put his hand over mine. He squeezed it.

"It's good to see you in sunlight, Emily," he said.

It was all very gorgeous. The food was fabulous, we had a lovely bottle of wine and all around us were people who looked like the people I knew in London, but more relaxed. And that was the problem. I couldn't relax.

Doing something so normal with Miles was making me feel incredibly tense. Coffee at the Fiera, even driving around sightseeing had been OK, but now I felt like we had stepped way over the boundaries I had set on our liaison, into something that was way too much like my real life.

I felt myself getting more and more inhibited as we sat there and it was all I could do to force down a mouthful of my grilled monkfish. I was relieved when it was time to leave. I was silent all the way back to the hotel and when I sneaked a glance at Miles he was looking fairly stony-faced too. He pulled up in front of the hotel and stopped the engine.

"What's up, Em?" he said, simply.

"Too real," I almost whispered.

I couldn't speak more loudly or say more, because I was too frightened what might come out. The thing we have is too precious. You don't know what it means to me. I can't risk spoiling it. All of those things I couldn't tell him, because I could hardly admit them to myself.

He stayed looking ahead. Was it hurt or disappointment I could see on that handsome face? I wasn't sure, but after a moment, he turned to me, sighing loudly, and patted my knee.

"I understand, Em," he said. "I went too far. I got a bit pushy there. I was just excited about showing you my city. Well, I won't do it again. I'll let you take charge. As always, Emily, you're driving. You know my number. And you know where I will be for the next four days. Your call." He shrugged. "Or not."

He totally got it, I thought, and I leaned over to kiss him on the cheek as I got out of the car.

I didn't call Miles. I was having too much fun. Australian Fashion Week was a blast and I felt so freed from the pressures of Paris and Milan. I had no bossy editor-in-chief, or moody fashion director to worry about and—apart from Miles—nobody knew me, so I didn't have any expectations to live up to. There were quite a few other people there from London, but they were all buyers and total strangers. It was so liberating.

I was also blissfully unaware of any front-row politics. I'm sure the usual jockeying for status and position was going on, but I wasn't part of it. And I didn't have to worry about bloody advertisers either.

Adding to my relaxed state, at the beginning of the week they had given me a pass with all my seat placements on it and, apart from one or two shows each day away from the official venue, I basically had the same front-row seat for the entire time. That made life brilliantly simple and, on top of that, the shows didn't run late, starting just about fifteen minutes, or so, after the stated time. I was so unprepared for that I nearly missed the first one.

The final treat was having a limo and driver to myself, laid on by the sponsors. It was such a treat after years of having to fit round other people's moods and schedules, I felt quite giddy.

When I say I didn't ring Miles, I didn't ignore him—in fact I saw him every day. The shows were so small compared to the ones in Europe, I'd bump into him constantly, going in and out of them and just hanging around the venue. I just didn't ring him, or see him, in our usual way.

It did feel a little strange, to be honest, to see him in public like that—and not to see him alone as well—and my heart did give a little leap every time he strayed casually into view, so on the second day I sent him a text saying that I hadn't forgotten him, but I just needed some space.

He replied that it was cool—but that he did want to see me again before I left. In fact, he said, he insisted on it. That was fine with me and I just assumed that he understood that it was the same deal as London. And then, with my usual talent for keeping things separate in my head, I just got on with it.

To keep me distracted, as well as all the actual fashion shows, there seemed to be another whole schedule of parties to go to. The first few evenings I'd been too jet lagged to do anything beyond cocktail events and dinners, but by the last night I was seriously ready to get on down at designer Wayne Cooper's after-show party.

I'd made what seemed like loads of new best friends at Bar Bazaar, the VIP delegates' bar out at the main shows venue, so I didn't feel shy to go on my own. Adding to my self-confidence, a make-up artist I'd met there had done my face and hair and I was wearing the emerald green Dolce & Gabbana toga dress I'd bought for the *Chic* Christmas party, with my highest gold Prada shoes.

Combined with a swift visit to a salon for a spray-on tan and a head full of compliments from people who'd only seen my dress before in internet shots of the Milan catwalk, I was feeling pretty happy about life.

It was quite late and I seemed to have been on the dance floor all night, shaking my thing with my new friends, when I felt someone come up behind me. Strong arms wrapped round me, lips nuzzled my neck and I breathed in the warm musky smell of hot man. I knew exactly who it was and I closed my eyes and breathed deeply as Miles nibbled my ear. Then he turned me round and kissed me— really kissed me—right there on the dance floor.

Maybe it was the Möet, maybe it was the scent of him, but as I kissed him back, one hand on the back of his head, pushing it into mine, as we swayed to the music, it did cross my mind that I was a married woman, kissing a man who was not my husband—in public. I didn't care.

After that, Miles led me off the dance floor and into a corner of the nightclub where he sat down on a banquette and pulled me on to his lap.

"Now where were we?" he said, his cheekiest grin back in place, and he kissed me again. We sat there snogging like a pair of teenagers, right down to the hard-on I could feel straining against my thigh through his jeans. Drunk on champagne and pheromones, I surrendered entirely to him and it was lucky it was dark in that corner, because he had his hand inside my new Collette Dinnigan knickers and was quickly bringing me to a climax.

After that he just held me on his knee, my arms around his neck, as the pounding music washed over us. I don't know how long we sat there like that, but I loved every minute of it. I was vaguely aware of other people passing by en route to the bar, but I didn't care. I was wrapped up in a world no bigger than the piece of Miles's shoulder my head was resting on.

"Em," he said softly, after a while, maybe a few hundred years. "Let's go."

I felt slightly odd in his tatty old panel van in my Dolce dress, but not enough to snap out of my blissful state of euphoric wellbeing. We seemed to drive for a long time. I'd got used to the trip from the main venue back to my hotel in my chauffeured car and had started to recognize landmarks, but now I had no bearings.

"Where are we going?" I asked him eventually.

"My place," said Miles, firmly.

I opened my mouth to speak, although I wasn't sure what I was going to say. I'd just assumed we'd be going back to the hotel. Miles and I always met in hotels.

"I'm taking charge tonight, Emily," he said. "Just go with it. Trust me."

And against all my better instincts, I did.

I woke up the next morning to sunlight streaming on to my face, the smell of coffee and music playing. Lifting my head from the pillow, I saw Miles walking around in a batik sarong. He was cutting up fruit and putting it into two bowls.

I looked round his place. It had seemed pretty amazing at night, with just a few candles lit, enough to illuminate a whole wall of books, and another two covered in artworks. The fourth wall was mainly window and at night it had just been black with a few lights twinkling, before he closed the blinds. In daylight I could see it looked straight out over water. It seemed to be the harbour, but not any part of it I had seen before.

His place was half a floor of an old warehouse building that had miraculously escaped the hands of developers, who would have turned it into about five separate rabbit hutches. It still had its original old worn floorboards and apart from the loo and a darkroom, it was completely open plan. Even the bath and glass shower cubicle were out in the middle of the space.

Miles saw I was awake and smiled broadly at me as he brought the bowls of fruit over to the bed. He climbed in beside me.

"That's yours," he said, handing me a groaning pile topped with yogurt, honey, and nuts. "I've put extra honey and yogurt on it. You're getting a bit thin. I like enough of you to get hold of, you know."

And he kissed me on the end of my nose.

"This is a great place, Miles," I said. "Where are we?"

"Glebe. That's the old industrial harbour out there. Great, isn't it? I'm renting this place from a friend who's living overseas. I was really lucky."

"I love this track," I said, as The Coral came on.

He turned and looked at me.

"I love you," he said.

I just looked back at him.

"I do," he said. "I'm not going to pretend any more. This may have started as a casual shows shag, but it has turned into something much more for me and I can't lie about it any more."

I opened my mouth to speak, but he put his fingers on my lips to stop me.

"I know it's against the rules we set ourselves," he said. "But it's the truth. I've been wretched all week, Emily, watching you walk in and out of those fucking shows, the most amazing woman I've ever known, but out of bounds to me, like you were behind glass."

I tried to speak, but he stopped me again. I decided to shut up and listen.

"I know men are supposed to be sex beasts who can turn it on and off like a tap, but I can't, Emily. Not with you. When we make love, it's not just sex, it's something much more and I know you know that. Like I told you in Paris, it has never been like this for me before with anyone and I'm not going to pretend any more whatever the fucking rules are."

Finally it seemed I could speak.

"Come here," I said.

I never did eat that fruit.

23

I DIDN'T eat the fruit and I didn't stay another night in the hotel. I moved in with Miles for the rest of the trip, which I extended for another week even beyond the extra days I was already officially staying for the fashion shoots.

Rosie didn't seem to care. I told her I was doing some additional shots and I'd be out and about on location, so just to call me on the mobile if she needed me. She never asked another question. Ollie didn't seem that bothered either. He seemed more excited about the fact that *Chic Interiors* was shooting our "apartment" the following day.

"I hope you don't mind not being in the pictures, Emily," he was saying. I was standing outside a café in a cool suburb called Surry Hills, making the calls, while Miles sat inside. "But Felicity thought it probably wasn't a very good idea, as you have recently left the *Chic* stable."

"Neeeeigh," I said. "Gee up, neddy. It doesn't bother me in the slightest. I'm just glad you got what you wanted out of her, Ollie. I hope it does wonderful things for the *brand*."

If he noticed the slight edge in my voice, he didn't react, but it was a conversation that made me feel a lot less guilty about what I was up to. If Ollie didn't give a damn when I came home that was fine with me. I was having such a lovely time with Miles. It was so good just to surrender to how I felt about him, although I hadn't gone quite as far as he had. I hadn't told him I loved him, because I didn't know if I did. But I loved being with him and for those all too brief days, I loved leading his kind of life, it was all so much more relaxed than what I was used to.

I did have to do the shoots for *Surface,* of course, and they went off really well, probably because I was so laid-back on them. I was using an Australian photographer who was starting to make a name for himself in New York and had come back to Sydney for Fashion Week, with a fantastic Brazilian model who happened to be his girlfriend.

Between the loved-up lot of us, it made for a very happy atmosphere on those shoots and a look in the model's eyes that could never have been faked, as she stared down the lens at her lover.

I did tack one extra session on to the ones I had gone out there planning to do. It was an accessories still-life series in rich colour, that we shot on a deserted beach somewhere north of Sydney. The photographer was Miles.

At first he'd been really reluctant to show me his "real" work, as opposed to the catwalk shots, but when he eventually did I was blown away. I knew he was an "art" photographer and that his subjects were natural phenomena and formations he found on beaches, mainly to do with the shapes of waves and the effect of water on sand and pebbles, but I'd expected them to be classic—i.e. boring— "arty" grainy black and white prints. Instead they were in the most amazing saturated colour, printed on superglossy paper and then worked into collages, some of it done by hand, other parts scanned in and manipulated on a computer. They were rich, sensuous and gorgeous, almost vibrating with life force.

Miles pinned them up on the walls of his loft and I just stood and drank them in. They had the same explosive sense of energy I had felt when I'd first seen Sydney Harbour in all its glory. Not dead-at-heart intellectual "art" photos at all, they were alive and throbbing with energy.

"Wow," was all I could say. "These are amazing, Miles. I love them."

I looked at an extraordinary close-up of the curl of a wave fractured into a thousand tiny pieces and then back at Miles.

"They're like you," I said. "A force of nature."

Something shifted inside me. I turned to him and took his hands in mine.

"My dad was an artist, you know," I started.

"And your mum is a really good poet," he replied.

I looked at him mystified.

"I saw her book in your bag," he explained. "I read it while you were out the other day. I hope you don't mind. I saw her picture on the back and had to have a look. She looks so like you. She's beautiful. And I really liked the poems, especially the one about you—buddy."

He took me in his arms and kissed me. I had been about to tell him my whole hideous family story, but instead I decided just to enjoy the moment and to leave that can of festering maggots unopened.

As the end of my stay drew nearer we both grew quiet. I knew he was feeling the same as me. It was almost unbearable to think of that special time ending, but I couldn't just stay. And the funny thing was, that although Miles had thrown our rulebook out that night at the party, we were still observing two of them very strictly. We never talked about my life with Ollie and how I felt about him, and we never discussed any kind of future relationship between us beyond the here and now. We lived entirely in the moment.

Until the last night, that is, when Miles brought it all up in one go. I felt like a brick wall had just fallen on my head.

"So, Emily," he said, leaning across the table towards me. I could tell by his tone of voice something was coming I didn't want to hear. Particularly not then.

We were eating a dinner we'd cooked together. We'd gone to the fish market to get all the ingredients and it had been a wonderful day, chopping, grating, slicing and sauté-ing with the windows open, a bottle of dry Riesling on the go and everything from Outkast to

Chopin blaring out of the stereo. Every now and then he'd taken me in his arms and we'd danced around the room.

Then, as we were eating our main course, he shattered it all with just a few dumb-ass questions.

"So what's next, Emily?" he said. "You're going home tomorrow, back to a job you hate and a husband you never talk about. Where does that leave me? Where does it leave us? When am I going to see you again? For a quick root in a hotel room in Milan in September? Is that going to be enough for you? Because I'll tell you straight up, it's not enough for me."

I didn't know what to say, so I said nothing. I sat there with my mouth open, feeling like a goldfish, but I couldn't fill the air with babble just for the sake of it. It was too serious.

"Well?" he said.

"I don't know," I said.

"Well, let's work it out. Starting with Mr. Husband. I've seen him, you know. He looks like a complete arse. What's with that make-up he wears?"

I put my fork down. I had to take a big gulp of wine to force down the piece of prawn I was chewing. It had turned to Play-Doh in my mouth.

"It's a work thing for him," I said, quietly.

Miles laughed.

"Is he a clown?"

"No," I said, tersely.

I felt weirdly offended on Ollie's behalf. He did look ridiculous in that make-up, but it was just part of the whole career persona that defined him and if you knew him, it made sense somehow. And although I was the one who was gallivanting with another man, I had been with Ollie for so many years and I still loved him. Or something.

"Please don't be horrible about him, Miles," I said quietly. "I am married to him. He may seem like an arsehole to you, but he's been very good to me."

"So good he hasn't rung you once while you've been here?" said Miles, clearly not ready to let it go.

It was true. Ollie was too caught up in that stupid shoot to call me, and when I thought about it, how did that sound? My husband hadn't rung me while I was on the other side of the world, because he was having his house photographed. Great.

"Do you really love him, Emily?" said Miles, his brow all bunched up in an uncharacteristic frown. "Do you love being with him?" He paused, then spoke again, more softly. "Do you love being with him, as much as you love being with me?"

My brain span just thinking about it all. Yes, but no, well, sort of. No, no, no. It didn't look that good when you studied it, but on the other hand, what was I supposed to do? Leave Ollie and move to Sydney? It was too much. My mind suddenly tripped back to the first night with Miles in Milan, when he'd told me he'd been watching me for a year. I had felt stalked then and that suffocated feeling returned.

"I don't know," I said again. "I love being here with you, but I love my life in London. I'm not ready to give it up."

"Really? Does it really make you happy? Would a woman who was really happy be starving herself? Slim is one thing and you had a beautiful figure when I met you, but you're fading away in front of me. You're just bones now, Emily, and you're thinner every time I see you. Is that a sign of a happy woman?"

Oh, not Miles as well now, I thought, telling me I was too thin. That made Ollie just about the only person who didn't go on at me about that. He might not have rung me since I'd been in Sydney, but at least he understood I just wanted to look good in my clothes, which was part of my job after all.

On top of everything else, it was too much. I did the only thing I could do in the circs. I burst into hysterical tears and then, to my great shame, I had a big sulk. I just couldn't cope with everything that Miles had thrown at me and I sulked for the rest of the night. I didn't make love with him then, or the next morning and then it was too late, it was time to get the plane. Stupid, stupid girl.

Considering that those days in Sydney had probably been the happiest times of my life, my parting from Miles was horrendous. He saw me off, looking grey in the face and I just felt like I was made of stone.

I wanted to throw myself at him and beg his forgiveness and ask him to keep me there for ever, but I couldn't. I could only go through the motions of checking in, buying magazines, kissing him on the cheek like some kind of acquaintance and pushing my trolley through that horrendous point of no return to passport control.

I turned round and looked at him just before there was a curve in the corridor and he would disappear from view. He was standing staring down at his boots, looking completely stricken. I hurried on before he looked up and I would have had to rush back to him.

I felt numb all the long flight home and the only thing that got me through it was watching terrible films and obsessively reading *Paeanies*. There was something about going over the same rhythmic words again and again that was amazingly comforting. It did make me have the odd unwelcome thought about my mother—and Toby—but mainly it made my brain switch into neutral, which is exactly where I wanted it to be.

When I finally got back, wrung out from the flight and the emotional spin cycle I'd been through, I found getting home was not the comfort it usually was for me. Normally just being in Westbourne Grove and sliding into my life there made me feel instantly grounded again, but this time I was like a dog turning round and round in my basket but not able to get comfortable. Ollie didn't seem to notice, he was too wrapped up in the stupid shoot of our flat. He was so overexcited about it you would have thought it was something important.

At that stage the *Chic Interiors* art department had started to lay out the pictures and he was going into their offices all the time to help with the captions and stuff like that. Combined with his usual workload and the continuing saga of Slap for Chaps, which was now part of a major charity fund-raising event, I hardly seemed to see him. And it suited me. It took the pressure off having to pretend I was fine, when I was anything but.

It wasn't until I'd been home for nearly two weeks that I realized he hadn't even tried to make love to me since I'd got back, which was unusual. I was perfectly happy about it, because at that point

I never wanted to have sex ever again, but it was still odd. We normally went through the motions whenever we'd been apart and this had been a longer separation than most. I reckoned Ollie must have been picking up on my low mood in some way and was giving me some space.

If things were tense at home, there wasn't any relief to be found in the *Surface* office. The launch date was getting closer and closer, but Rosie was still in the same state of chaotic bravado. She'd written up her piece on Junya Watanabe and Steve was in the process of organizing a portrait of him, but apart from that the only material we had in was the pictures I'd shot in Sydney. At least they liked them—even grumpy Steve was impressed by Miles's pictures.

Their enthusiastic reaction to his shots was just about the only nice thing that had happened since I had got home, until I received an email from him with no message, just a picture attachment. It was a photo of me, asleep and naked. Using his collage technique, he'd fanned my hair out around my shoulders, taken the flowers that had been in a vase on the bedside cabinet and scattered them in the air around me and chopped up the blue and white of the sheets, so I looked like some kind of twenty-first-century Venus rising from the waves. He'd called it "Bud."

It was such a beautiful gesture I wanted to respond but I just couldn't find the right words, so I went on the internet and trawled through those out-of-print book search sites, until eventually I found a copy of my mother's anthology and had them send it straight to him.

Life went on like this for a few more weeks until something happened to shock me out of my self-obsession. Frannie rang me at *Surface* one afternoon and said she had some horrible news.

"There's nothing wrong with the baby, is there?" I asked, immediately.

"No, no, he or she is growing like a little champion—it's Alice. She's taken an overdose. She nearly died, Emily."

"Oh, fuck me," I said, feeling really shocked. "When did it happen?"

"A couple of days ago, but we've only just heard. It seems Alice called her neighbour just in time, or she'd be dead. She'd taken masses of painkillers, but something made her change her mind, thank God. She's been in intensive care, but she's stable now, whatever that means."

"Oh, poor Alice," I said. My eyes filled with tears. For all my complicated feelings about her, I felt deeply sad that she'd felt bad enough to try and kill herself. No one deserved that. Plus it set off a lot of painful associations to do with my mother. Ouch.

"So we were right about her being depressed," I said.

"We bloody well were. The silly cow. Why didn't she tell you, when you asked her that time in Milan?"

I just exhaled loudly. What a mess we stupid humanoids were, I thought. All scurrying along in our private pods of misery and not telling each other.

"I think she couldn't admit it to herself," I said, still not wanting to tell Frannie what had really passed between me and Alice that dark day in Milan, or any of the other baggage I was carrying in relation to Miss Alee-chay Pettigrew.

"Which hospital is she in?" I asked Frannie, thinking I might send some flowers. It seemed the least I could do.

"She's in St. Mary's and actually, that's one of the reasons I'm ringing. Bee told me to—she's been asking for you."

"Alice has? Me? That's weird."

"That's what I thought. I always thought she hated your guts, but that's what Bee said, she wants you to go and see her. Will you? I know how you feel about hospitals, but Bee is pretty firm that you've got to go. Not that you work here any more, but . . ."

Frannie didn't need to say any more. She knew all about my mum and how I felt about visiting her, and my blood phobia didn't exactly predispose me towards medical institutions either, but in the circumstances—and if Bee wanted me to—I thought I'd better go.

I got a taxi straight over there and forced myself to get in the lift up to the ward where she was. Just the smell of the place was enough to bring me to the brink of running out again, but I didn't. I just wanted to get it over with.

After a few wrong turns I finally found Alice in a room on her own. I peeped round the door before I went in and she looked tiny lying there, without any of her usual extravagant accessories, and so pale, just gazing fixedly into space.

"Alice?" I said quietly.

She turned her head and blinked when she saw me. Then she extended a hand. I went and sat next to her and took her hand in mine. Her eyes were full of tears.

"How are you?" I said quietly.

She just closed her eyes and shook her head.

"Thank you for coming," she said eventually, sighing deeply. "I had to see you."

I squeezed her hand. This was seriously weird.

"If there's anything I can do . . ." I started to say, but she just shook her head to stop me.

"I just need you to listen to me," she said.

"OK," I said, nodding.

"I owe you an apology," she said. "I did a terrible thing to you. I stole your ideas. I did it deliberately. I wanted to fuck you up. I wanted you to leave *Chic*." She paused a moment and then spoke in a whisper. "I was so jealous of you, Emily." She turned her big blue eyes to me, staring intensely into mine. I felt really uncomfortable.

"You've got it all," she continued. "Everything I want. The looks, the husband, the money, the flat—all the security I so desperately need and you've got the brilliant ideas too. That's what I couldn't stand. You had all that and you were more truly creative than me too. I knew Bee liked you better than me as well, because you've got a sense of humour and I haven't. It was so unfair, I couldn't let you win. I couldn't let you have everything. I had to hold on to my job, because it's all I have. I don't have any of that other stuff you have. And I never will."

She looked wretched. If only she knew, I thought. I had all that and I was desperately unhappy too, because I was doing my best to fuck it up.

"Don't say that, Alice," I said. "You don't know what's going to happen. You could meet the right man any day. He might be your doctor here."

It was pathetic, but it was the best I could do. She ignored me.

"I need you to forgive me," she said.

"Oh, forget all that," I said. "Of course I forgive you. It's all in the past. But if you could just tell me one thing, Alice, it would really help me."

"Ask me," she said.

"What I never understood was—how did you do it? How did you find out my ideas before the meetings?"

"I got Natalie to do it," she said blankly.

"But how did she get them, when I hadn't even typed them out on my computer? I could never work that out."

"She looked in your shows notebooks," said Alice, simply. "It wasn't hard."

Well, at least that explained why I had found the little shit snooping round my office so much.

"I never did like Natalie," I said.

"You don't know the half of it," said Alice, quietly, her face looking momentarily even more stricken.

I didn't say anything, I had a feeling she had more to tell me. She did.

"She blackmailed me," said Alice, almost whispering. "She threatened to tell Bee what I'd been doing. But by then it was too late for me to stop. I was so terrified about being found out I couldn't even think straight, let alone come up with any ideas, so I had to carry on stealing yours and she got more and more demanding. How do you think she got your job? She made me recommend her."

Alice looked stricken. I patted her hand.

"It's OK, Alice," I said. "She'll get found out for what she is. People who scheme and plot like that never really get ahead in the end. All that matters is that you get better. Your ideas will come back again."

I wasn't entirely sure I believed any of it, but I hoped it might comfort her. She seemed to make an effort to collect herself.

"Anyway, Emily, thank you for listening. I am truly sorry. It was a terrible thing to do, but I was desperate. And you were so nice that time in Milan, when you asked if I was OK. I wasn't, but I couldn't take sympathy from you. You were the worst person to have asked me. Can you forgive me?"

"Of course," I said, although it actually made it even more unbearable that Fatalie now had my job, but I wasn't going to tell Alice that. She was suffering enough.

"Don't think about it any more," I said. "It's all in the past. Just concentrate on yourself and getting better, and if you ever need someone to talk to, just call me. You've got my numbers."

I think I meant it.

I left St. Mary's feeling stunned and rather tainted. I wanted to go home and have a hot shower to wash that hospital atmosphere off my skin. It made me shudder. But I also felt strangely relieved—at least I wasn't nuts. I wasn't paranoid and delusional, Alice and Natalie *had* been stalking me; which, with my family history, was quite a relief. I had seriously started to wonder.

But before I could even start to process any of this new information, I had a very unwelcome phone call. I had just turned my mobile on after leaving the hospital when it rang. I fished it out of my bag and saw Ursula's number on the display.

"Ursa Major!" I cried, delighted to hear from her so unexpectedly.

"Hey, kiddo," she said, getting straight to the point. "Spoken to your brother recently?"

"Not since Christmas," I said, guardedly. I was still upset about that conversation with Toby, and with what had happened since at *Chic*, with Miles, and the ongoing catastrophe that was *Surface*, I'd just put it in a mental pending file.

Toby had called me a few times since then, but I hadn't rung him back. I'd been too busy and with everything else that was going on I was not in the mood to be nagged about my mum as well. In fact Toby was seriously pissing me off. I couldn't understand why he couldn't just leave me alone like he used to.

"I think he called, but I haven't got back to him yet," I said, trying to sound vague.

"That's what Toby said," said Ursula, quite tersely. "He said he's called you at least ten times and you have never called him back and one time, you actually hung up on him. Your mother is asking for you, Emily. She really wants to see you. She's a sick woman and she needs to see you. Toby rang me to ask me to intervene. He said he just couldn't get through to you about it."

"I suppose you think I should go and see her as well," I said, the old anger and resistance rising inside me.

"As I have always said," said my un-mother, "it's up to you, kiddo, only you can decide, but it might do you more good than endlessly shopping and starving yourself."

"I don't want to see her," I spat down the phone. "Why can't you all leave me alone about it?"

And she just beat me in the race to hang up first.

I was furious with Ursula. Furious and hurt. She'd stepped over an invisible line in our relationship—the line between being my virtual parent and telling me what to do with regard to my real "mommie dearest." And my anger with Toby was off the scale for involving her in it.

Great, I thought. First Ursula gets Paul on to me and now Toby has recruited Ursula to nag me as well. It was like some kind of international conspiracy to interfere with my life and to stir up shit that was much better left well alone. I felt betrayed by the lot of them. Between all the stuff that was going on in my life already and now what had happened with Alice, I was beginning to feel like an emotional squash ball. Just too many hard hits too close together.

I stomped along Praed Street fighting tears, until I saw a cab coming along. I hailed it and went straight to the Chloé boutique in Sloane Street and bought the high-waist linen pants I had been lusting after ever since I'd seen them in the spring/summer show.

Then I powerwalked down to the end of the King's Road and the haven that was Manolo Blahnik, to pick up a couple of pairs of flat sandals, to get me through summer. After a pedicure at Bliss, to set them off to their finest advantage, I felt I had myself under control again. I needed it all anyway because I was going on another trip, as Rosie finally seemed to have realized we had a magazine to put out in just a few weeks and very little to go in it.

Tunisia in mid-July would not have been my first choice of location for shooting three autumn trends stories, but it was the cheapest option that would at least provide guaranteed light and some exotic backdrops. I already felt sorry for the model who would have to wear tweed suits in sub-Saharan summer temperatures, but needs must.

I had managed to scam the accommodation from the Tunisian tourist board and the *Surface* budget could just about stretch to five charter flights out there for me, Nivek and his assistant, a hairdresser and a make-up artist, but not for an assistant for me.

The thought of doing all the ironing in that heat made me feel quite queasy, but I was seriously looking forward to getting away and losing myself in work for a while. I felt quite cheerful as I assembled my packing wardrobe in neat piles on the bed, ready to leave the next day. This was what I was best at, I thought, as I stood back to admire what I had put together.

It had a white and navy linen theme with turquoise accents and flashes of burnt ochre in a bikini and a fine cotton shawl. I had a couple of caftans I'd had made once on a trip to Vietnam, which were perfect for keeping cool in Muslim countries, without offending the locals, plus my big squashy straw hat and my blackest sunglasses to keep the sun damage off my face. Orange Converse All Stars to fly in, my trusty Birkenstocks and the new Manolos, of course. I was such a pro.

As I was packing my inflight tote, I automatically reached inside my bedside cabinet for *Paeanies,* but after studying the cover for a moment I put it back. It had become a bit of a routine to read it on planes, but I decided not to take it this time, because it was starting to get a little dog-eared. I decided I would get hold of another copy for reading and save the inscribed one. It was too special to spoil.

Then, on an impulse, I took it through to the sitting room, where Ollie was watching TV. I hadn't shown it to him before and it just seemed like the right time to do it. I hadn't told him about her ask-ing for me—I hadn't told anyone—but this was my way of ac-knowledging her, without actually having to go and see her. Ollie made all the right noises and was suitably complimentary about my mother's photograph and the poem she had written about me, so I left the book with him to look at.

When I went back into the sitting room later I saw he had left it lying on the sofa, so I picked it up and placed it on the kilim-covered ottoman that was our book display area. It looked very nice sitting between a copy of *Derek Jarman's Garden* and a new book about Yves Saint Laurent. I didn't think any more of it until I went to bed that night and found it sitting on my bedside table.

"Did you bring this back through here?" I said to Ollie, al-though it was obvious he had.

"Yes, darling," he said.

"Why?" I asked him.

"Well, it's not something we should prominently display, is it? I'll probably have a Sunday salon while you're away and we don't want to prompt any questions about your mother, do we?"

I just stood there stunned, as he carried on getting ready for bed, like nothing had happened. A geyser of red-hot anger shot through me. How dare he insult her like that? I wanted to kill him. I wanted to run at him like a shrieking banshee and tear his limbs off. But Ollie and I never rowed.

Right from the start of our relationship we had always found a way of dissipating tension through a joke, or just by silently fuming for a while, until we got over it. We might have a few cross words, but we never had slanging matches. People like Ollie simply didn't, and up until then I had been perfectly happy to avoid anything that reminded me of the heavy mortar fire that used to go on between my parents when they were drunk. Anger frightened me.

I stood there feeling gagged, shaking with fury, and starting to feel sick from the adrenaline rush, but still I couldn't let it out. I wanted to scream and shout and claw him to death, but I just couldn't. I felt the rage within me turn from fire into cold steel.

"What?" he said, finally noticing something was wrong. "Why are you looking at me like that?"

"You cunt," I said slowly. "You self-satisfied, judgemental, superficial cunt."

Before he could reply, I grabbed the book from my bedside
table and stalked out of the room, slamming the door behind me.
By the look I saw on Ollie's face as I turned, I knew those words
had done the trick more effectively than any pyrotechnic display
could have. Fuck him.

24

TUNISIA was really beautiful. Bloody hot, but really beautiful. And although it was a bit like shooting fashion in a pizza oven, we were doing great pictures.

Since our session in New York, Nivek and I had rubbed along pretty well together; he knew how important these tear sheets were for building his name, and appearing in the first issue of a high-profile new magazine was the perfect platform to get his work seen internationally. But he was still no breeze to work with.

Even after our conversation about his attitude, he was still capable of throwing a foul tantrum if he didn't feel a shoot was going exactly as he wanted it, but I put up with him because his photographs were so damn good. I still had enough pride in my work to want to make sure that my pages in the launch issue of *Surface* would be brilliant.

And it was worth putting up with ironing in the heat and a sulky photographer to be away from all the things that were going on at home. I was still furious with Ollie for what he had said about my mother's book. And he wasn't talking to me at all because of those—and I quote—"unacceptable" words I had said to him.

"Frankly, I'm astonished," he'd said, in a message he'd left on my mobile voicemail the next day, after leaving for work while I was still asleep in the spare room. "I'm deeply hurt and speechless," he'd said. "That you could speak to me like that. It's completely unacceptable. I don't know what's happened to you, but any woman who could use that kind of gutter language is not the Emily I married. God, if my parents knew . . . Anyway, I am really not inclined to speak to you again until you apologize. So perhaps you will have some opportunity to think about that while you are away. Until then, don't bother to call me. Goodbye."

I'd given my phone the finger after getting that message. If he thought I was from the gutter, that's the way I would behave. Because until he apologized to me for what he had said about my mother, I didn't really want to speak to him either.

So there was all that, the disaster that was *Surface,* and, of course, the ongoing anxiety about all the credit-card bills I couldn't pay. And then there was the not inconsiderable issue of the pressure on me to visit the woman who that whole fracas with Ollie had been about. But while I couldn't allow him to insult her, I still didn't want to go and see her. That's just the way it was.

But as I looked out of my hotel-room window, over the cubic shapes of the Tunisian townscape, blindingly white in the African sun, I felt perfectly happy. Somehow, just having three jet hours between me and home made all those worries dissolve like the vitamin C tablet I had for breakfast each morning. Until Peter Potter called me.

It was the second to last day of the trip. I had just gone down to the market to buy some bottled water for the day's shooting when my mobile rang.

"Hi, Emily," said his familiar snide voice. "Peter Potter here."

I was surprised to hear from him, although it wasn't unknown for us to speak and he didn't know I was away. My mobile calls just came through as though I was in London, so he probably thought I was in Westbourne Grove.

"Hi, Peter," I said enthusiastically, slipping into our usual faux best friends mode. He didn't even bother. He went straight for the jugular.

"I just wondered how you felt about your husband having an affair with your former colleague, Felicity Aldous?"

I laughed. It was the only possible reaction.

"Don't be daft," I said. "Come off it. Anyway what did you really ring about?"

"I'm calling about the affair your husband is having with the editor of *Chic Interiors.*"

I began to feel a little uneasy, but it was so ridiculous. Ollie was so looks-ist, he would never have an affair with someone as plain as her.

"Come off it, Peter. Spitty Felicity? Now what's the real goss?"

Oh, my big mouth.

"Spitty Felicity?" said Peter sounding thrilled. "Is that what you call her? Well, you may find it hard to believe but your darling Ollie has been shagging 'Spitty,' as you call her, for nearly a year. He clearly doesn't find her spitty at all, or maybe it's just all her famous friends he likes, because he keeps a toothbrush, underwear and a whole set of duplicate shirts at her place, for all these times when you're out of town, isn't that cosy? Quite the little Brick Lane love nest apparently."

Duplicate shirts. It all started to seem hideously possible. I felt dizzy.

"But he can't be . . ." I spluttered.

"But he is, darling, and you can read all about it in my column tomorrow." He paused. "Peter's gonads never wrong, Emily."

And with a bitter laugh he put the phone down. I just sat down where I was, in the middle of the street. So this was what shock felt like. I still didn't really believe it, but at the same time I felt a dawning possibility that it could be true. Ollie's sudden fascination with Brick Lane and its just as sudden end—Felicity had first come over to our place around that time. He had put her next to him at our table. All the stupid decorators suddenly at our salons.

Then it hit me, like a poleaxe—the trip to the Milan Furniture Fair and all his excitement about that stupid shoot. It was true. My handsome, successful, secure husband was schtupping a human lawn-sprinkler.

My brain went into overdrive. Ollie was being unfaithful to me—but could I really complain when I was being unfaithful to him too? And frankly, the way he'd been behaving recently, did I really care? I didn't know, I didn't know what to think about anything, so I did the only thing I could do. I rang him. I didn't care if he was talking to me or not, I wanted some answers.

I was quite surprised when he picked up—he was in so many "phone off" meetings these days, I rarely got him live. Oh no, I thought simultaneously, more evidence. And there was more, when I heard his voice. I'd never heard him sound like that before. He kept clearing his throat.

"Ollie, it's Emily."

"Ah, ahem, yeah, Emily."

"Emily," I said. "Your *wife.*"

"Ahem, yeah."

" 'Ahem, yeah?' Is that all you can say? Am I to take it that this ridiculous story is true then?"

Ollie regained hold of his usual smoothie tactics.

"Now what story would that be?"

"The story that you have been shagging Spitty Felicity for over a year and that you even keep shirts—duplicate shirts, Ollie, I've *seen* them—in her Spitalfields house."

There was a pause. I could just imagine his calculating brain trying to work out the best damage limitation strategy.

"Who told you that?" he finally responded, with a new coldness in his voice.

I had to admire him. The man should be in politics. Never admit anything, was the way he worked.

"Peter Potter told me. He also told me it's going to be in his column tomorrow and judging by your tone of voice, he's told you that too, so you'd better tell me—is it true, Ollie? Really, I find it hard to believe that you could be unfaithful to me for someone quite so unattractive and humourless—and frankly, I'm not even sure how much I care—but I would like to know one way or the other."

Actually, I didn't want to know, but it just seemed like the thing I had to say.

"OK," said Ollie. "It is true. I am involved with Felicity and for your information, she is not unattractive and humourless. She's wonderful. She's a very striking and creative woman—and I'm leaving you for her."

I had already started to believe it, but hearing Ollie actually say those words knocked me down all over again. I couldn't breathe. I'd be single. I'd have to leave the flat. Where would I go?

"Is that it?" I said, when I could speak again. "Is that all you have to say after all our years together? That you're shagging someone else and you're just dumping me? Is that how gentlemen behave, Ollie? What will your parents say?"

"I wouldn't get too much on my moral high horse, if I were you, Emily," he replied, in a tone of pure ice. "I know what you got up to in Sydney."

Another wave of shock crashed over me. I felt like someone was holding my head down a loo and repeatedly flushing it. I tried to speak, but it just came out like a strangled gurgle.

"I heard all about you practically humping some Australian oik in full public view at a party. Unbelievable."

"Who told you that?" I finally managed to squeak out.

"The chief fashion buyer from Storridges told Maeve—you remember Maeve, the Storridges cosmetics buyer who came to our salon, that time? And Maeve told one of my Slap people and I overheard her telling the entire office and tomorrow the whole of London will know, because I'm going to tell Peter Potter."

My head was down the loo again. Of course he would tell Rotter. He wouldn't look nearly so bad in print, if I'd been unfaithful to him too. But Ollie hadn't finished.

"Really, Emily," he said, sounding like he was starting to enjoy himself. "What a way to behave. At least Felicity and I have been discreet and adult about our affair, but to do that in public like a common little tart . . ."

It was then—when he said her name—that another really horrible thought struck me.

"That's why you made me leave *Chic*," I said, the whole situation suddenly becoming clear. He'd wanted me out of the offices where she worked. "You made me leave *Chic*, to get me out of the way."

"Now Emily . . ." he started, but I knew I was right. OK, so I was as bad as him in the adultery department, but making me leave my job like that was pure treachery.

"You know what, Ollie?" I said, fury suddenly rising in me. "I stand by what I said the other night. You really are a cunt—and you can tell your fascist fucking parents I said that."

And I threw my phone down on to the cobbled street.

After that I just sat there panting, on the hot, hard stones. I sat there, until people were starting to stop and stare. Then I stood up and started to stumble back to the hotel, but in my confusion and the heat and noise of the busy market quarter I got all turned around and lost my way.

The labyrinthine streets of the old town were bewildering at the best of times and in my traumatized state I just couldn't find my way. I seemed to be turning into narrower and narrower back lanes, but then I saw a blue filigree door I thought I recognized. I made for it, then turned left, fairly certain it would bring me out on to the main market square, but I was wrong. Horribly wrong.

Instead I found myself looking straight into a yard behind what must have been a butcher's shop. There was a small goat hanging up by its back legs making horrible squealing noises and as I looked, the butcher picked up a large steel knife and cut its throat.

Blood spurted out in a great scarlet arc and as I saw it another image flashed into my head. It was my father, with blood pumping out of his neck. The two images kept flashing on and off in my head, like a strobe light. The dying goat and my father, lying on the floor of his studio with a knife in his hand and blood pouring out of his throat. And me, ten years old, standing in the doorway, watching.

I heard myself scream as I stumbled and fell forward to the ground. I felt the impact of my head against the cobbles and that was the end of it.

I woke up in a dark room, which I took a while to realize was a hospital, or some kind of clinic. I just lay there for a few moments trying to work out where I was and then it all flooded back like a tidal wave crashing over my head. Peter Potter's call. My conversation with Ollie. And then the goat and the blood and the memory of my father, dying in front of me. I started to shake and before I was even fully aware of it, I was calling out.

A nurse came into the room. She couldn't speak any English, but she calmed me with soothing tones and made me drink some water. As I sat up to sip it, I realized my head was splitting with pain. I tentatively put my hand up and found I had a big dressing on my forehead, where I must have hit the hard ground.

I closed my eyes to try and make it all go away, but it wouldn't. It just went round and round in my head like some kind of psychedelic light show. My father killing himself, not knowing I was watching. How had I managed to convince myself for so many years it was a brain haemorrhage? Had I really believed that?

Then the rest of it came back. My husband was leaving me, after tricking me into leaving my job. I'd alienated the man who really did care about me—Miles. I was alone in a Tunisian hospital. My mother was alone in a mental hospital. Nobody knew where I was.

I knew I was semi-delirious, but I couldn't stop myself jabbering on, holding on to the nurse's sleeve and pleading with her to get Ursula for me. Eventually she went out and came back a few minutes later with a man in a white coat, who I assumed was a doctor. He spoke English and he knew my name. I grabbed his hand and wouldn't let go.

"Miss Pointer," he said, kindly. "You have had a serious concussion. You have a lesion to your forehead and I have had to use stitches. You have been here for two days under sedation. You will have another skull X-ray later and if it is satisfactory you will be able to leave."

"Does anyone know I'm here?" I asked him.

"Your passport was in your bag and we have informed the British Embassy in Tunis. We have also contacted the people you were travelling with, as your hotel key was also in your bag. They know where you are."

But no one came to see me. I was taken for the X-ray, but apart from that I just lay in that bed for another day and still no one came. I kept asking for my mobile, until I remembered I had smashed it down on to the stony ground, and eventually a nurse took pity on me and let me use the telephone in the doctor's office.

I rang Ursula and told her what had happened. At first I just sobbed down the phone until I could get the story out.

"Oh, my poor girl," she said. "My poor baby. You must come here immediately. God, I wish I could come and get you, but I can't, Emily. I can't do that flight, you know I can't."

She paused for a moment, clearly thinking it through. I just sobbed a bit more, mainly from relief at hearing her voice.

"OK, kiddo," she said. "Here's what we'll do. I will call the British Embassy and arrange for someone to take you to the airport and I will make sure you are looked after on the flight, OK? Just tell me the name of your hotel and I will call back with the details. Above all, don't worry. I will look after you."

And I knew she would.

After another day, when the doctor had seen the X-ray and said I was OK to leave, they put me in a taxi to the hotel. When I got there the receptionist handed me an envelope.

It was a note from Nivek saying he hoped I would be OK and to call him when I got back, but he was afraid he'd had to leave for another job. He also said he'd taken the film and would deliver it to Rosie, which pretty much summed up his priorities. And that was it, they'd all just gone, leaving me there with a cracked head in a Tunisian hospital.

When I got up to my room I found they'd left all the clothes from the shoot behind too. They'd just dumped it all on my bed and split. It looked like a sample sale in there. I threw all the clothes on the floor and got into bed, my head spinning from both the concussion and the shock of everything that had happened in the last few weeks. I desperately wished I had my mum's book with me and lay there muttering the poems I knew off by heart over and over again.

After a while saying them wasn't enough, so I got up and found the hotel stationery and started writing them down. Then without really realizing it I was writing a letter. To my mother.

I don't know how long passed, but the letter went on and on until I had to ring reception to ask them to bring up more paper. The young man who brought it also handed me an envelope, which contained a fax from Ursula. She told me she'd booked me on the first available flight to New York, which wasn't for another two days, but that she had arranged for me to be taken to the airport and to be looked after. She'd meet me at JFK. I wasn't to worry about a thing, she said. It was all taken care of.

I had a fretful night, most of which I spent sitting up in bed adding to the letter to my mother. I told her everything. How I felt utterly abandoned by her and my father. How I felt desperately ashamed of them, but incredibly proud too. I told her I had now remembered the real circumstances of my father's death and wondered how I had managed to repress it for twenty years, to the point where I really had believed he'd died from natural causes.

I begged her to understand how traumatic my few visits to see her had been—especially the last one—and how I missed her too much to risk it again. I told her how much I loved her and how much I hated her. How I still grieved for my ruined childhood and that I had decided never to have children myself in case I had post-natal depression like she had. I told her everything. I told her the truth.

I even told her about Ollie—who she had never even met—and how I felt more betrayed about him tricking me into leaving my job, than I did about his marital infidelity. And then I told her about my affair with Miles, the wonderful time I'd had with him in Sydney and how it had made me start to realize that perhaps my marriage to Ollie was just another superficial accessory, like my Luella Bartley Baby Gisele bag, that I was clinging on to for a deluded sense of security.

I sobbed all over that letter until the paper was wrinkled and blotched, but I kept on writing. As the sun came up, I finally finished and after sealing and addressing the envelope—I hadn't realized I knew that address by heart, until I saw myself writing it—I fell into a dead sleep.

I was woken what seemed like moments later by a gentle knocking on my door. I didn't answer, hoping housekeeping, or whoever it was, would just go away, but they kept knocking and when I realized someone was saying my name, I finally stumbled over and opened the door.

It was Miles.

I collapsed into his arms too exhausted even to speak. He carried me over to the bed and held me, rocking me in his arms like a child.

"You poor baby," he kept saying. "Everything is going to be all right."

I couldn't really take it in. Where had he come from? How did he know where I was? At first I couldn't even summon the energy to ask him. I was just so incredibly glad he was there. He called down to room service and had them send up some soup and bread, which he forced me to eat, against my protests. Only then did I ask him how he'd known to come and find me.

"Ursula called me," he said, moving the tray and sitting on the bed beside me.

"Ursula?" I said, bewildered. "How did she get your number?"

"She knew my name and she knew what I did," he said. "Because you told her." He smiled at me. That wonderful crooked grin. I nodded.

"So she called Paul to see if he knew where to find me and Paul called Frannie and Frannie called Nelly and Nelly called Seamus and Seamus handed the phone to me, because I was standing next to him at the Dior couture show in Paris. I got the next plane to Tunis and here I am. I'm going to take you home."

"Where's that?" I asked, in alarm. I really didn't know if he meant New York, Sydney, or Westbourne Grove. I hoped he wasn't planning to deliver me back to Ollie.

"New York," he said. "Ursula's place. I like the sound of Ursula."

"She liked the sound of you," I said, feeling able to smile for the first time in days.

"That is—unless, you'd rather go back to London," said Miles tentatively.

"What? Back to my loving husband?"

"Well, I don't know," he said, slowly. "I hope you don't want to go back there, but you are married to him—and you did want to go back to him from Sydney."

I sighed and put my face in my hands, shaking my head. What a fuck-up. Miles pulled my hands gently down and held them in his.

"Does he even know where you are, Emily?" he said. "Does he know what's happened?"

"No," I said, shaking my head slowly. "I don't think Ollie knows anything about me and I think he cares even less."

Miles just looked at me steadily with his head on one side and squeezed my hands.

"Tell me about it," he said.

So I did. I told him the whole crazy story, how Ollie had been cheating on me the whole time I'd been cheating on him. How he had vilely tricked me into leaving my wonderful job, for his own convenience, and how I had abruptly been forced to realize, after years of kidding myself, that our marriage had about as much depth and meaning as a fashion shoot. Which, in a way, is what it had been. All style and no substance.

When I'd finished, Miles said nothing. He just took me in his arms and held me tight, until I fell asleep.

I slept for a while, but then woke suddenly, my heart pounding. I'd been having a horrible dream about my father. And the blood. I started to weep.

"Hey," said Miles, stroking my head gently. "It's all right, Emily. I'm here. I'm going to look after you now. You don't have to worry any more. I'm not letting you out of my sight. Ever."

But I couldn't stop crying.

"Don't get involved with me, Miles," I managed to choke out between sobs. "I'm too much trouble. Just take me to Ursula and go. You don't want me in your life. I'm a mess. Run away, while you can. Ollie's right—I'm not worth the bother."

"What are you talking about?" he said.

"My life, my childhood, you've got no idea what you're taking on, Miles. Even Ollie doesn't know the full story, but I can't pretend any more and it's too much shit for you to bother with."

"You mean your parents?" said Miles.

I just nodded.

"You mean all the stuff about your father's suicide and your mum being in a mental hospital?"

I just looked at him amazed. I was so shocked, I stopped crying.

"How do you know all that?" I asked. "Did Ursula tell you?"

"It's common knowledge, Emily," he said. "Your father was a pretty well-known artist and it's no secret that he committed suicide—and how he did it. Seamus told me you were Matthew Pointer's daughter and I already knew about him and what had happened. It was a shocking waste."

"What?" I croaked out. "You knew?"

He nodded.

"Well, how come you never mentioned it?" I asked.

"I didn't want to upset you. Especially after what happened at that fashion show, with the blood. Everyone was talking about it at the time and how vile it was of that fucker to write about you in the paper like that, after what had happened to your dad."

"But no one said anything to me."

Miles shrugged. "It's a touchy subject. People are sensitive about these things, believe it or not, and I always thought that if you wanted to talk about it, you'd bring it up yourself."

I sat and took this information in for a bit. Then something else struck me.

"But what about my mum?" I said. "How did you know about her? Does everyone know about that too?"

Miles looked a bit sheepish.

"I don't know about anyone else, but I did a Google search on her."

I just gawped at him.

"A Google search?"

"You see, after I read her poetry I was intrigued," he continued. "But you are so closed up about your family—which is under-standable, in the circs—that I didn't want to push it with you, but it's all there on the web. Her work is well thought of, you know, in poetry circles. They call her the English Sylvia Plath. There are whole websites about her. I guess some people are just fascinated by the romance of mental illness," he added cautiously, gauging my reaction, but I was still stuck several thoughts behind him.

"My mother is on the internet?" I asked him in amazement. "There are websites?"

He nodded, like an earnest schoolboy.

"She sounds a fascinating character," he said. "I'd really like to meet her."

And the only thing I could do was laugh. I laughed so much I had tears pouring down my cheeks. It was all so ridiculous. A little while later, after I could breathe normally again, I noticed Miles had a particularly twinkly look in his eye.

"What?" I said cautiously, wondering what was coming next.

"As you're in the mood for a laugh," he said. "Do you want to hear something else funny?"

I nodded, still wiping my eyes.

"Well, according to Seamus, the latest hot goss from the London fashion scene concerns your old editor, Bee."

"Go on . . ." I said, intrigued.

"Well, apparently she's shacked up with that Italian guy who used to drive you lot around."

"Luigi?" I almost screamed at him.

"Yeah, I think that was his name. The limo driver. Turns out she's been shagging him for years while she was at the shows and now she's left her husband for him."

And that just started me off all over again.

As we were checking out of the hotel the next morning, I stopped at the front desk, to ask them to post the letter to my mother for me. I knew if I didn't send it there and then, I never would.

I handed the concierge the envelope and the money for the stamps, and started to walk away, but then I turned round and asked for it back. I picked up a pen that was lying on the counter and added a postscript to the back of the envelope.

> *A butterfly*
> *on a dung heap*
> *A cobweb*
> *on barbed wire*

A rainbow
on an oil slick
A snowflake
on a pyre

I read it over again and then I handed it back to the concierge.
I knew it was pretty lame, but it was a start.

About the Author

Maggie Alderson has worked on nine magazines and three newspapers, and has been covering the international fashion shows for many years. Her first novel, *Pants on Fire*, was a UK bestseller and she was a co-editor of the charity anthology *Big Night Out*. *Pants on Fire* and her most recent novel, *Mad About the Boy*, are both published by Penguin.